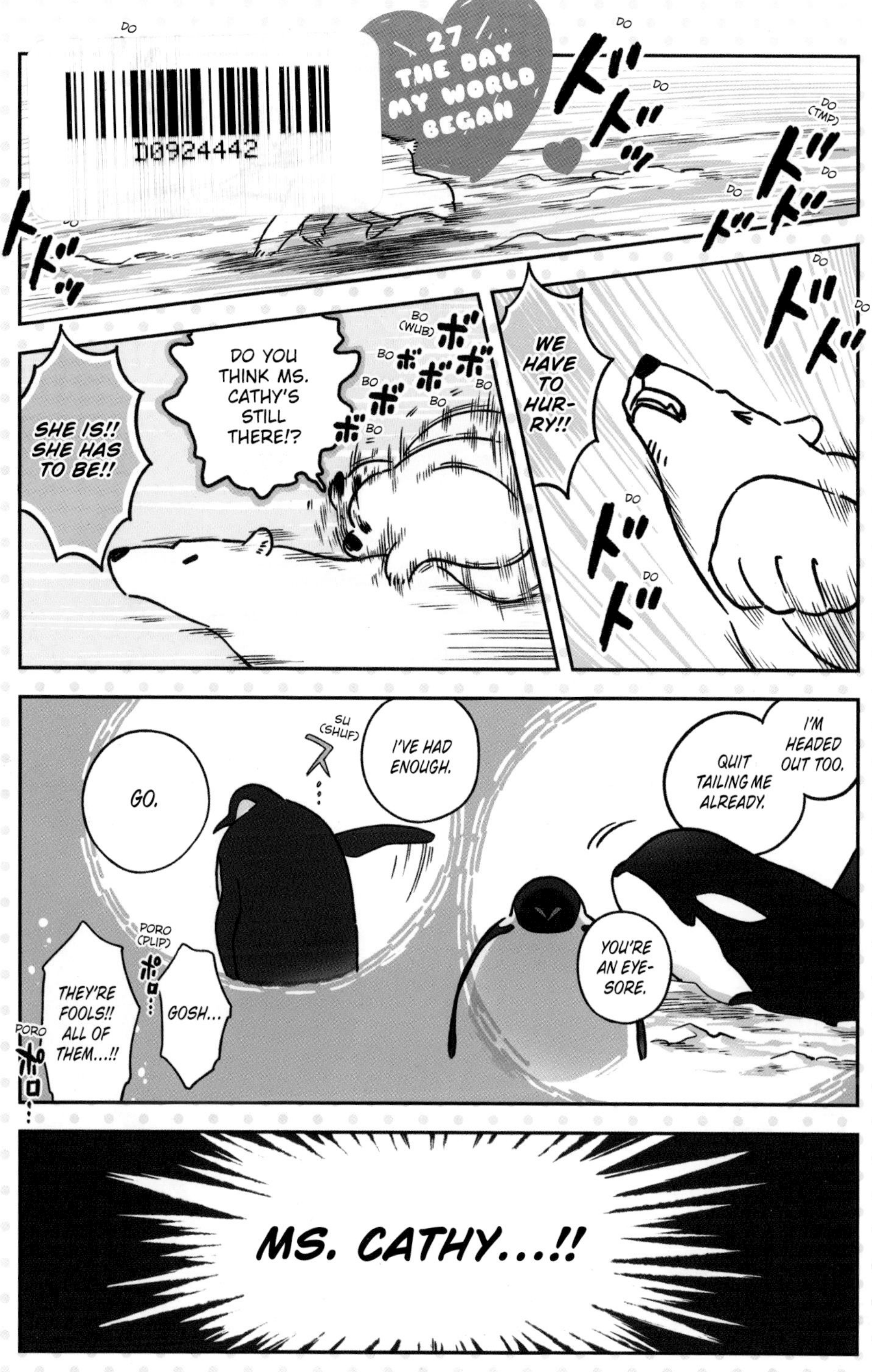
27
THE DAY MY WORLD BEGAN
DO (TMP) ドドド
DO ドドッ
WE HAVE TO HURRY!!
DO ドド
DO YOU THINK MS. CATHY'S STILL THERE!?
BO (WUB) ボボボ
SHE IS!! SHE HAS TO BE!!
I'M HEADED OUT TOO.
QUIT TAILING ME ALREADY.
YOU'RE AN EYE-SORE.
I'VE HAD ENOUGH.
SU (SHUF) ス…
GO.
PORO (PLIP) ポロ…
GOSH…
THEY'RE FOOLS!! ALL OF THEM…!!
PORO ポロ…
MS. CATHY…!!

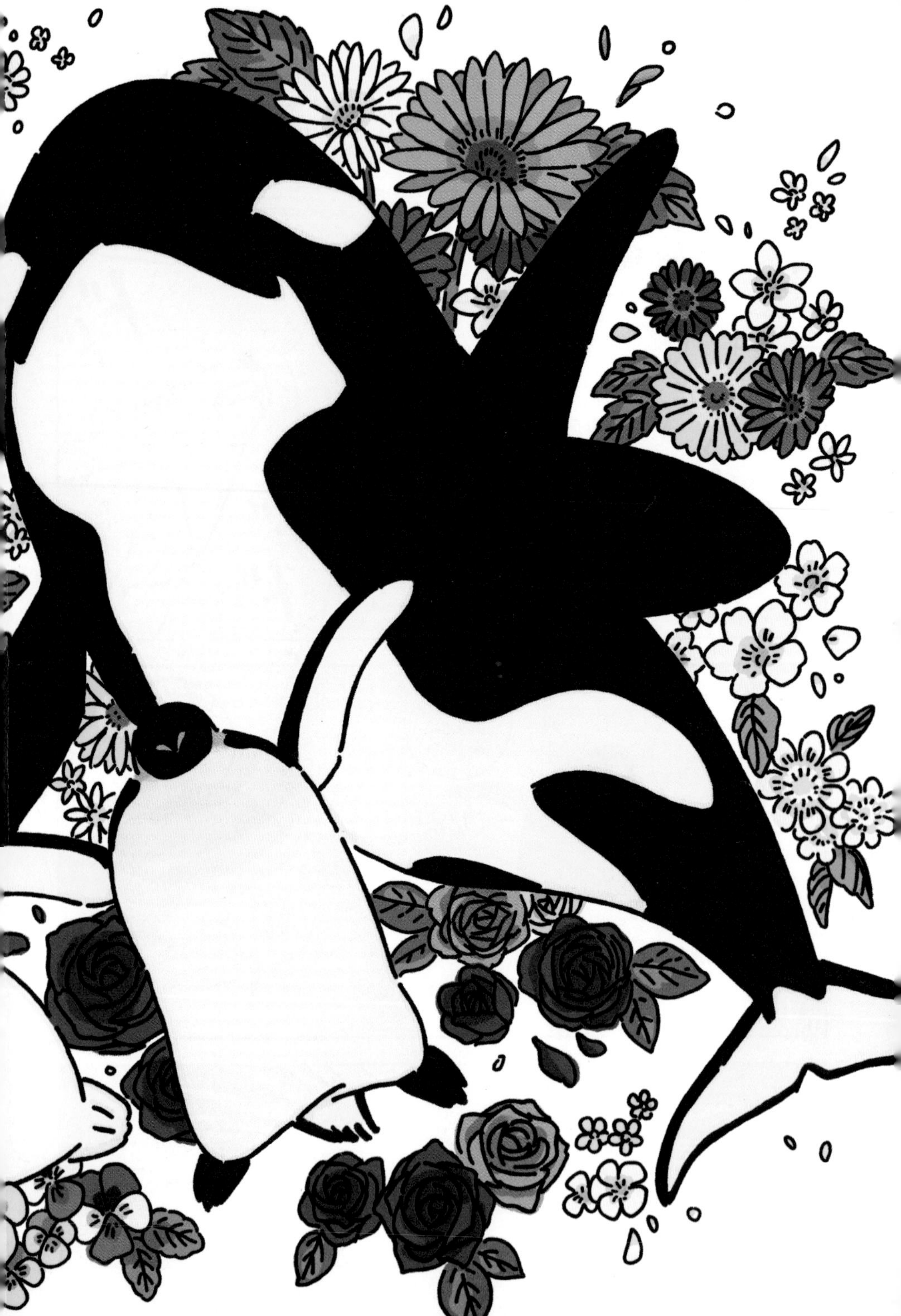

A POLAR BEAR in LOVE

5

KOROMO

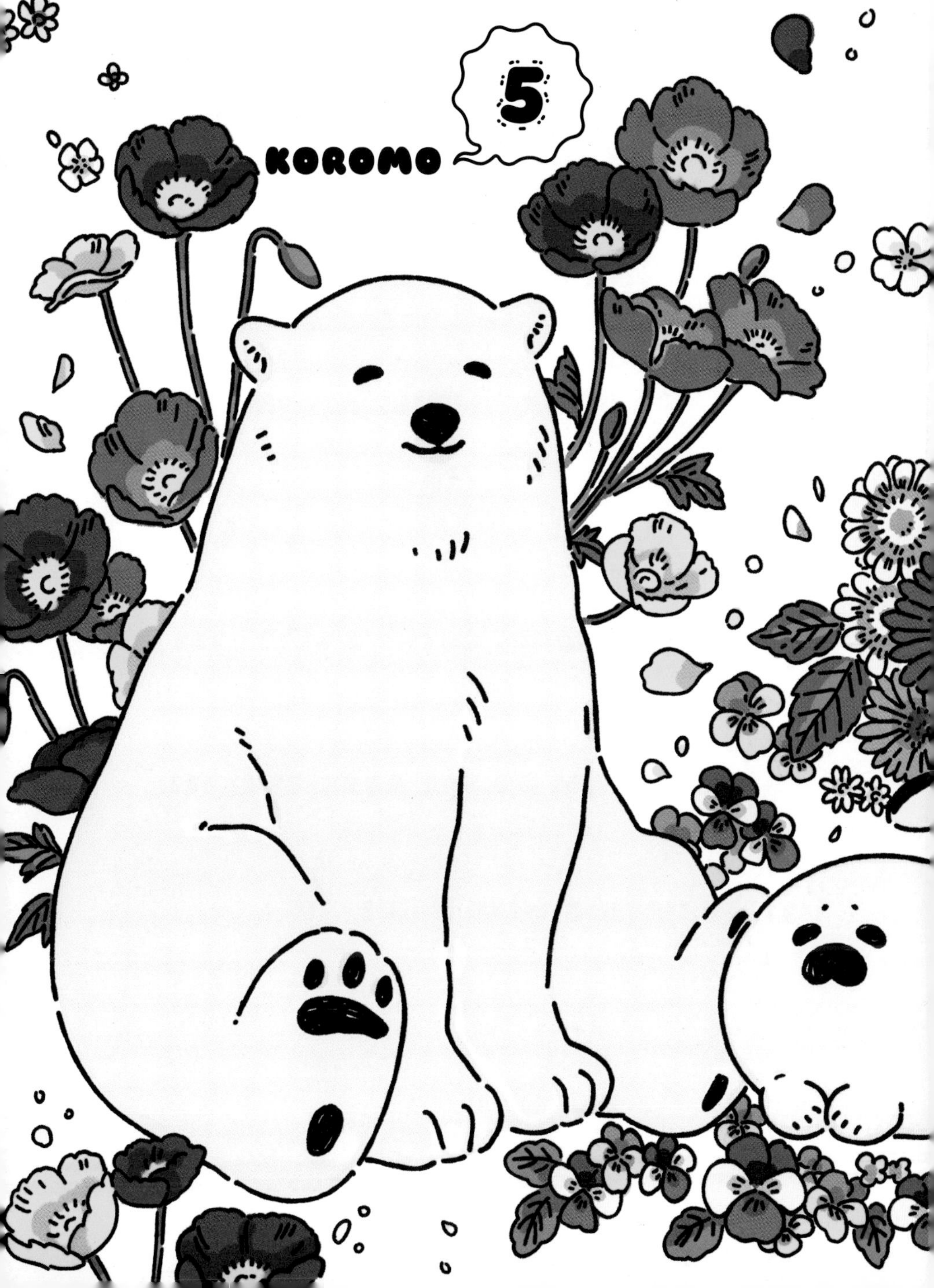

c o n t e n t s

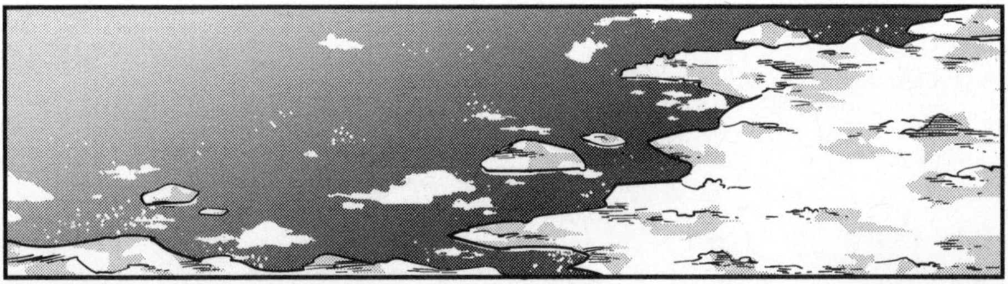

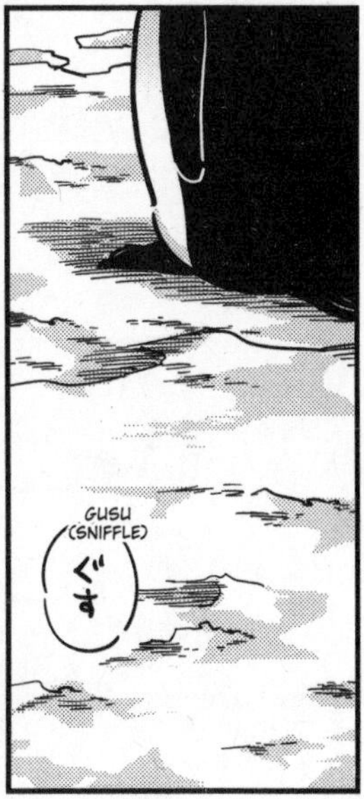
GUSU (SNIFFLE)
ぐす

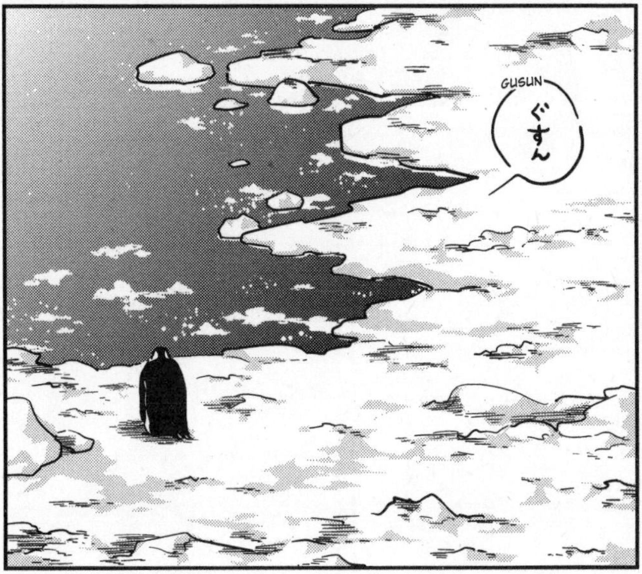
GUSUN
ぐすん

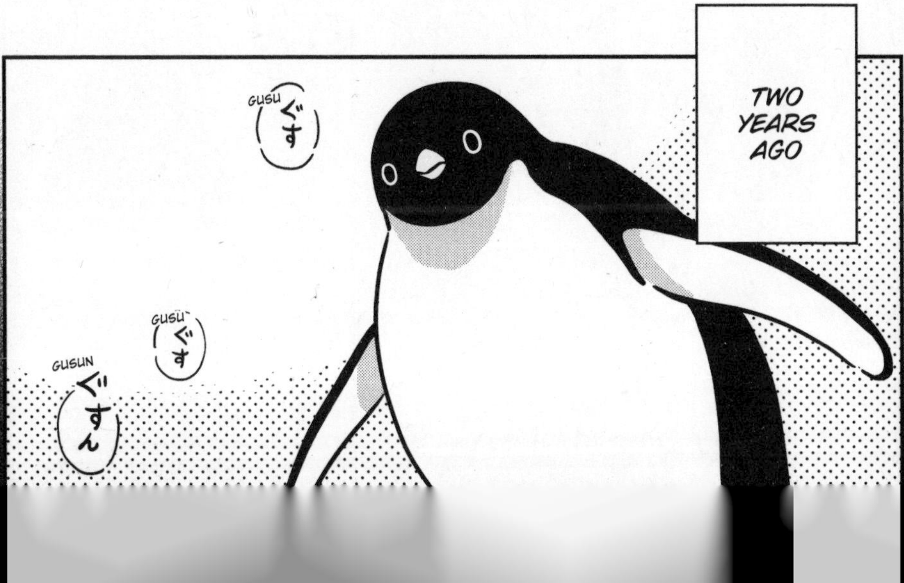
TWO YEARS AGO
GUSU
ぐす
GUSU
ぐす
GUSUN
ぐすん

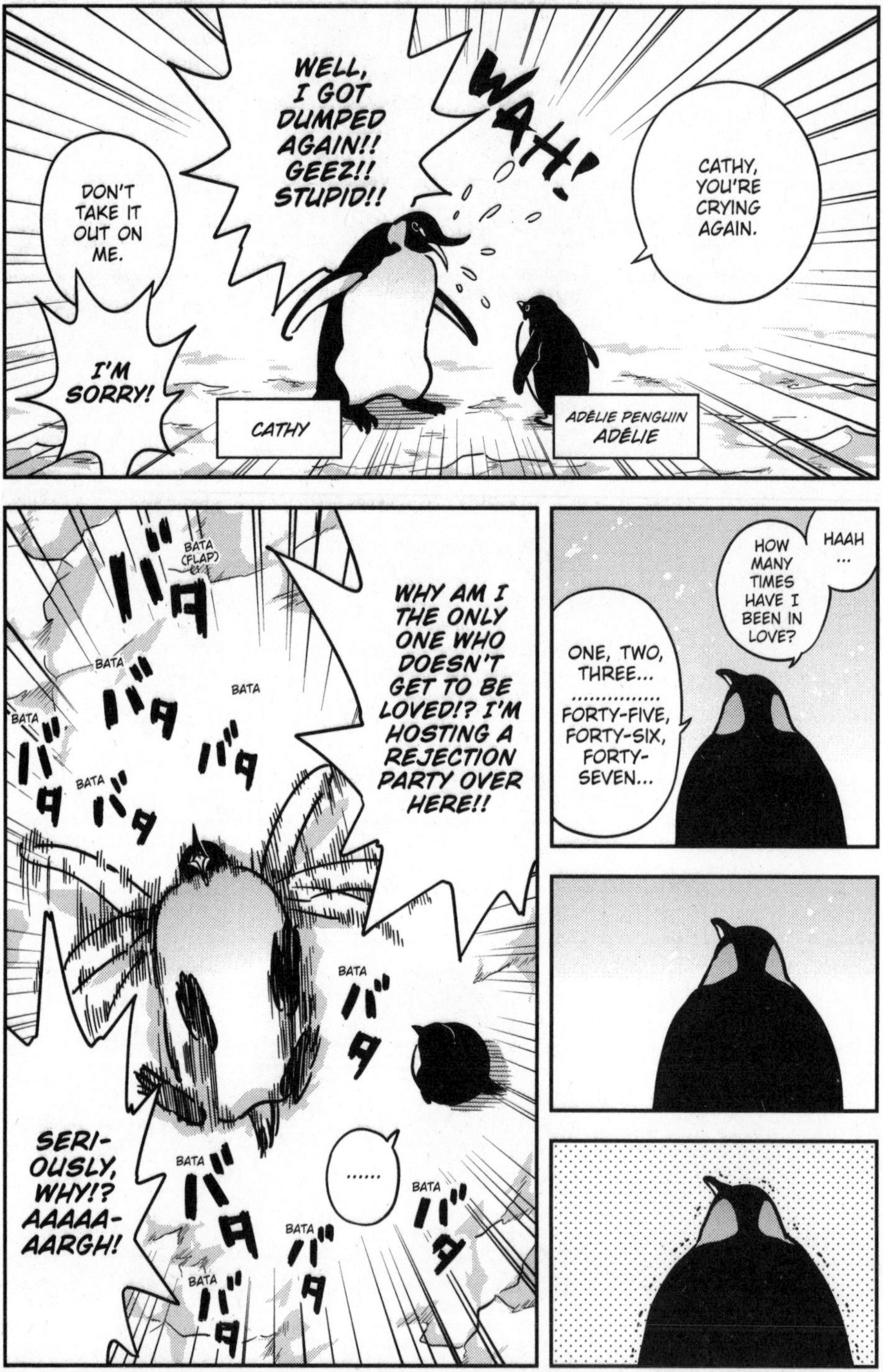
CATHY, YOU'RE CRYING AGAIN.
WAH!
WELL, I GOT DUMPED AGAIN!! GEEZ!! STUPID!!
DON'T TAKE IT OUT ON ME.
I'M SORRY!
ADÉLIE PENGUIN ADÉLIE
CATHY
HAAH ...
HOW MANY TIMES HAVE I BEEN IN LOVE?
ONE, TWO, THREE... .... FORTY-FIVE, FORTY-SIX, FORTY-SEVEN...
WHY AM I THE ONLY ONE WHO DOESN'T GET TO BE LOVED!? I'M HOSTING A REJECTION PARTY OVER HERE!!
バタ BATA (FLAP)
バタ BATA
バタ BATA
バタ BATA
バタ BATA
バタ BATA
......
バタ BATA
バタ BATA
バタ BATA
バタ BATA
SERI-OUSLY, WHY!? AAAAA-AARGH!

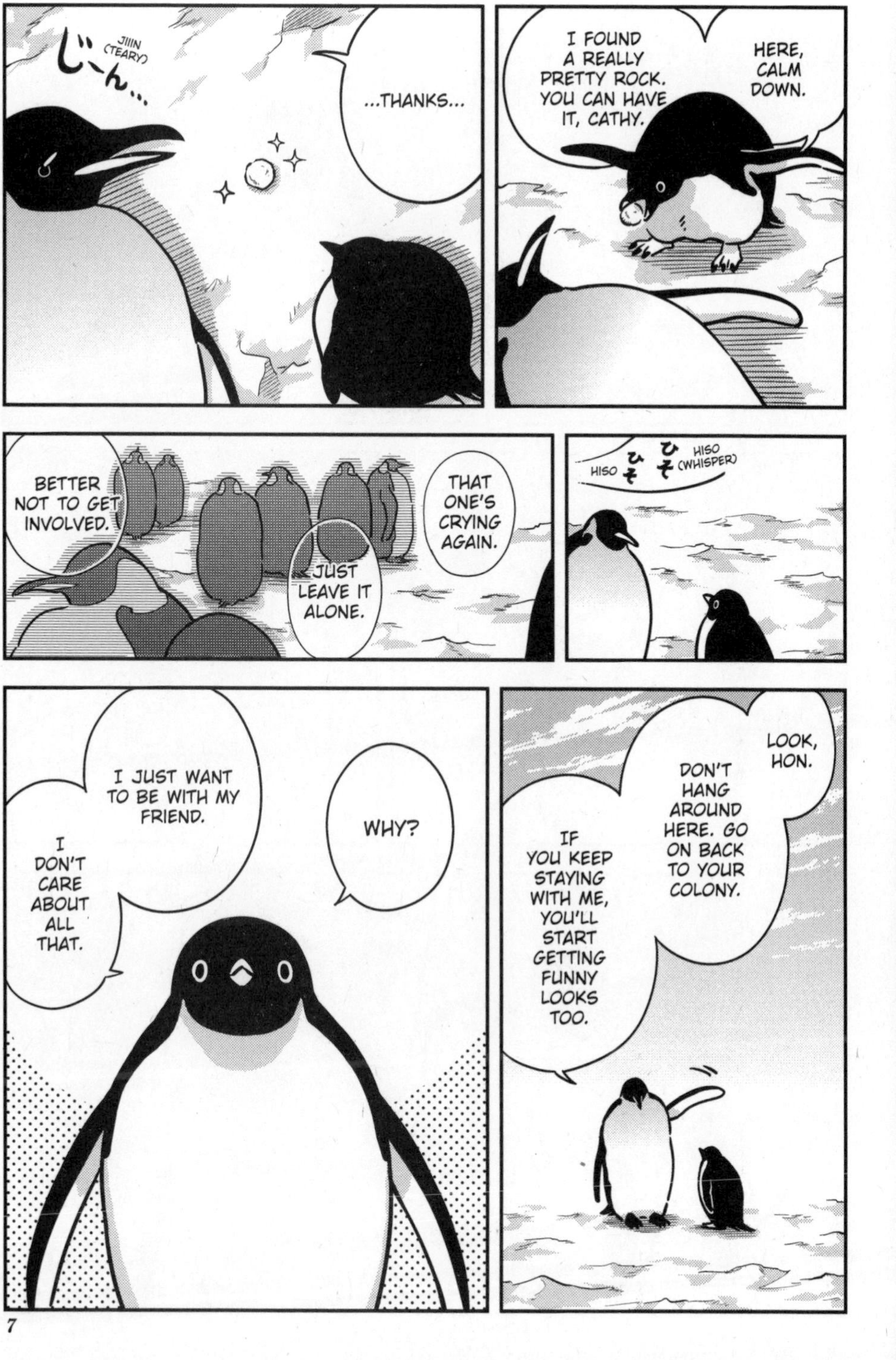
HERE, CALM DOWN.
I FOUND A REALLY PRETTY ROCK. YOU CAN HAVE IT, CATHY.
...THANKS...
じ～ん…
JIIN (TEARY)
ひそ ひそ
HISO (WHISPER)
HISO
THAT ONE'S CRYING AGAIN.
JUST LEAVE IT ALONE.
BETTER NOT TO GET INVOLVED.
LOOK, HON.
DON'T HANG AROUND HERE. GO ON BACK TO YOUR COLONY.
IF YOU KEEP STAYING WITH ME, YOU'LL START GETTING FUNNY LOOKS TOO.
WHY?
I JUST WANT TO BE WITH MY FRIEND.
I DON'T CARE ABOUT ALL THAT.

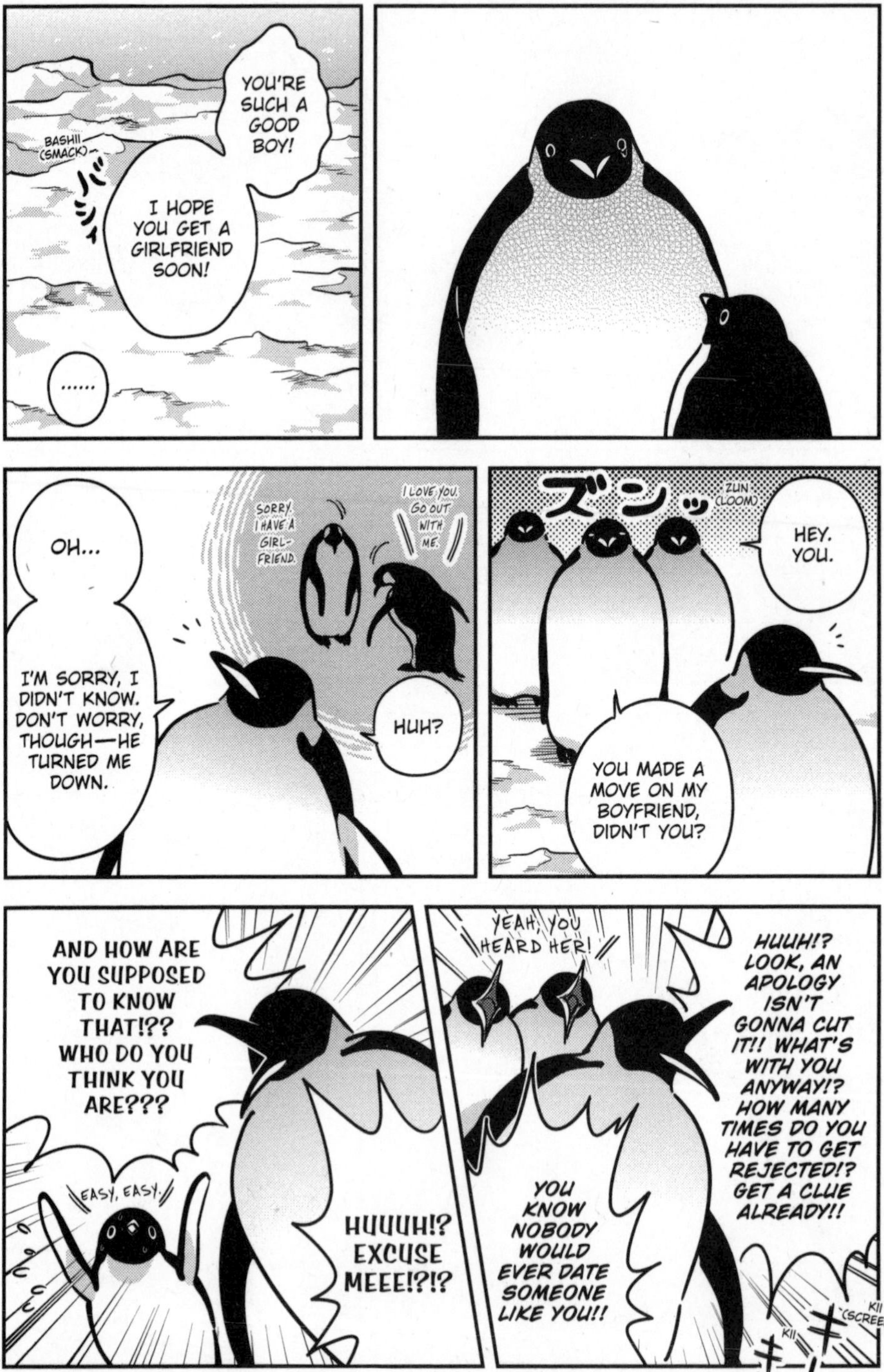
YOU'RE SUCH A GOOD BOY!
BASHII (SMACK)
I HOPE YOU GET A GIRLFRIEND SOON!
......
ZUN (LOOM)
HEY. YOU.
YOU MADE A MOVE ON MY BOYFRIEND, DIDN'T YOU?
I LOVE YOU. GO OUT WITH ME.
SORRY. I HAVE A GIRLFRIEND.
OH...
I'M SORRY, I DIDN'T KNOW. DON'T WORRY, THOUGH—HE TURNED ME DOWN.
HUH?
HUUH!? LOOK, AN APOLOGY ISN'T GONNA CUT IT!! WHAT'S WITH YOU ANYWAY!? HOW MANY TIMES DO YOU HAVE TO GET REJECTED!? GET A CLUE ALREADY!!
YEAH, YOU HEARD HER!
YOU KNOW NOBODY WOULD EVER DATE SOMEONE LIKE YOU!!
KII (SCREECH)
KII
HUUUH!? EXCUSE MEEE!?!?
AND HOW ARE YOU SUPPOSED TO KNOW THAT!?? WHO DO YOU THINK YOU ARE???
EASY, EASY.

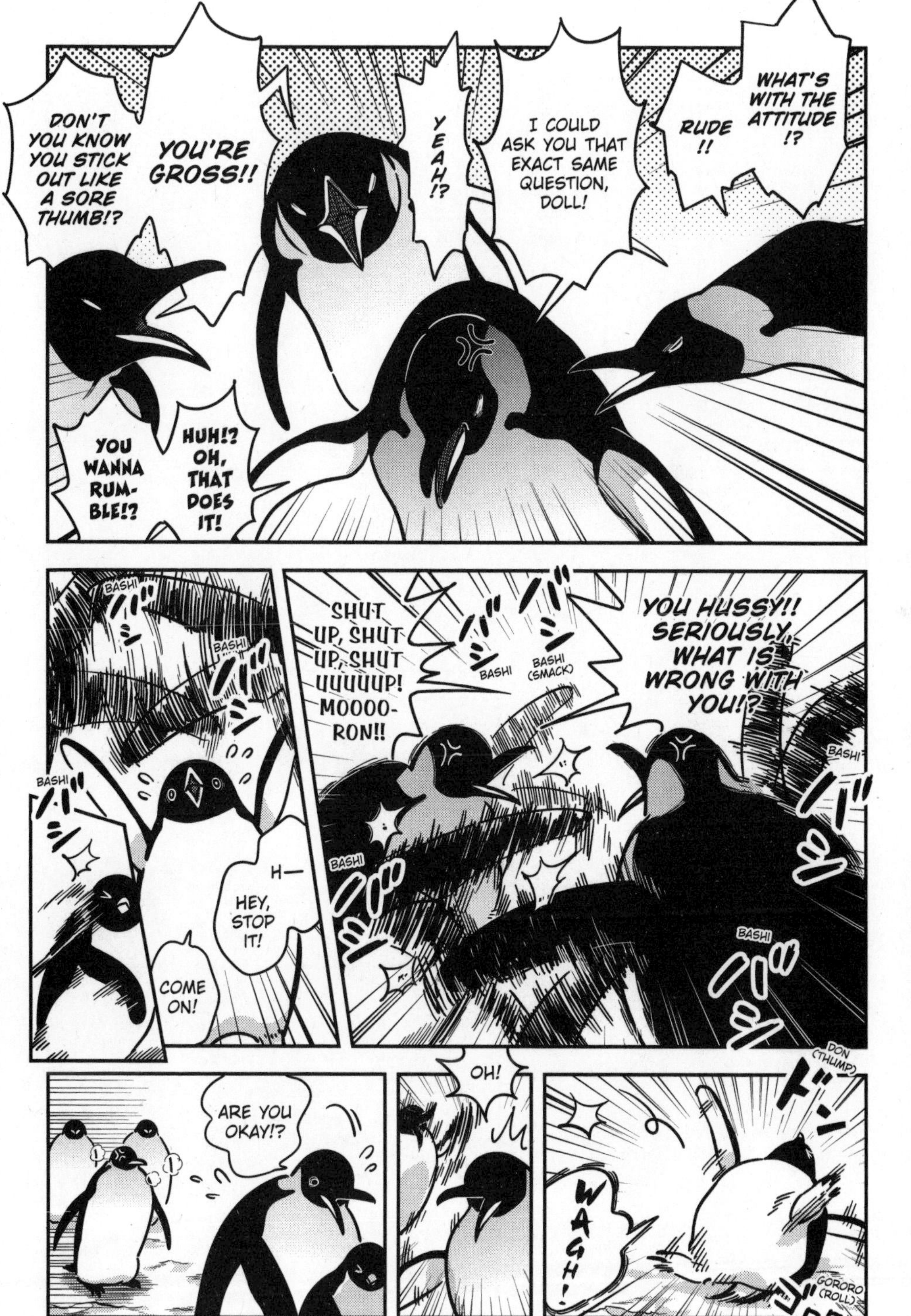
WHAT'S WITH THE ATTITUDE!?
RUDE!!
I COULD ASK YOU THAT EXACT SAME QUESTION, DOLL!
YEAH!?
YOU'RE GROSS!!
DON'T YOU KNOW YOU STICK OUT LIKE A SORE THUMB!?
HUH!? OH, THAT DOES IT!
YOU WANNA RUM-BLE!?
YOU HUSSY!! SERIOUSLY, WHAT IS WRONG WITH YOU!?
BASHI
BASHI (SMACK)
BASHI
SHUT UP, SHUT UP, SHUT UUUUUP! MOOOO-RON!!
BASHI
BASHI
BASHI
BASHI
BASHI
H—
HEY, STOP IT!
COME ON!
DON (THUMP)
WAGH!
GORORO (ROLL)
OH!
ARE YOU OKAY!?

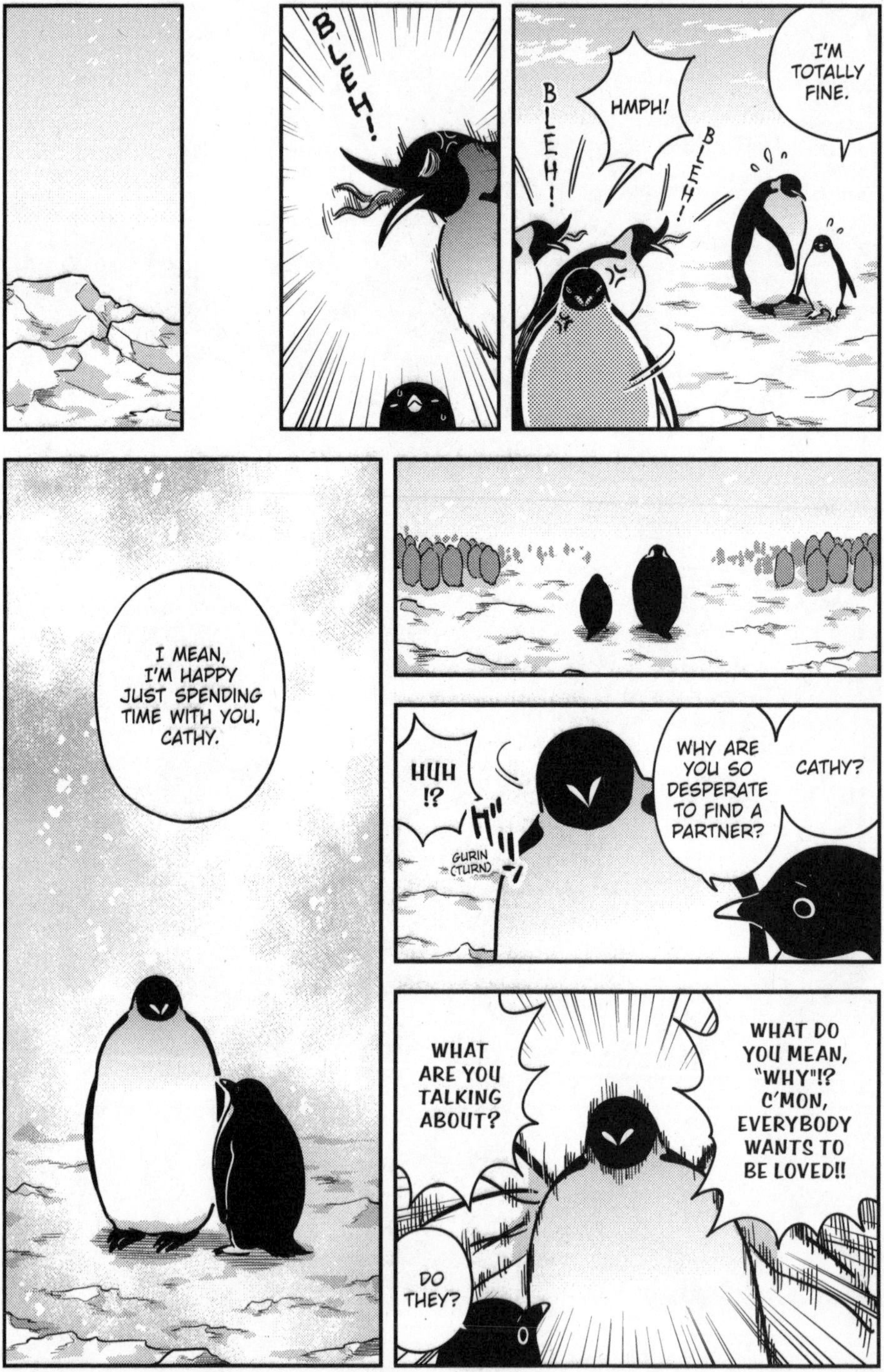
I'M TOTALLY FINE.
BLEH!
HMPH!
BLEH!
BLEH!
CATHY?
WHY ARE YOU SO DESPERATE TO FIND A PARTNER?
HUH!?
GURIN (TURN)
WHAT DO YOU MEAN, "WHY"!? C'MON, EVERYBODY WANTS TO BE LOVED!!
WHAT ARE YOU TALKING ABOUT?
DO THEY?
I MEAN, I'M HAPPY JUST SPENDING TIME WITH YOU, CATHY.

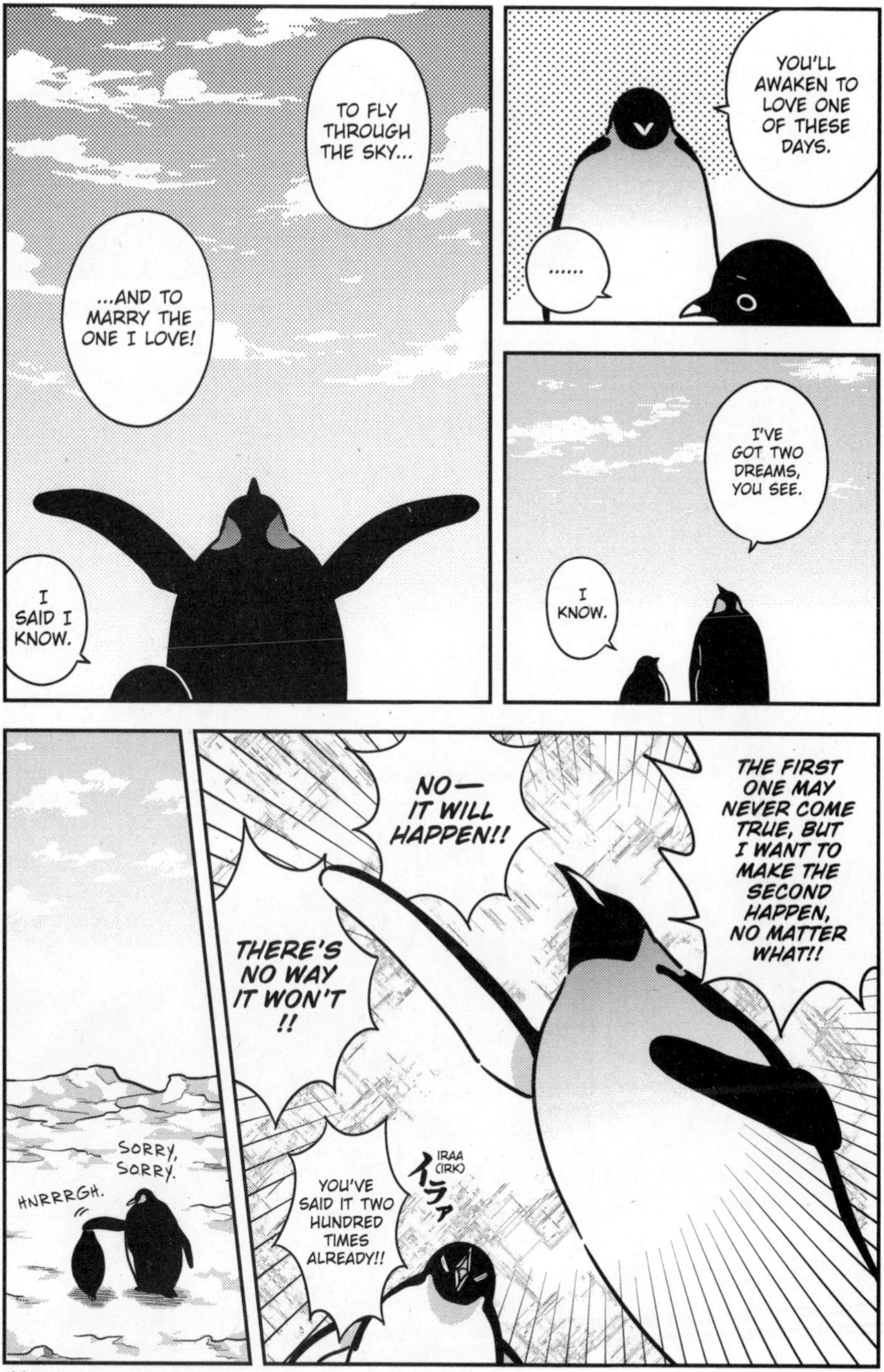
YOU'LL AWAKEN TO LOVE ONE OF THESE DAYS.
......
I'VE GOT TWO DREAMS, YOU SEE.
I KNOW.
TO FLY THROUGH THE SKY...
...AND TO MARRY THE ONE I LOVE!
I SAID I KNOW.
THE FIRST ONE MAY NEVER COME TRUE, BUT I WANT TO MAKE THE SECOND HAPPEN, NO MATTER WHAT!!
NO— IT WILL HAPPEN!!
THERE'S NO WAY IT WON'T !!
IRAA (IRK)
YOU'VE SAID IT TWO HUNDRED TIMES ALREADY!!
SORRY, SORRY.
HNRRRGH.

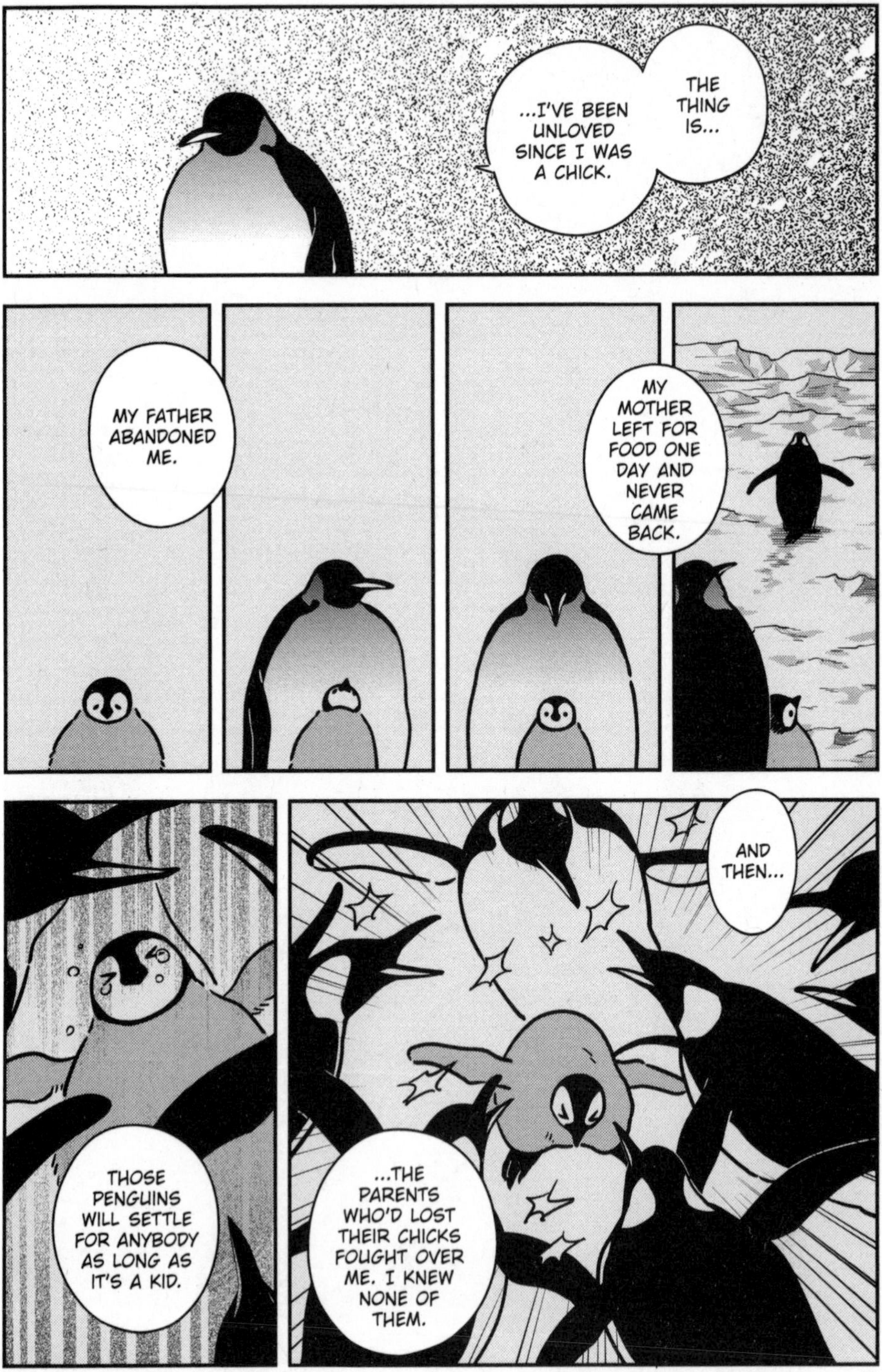
THE THING IS...
...I'VE BEEN UNLOVED SINCE I WAS A CHICK.
MY MOTHER LEFT FOR FOOD ONE DAY AND NEVER CAME BACK.
MY FATHER ABANDONED ME.
AND THEN...
...THE PARENTS WHO'D LOST THEIR CHICKS FOUGHT OVER ME. I KNEW NONE OF THEM.
THOSE PENGUINS WILL SETTLE FOR ANYBODY AS LONG AS IT'S A KID.

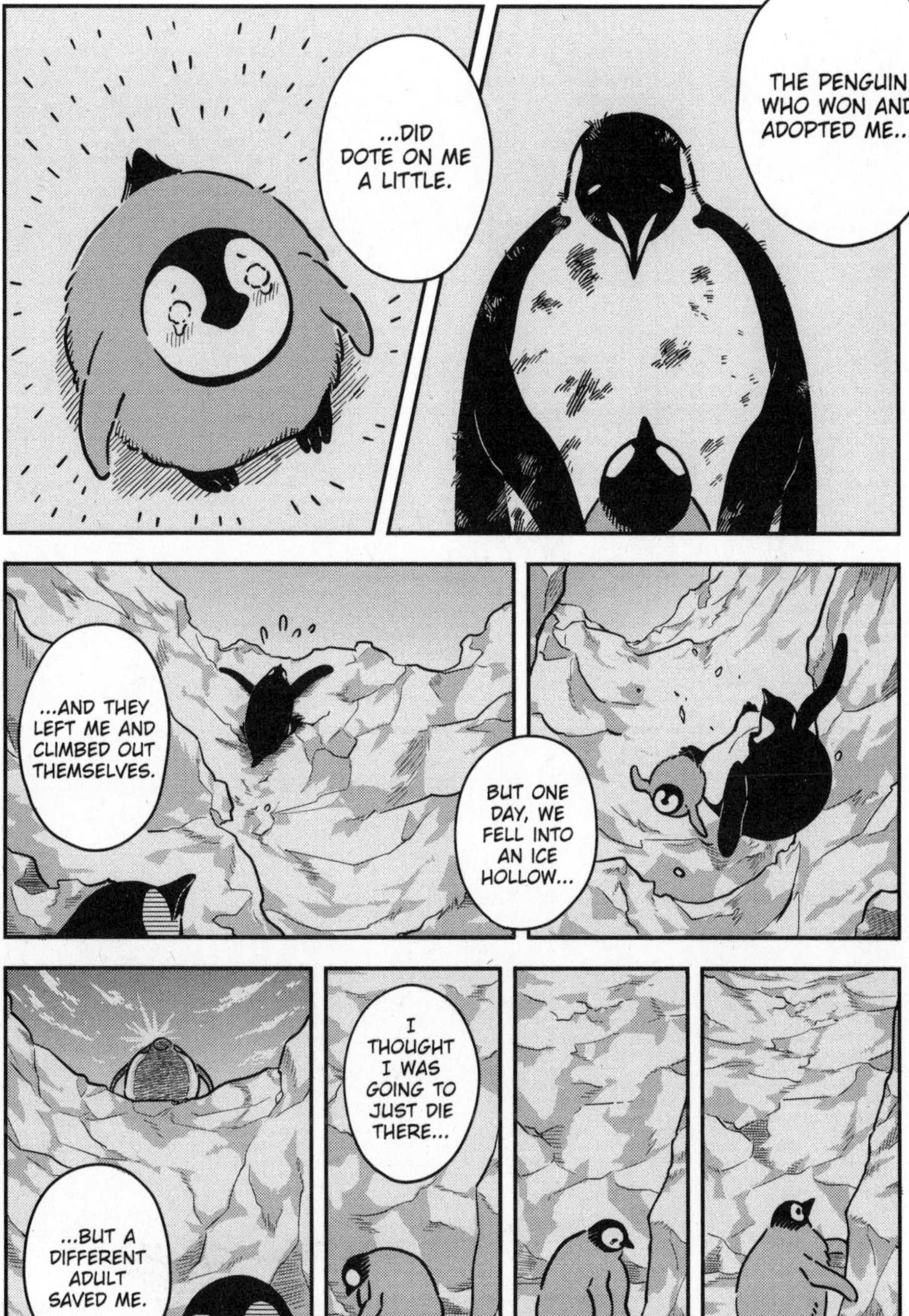
THE PENGUIN WHO WON AND ADOPTED ME...
...DID DOTE ON ME A LITTLE.
BUT ONE DAY, WE FELL INTO AN ICE HOLLOW...
...AND THEY LEFT ME AND CLIMBED OUT THEMSELVES.
I THOUGHT I WAS GOING TO JUST DIE THERE...
...BUT A DIFFERENT ADULT SAVED ME.

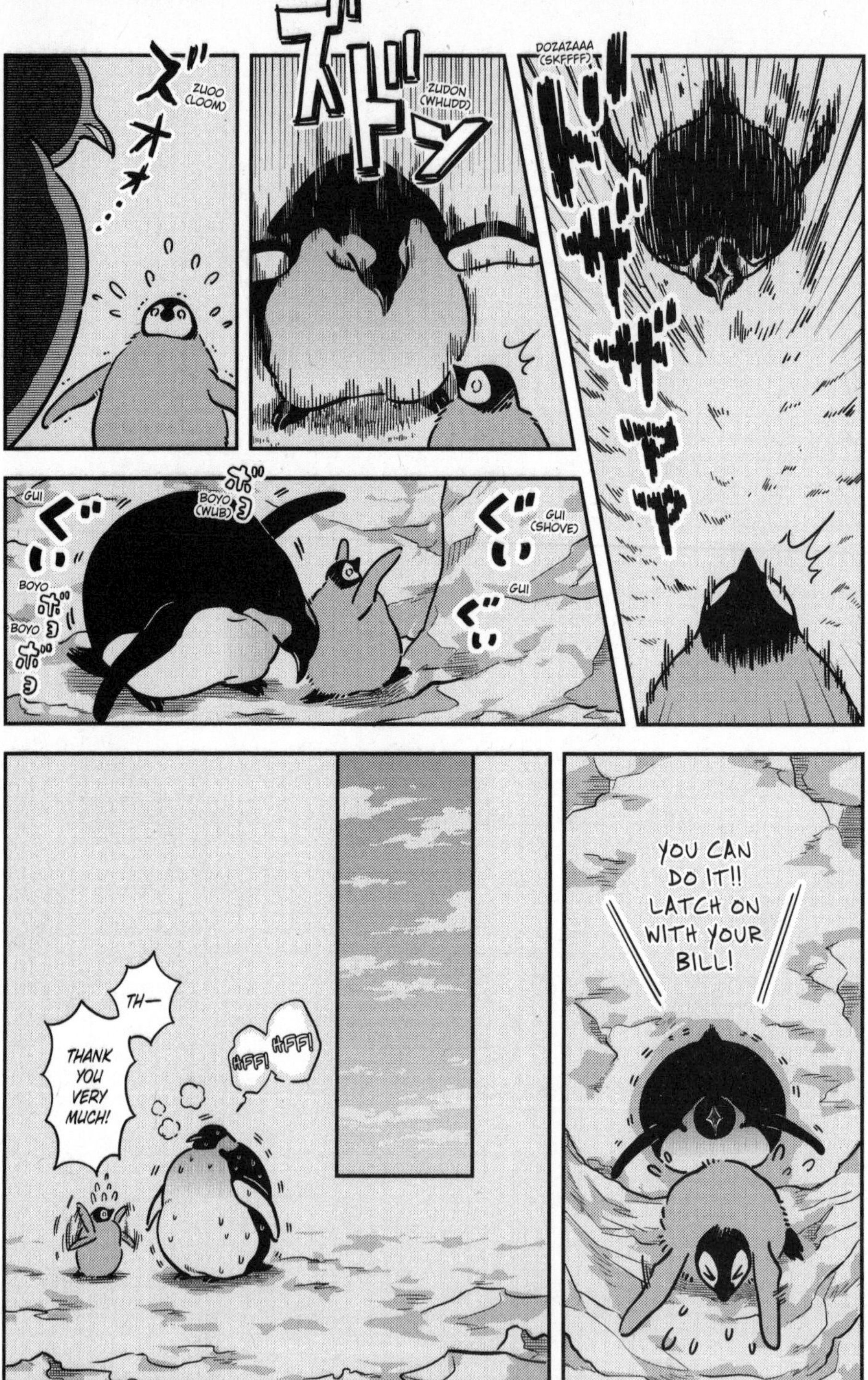

DOZAZAAA (SKFFFF)
ZUDON (WHUDD)
ZUOO (LOOM)
GUI (SHOVE)
GUI
BOYO (WUB)
GUI
BOYO
BOYO
YOU CAN DO IT!! LATCH ON WITH YOUR BILL!
HFF! HFF!
TH—
THANK YOU VERY MUCH!

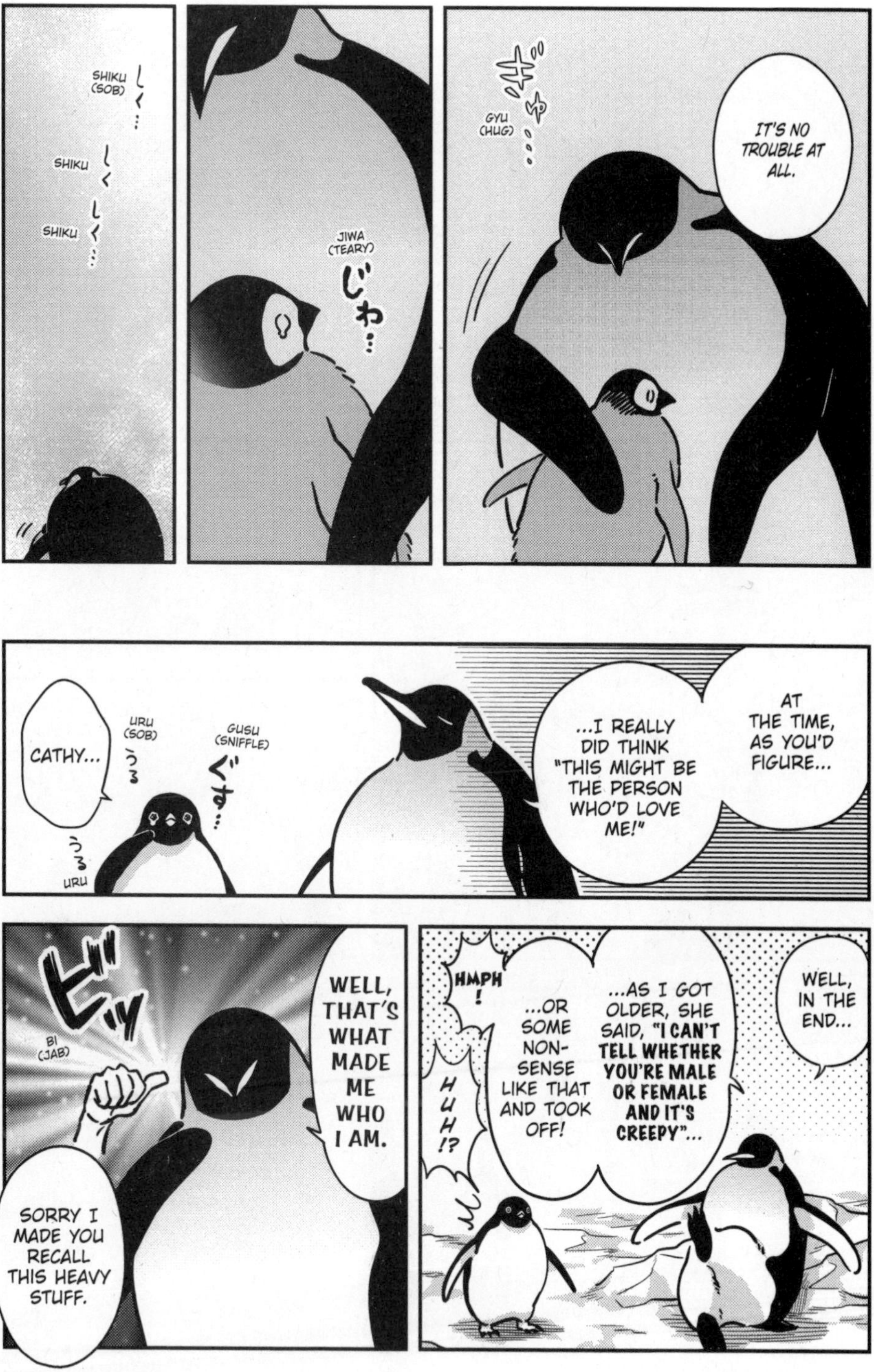

GYU (HUG)
ぎゅ…
IT'S NO TROUBLE AT ALL.
JIWA (TEARY)
じわ…
SHIKU (SOB)
しく…
SHIKU
しく
SHIKU
しく…
AT THE TIME, AS YOU'D FIGURE...
...I REALLY DID THINK "THIS MIGHT BE THE PERSON WHO'D LOVE ME!"
GUSU (SNIFFLE)
ぐす…
URU (SOB)
うる
CATHY...
うる
URU
WELL, IN THE END...
...AS I GOT OLDER, SHE SAID, "I CAN'T TELL WHETHER YOU'RE MALE OR FEMALE AND IT'S CREEPY"...
...OR SOME NON-SENSE LIKE THAT AND TOOK OFF!
HMPH!
HUH!?
WELL, THAT'S WHAT MADE ME WHO I AM.
BI (JAB)
ビッ
SORRY I MADE YOU RECALL THIS HEAVY STUFF.

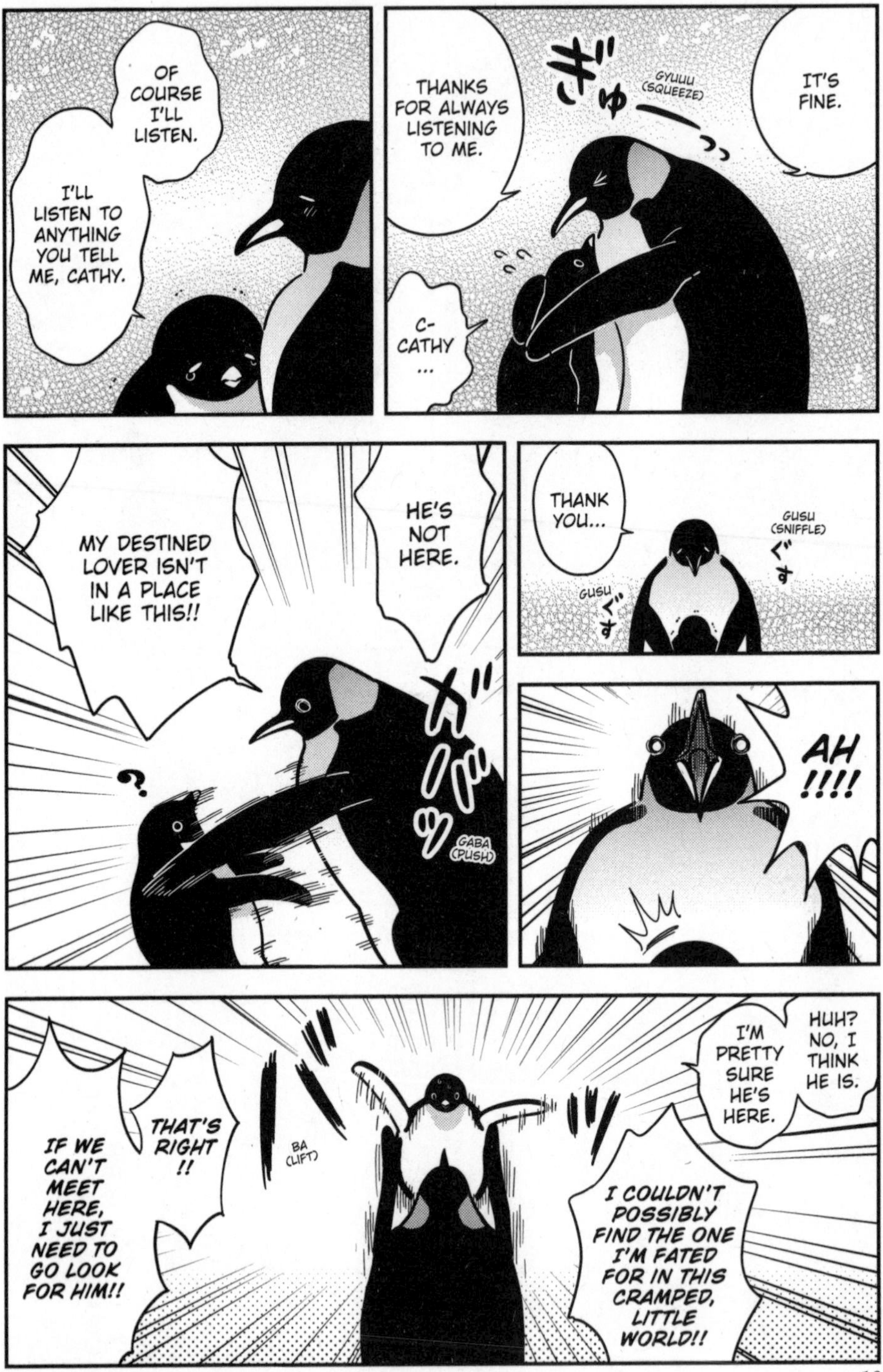
IT'S FINE.
GYUUU (SQUEEZE)
ぎゅーっ
THANKS FOR ALWAYS LISTENING TO ME.
C-CATHY...
OF COURSE I'LL LISTEN.
I'LL LISTEN TO ANYTHING YOU TELL ME, CATHY.
GUSU (SNIFFLE)
ぐす
THANK YOU...
GUSU
ぐす
AH!!!!
HE'S NOT HERE.
MY DESTINED LOVER ISN'T IN A PLACE LIKE THIS!!
GABA (PUSH)
HUH? NO, I THINK HE IS.
I'M PRETTY SURE HE'S HERE.
I COULDN'T POSSIBLY FIND THE ONE I'M FATED FOR IN THIS CRAMPED, LITTLE WORLD!!
BA (LIFT)
THAT'S RIGHT!!
IF WE CAN'T MEET HERE, I JUST NEED TO GO LOOK FOR HIM!!

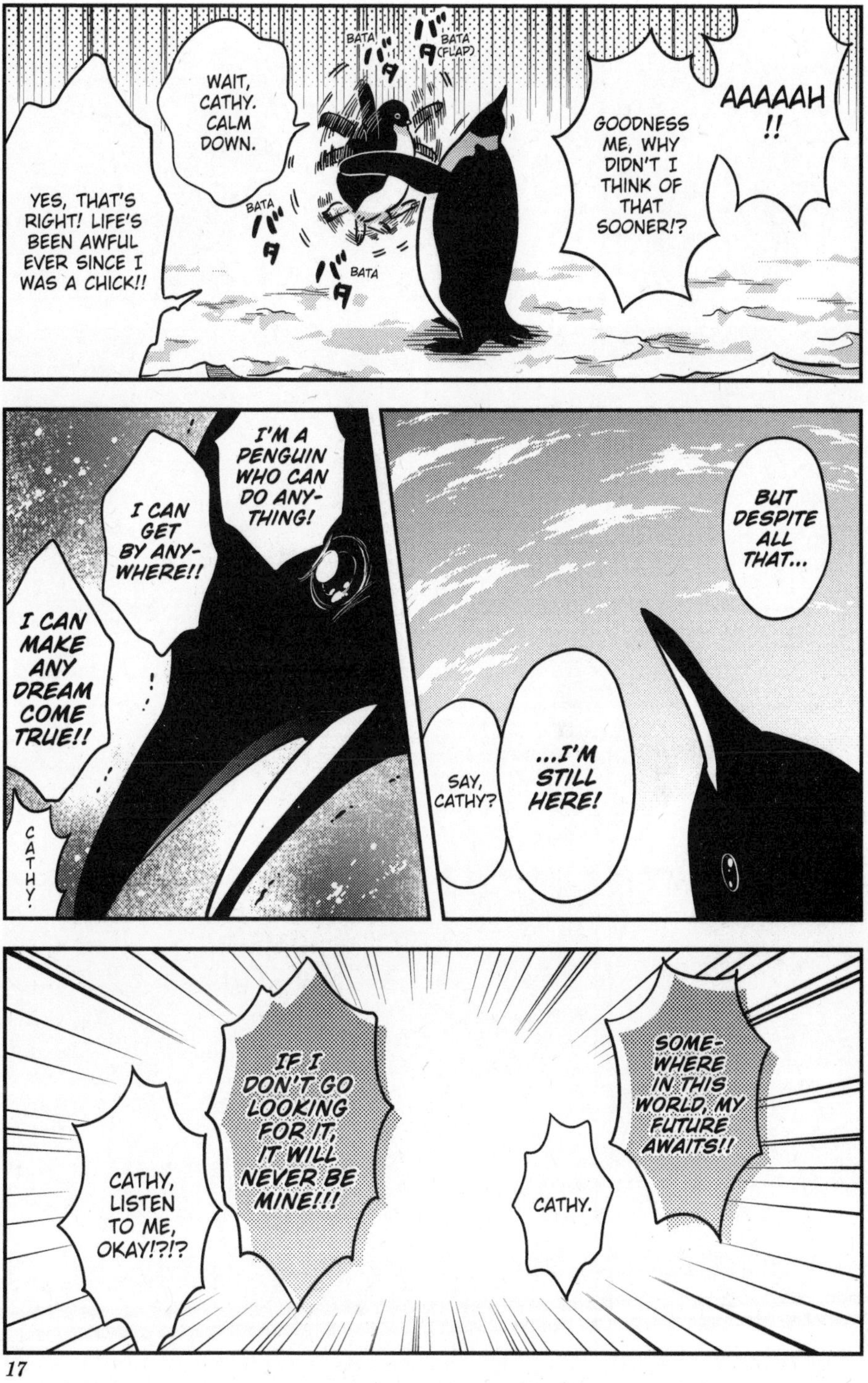
AAAAAH!!
GOODNESS ME, WHY DIDN'T I THINK OF THAT SOONER!?
BATA バタ BATA (FLAP) バタ
WAIT, CATHY. CALM DOWN.
BATA バタ BATA バタ
YES, THAT'S RIGHT! LIFE'S BEEN AWFUL EVER SINCE I WAS A CHICK!!
BUT DESPITE ALL THAT...
...I'M STILL HERE!
SAY, CATHY?
I'M A PENGUIN WHO CAN DO ANYTHING!
I CAN GET BY ANYWHERE!!
I CAN MAKE ANY DREAM COME TRUE!!
CATHY.
SOMEWHERE IN THIS WORLD, MY FUTURE AWAITS!!
CATHY.
IF I DON'T GO LOOKING FOR IT, IT WILL NEVER BE MINE!!!
CATHY, LISTEN TO ME, OKAY!?!?

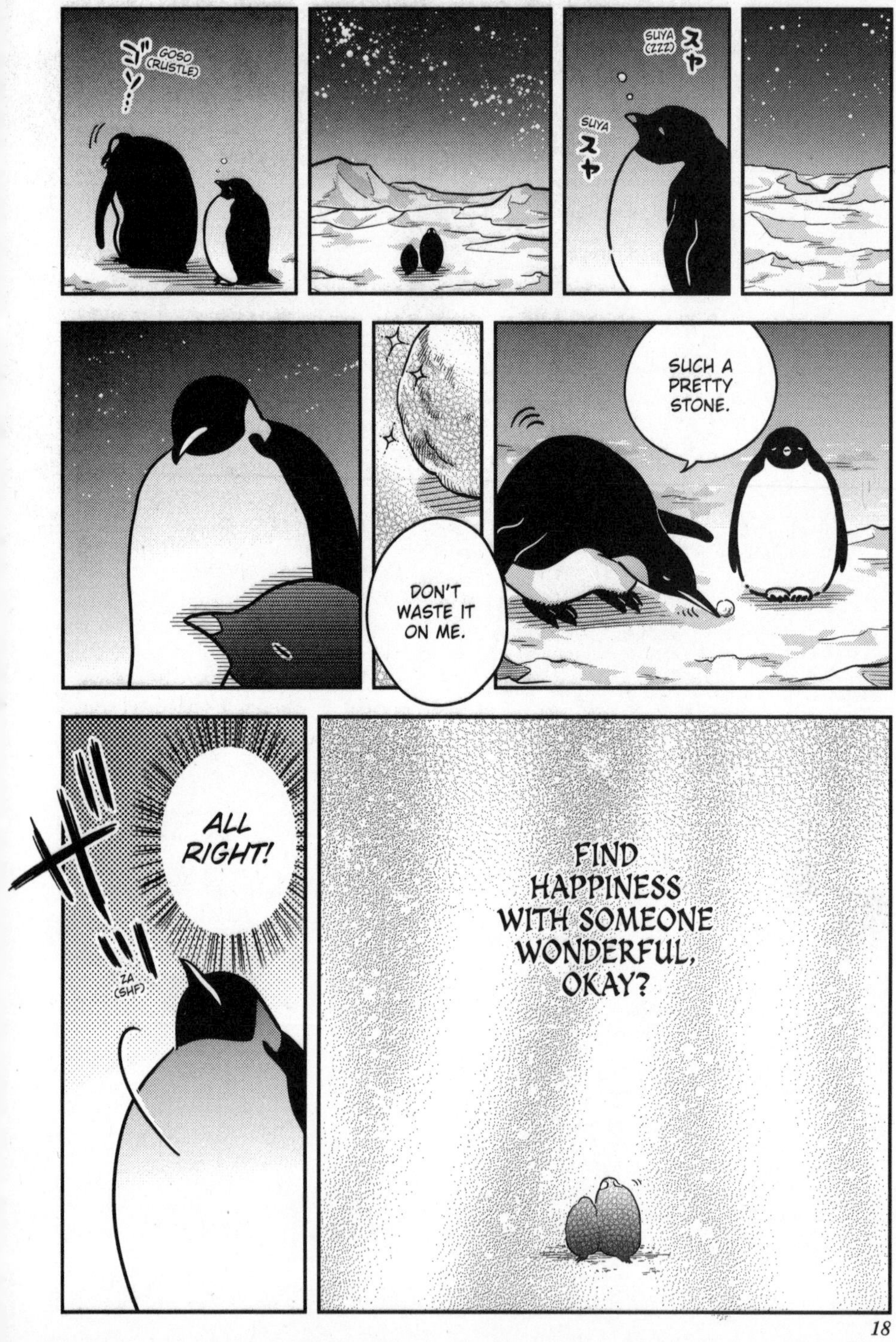
SUYA (ZZZ) スヤ
SUYA スヤ
GOSO (RUSTLE)
SUCH A PRETTY STONE.
DON'T WASTE IT ON ME.
FIND HAPPINESS WITH SOMEONE WONDERFUL, OKAY?
ALL RIGHT!
ZA (SHF)

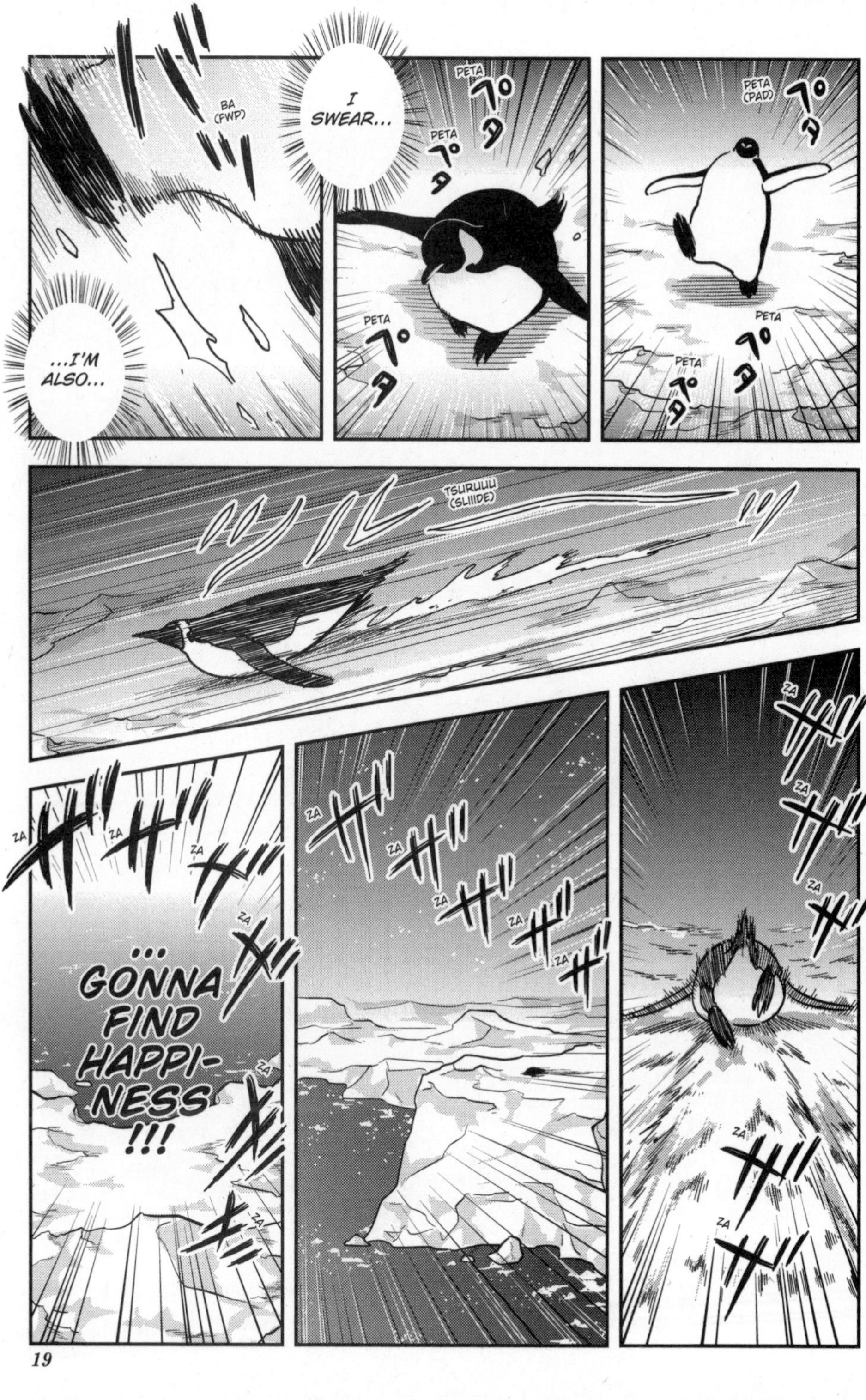
PETA (PAD)
PETA
PETA
I SWEAR...
PETA
PETA
PETA
BA (FWP)
...I'M ALSO...
TSURUUU (SLIIIDE)
ZA
ZA
ZA
ZA
ZA
ZA
ZA
ZA
ZA
ZA
ZA
ZA
ZA
ZA
...GONNA FIND HAPPINESS!!!
ZA
ZA

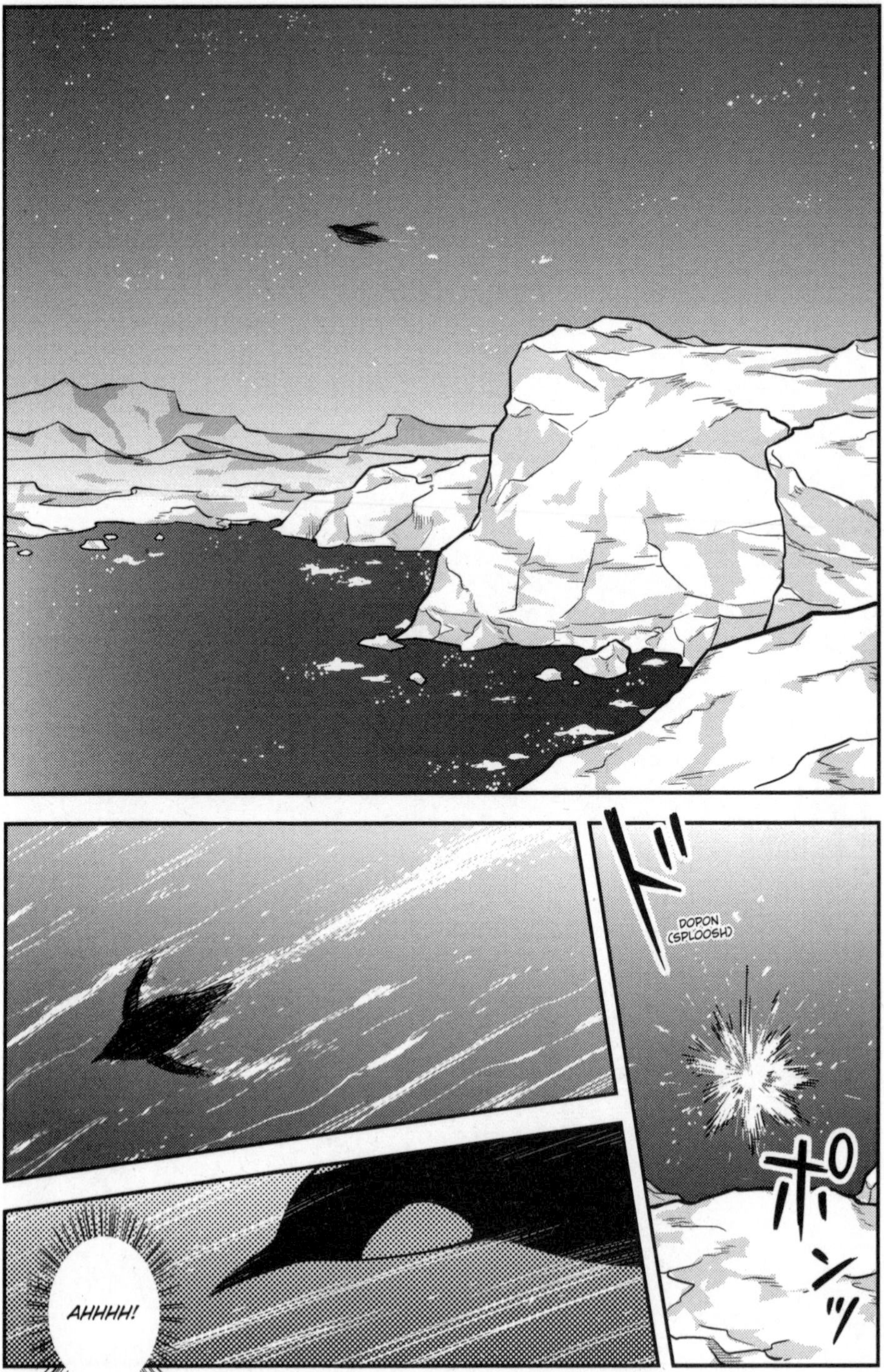
ド
DOPON
(SPLOOSH)
ポンッ
AHHHH!

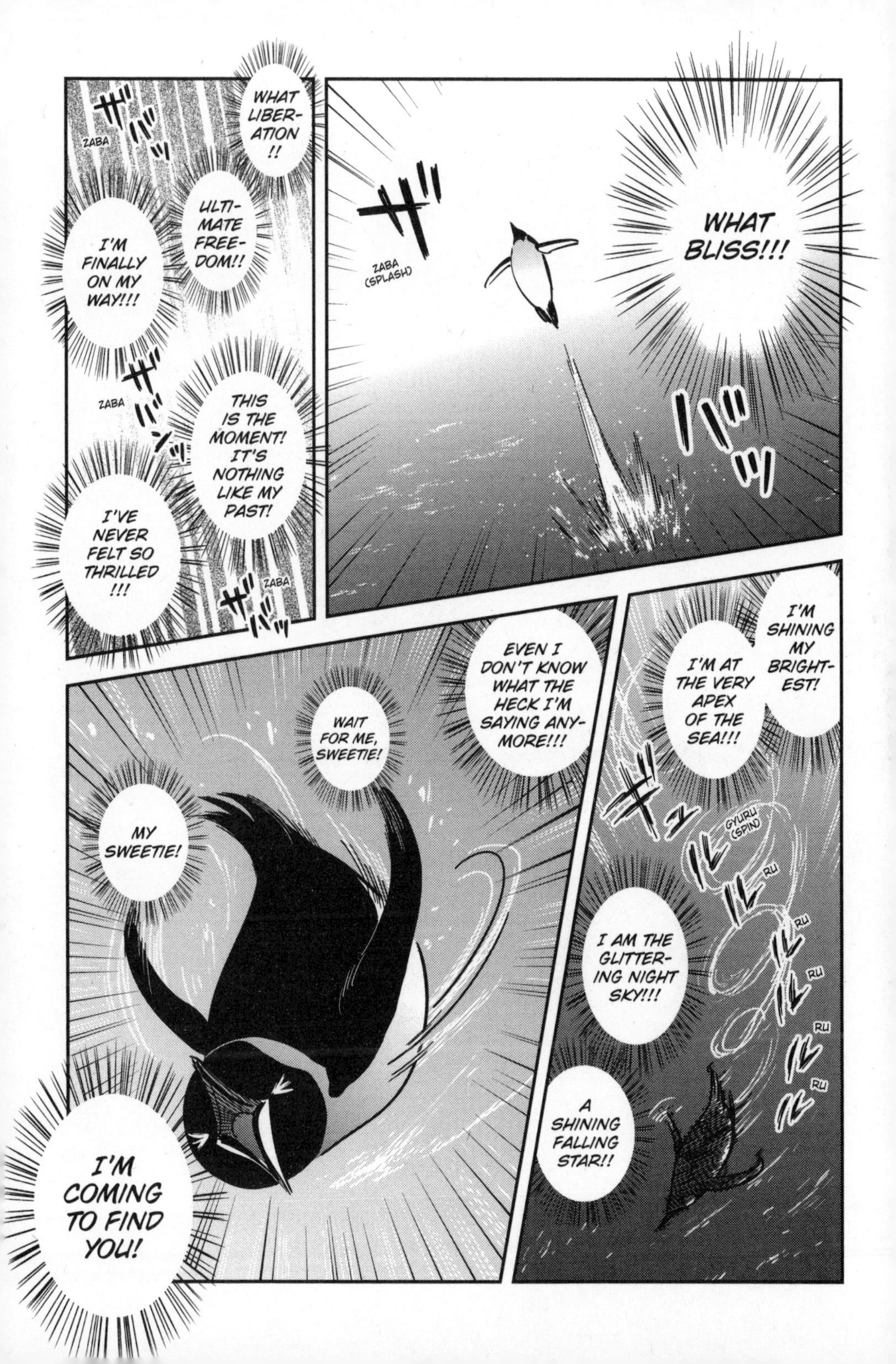
ZABA (SPLASH)
WHAT BLISS!!!
WHAT LIBERATION!!
ZABA
ULTIMATE FREEDOM!!
I'M FINALLY ON MY WAY!!!
THIS IS THE MOMENT! IT'S NOTHING LIKE MY PAST!
ZABA
I'VE NEVER FELT SO THRILLED!!!
ZABA
I'M SHINING MY BRIGHTEST!
I'M AT THE VERY APEX OF THE SEA!!!
GYURU (SPIN)
RU
I AM THE GLITTERING NIGHT SKY!!!
RU
RU
RU
RU
A SHINING FALLING STAR!!
EVEN I DON'T KNOW WHAT THE HECK I'M SAYING ANYMORE!!!
WAIT FOR ME, SWEETIE!
MY SWEETIE!
I'M COMING TO FIND YOU!

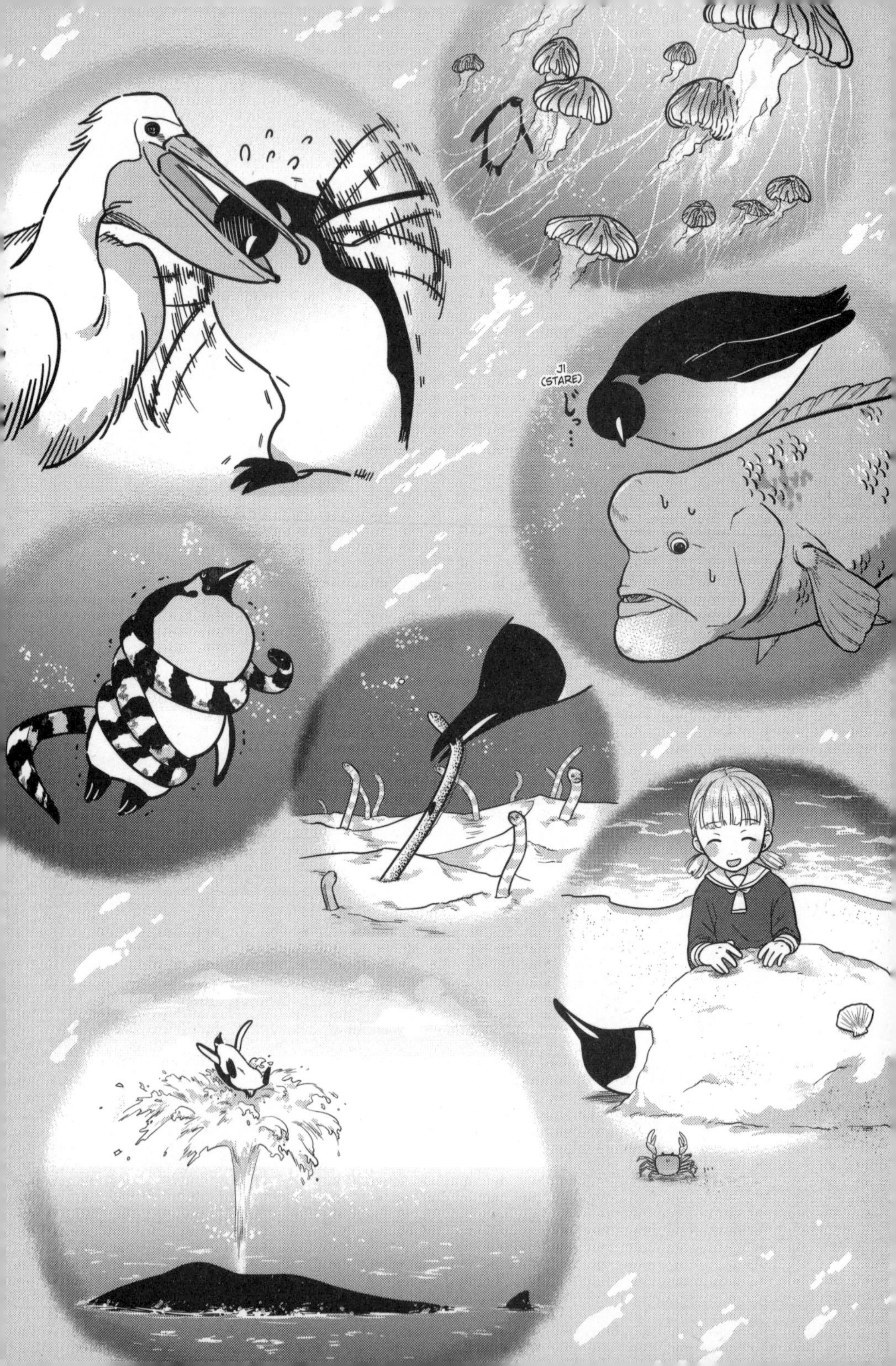
JI (STARE)
じっ…

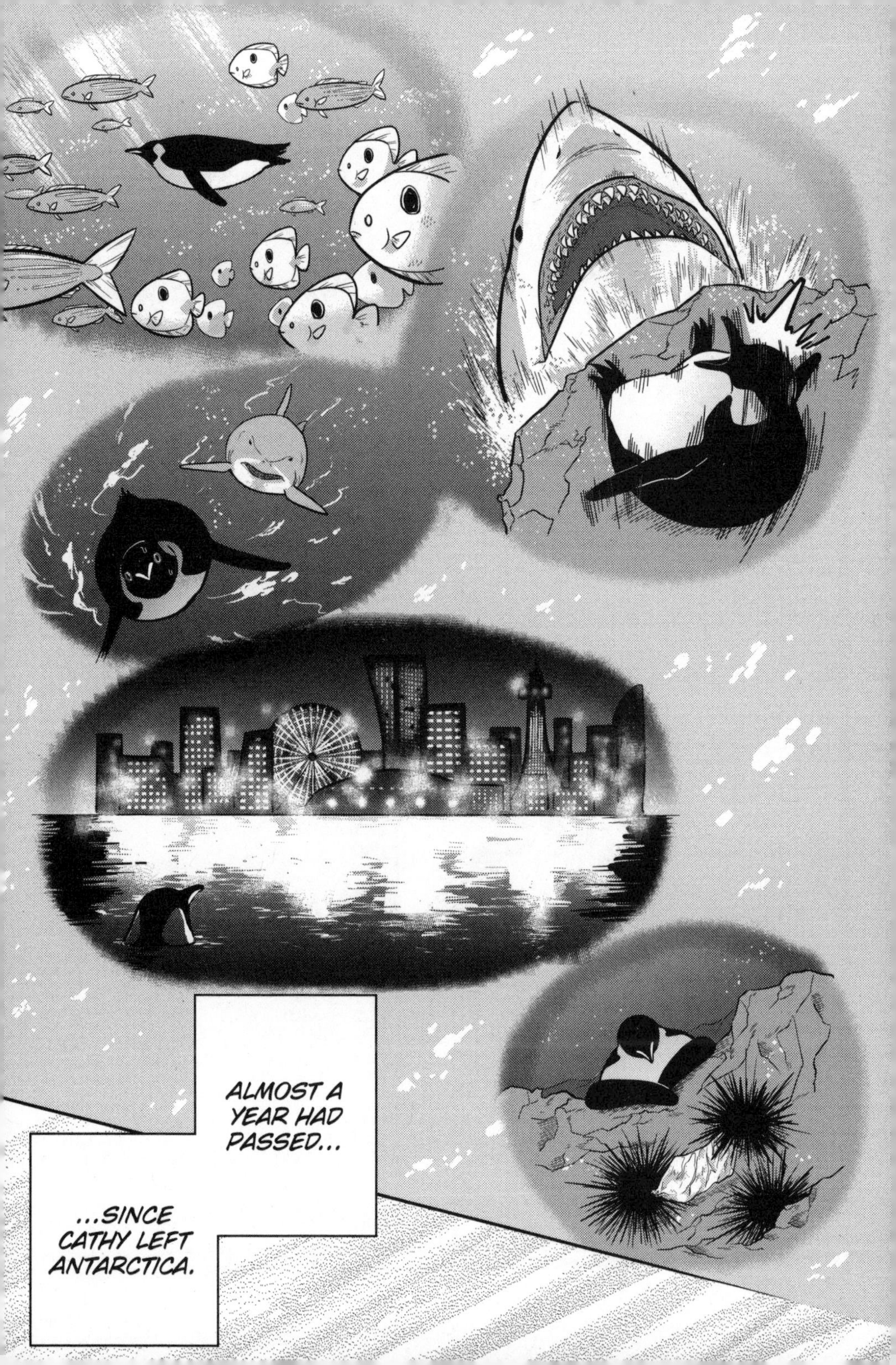
ALMOST A YEAR HAD PASSED...
...SINCE CATHY LEFT ANTARCTICA.

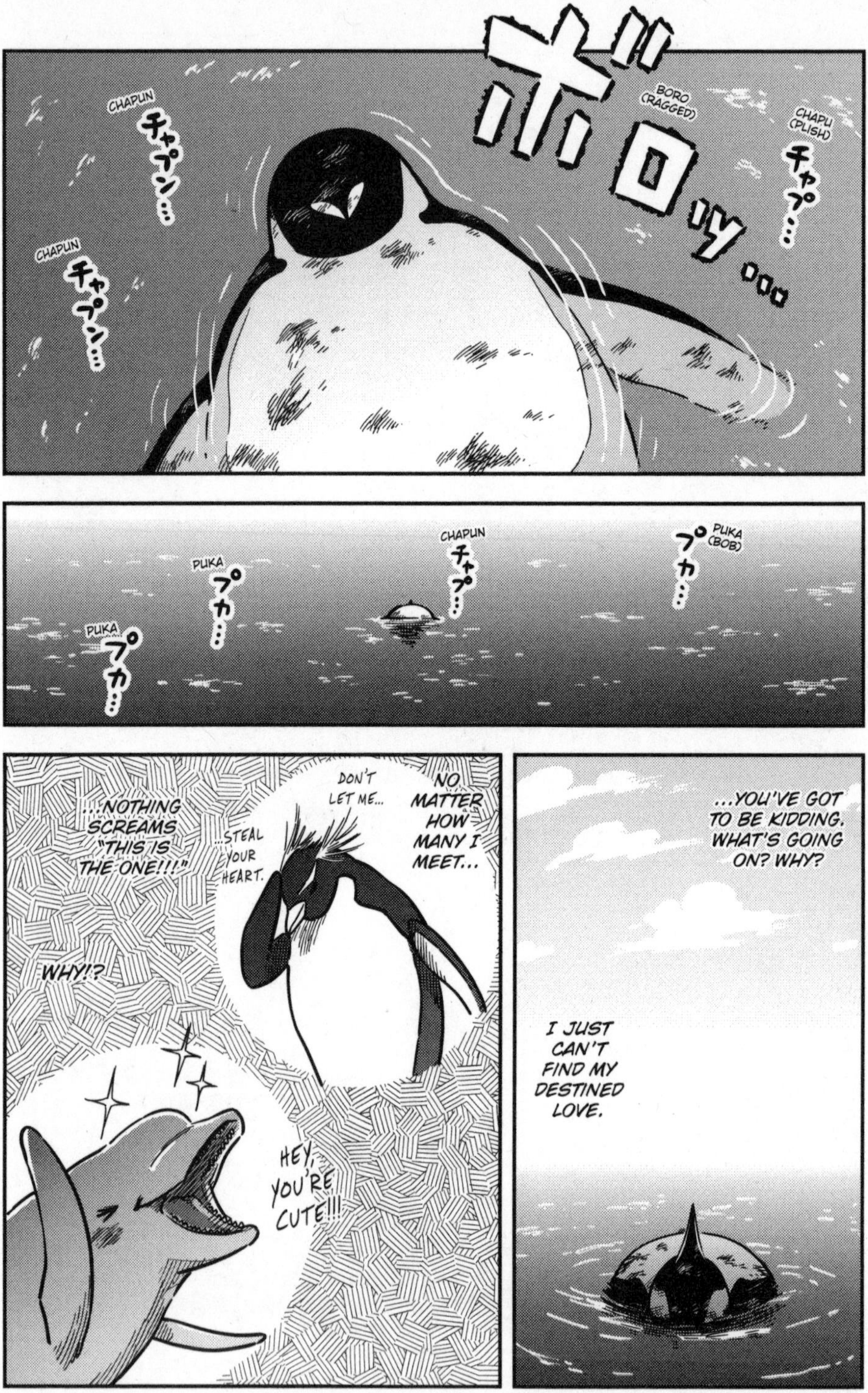
CHAPU (PLISH)
チャプ…
BORO (RAGGED)
ボロッ…
CHAPUN
チャプン…
CHAPUN
チャプン…
PUKA (BOB)
プカ…
CHAPUN
チャプ…
PUKA
プカ…
PUKA
プカ…
...YOU'VE GOT TO BE KIDDING. WHAT'S GOING ON? WHY?
I JUST CAN'T FIND MY DESTINED LOVE.
NO MATTER HOW MANY I MEET...
DON'T LET ME...
...STEAL YOUR HEART.
...NOTHING SCREAMS "THIS IS THE ONE!!!"
WHY!?
HEY, YOU'RE CUTE!!!

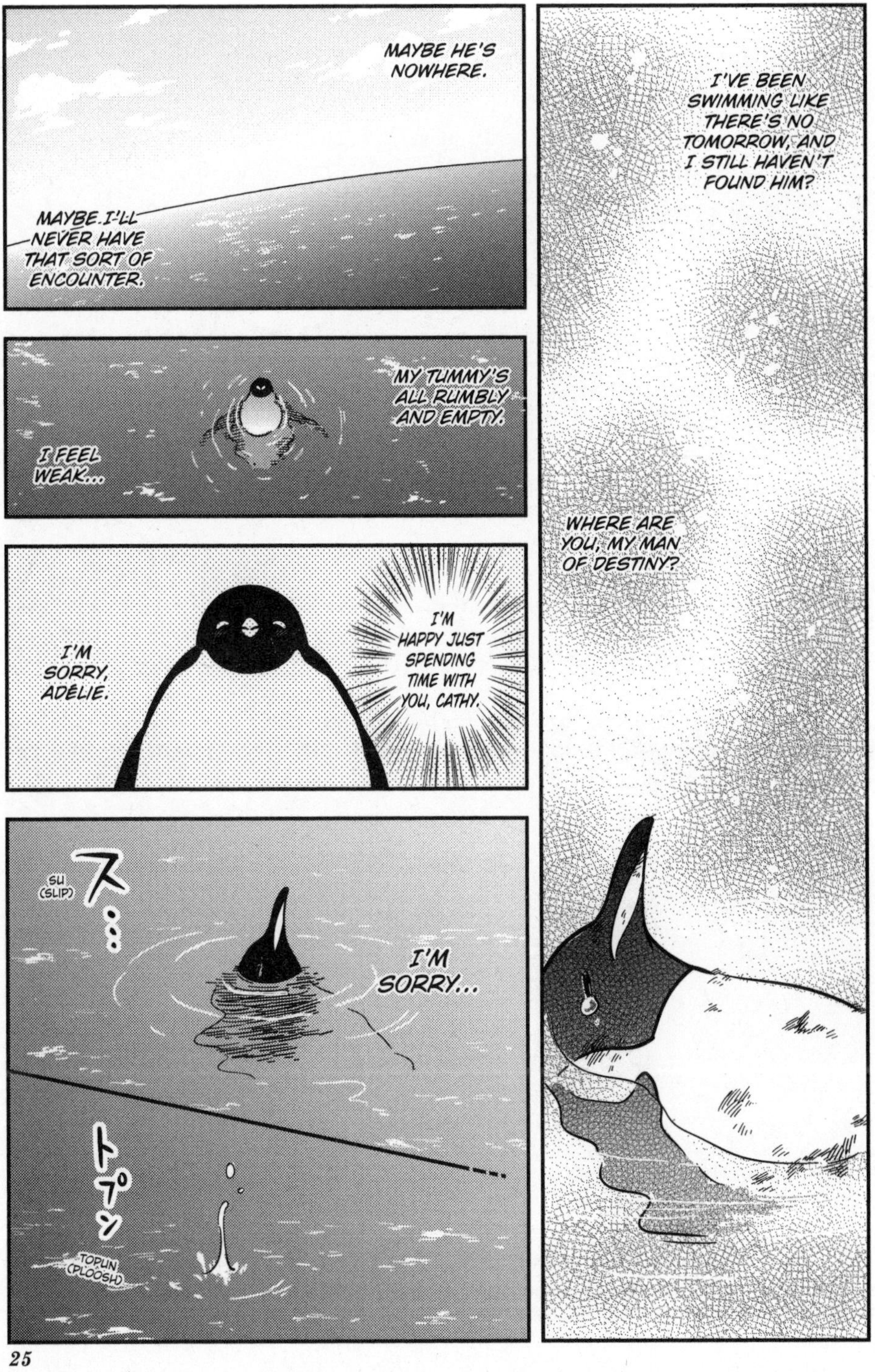
I'VE BEEN SWIMMING LIKE THERE'S NO TOMORROW, AND I STILL HAVEN'T FOUND HIM?
WHERE ARE YOU, MY MAN OF DESTINY?
MAYBE HE'S NOWHERE.
MAYBE I'LL NEVER HAVE THAT SORT OF ENCOUNTER.
MY TUMMY'S ALL RUMBLY AND EMPTY.
I FEEL WEAK...
I'M HAPPY JUST SPENDING TIME WITH YOU, CATHY.
I'M SORRY, ADÉLIE.
ス…
SU (SLIP)
I'M SORRY...
トプン
TOPUN (PLOOSH)

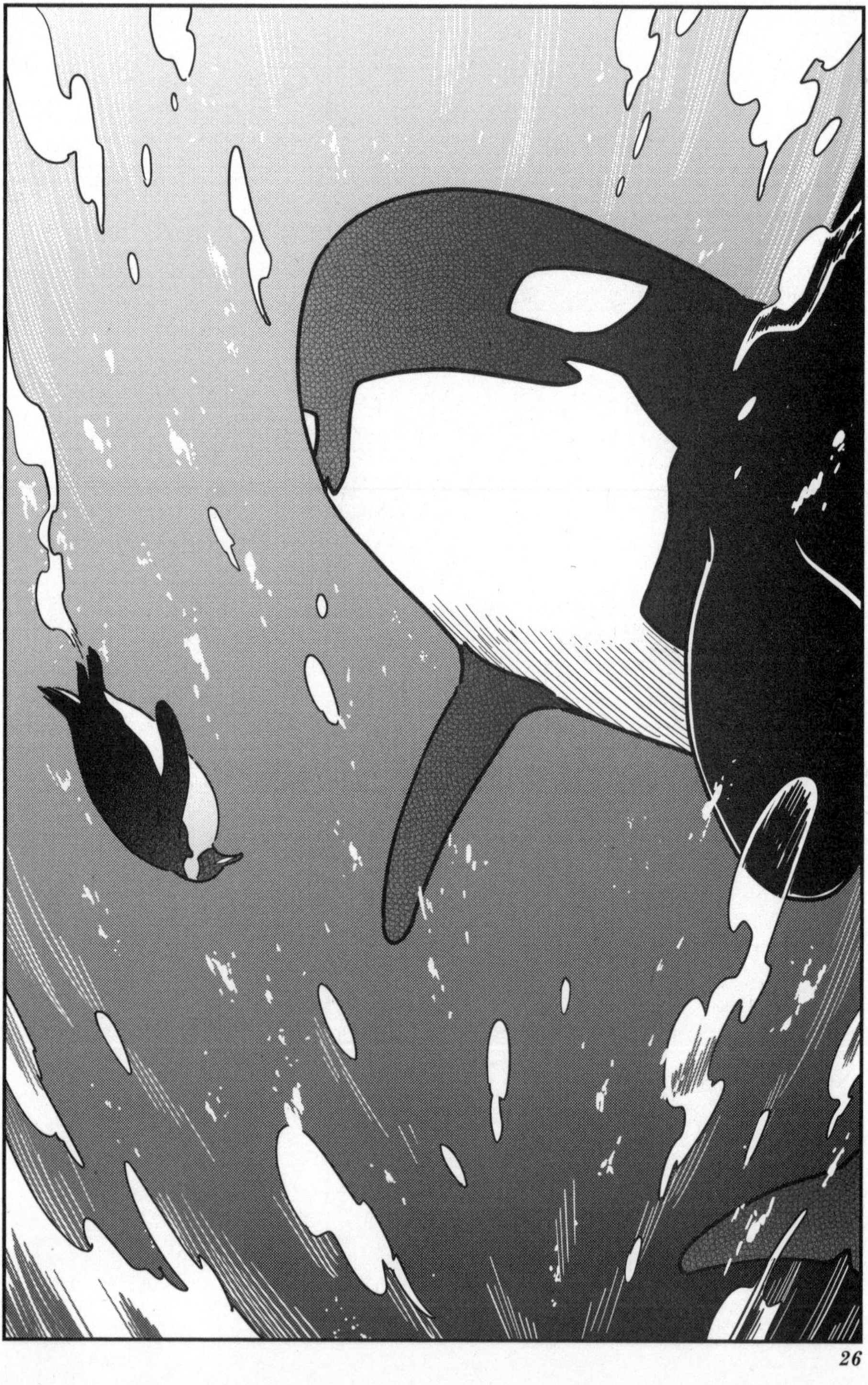

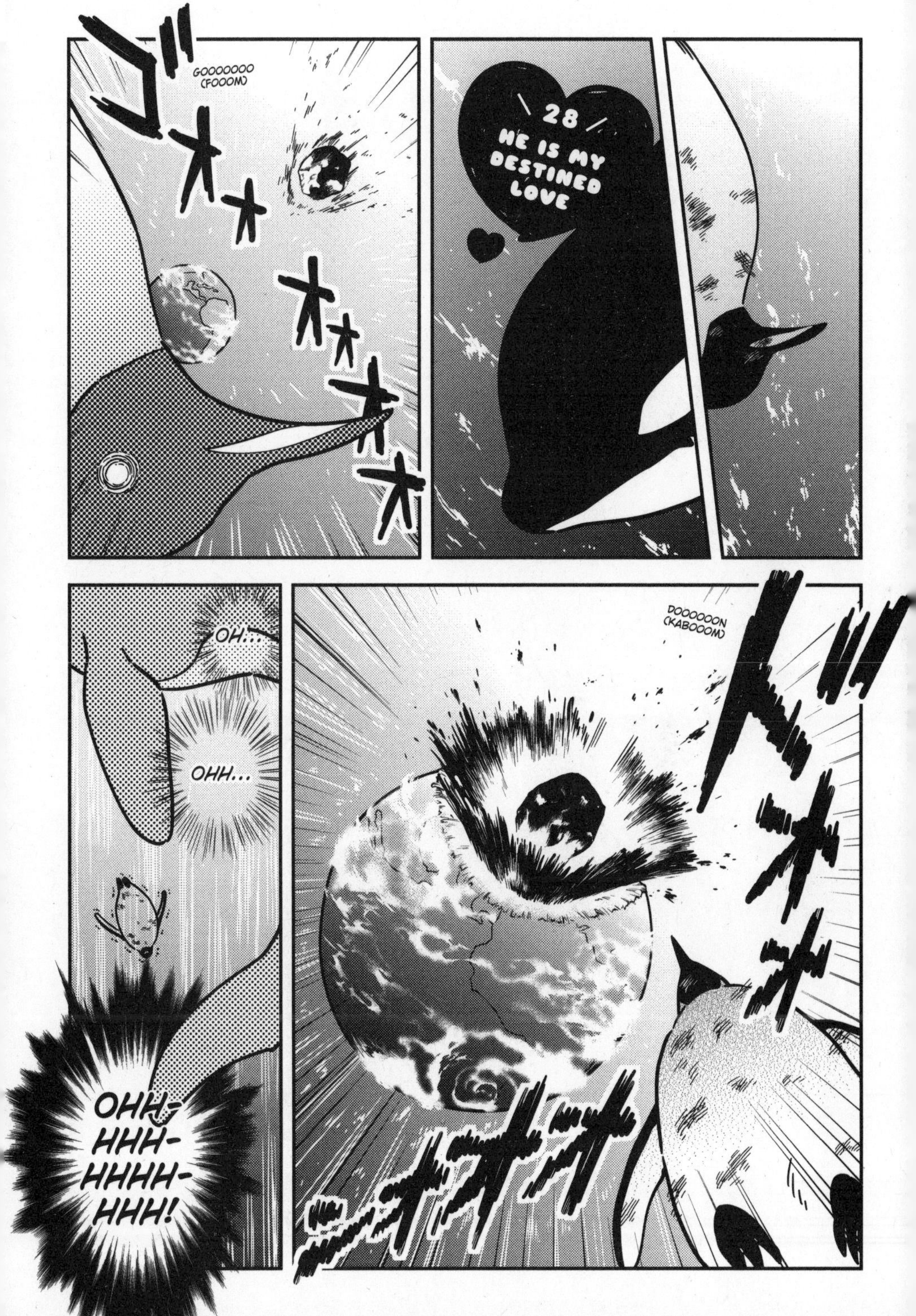
28
HE IS MY DESTINED LOVE
GOOOOOOO (FOOOM)
DOOOOOON (KABOOOM)
OH...
OHH...
OHH-HHH-HHHH-HHH!

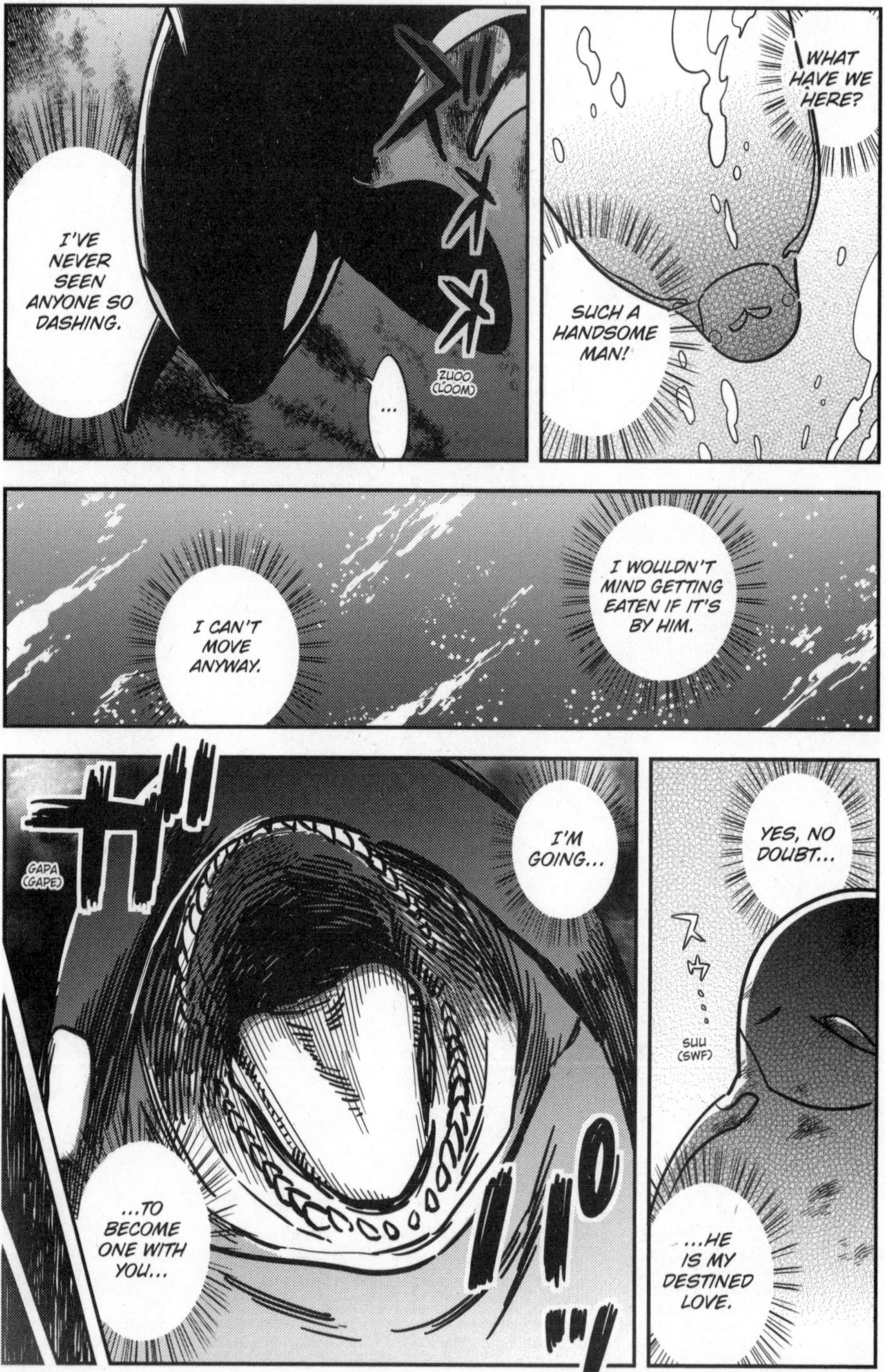
WHAT HAVE WE HERE?
SUCH A HANDSOME MAN!
I'VE NEVER SEEN ANYONE SO DASHING.
ZUOO (LOOM)
...
I WOULDN'T MIND GETTING EATEN IF IT'S BY HIM.
I CAN'T MOVE ANYWAY.
YES, NO DOUBT...
SUU (SWF)
...HE IS MY DESTINED LOVE.
I'M GOING...
GAPA (GAPE)
...TO BECOME ONE WITH YOU...

MUKU
(RISE)

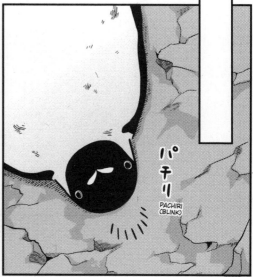

PACHIRI
(BLINK)

ZABAA
(SPLOOSH)

BARARARARA
(SCATTER)

......

?

?

KYORO
(PEEK)

KYORO

YURA
(RIPPLE)

?

A
DREAM
?

?

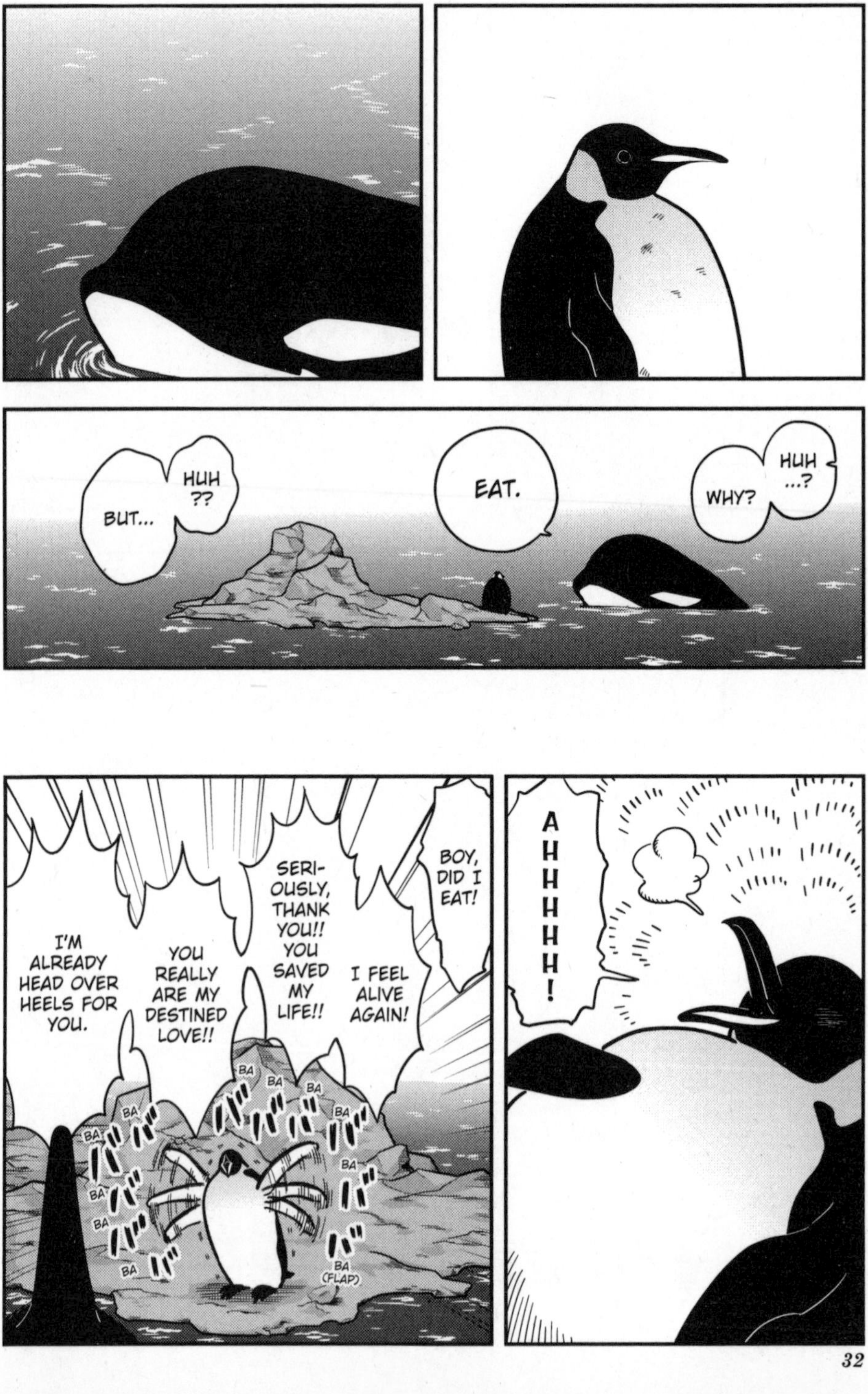
HUH ...?
WHY?
EAT.
HUH ??
BUT...
AHHHHHH!
BOY, DID I EAT!
I FEEL ALIVE AGAIN!
SERI-OUSLY, THANK YOU!! YOU SAVED MY LIFE!!
YOU REALLY ARE MY DESTINED LOVE!!
I'M ALREADY HEAD OVER HEELS FOR YOU.
BA BA BA BA BA BA BA BA BA BA
BA (FLAP)

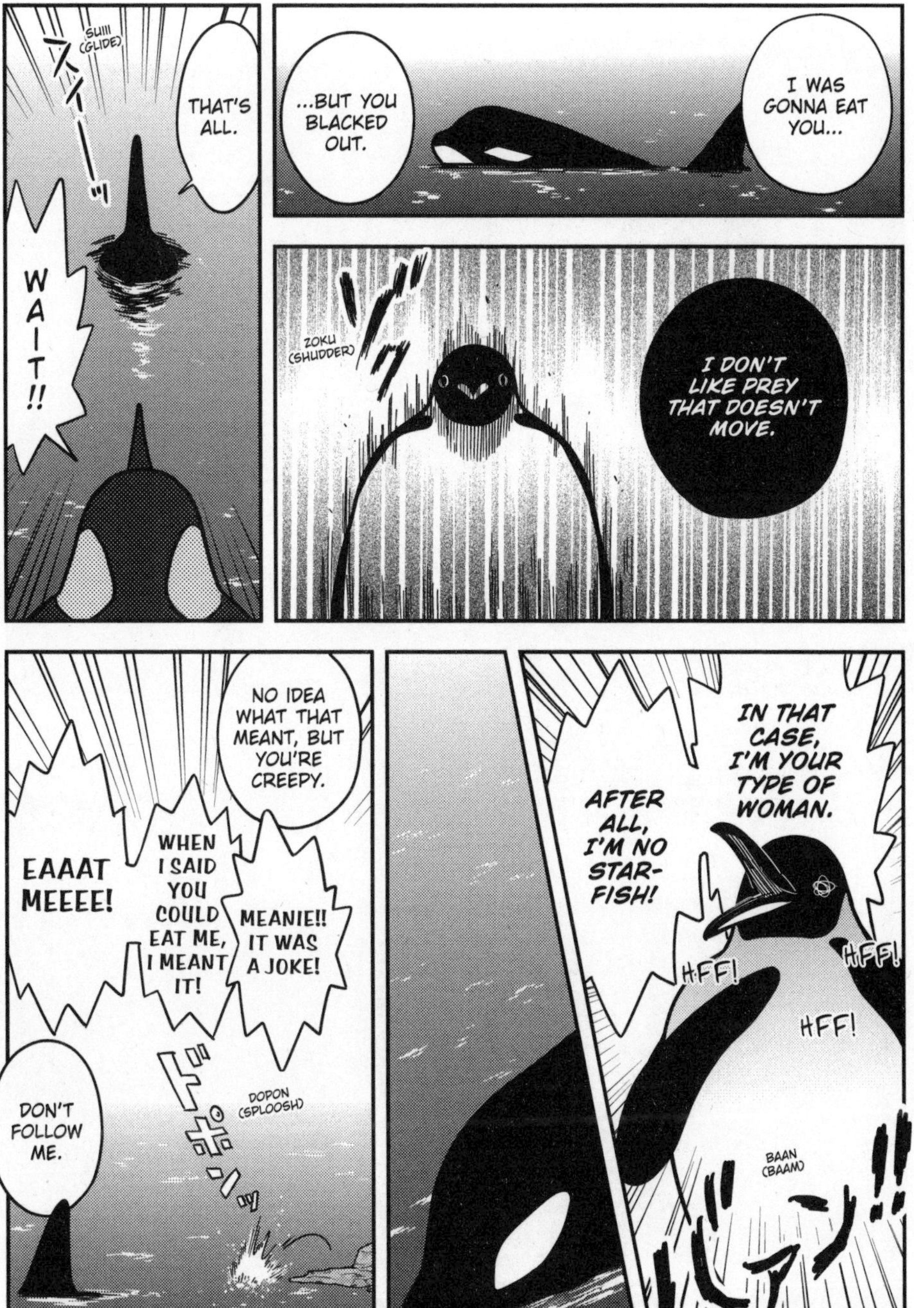
I WAS GONNA EAT YOU...
...BUT YOU BLACKED OUT.
I DON'T LIKE PREY THAT DOESN'T MOVE.
ZOKU (SHUDDER)
THAT'S ALL.
SUIII (GLIDE)
WAIT!!
IN THAT CASE, I'M YOUR TYPE OF WOMAN.
AFTER ALL, I'M NO STAR-FISH!
HFF!
HFF!
HFF!
BAAN (BAAM)
NO IDEA WHAT THAT MEANT, BUT YOU'RE CREEPY.
MEANIE!! IT WAS A JOKE!
WHEN I SAID YOU COULD EAT ME, I MEANT IT!
EAAAT MEEEE!
DOPON (SPLOOSH)
DON'T FOLLOW ME.

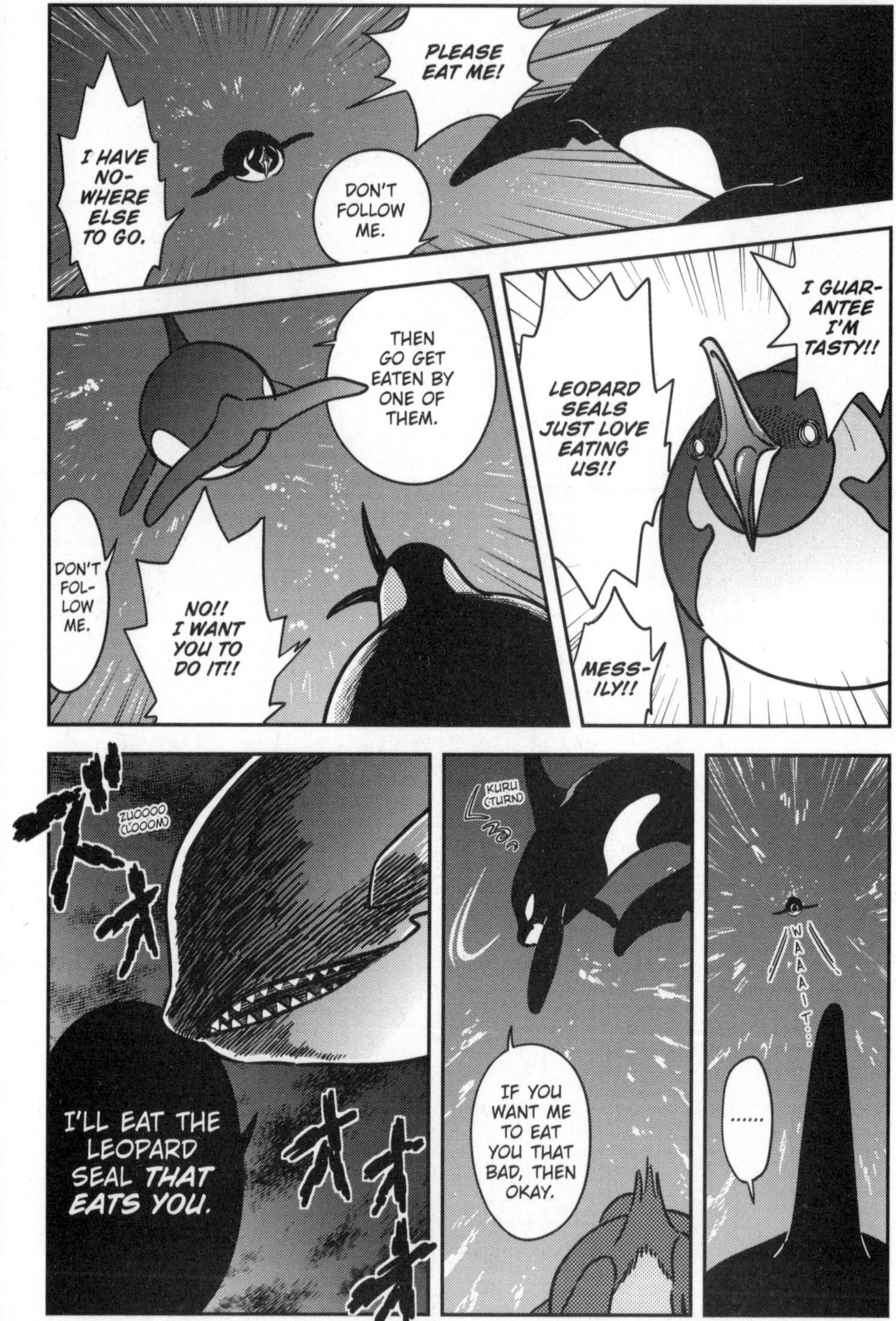
PLEASE EAT ME!
DON'T FOLLOW ME.
I HAVE NO-WHERE ELSE TO GO.
I GUAR-ANTEE I'M TASTY!!
LEOPARD SEALS JUST LOVE EATING US!!
MESS-ILY!!
THEN GO GET EATEN BY ONE OF THEM.
NO!! I WANT YOU TO DO IT!!
DON'T FOL-LOW ME.
WAAAIT...
......
KURU (TURN)
IF YOU WANT ME TO EAT YOU THAT BAD, THEN OKAY.
ZUOOOO (LOOOM)
I'LL EAT THE LEOPARD SEAL THAT EATS YOU.

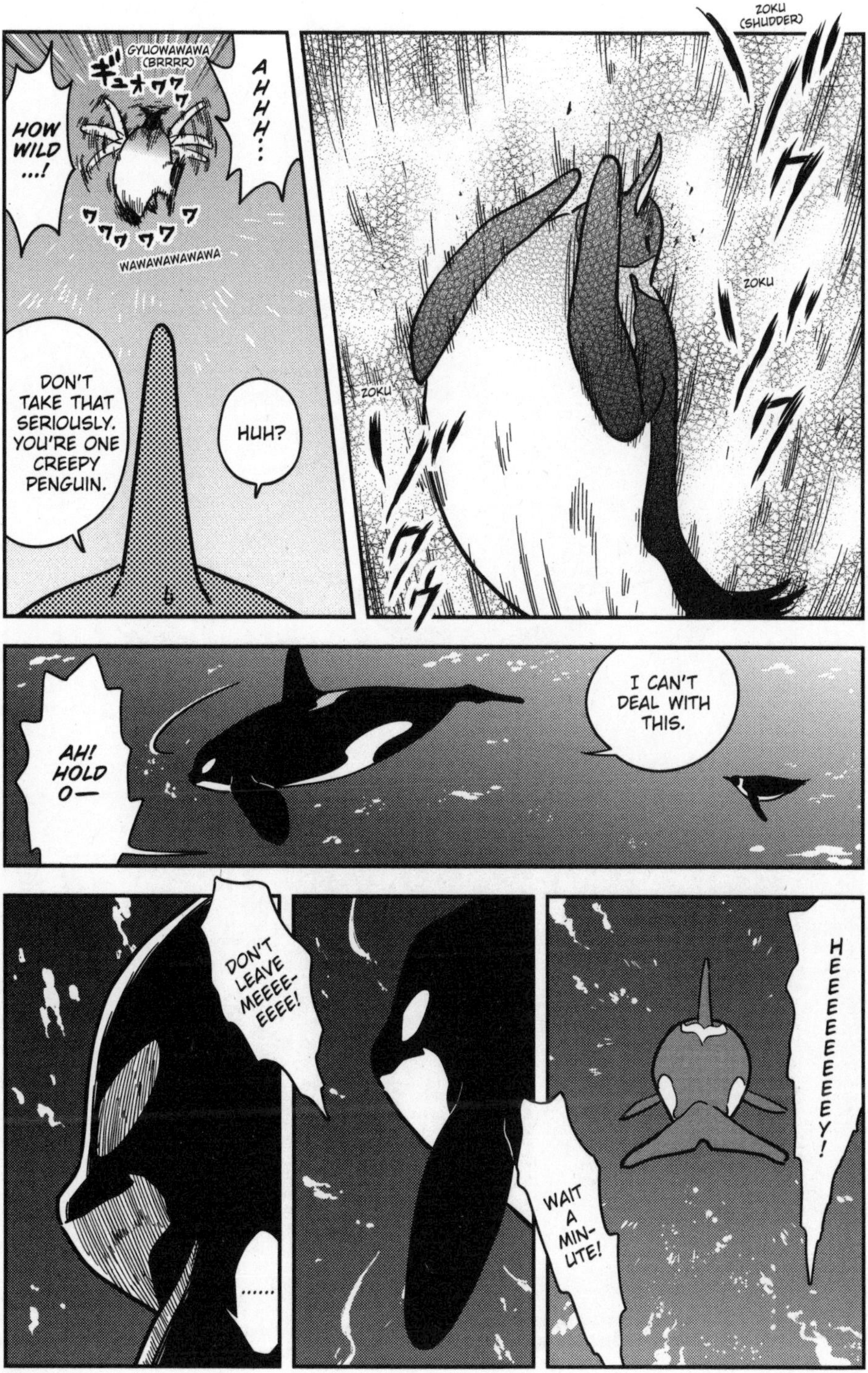
ZOKU (SHUDDER)
ZOKU
ZOKU
AHHH...
ギュオワワ
GYUOWAWAWA (BRRRR)
HOW WILD ...!
ワワワワワワ
WAWAWAWAWAWA
HUH?
DON'T TAKE THAT SERIOUSLY. YOU'RE ONE CREEPY PENGUIN.
I CAN'T DEAL WITH THIS.
AH! HOLD O—
HEEEEEEEEEY!
WAIT A MIN-UTE!
DON'T LEAVE MEEEE-EEEE!
......

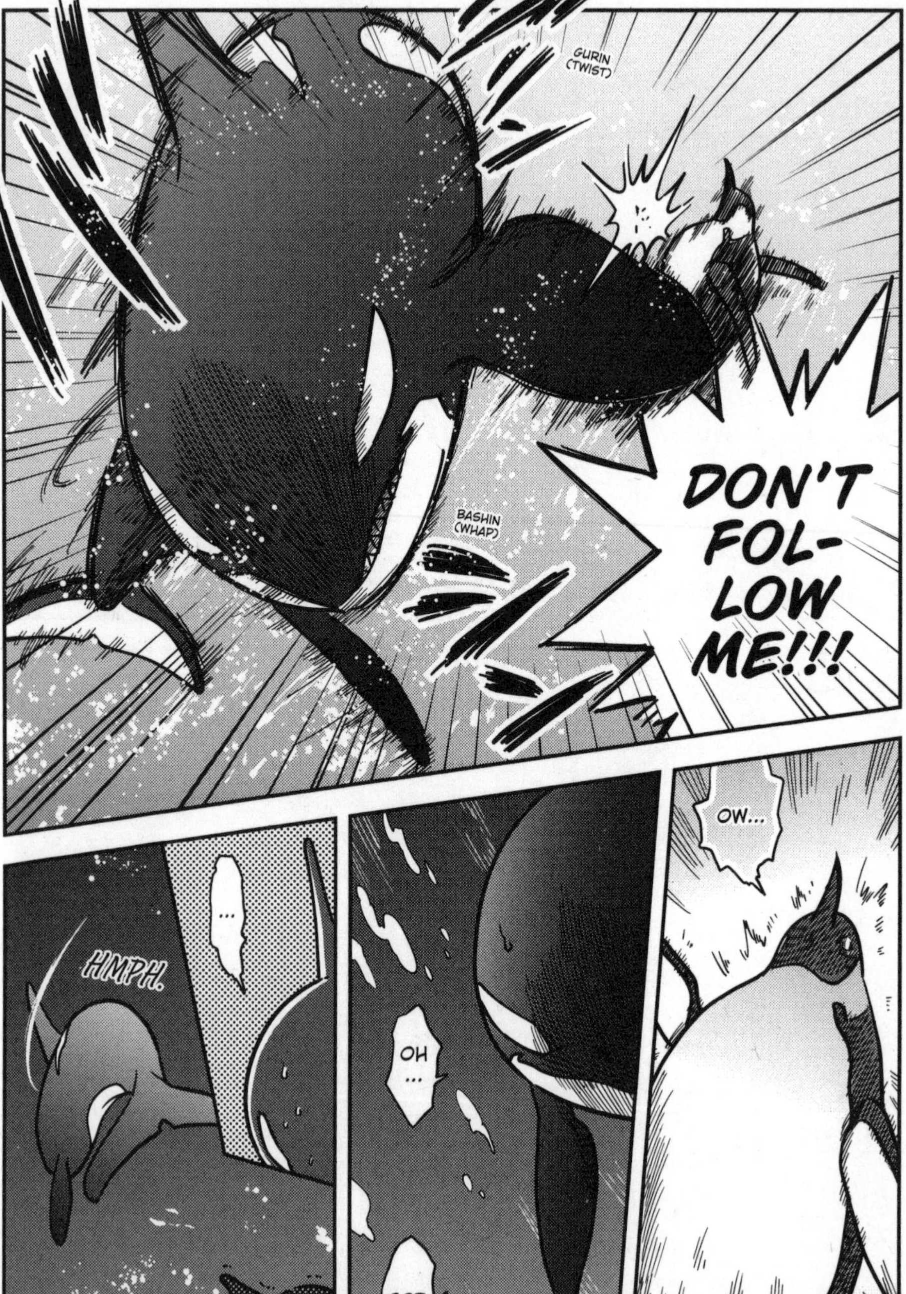
GURIN (TWIST)
DON'T FOL-LOW ME!!!
BASHIN (WHAP)
OW...
OH ...
SOR —
...
HMPH.

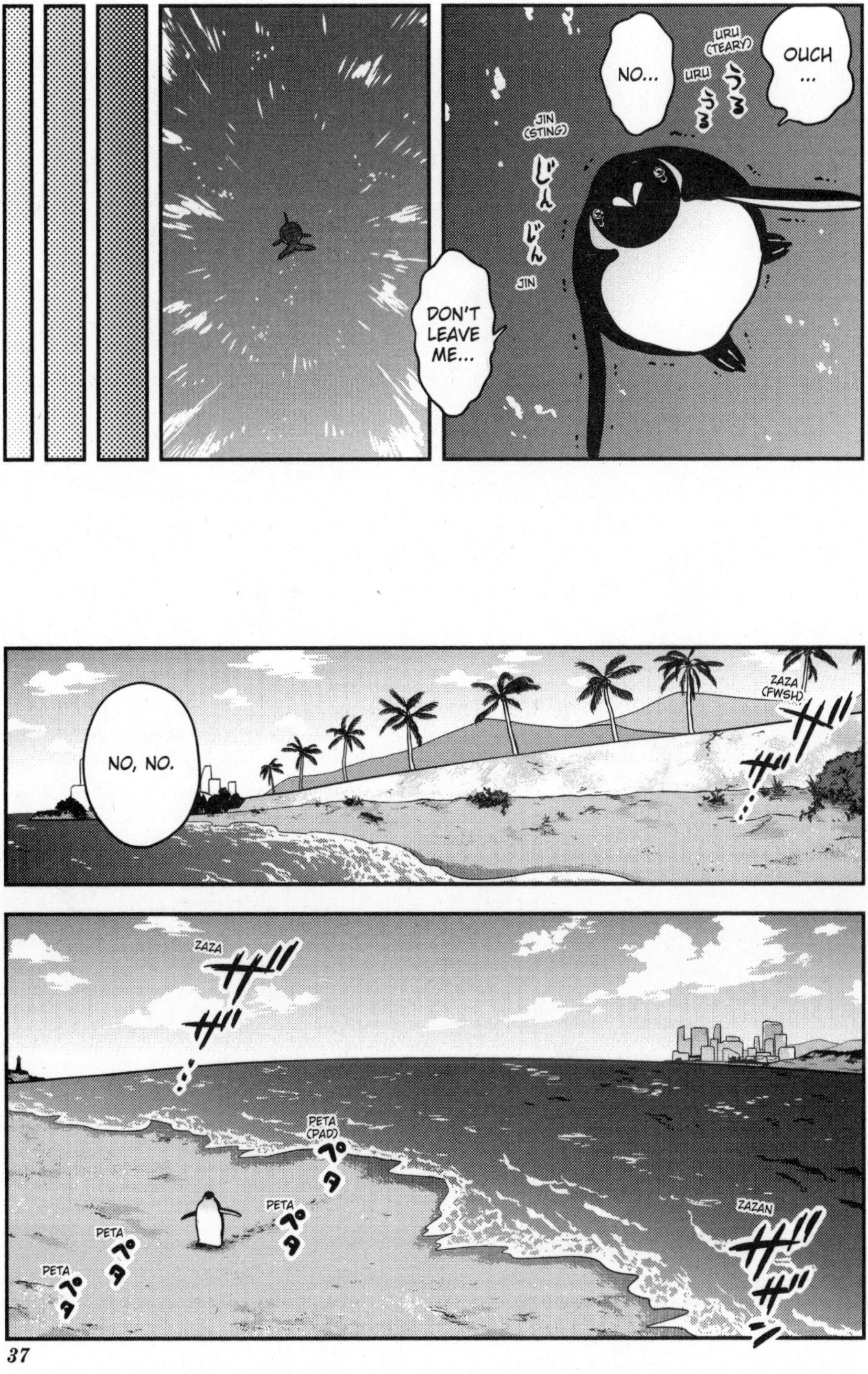
OUCH ...
URU (TEARY) うる
URU うる
NO...
JIN (STING) じん
じん JIN
DON'T LEAVE ME...
ZAZA (FWSH) ザザ...
NO, NO.
ZAZA ザザ...
ZAZAN ザザン
PETA (PAD) ペタ
PETA ペタ
PETA ペタ
PETA ペタ

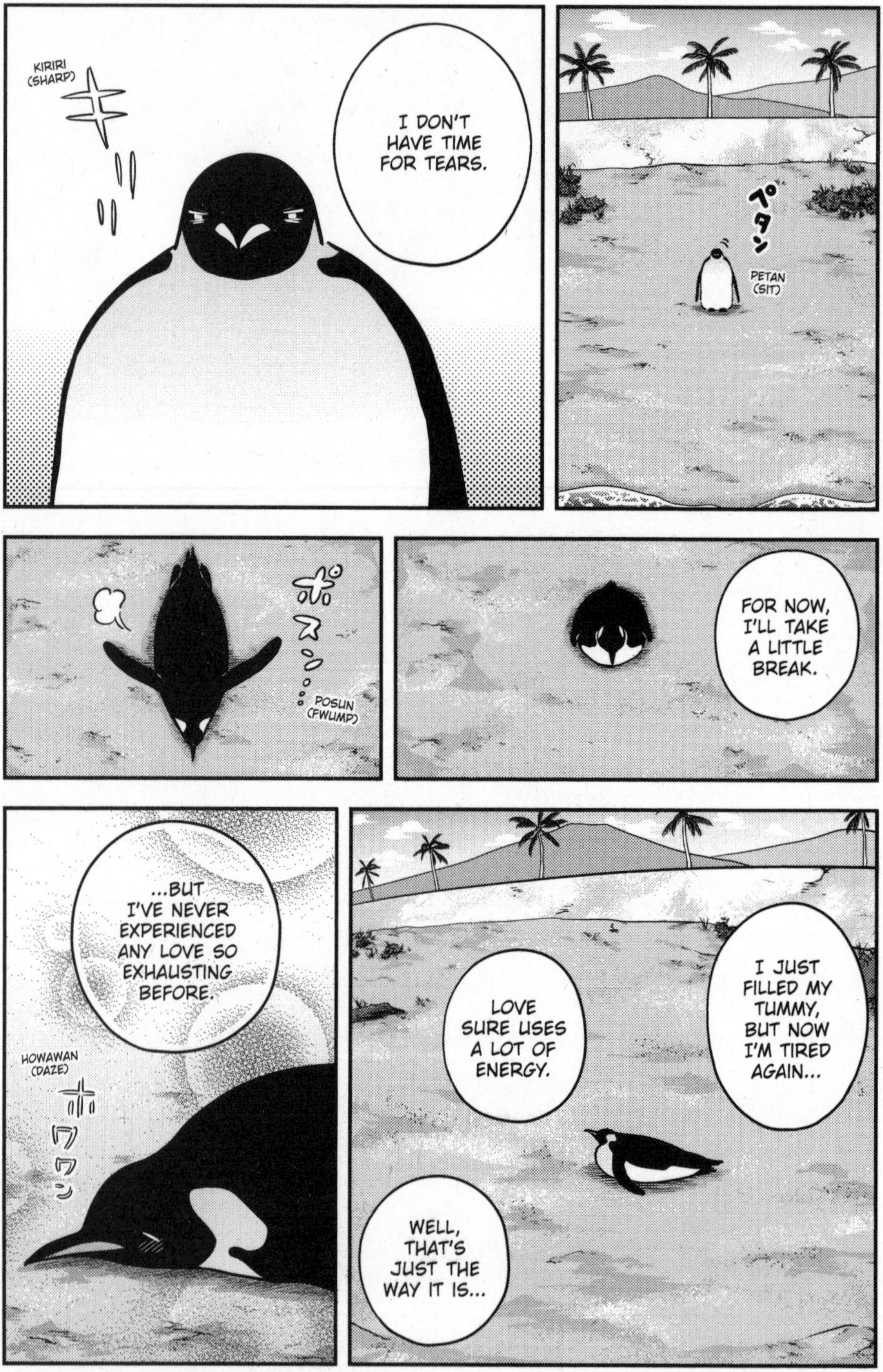
ペタン
PETAN (SIT)
KIRIRI (SHARP)
I DON'T HAVE TIME FOR TEARS.
FOR NOW, I'LL TAKE A LITTLE BREAK.
ポスン
POSUN (FWUMP)
I JUST FILLED MY TUMMY, BUT NOW I'M TIRED AGAIN...
LOVE SURE USES A LOT OF ENERGY.
WELL, THAT'S JUST THE WAY IT IS...
...BUT I'VE NEVER EXPERIENCED ANY LOVE SO EXHAUSTING BEFORE.
HOWAWAN (DAZE)
ホワワン

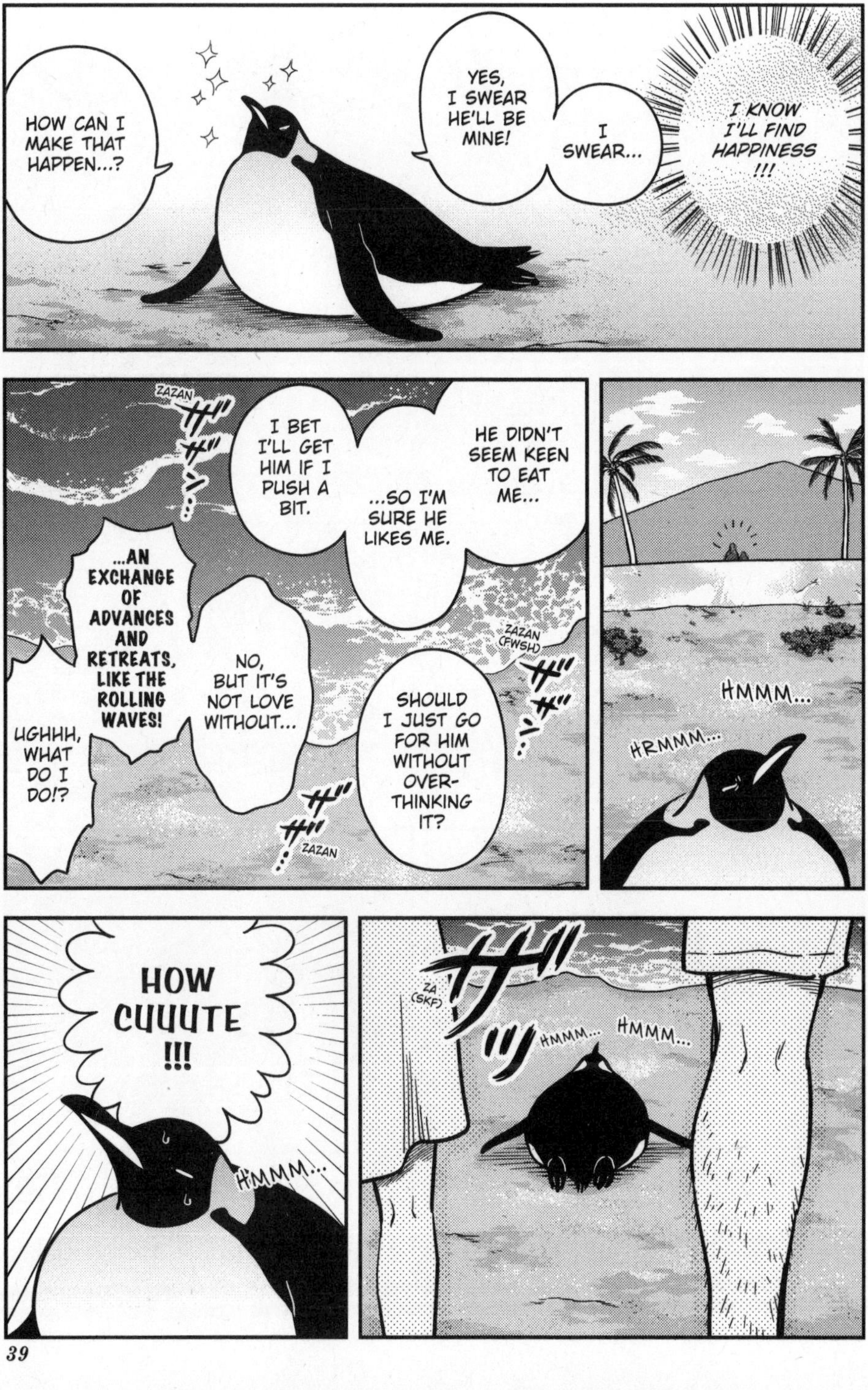
I KNOW I'LL FIND HAPPINESS !!!
I SWEAR...
YES, I SWEAR HE'LL BE MINE!
HOW CAN I MAKE THAT HAPPEN...?
HMMM...
HRMMM...
HE DIDN'T SEEM KEEN TO EAT ME...
...SO I'M SURE HE LIKES ME.
I BET I'LL GET HIM IF I PUSH A BIT.
ZAZAN
ZAZAN (FWSH)
SHOULD I JUST GO FOR HIM WITHOUT OVER-THINKING IT?
NO, BUT IT'S NOT LOVE WITHOUT...
...AN EXCHANGE OF ADVANCES AND RETREATS, LIKE THE ROLLING WAVES!
UGHHH, WHAT DO I DO!?
ZAZAN
HMMM...
HMMM...
ZA (SKF)
HOW CUUUTE !!!
HMMM...

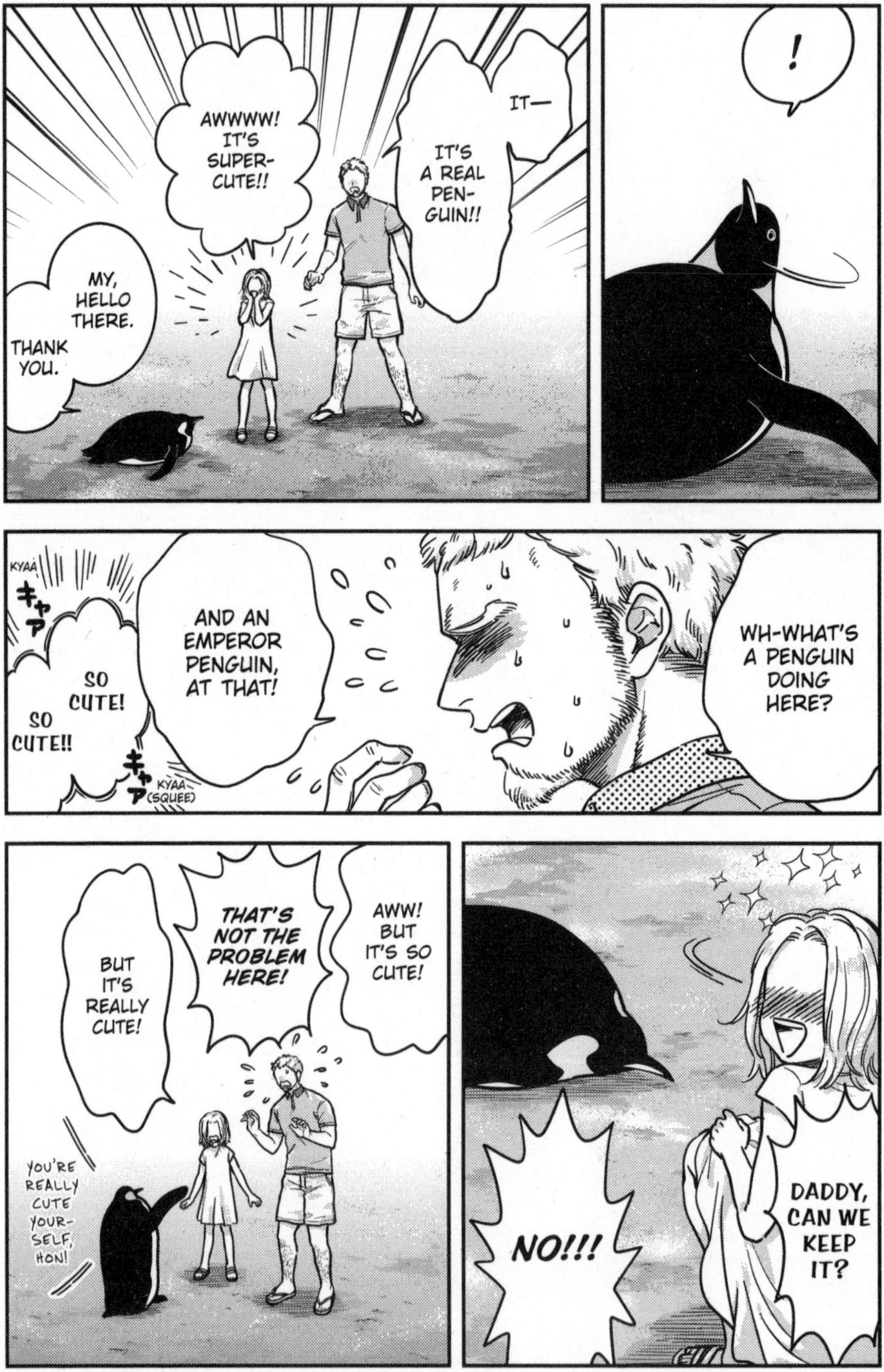
!
IT—
IT'S A REAL PENGUIN!!
AWWWW! IT'S SUPER-CUTE!!
MY, HELLO THERE.
THANK YOU.
WH-WHAT'S A PENGUIN DOING HERE?
AND AN EMPEROR PENGUIN, AT THAT!
KYAA!
キャア
SO CUTE!
SO CUTE!!
キャア
KYAA (SQUEE)
DADDY, CAN WE KEEP IT?
NO!!!
AWW! BUT IT'S SO CUTE!
THAT'S NOT THE PROBLEM HERE!
BUT IT'S REALLY CUTE!
YOU'RE REALLY CUTE YOURSELF, HON!

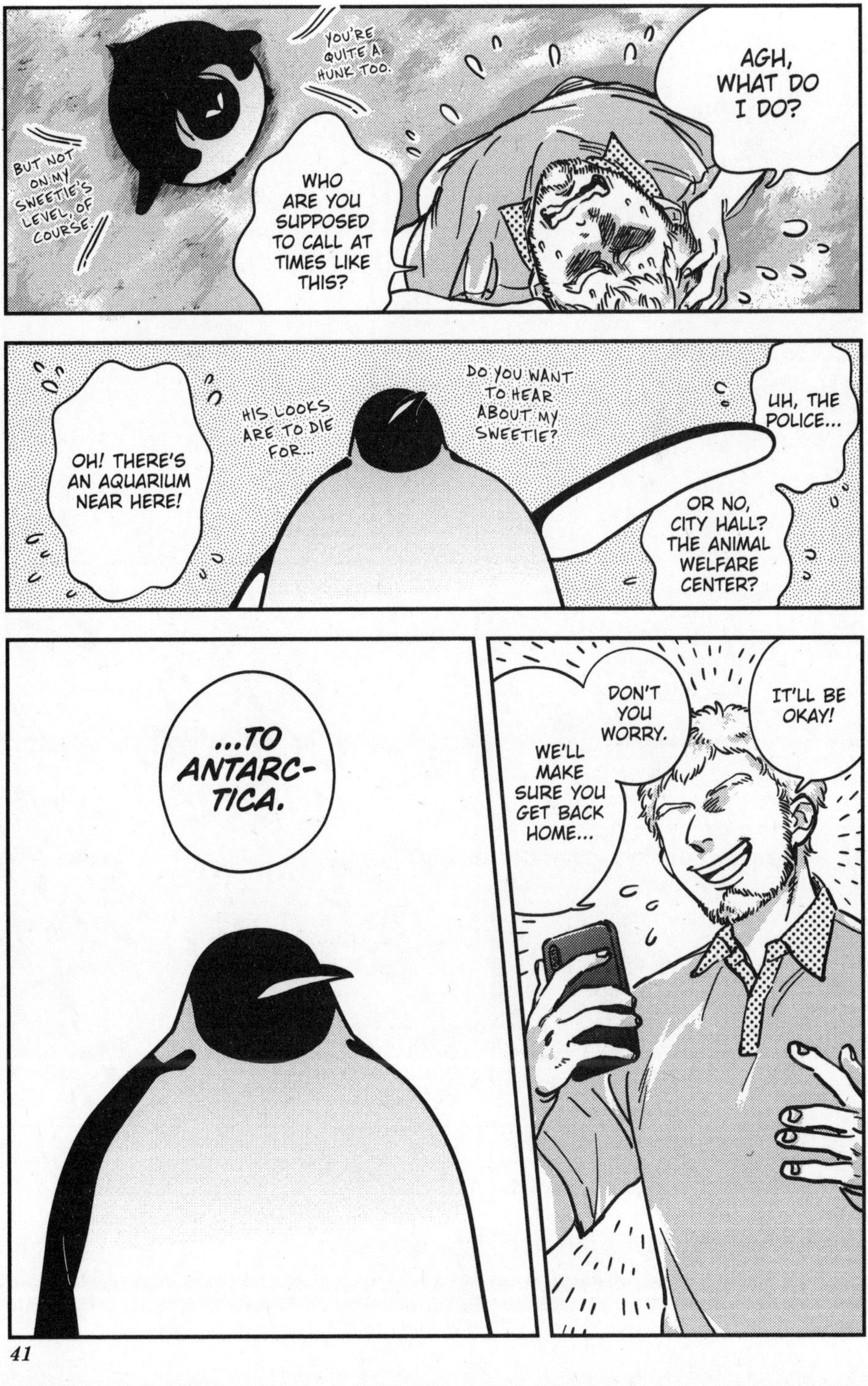
AGH, WHAT DO I DO?
WHO ARE YOU SUPPOSED TO CALL AT TIMES LIKE THIS?
YOU'RE QUITE A HUNK TOO.
BUT NOT ON MY SWEETIE'S LEVEL, OF COURSE.
UH, THE POLICE...
OR NO, CITY HALL? THE ANIMAL WELFARE CENTER?
DO YOU WANT TO HEAR ABOUT MY SWEETIE?
HIS LOOKS ARE TO DIE FOR...
OH! THERE'S AN AQUARIUM NEAR HERE!
IT'LL BE OKAY!
DON'T YOU WORRY.
WE'LL MAKE SURE YOU GET BACK HOME...
...TO ANTARCTICA.

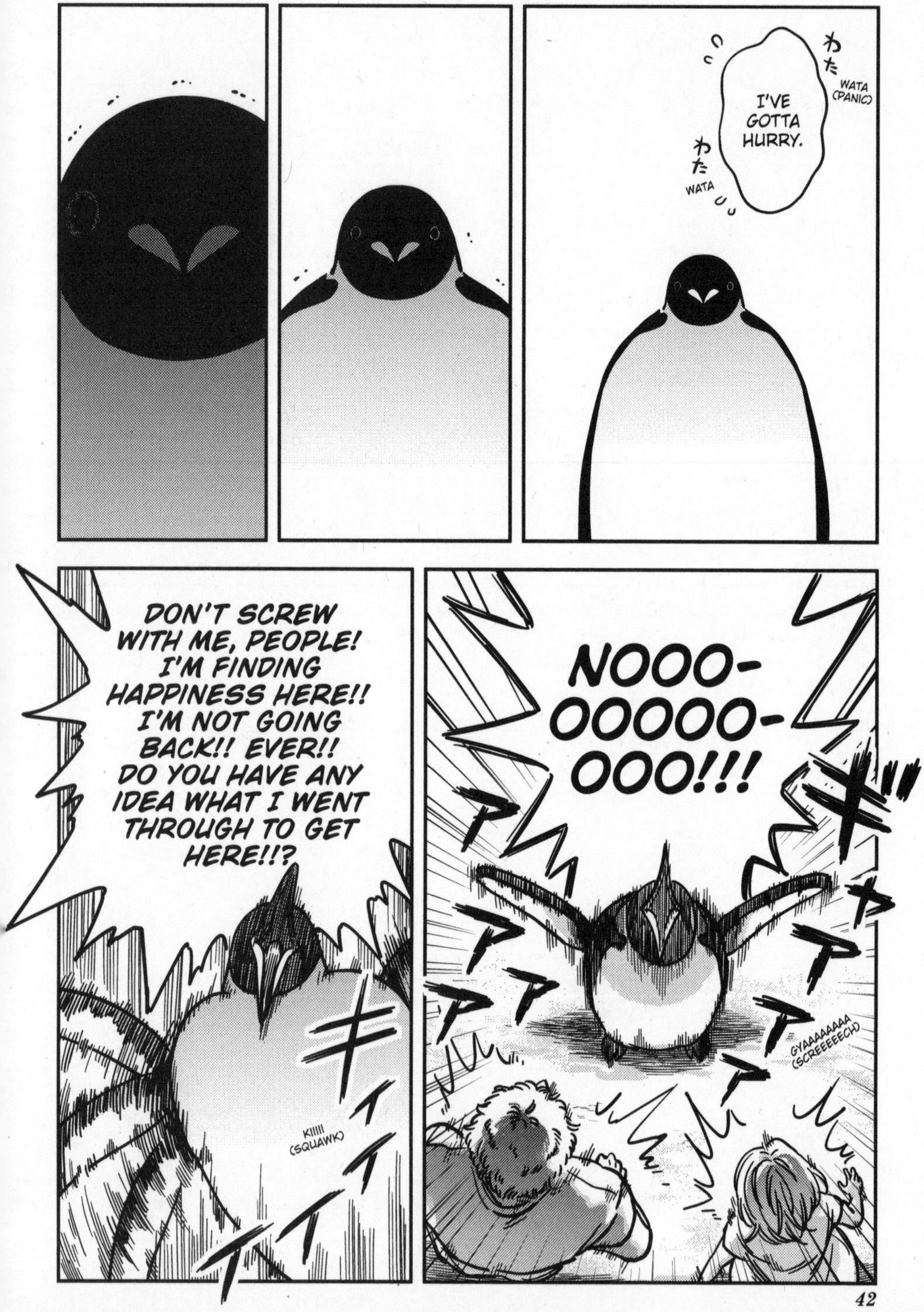
わた
WATA (PANIC)
I'VE GOTTA HURRY.
わた
WATA
NOOO-OOOOO-OOO!!!
GYAAAAAAAA (SCREEEEECH)
DON'T SCREW WITH ME, PEOPLE! I'M FINDING HAPPINESS HERE!! I'M NOT GOING BACK!! EVER!! DO YOU HAVE ANY IDEA WHAT I WENT THROUGH TO GET HERE!!?
KIIIII (SQUAWK)

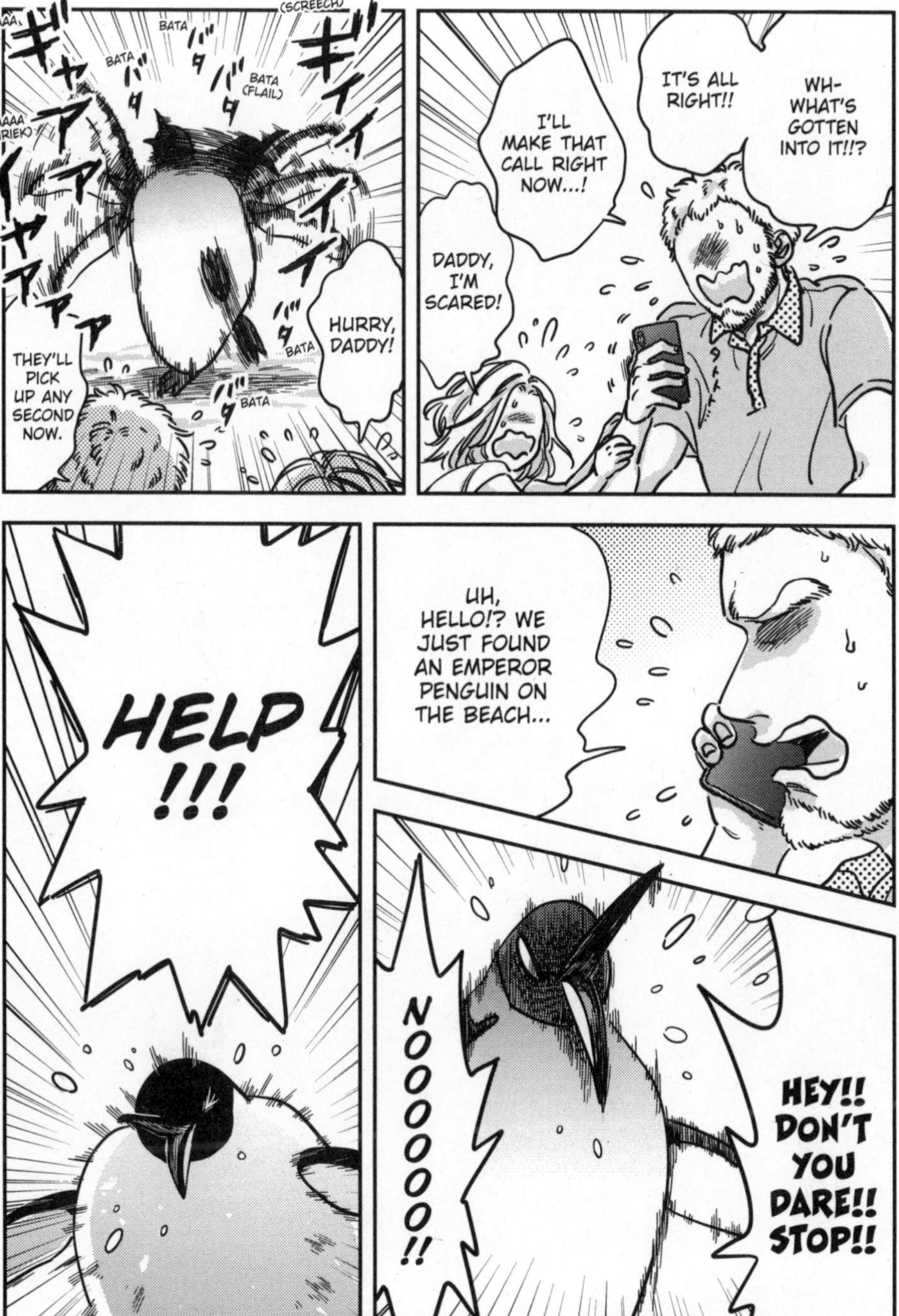
WH-WHAT'S GOTTEN INTO IT!!?
IT'S ALL RIGHT!!
I'LL MAKE THAT CALL RIGHT NOW...!
DADDY, I'M SCARED!
GIIIII (SCREECH)
BATA
BATA
BATA (FLAIL)
GYAAA
IYAAAA (SHRIEK)
HURRY, DADDY!
BATA
BATA
THEY'LL PICK UP ANY SECOND NOW.
UH, HELLO!? WE JUST FOUND AN EMPEROR PENGUIN ON THE BEACH...
HEY!! DON'T YOU DARE!! STOP!!
NOOOOOOOO!!
HELP !!!

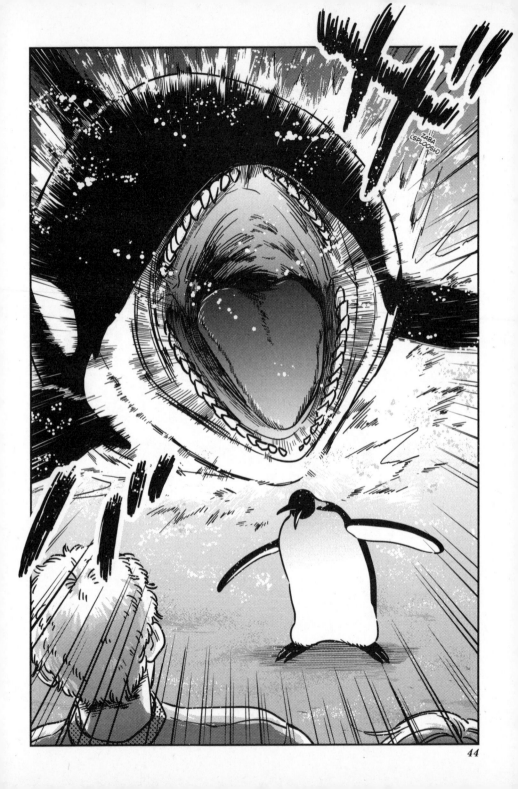

ZABA
(SPLOOSH)

44

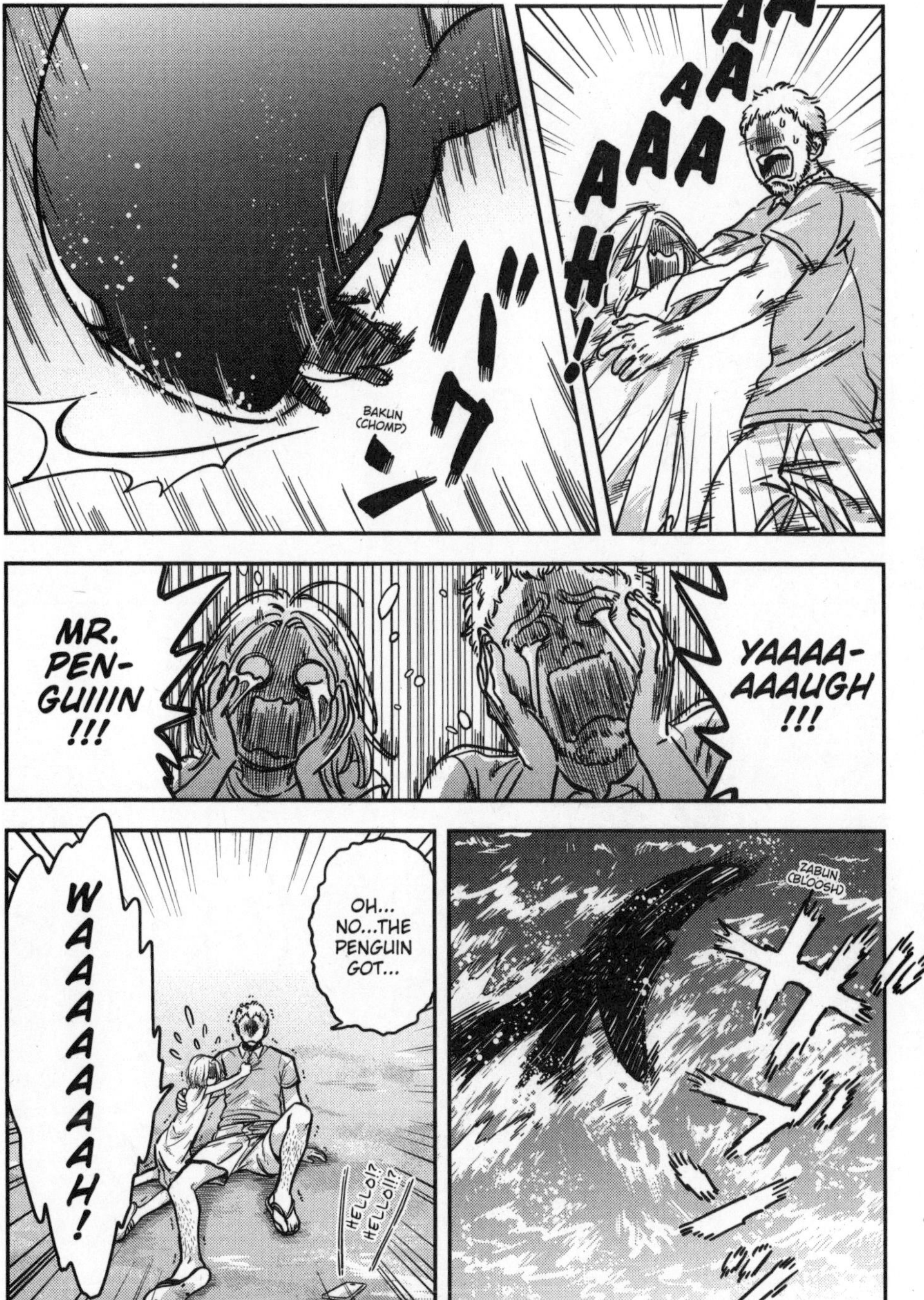
AAAAAAAH!!
BAKUN (CHOMP)
バクン
YAAAA-AAAUGH!!!
MR. PEN-GUIIIN!!!
ZABUN (BLOOSH)
OH... NO...THE PENGUIN GOT...
WAAAAAAAH!
HELLO!? HELLO!?

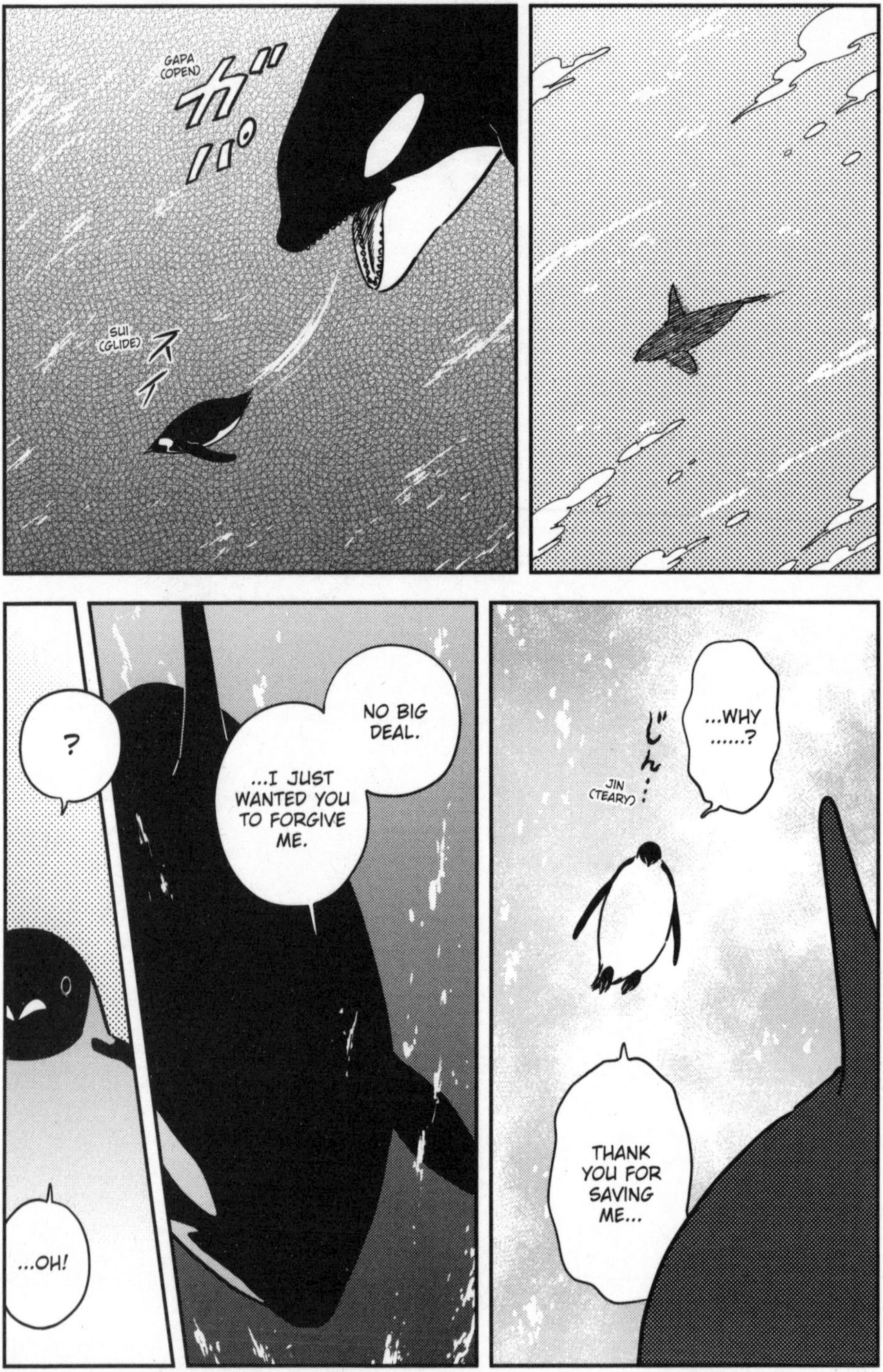
GAPA (OPEN)
ガパ
SUI (GLIDE)
スイ
...WHY ......?
じん..
JIN (TEARY)
THANK YOU FOR SAVING ME...
NO BIG DEAL.
...I JUST WANTED YOU TO FORGIVE ME.
?
...OH!

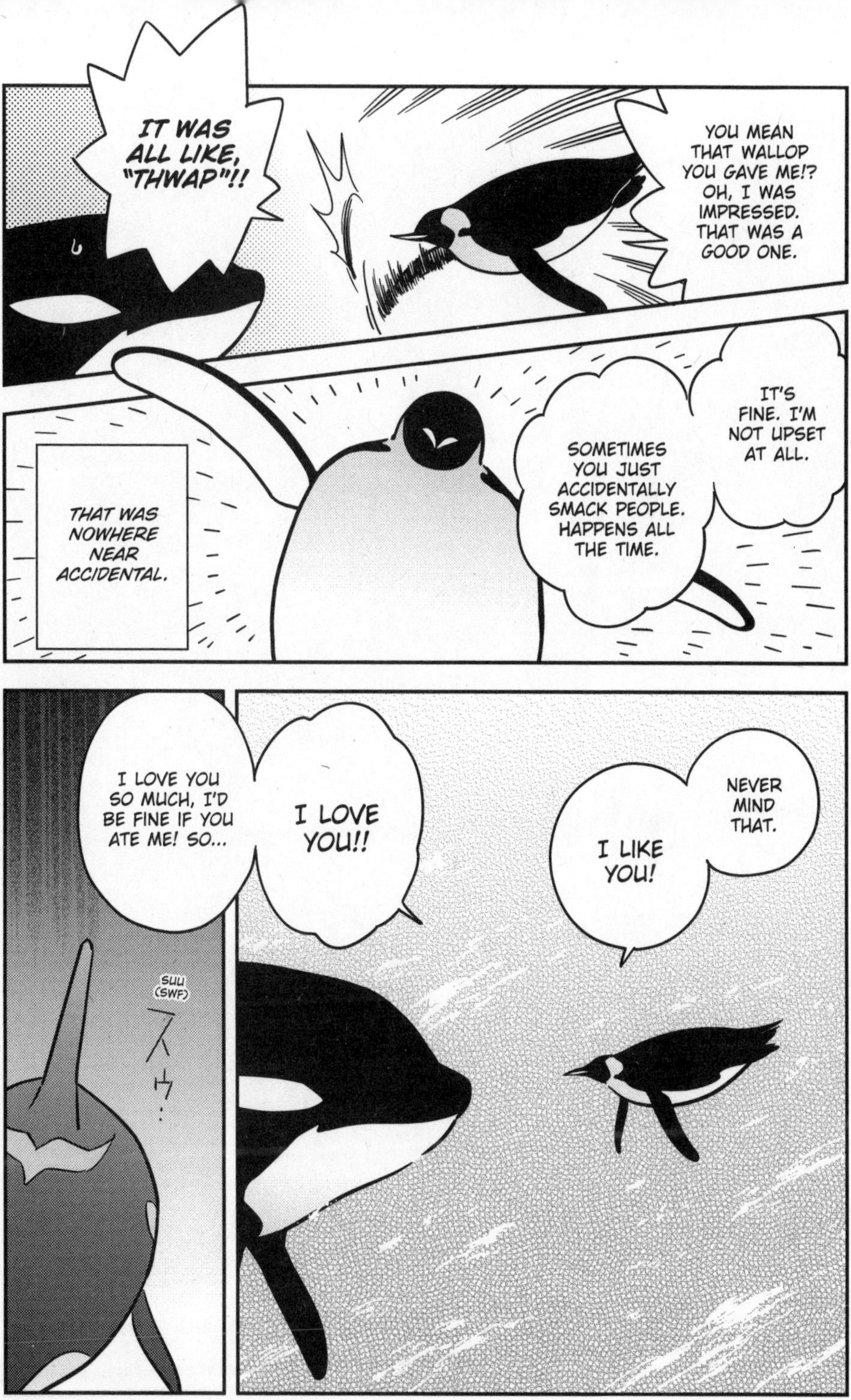
IT WAS ALL LIKE, "THWAP"!!
YOU MEAN THAT WALLOP YOU GAVE ME!? OH, I WAS IMPRESSED. THAT WAS A GOOD ONE.
IT'S FINE. I'M NOT UPSET AT ALL.
SOMETIMES YOU JUST ACCIDENTALLY SMACK PEOPLE. HAPPENS ALL THE TIME.
THAT WAS NOWHERE NEAR ACCIDENTAL.
NEVER MIND THAT.
I LIKE YOU!
I LOVE YOU!!
I LOVE YOU SO MUCH, I'D BE FINE IF YOU ATE ME! SO...
SUU (SWF)
スゥ…

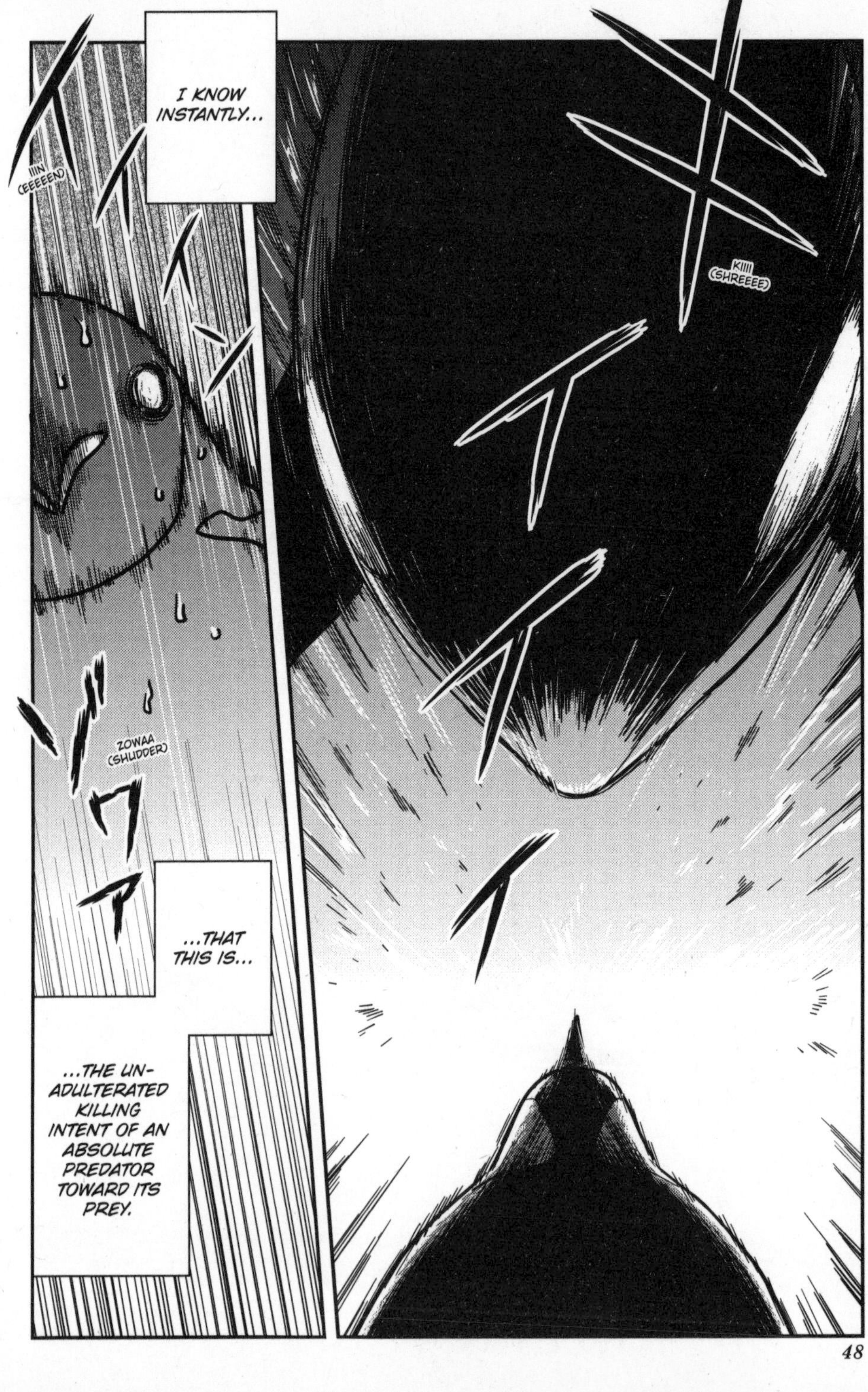
KIII
(SHREEEE)
I KNOW INSTANTLY...
IIIN
(EEEEEND)
ZOWAA
(SHUDDER)
...THAT THIS IS...
...THE UN-ADULTERATED KILLING INTENT OF AN ABSOLUTE PREDATOR TOWARD ITS PREY.

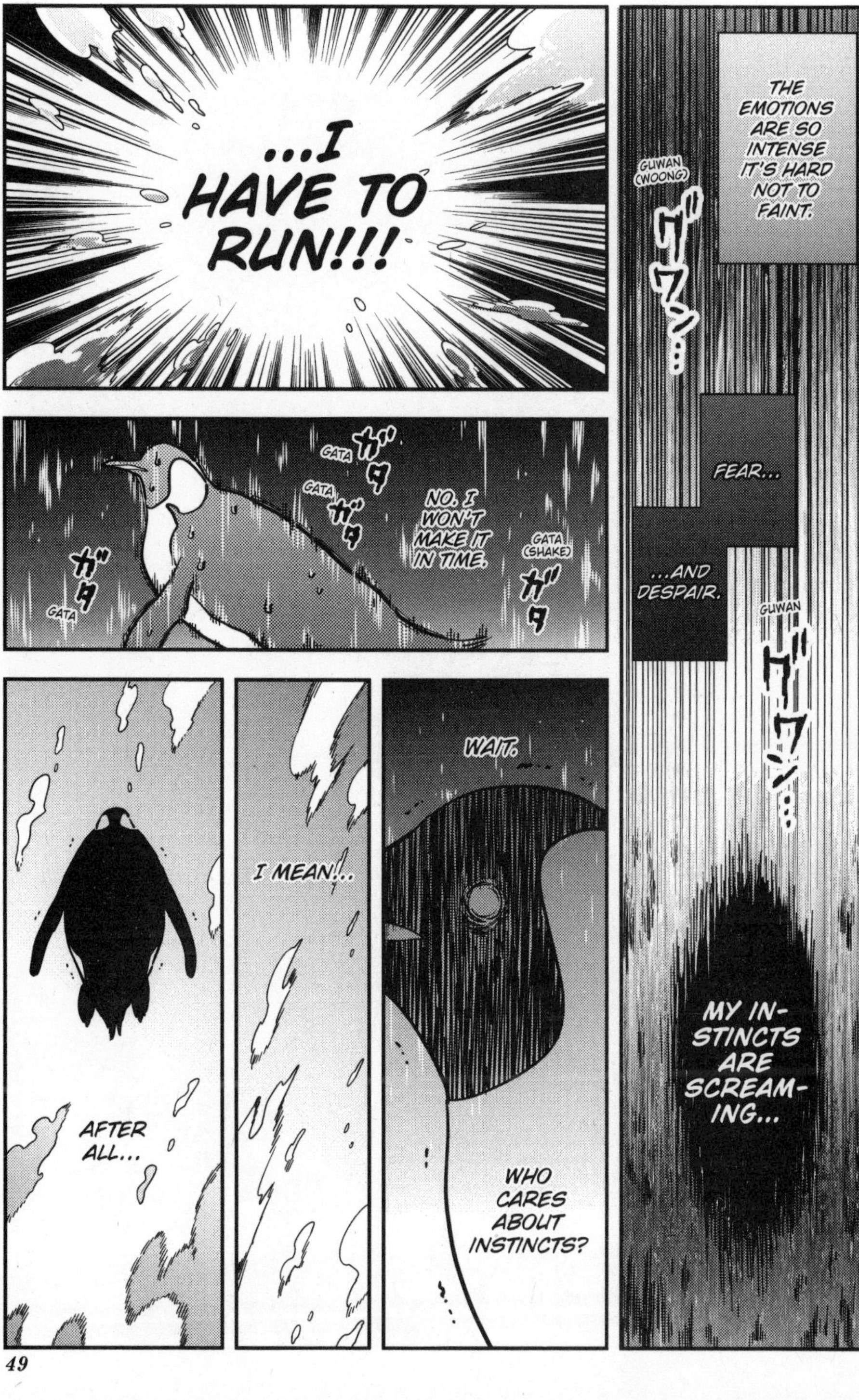
THE EMOTIONS ARE SO INTENSE IT'S HARD NOT TO FAINT.
GUWAN (WOONG)
グワン…
FEAR...
...AND DESPAIR.
GUWAN
グワン…
MY IN-STINCTS ARE SCREAM-ING...
...I HAVE TO RUN!!!
GATA (SHAKE)
ガタ
NO. I WON'T MAKE IT IN TIME.
GATA
ガタ
GATA
ガタ
GATA
ガタ
WAIT.
WHO CARES ABOUT INSTINCTS?
I MEAN...
AFTER ALL...

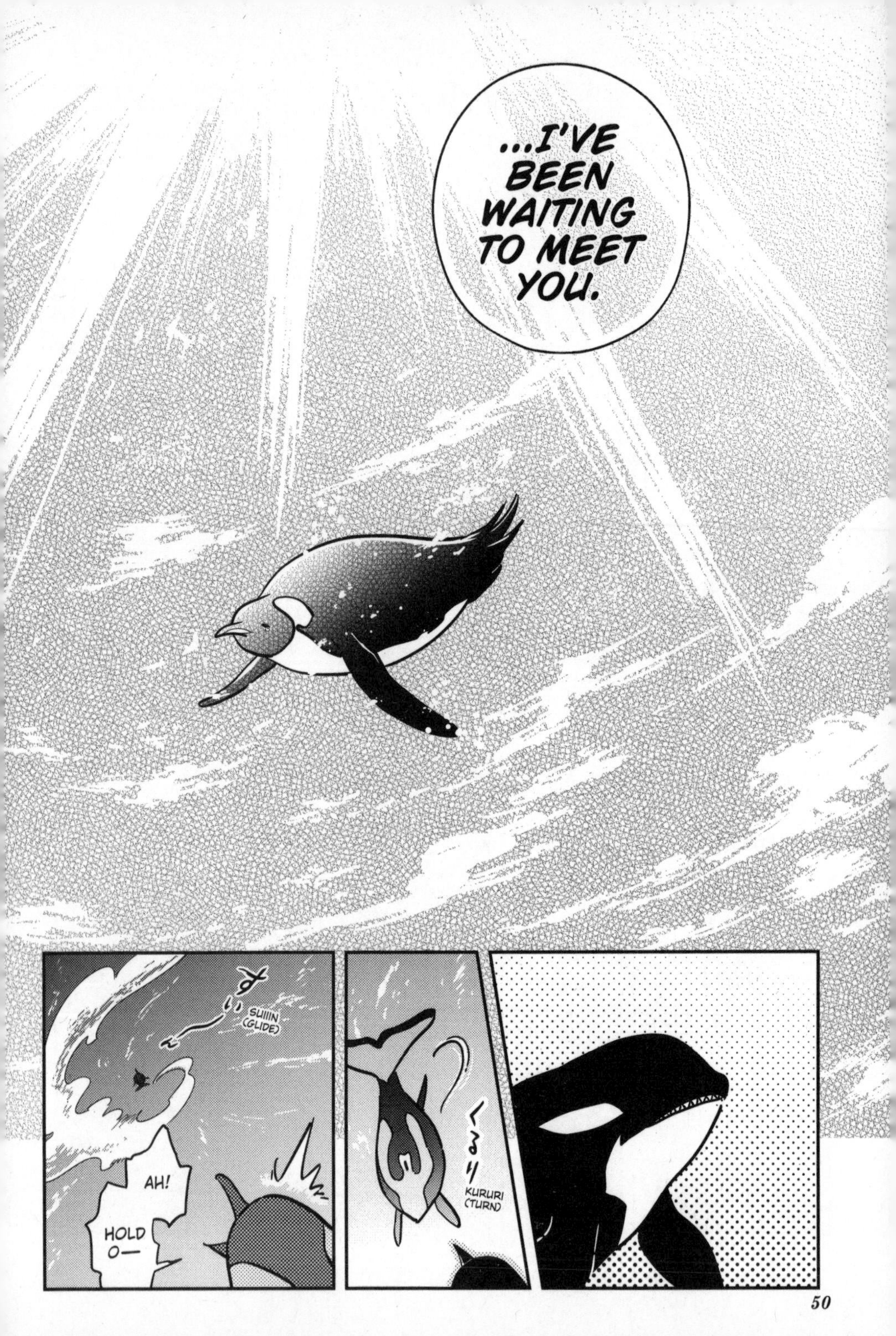
...I'VE BEEN WAITING TO MEET YOU.
くるり
KURURI (TURN)
SUIIIN (GLIDE)
AH!
HOLD O—

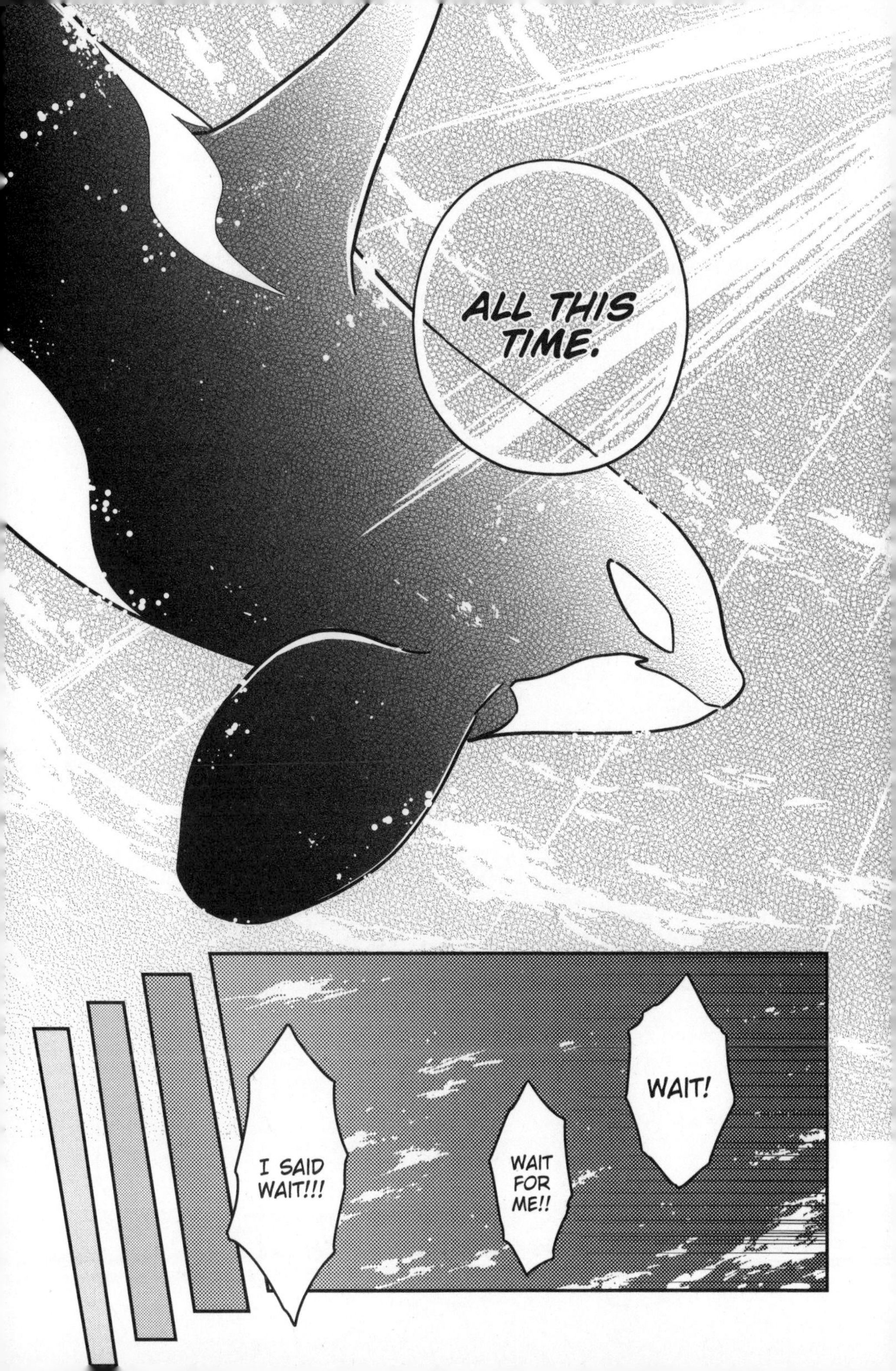
ALL THIS TIME.
WAIT!
WAIT FOR ME!!
I SAID WAIT!!!

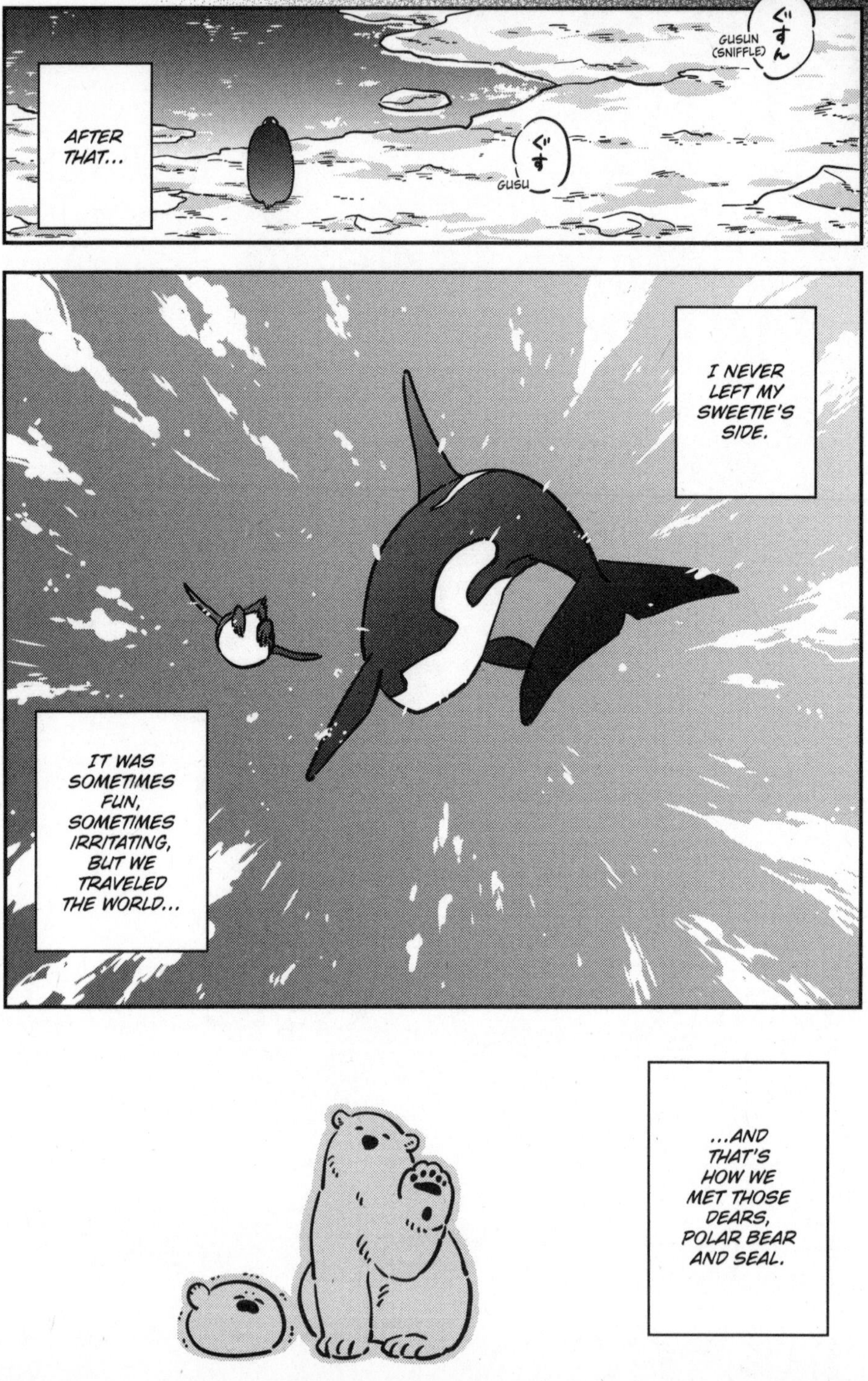
ぐすん
GUSUN (SNIFFLE)
ぐす
GUSU
AFTER THAT...
I NEVER LEFT MY SWEETIE'S SIDE.
IT WAS SOMETIMES FUN, SOMETIMES IRRITATING, BUT WE TRAVELED THE WORLD...
...AND THAT'S HOW WE MET THOSE DEARS, POLAR BEAR AND SEAL.

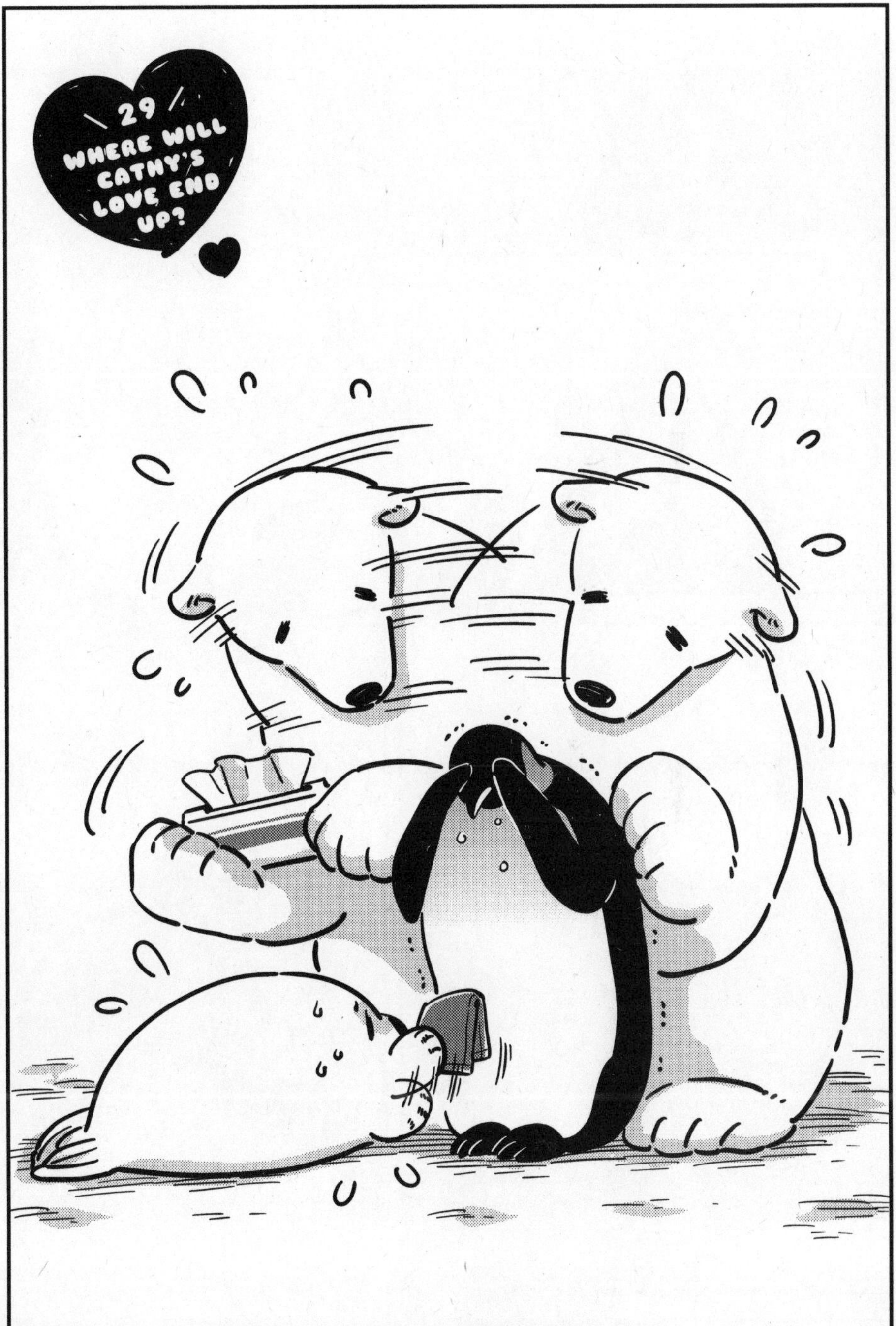
29
WHERE WILL CATHY'S LOVE END UP?

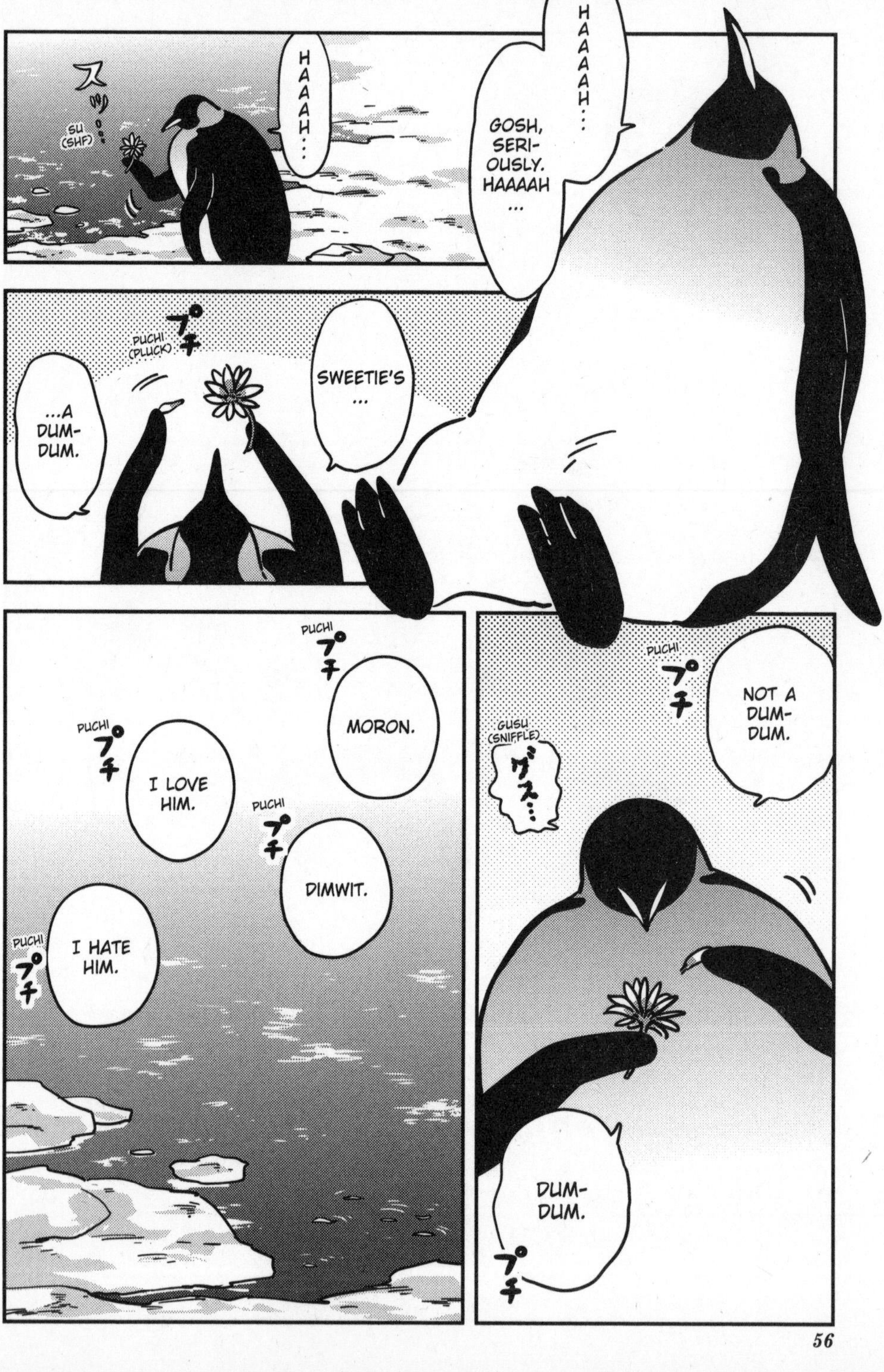
HAAAAH...
GOSH, SERI-OUSLY. HAAAAH...
HAAAH...
ス
SU (SHF)
プチ
PUCHI (PLUCK)
SWEETIE'S...
...A DUM-DUM.
PUCHI
プチ
NOT A DUM-DUM.
GUSU (SNIFFLE)
グス…
DUM-DUM.
プチ
PUCHI
プチ
MORON.
PUCHI
プチ
I LOVE HIM.
PUCHI
プチ
DIMWIT.
PUCHI
プチ
I HATE HIM.

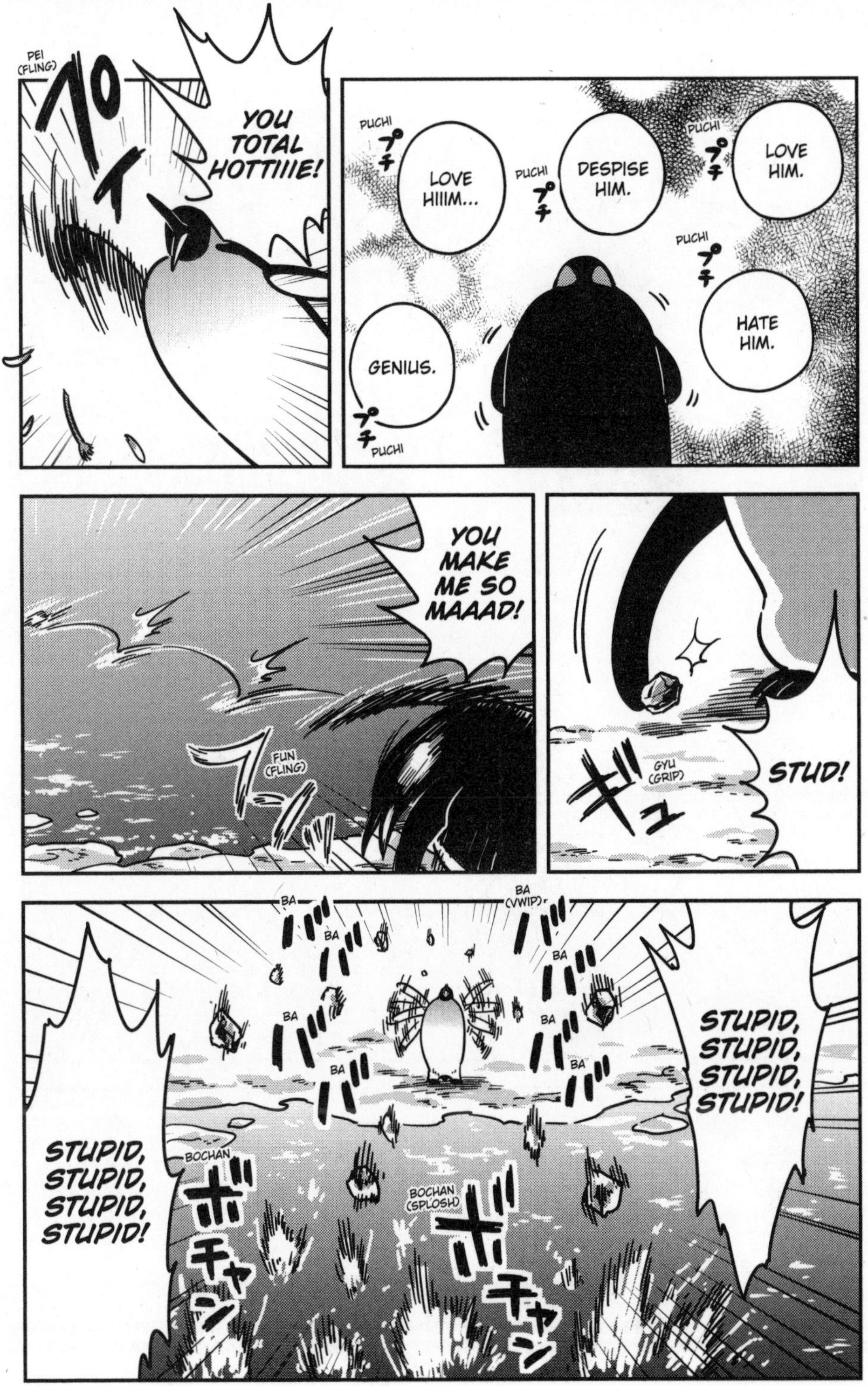

PUCHI
LOVE HIM.
PUCHI
DESPISE HIM.
PUCHI
LOVE HIIIM...
PUCHI
HATE HIM.
GENIUS.
PUCHI
PEI (FLING)
YOU TOTAL HOTTIIIIE!
GYU (GRIP)
STUD!
YOU MAKE ME SO MAAAD!
FUN (FLING)
BA (VWIP)
BA
BA
BA
BA
BA
BA
BA
STUPID, STUPID, STUPID, STUPID!
BOCHAN (SPLOSH)
BOCHAN
STUPID, STUPID, STUPID, STUPID!

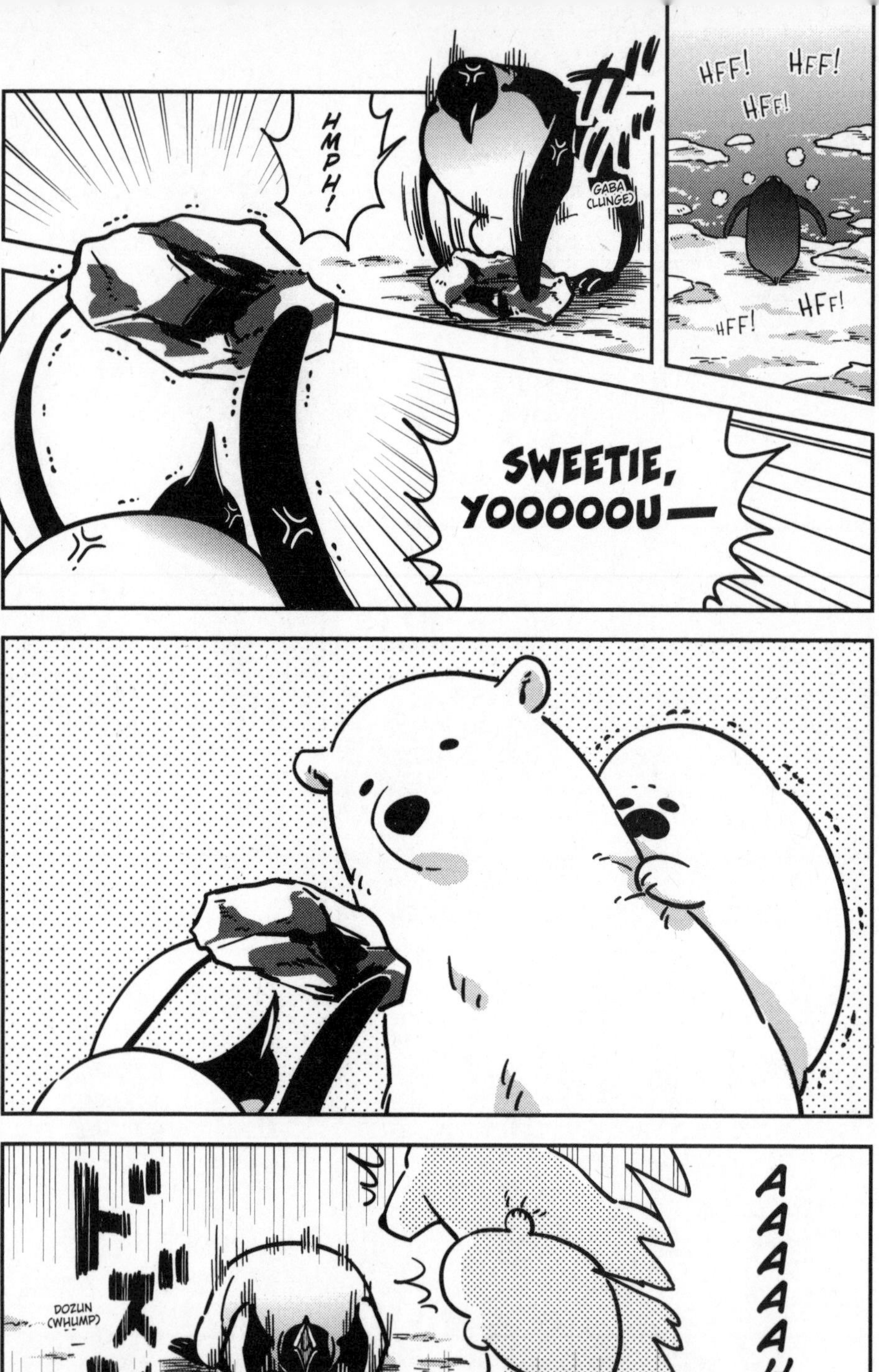
HFF! HFF!
HFF!
HFF! HFF!
GABA (LUNGE)
HMPH!
SWEETIE, YOOOOOU—
AAAAAAH!!!
DOZUN (WHUMP)

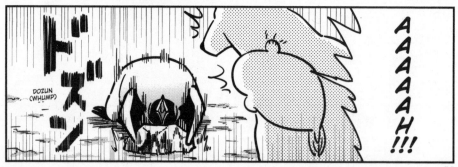

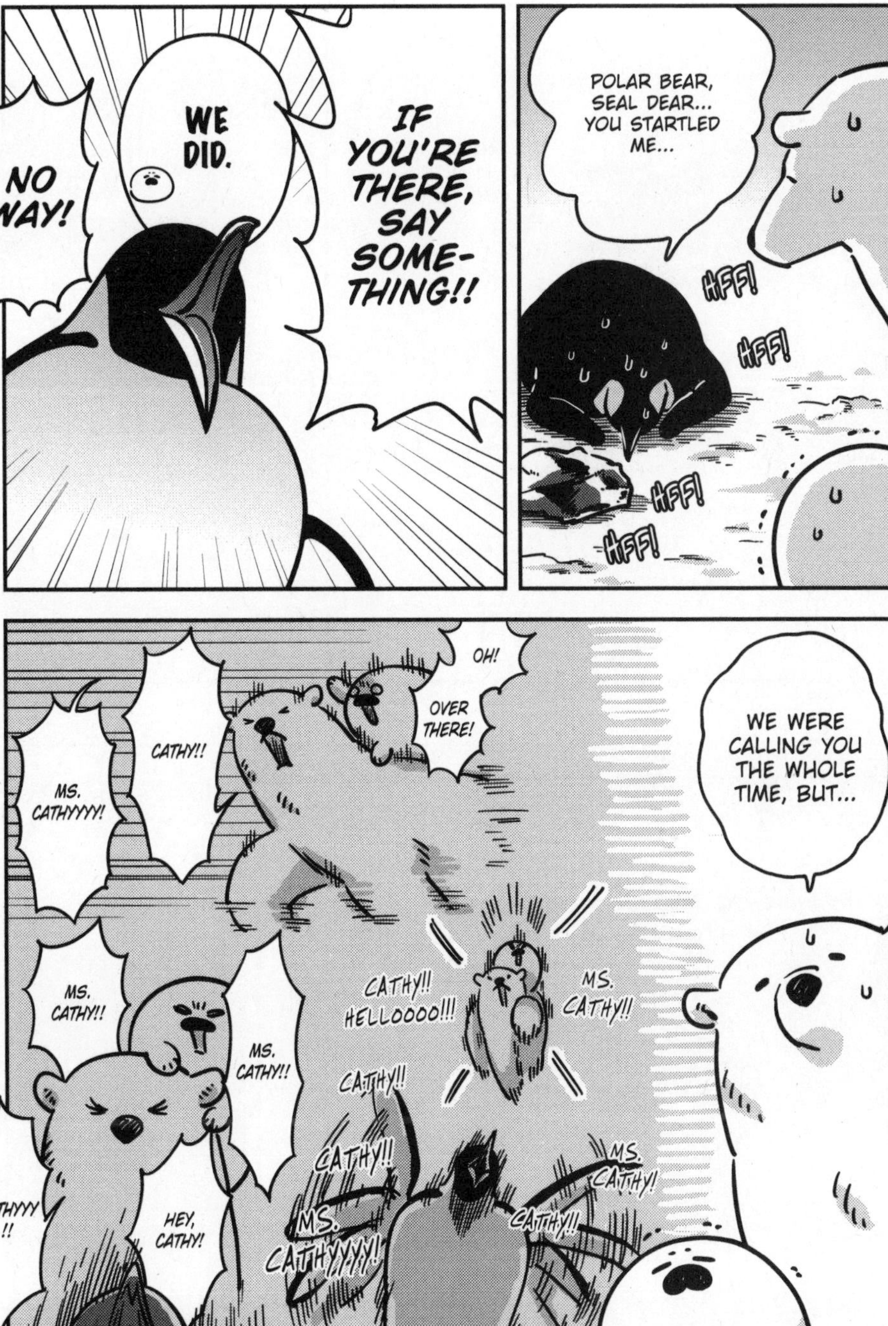
POLAR BEAR, SEAL DEAR... YOU STARTLED ME...
HFF!
HFF!
HFF!
HFF!
IF YOU'RE THERE, SAY SOME-THING!!
WE DID.
NO WAY!
WE WERE CALLING YOU THE WHOLE TIME, BUT...
OH!
OVER THERE!
CATHY!!
MS. CATHYYYY!
MS. CATHY!!
CATHY!! HELLOOOO!!!
MS. CATHY!!
CATHY!!
MS. CATHY!!
MS. CATHY!
CATHY!!
CATHY!!
MS. CATHYYYY!
HEY, CATHY!
CATHYYY !!

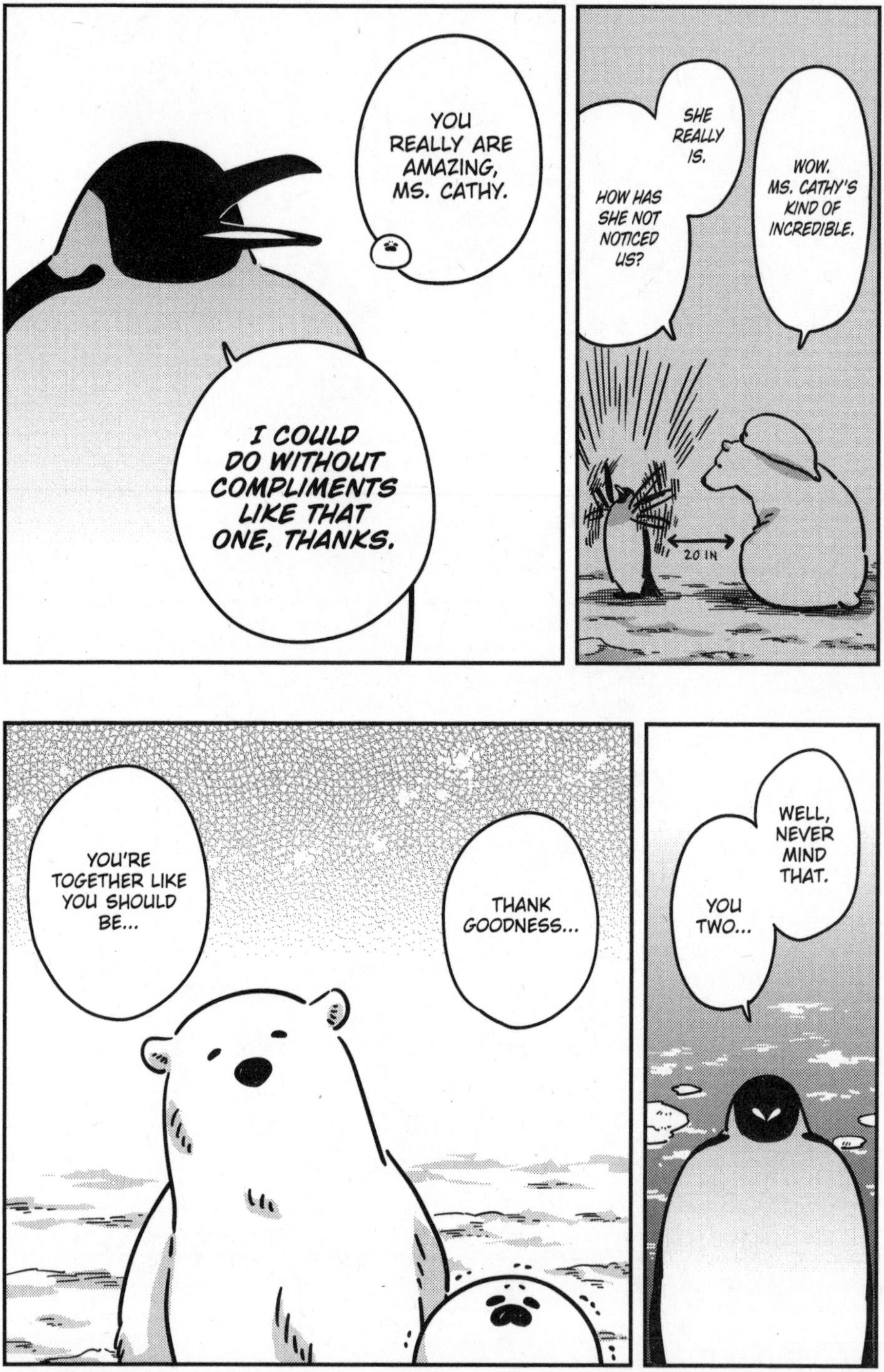
WOW. MS. CATHY'S KIND OF INCREDIBLE.
SHE REALLY IS.
HOW HAS SHE NOT NOTICED US?
20 IN
YOU REALLY ARE AMAZING, MS. CATHY.
I COULD DO WITHOUT COMPLIMENTS LIKE THAT ONE, THANKS.
WELL, NEVER MIND THAT.
YOU TWO...
THANK GOODNESS...
YOU'RE TOGETHER LIKE YOU SHOULD BE...

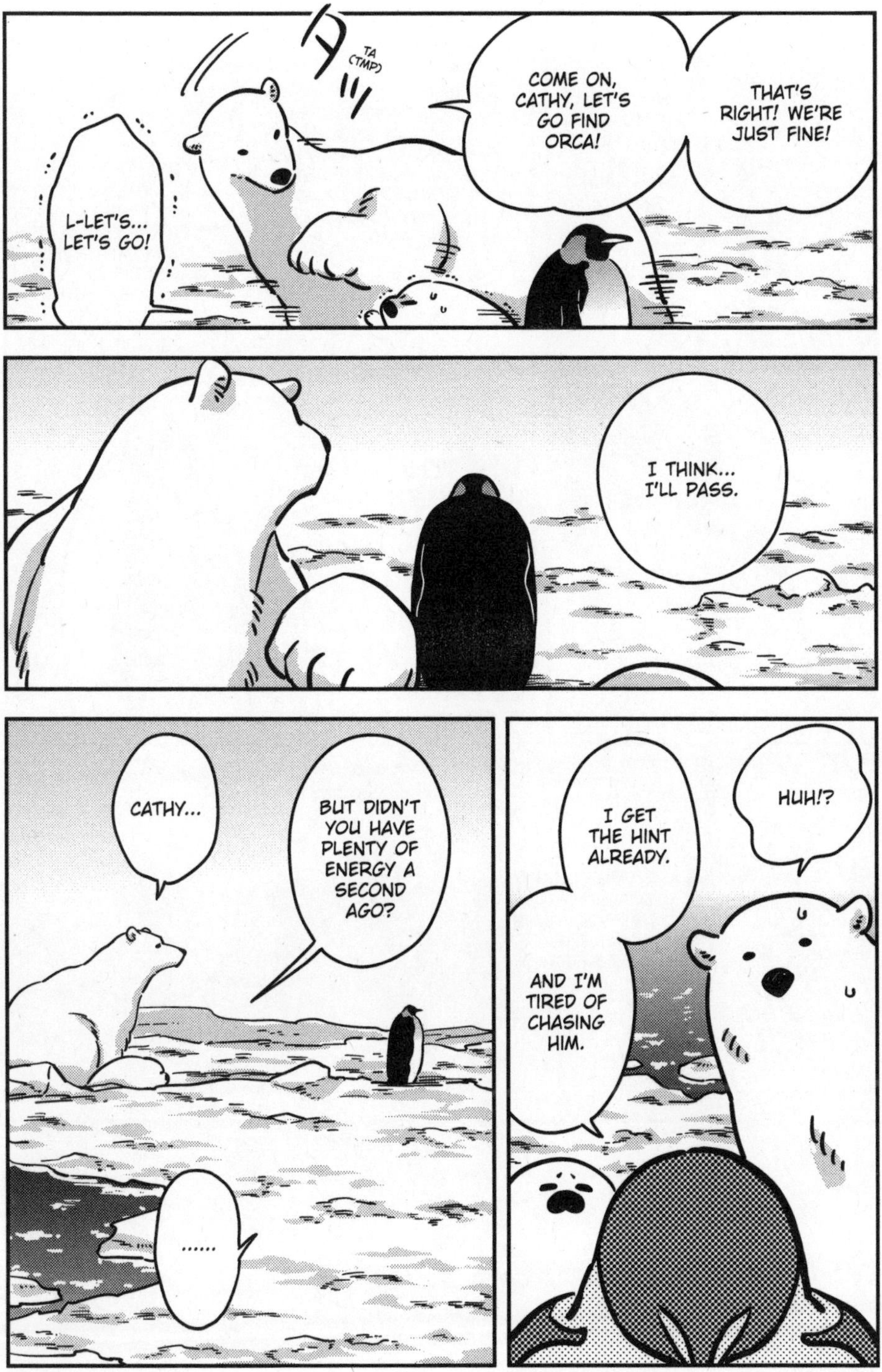
THAT'S RIGHT! WE'RE JUST FINE!
COME ON, CATHY, LET'S GO FIND ORCA!
TA (TMP)
L-LET'S... LET'S GO!
I THINK... I'LL PASS.
HUH!?
I GET THE HINT ALREADY.
AND I'M TIRED OF CHASING HIM.
BUT DIDN'T YOU HAVE PLENTY OF ENERGY A SECOND AGO?
CATHY...
......

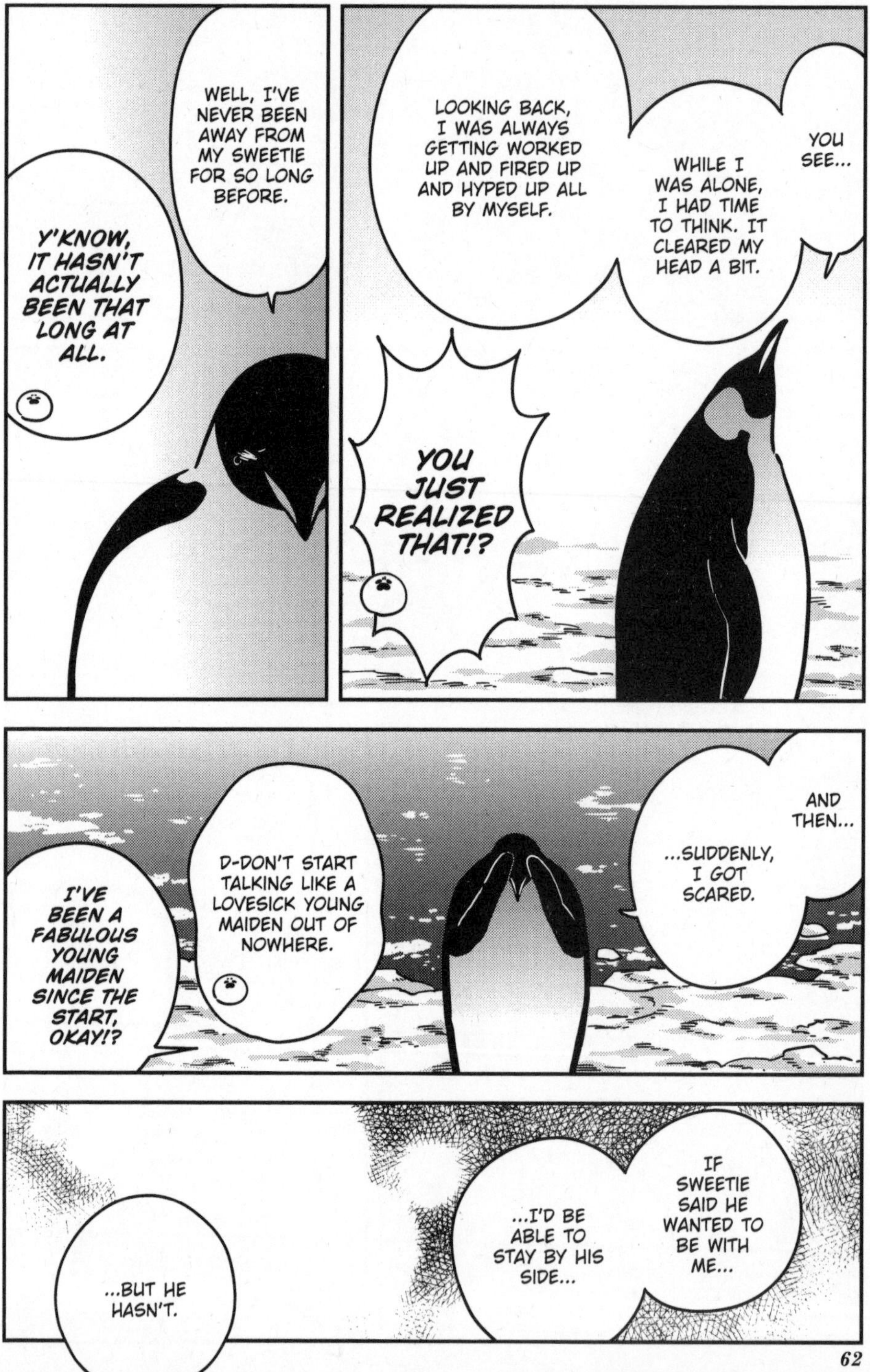
YOU SEE...
WHILE I WAS ALONE, I HAD TIME TO THINK. IT CLEARED MY HEAD A BIT.
LOOKING BACK, I WAS ALWAYS GETTING WORKED UP AND FIRED UP AND HYPED UP ALL BY MYSELF.
YOU JUST REALIZED THAT!?
WELL, I'VE NEVER BEEN AWAY FROM MY SWEETIE FOR SO LONG BEFORE.
Y'KNOW, IT HASN'T ACTUALLY BEEN THAT LONG AT ALL.
AND THEN...
...SUDDENLY, I GOT SCARED.
D-DON'T START TALKING LIKE A LOVESICK YOUNG MAIDEN OUT OF NOWHERE.
I'VE BEEN A FABULOUS YOUNG MAIDEN SINCE THE START, OKAY!?
IF SWEETIE SAID HE WANTED TO BE WITH ME...
...I'D BE ABLE TO STAY BY HIS SIDE...
...BUT HE HASN'T.

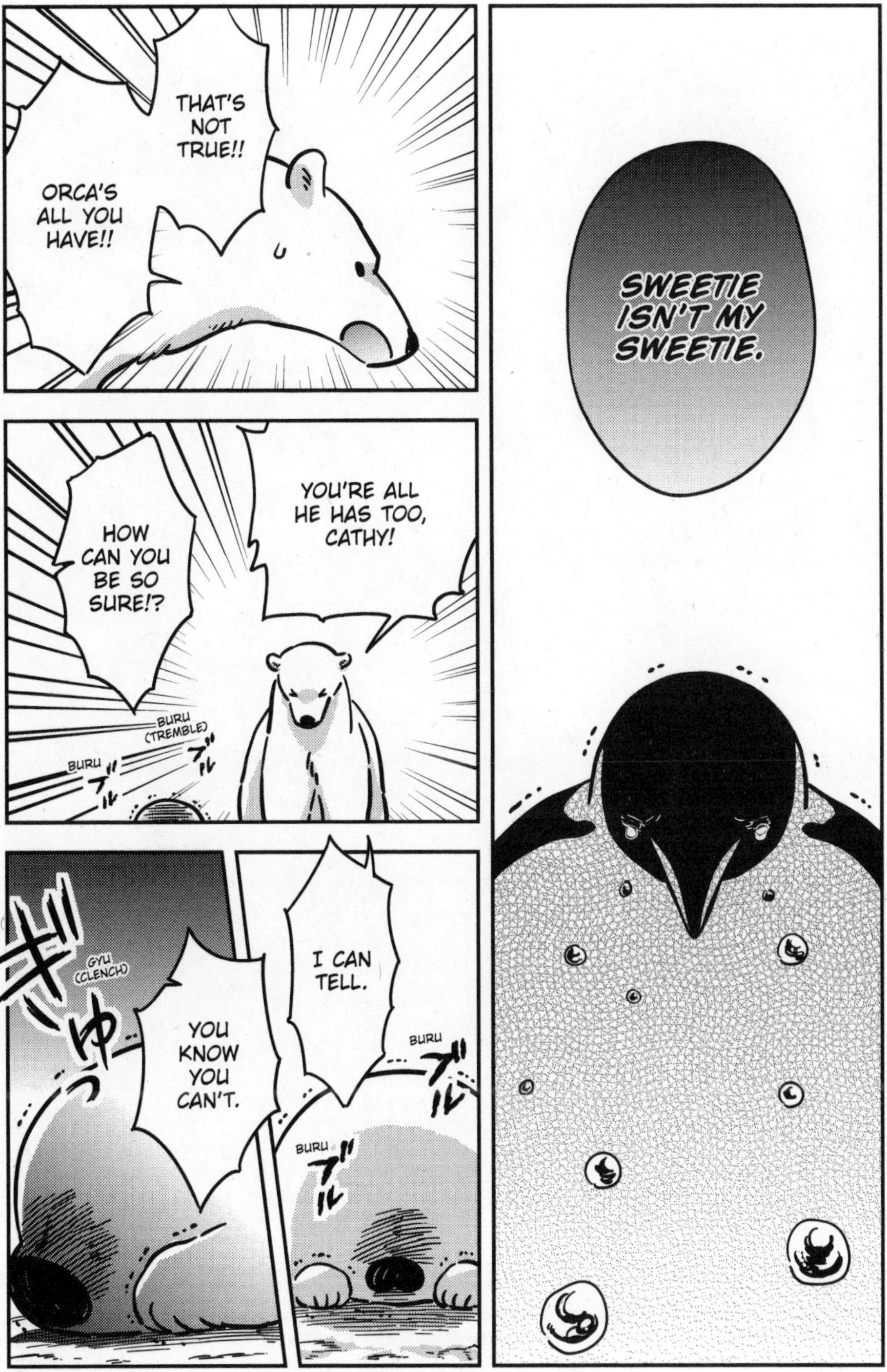
SWEETIE ISN'T MY SWEETIE.
THAT'S NOT TRUE!!
ORCA'S ALL YOU HAVE!!
YOU'RE ALL HE HAS TOO, CATHY!
HOW CAN YOU BE SO SURE!?
BURU (TREMBLE)
BURU
I CAN TELL.
BURU
BURU
GYU (CLENCH)
YOU KNOW YOU CAN'T.

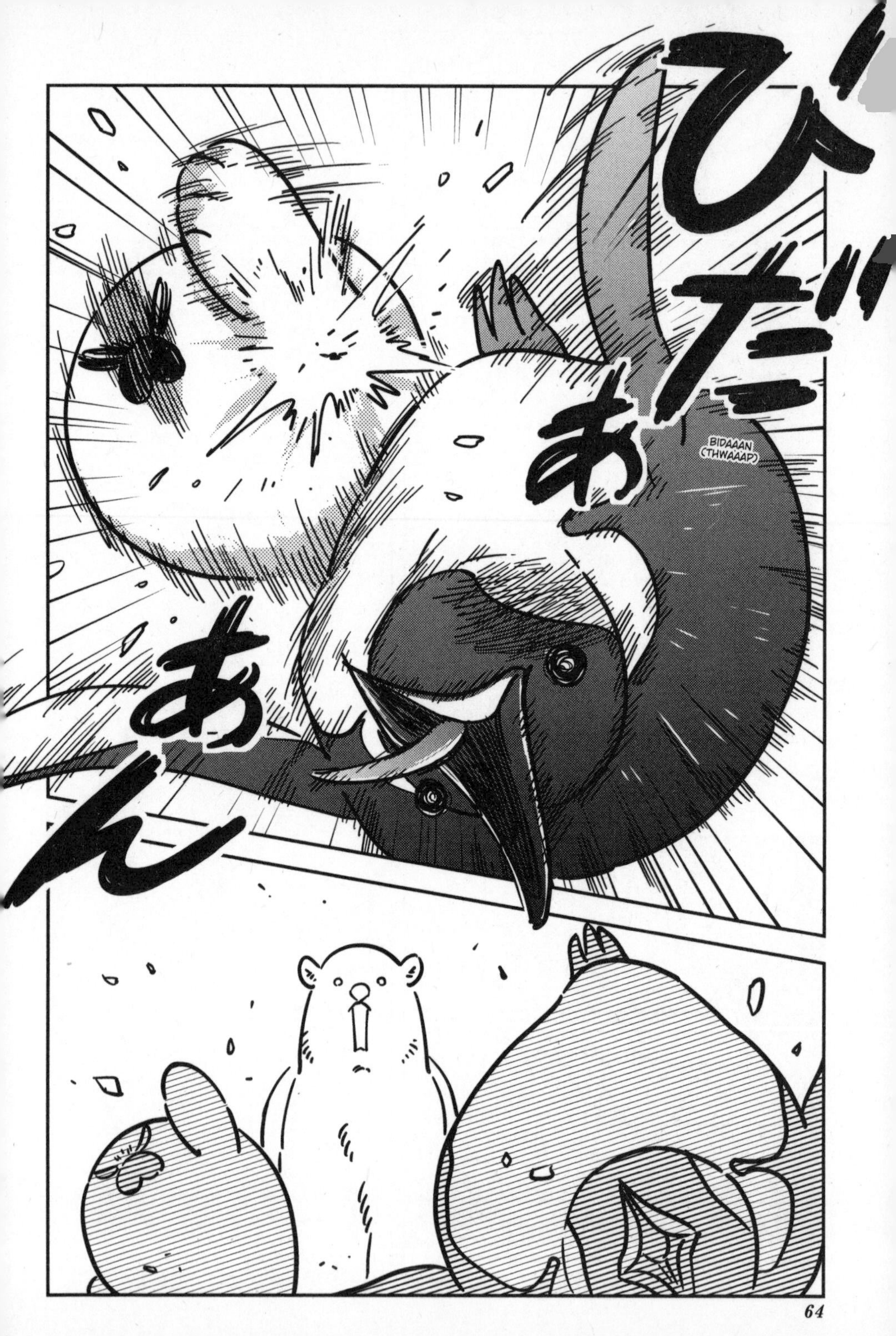
BIDAAAN
(THWAAAP)

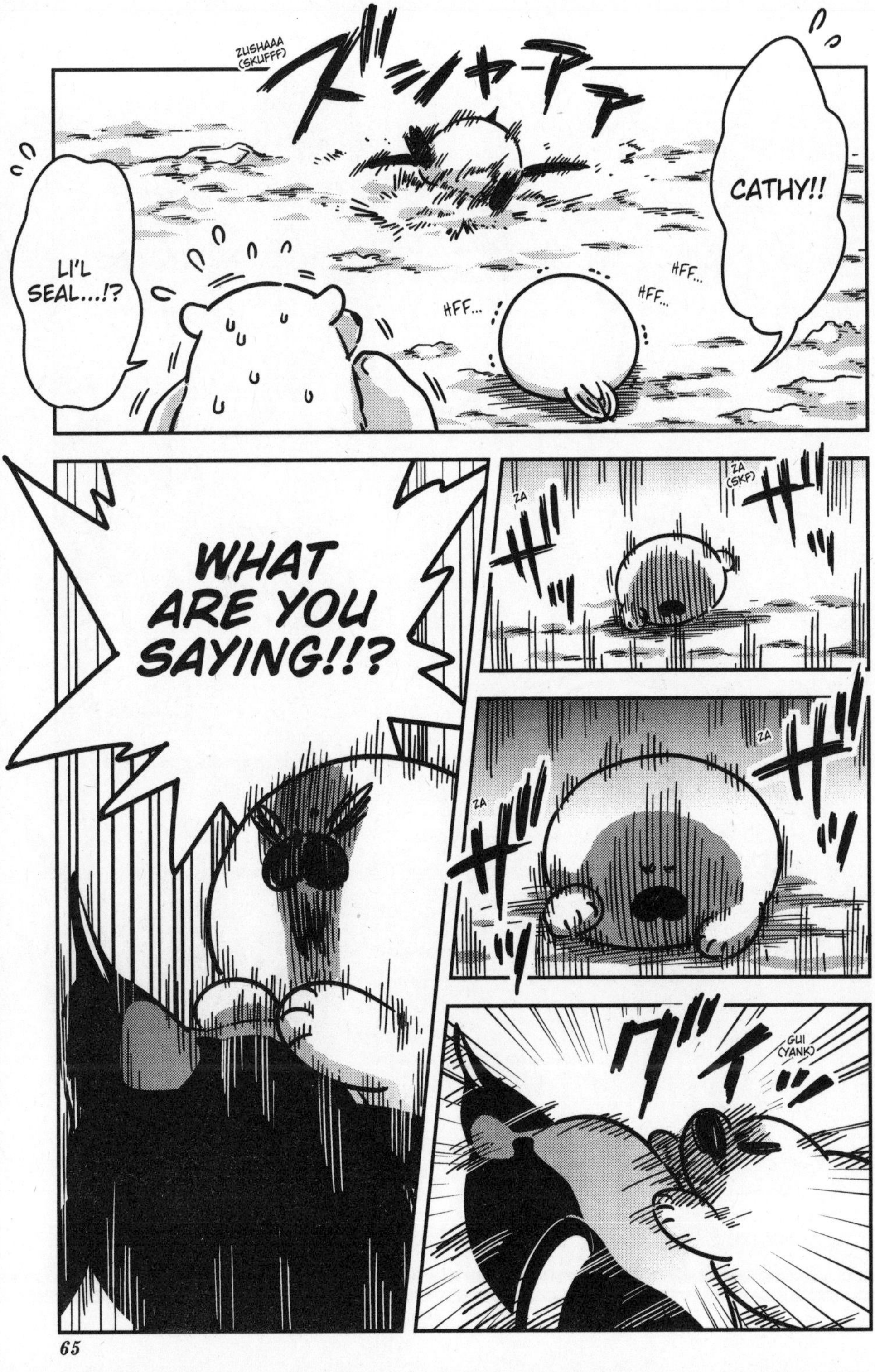
CATHY!!
ZUSHAAA (SKUFFF)
HFF...
HFF...
HFF...
LI'L SEAL...!?
ZA (SKF)
ZA
ZA
ZA
GUI (YANK)
WHAT ARE YOU SAYING!!?

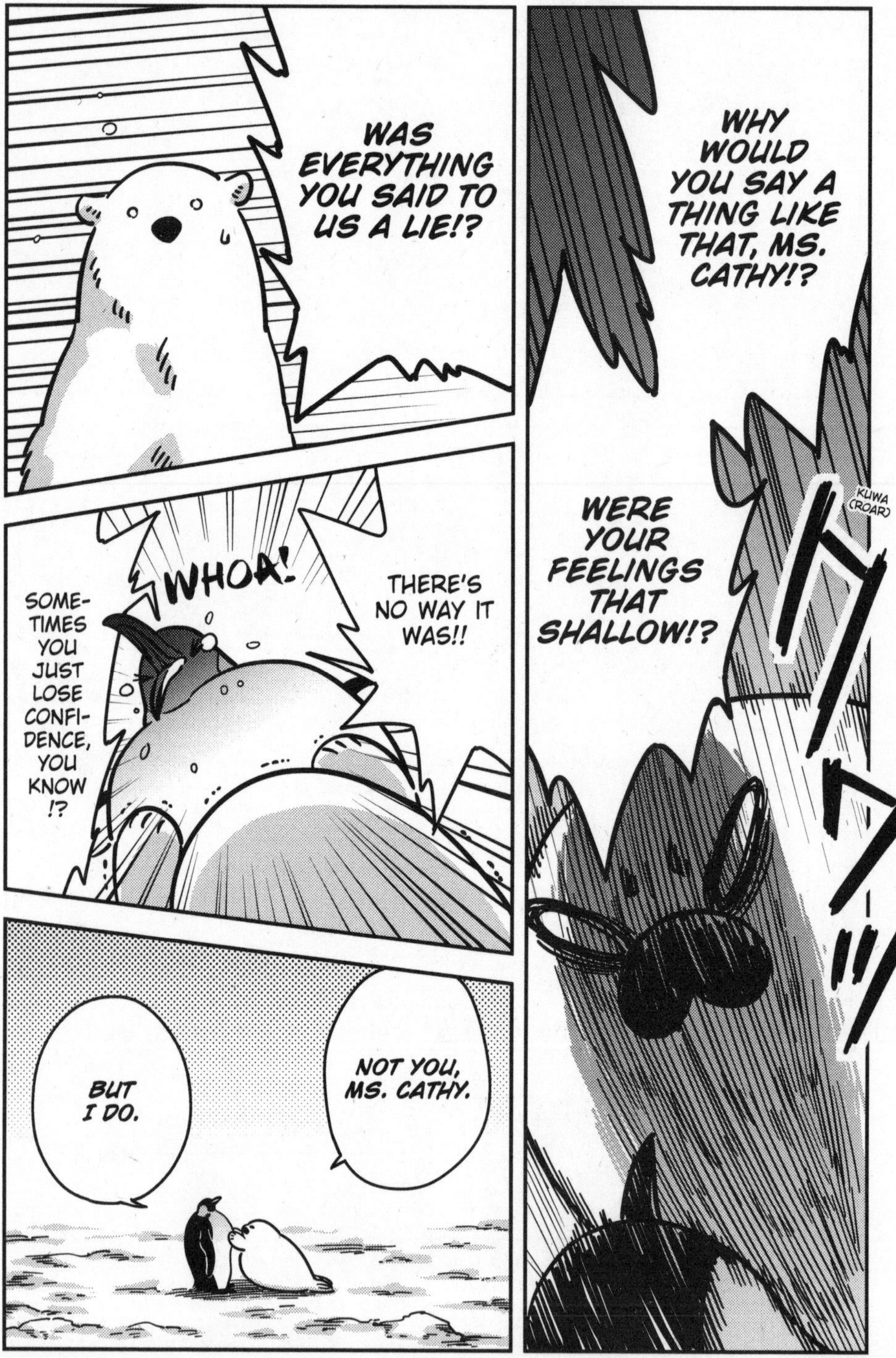
WHY WOULD YOU SAY A THING LIKE THAT, MS. CATHY!?
WERE YOUR FEELINGS THAT SHALLOW!?
KUWA (ROAR)
WAS EVERYTHING YOU SAID TO US A LIE!?
WHOA!
THERE'S NO WAY IT WAS!!
SOMETIMES YOU JUST LOSE CONFIDENCE, YOU KNOW!?
NOT YOU, MS. CATHY.
BUT I DO.

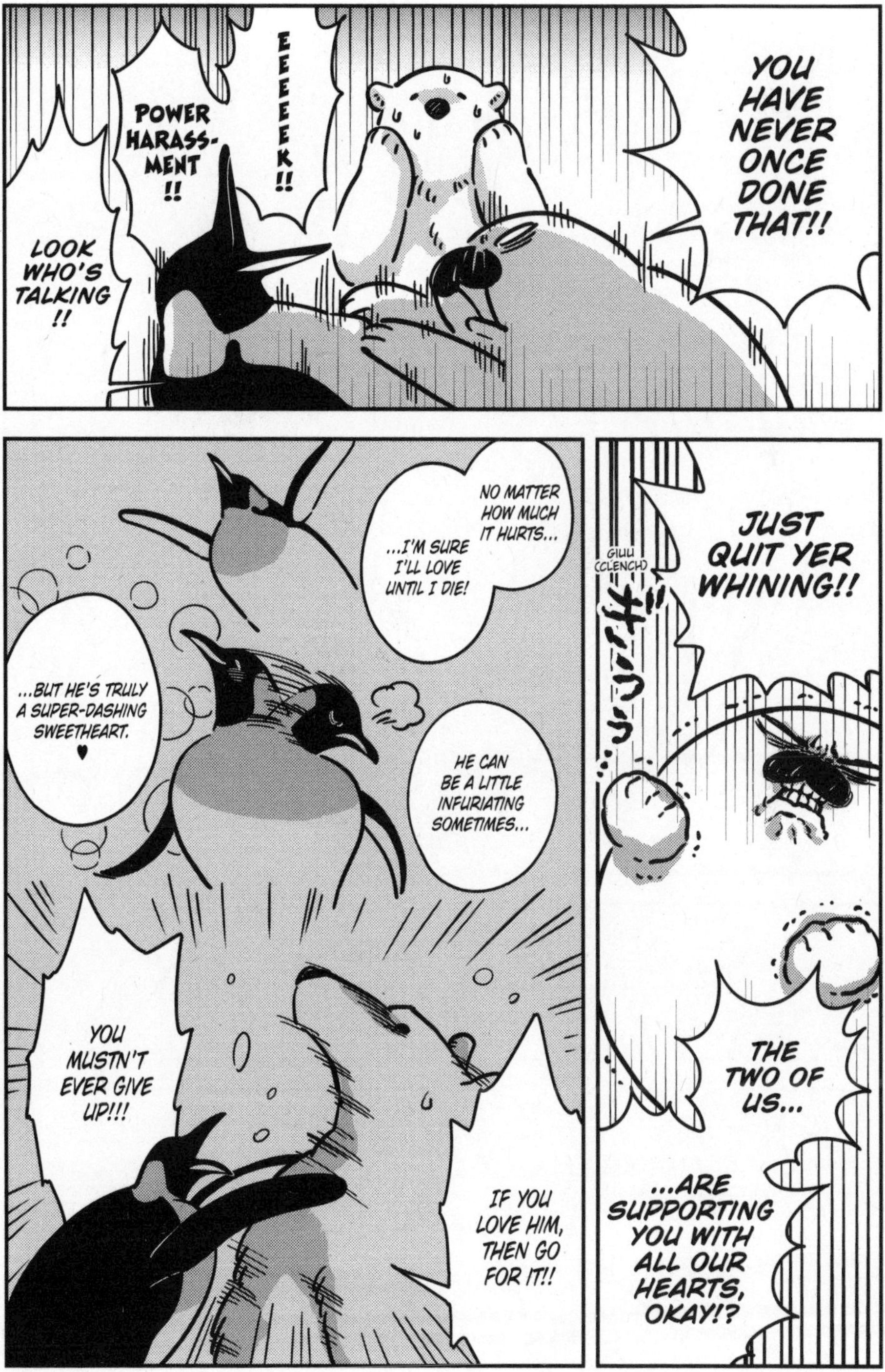
YOU HAVE NEVER ONCE DONE THAT!!
EEEEEEK!!
POWER HARASS-MENT!!
LOOK WHO'S TALKING!!
JUST QUIT YER WHINING!!
GIUU (CLENCH)
THE TWO OF US...
...ARE SUPPORTING YOU WITH ALL OUR HEARTS, OKAY!?
NO MATTER HOW MUCH IT HURTS...
...I'M SURE I'LL LOVE UNTIL I DIE!
HE CAN BE A LITTLE INFURIATING SOMETIMES...
...BUT HE'S TRULY A SUPER-DASHING SWEETHEART. ♥
IF YOU LOVE HIM, THEN GO FOR IT!!
YOU MUSTN'T EVER GIVE UP!!!

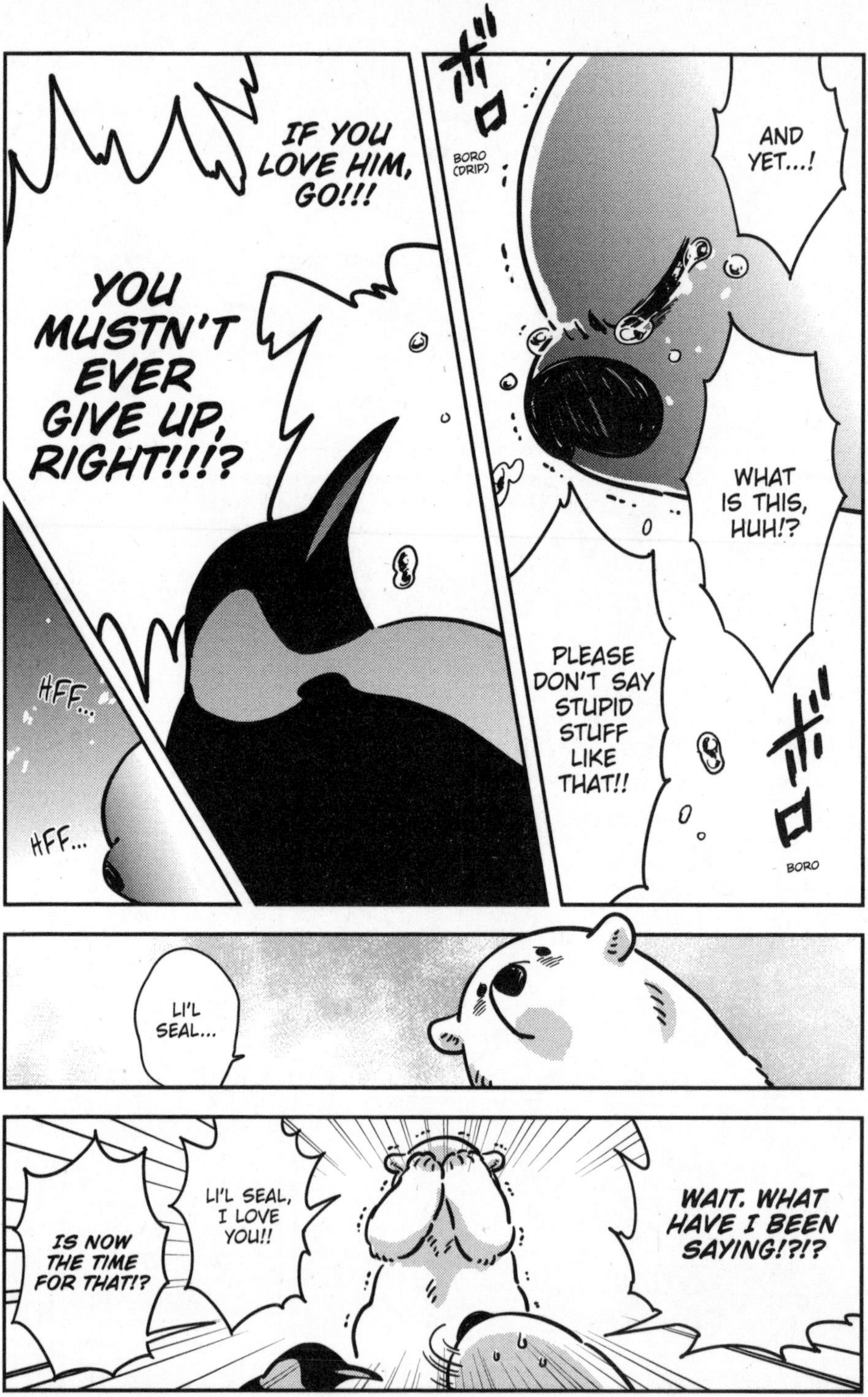

AND YET...!
ボロ
BORO (DRIP)
WHAT IS THIS, HUH!?
ボロ
BORO
PLEASE DON'T SAY STUPID STUFF LIKE THAT!!
IF YOU LOVE HIM, GO!!!
YOU MUSTN'T EVER GIVE UP, RIGHT!!!?
HFF...
HFF...
LI'L SEAL...
WAIT. WHAT HAVE I BEEN SAYING!?!?
LI'L SEAL, I LOVE YOU!!
IS NOW THE TIME FOR THAT!?

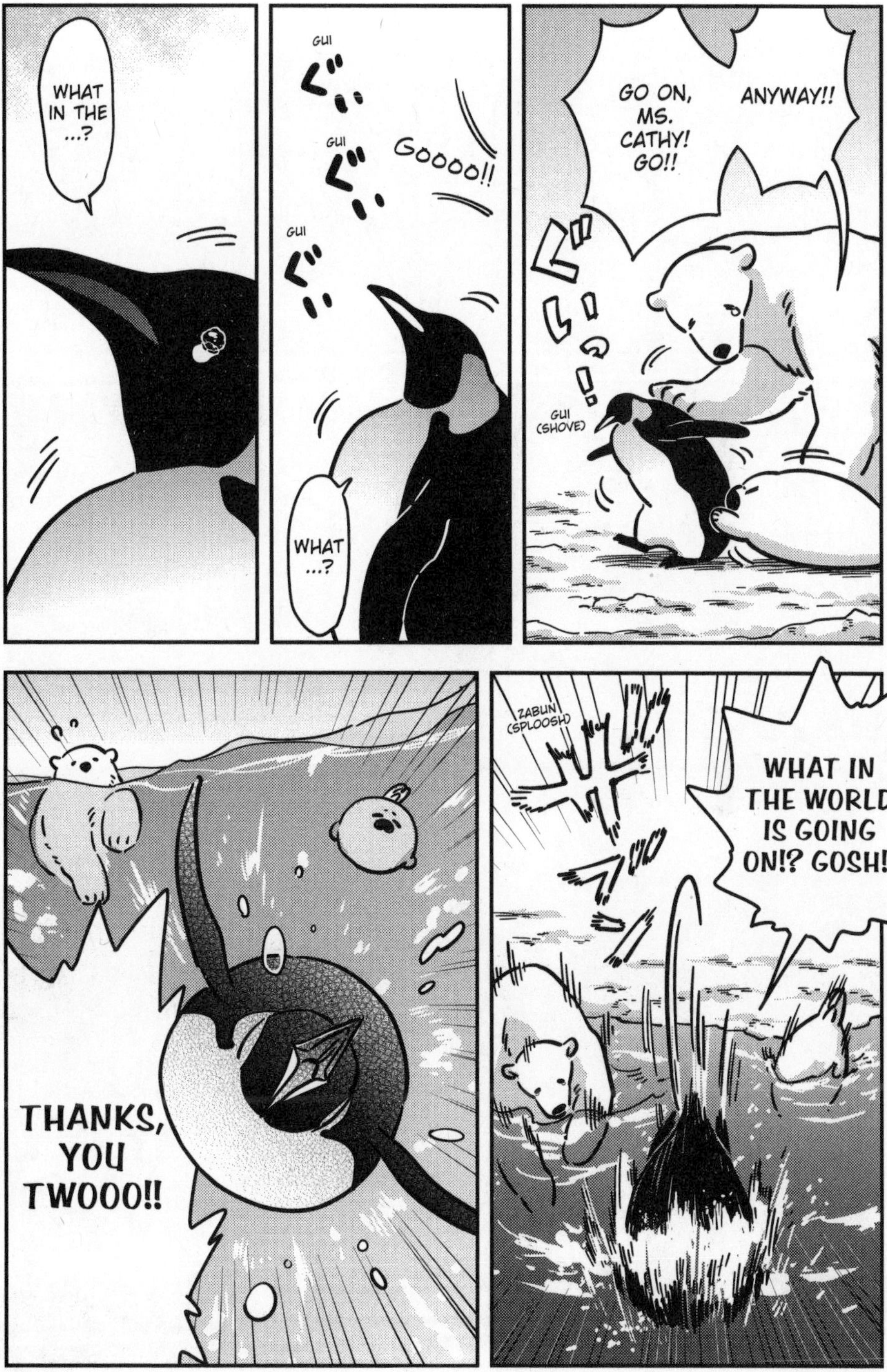
ANYWAY!!
GO ON, MS. CATHY! GO!!
GUI (SHOVE)
GUI
GUI
GUI
GOOOO!!
WHAT ...?
WHAT IN THE ...?
ZABUN (SPLOOSH)
WHAT IN THE WORLD IS GOING ON!? GOSH!!
THANKS, YOU TWOOO!!

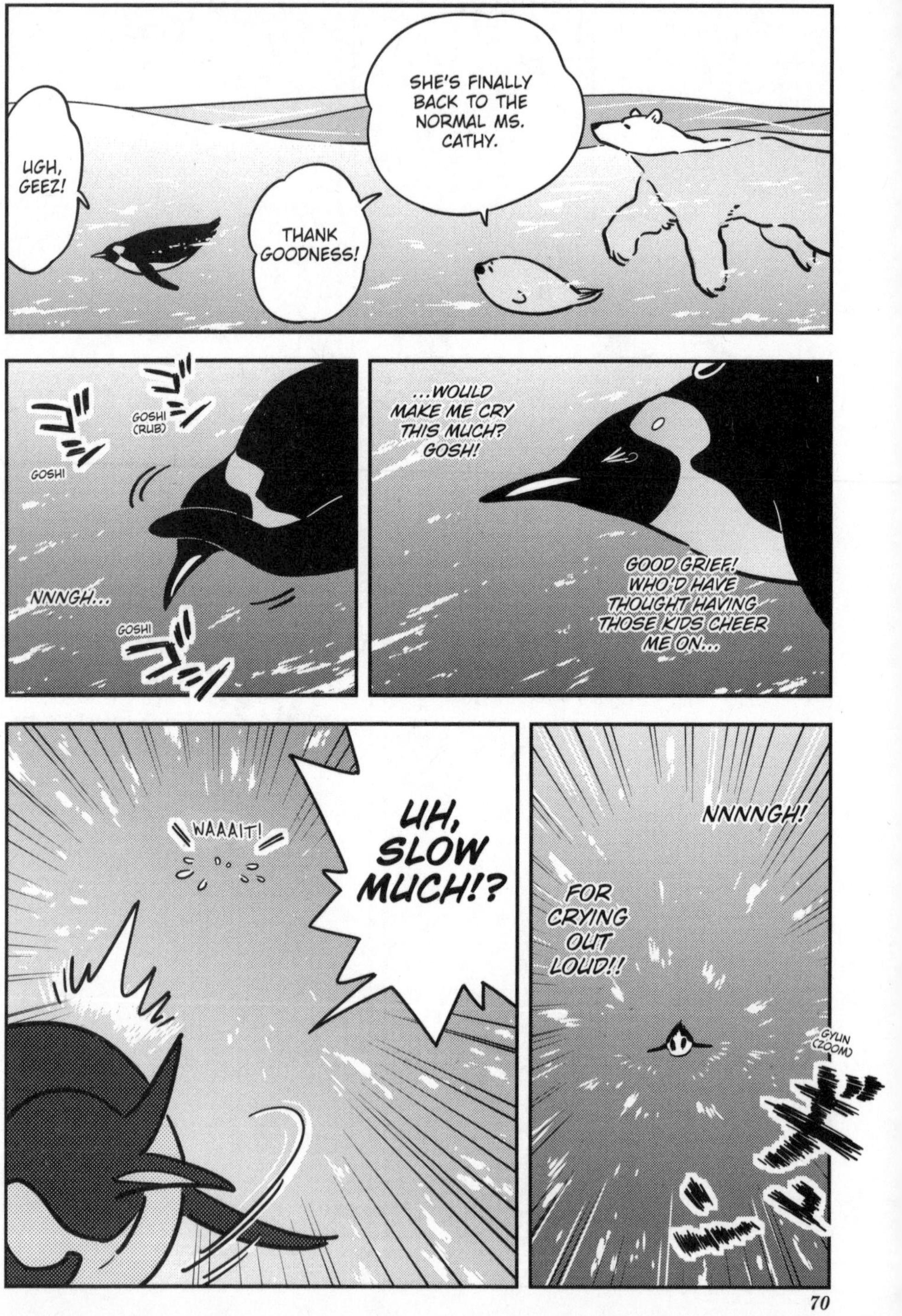
SHE'S FINALLY BACK TO THE NORMAL MS. CATHY.
THANK GOODNESS!
UGH, GEEZ!
GOOD GRIEF! WHO'D HAVE THOUGHT HAVING THOSE KIDS CHEER ME ON...
...WOULD MAKE ME CRY THIS MUCH? GOSH!
GOSHI (RUB)
GOSHI
NNNGH...
GOSHI
NNNNGH!
FOR CRYING OUT LOUD!!
GYUN (ZOOM)
UH, SLOW MUCH!?
WAAAIT!

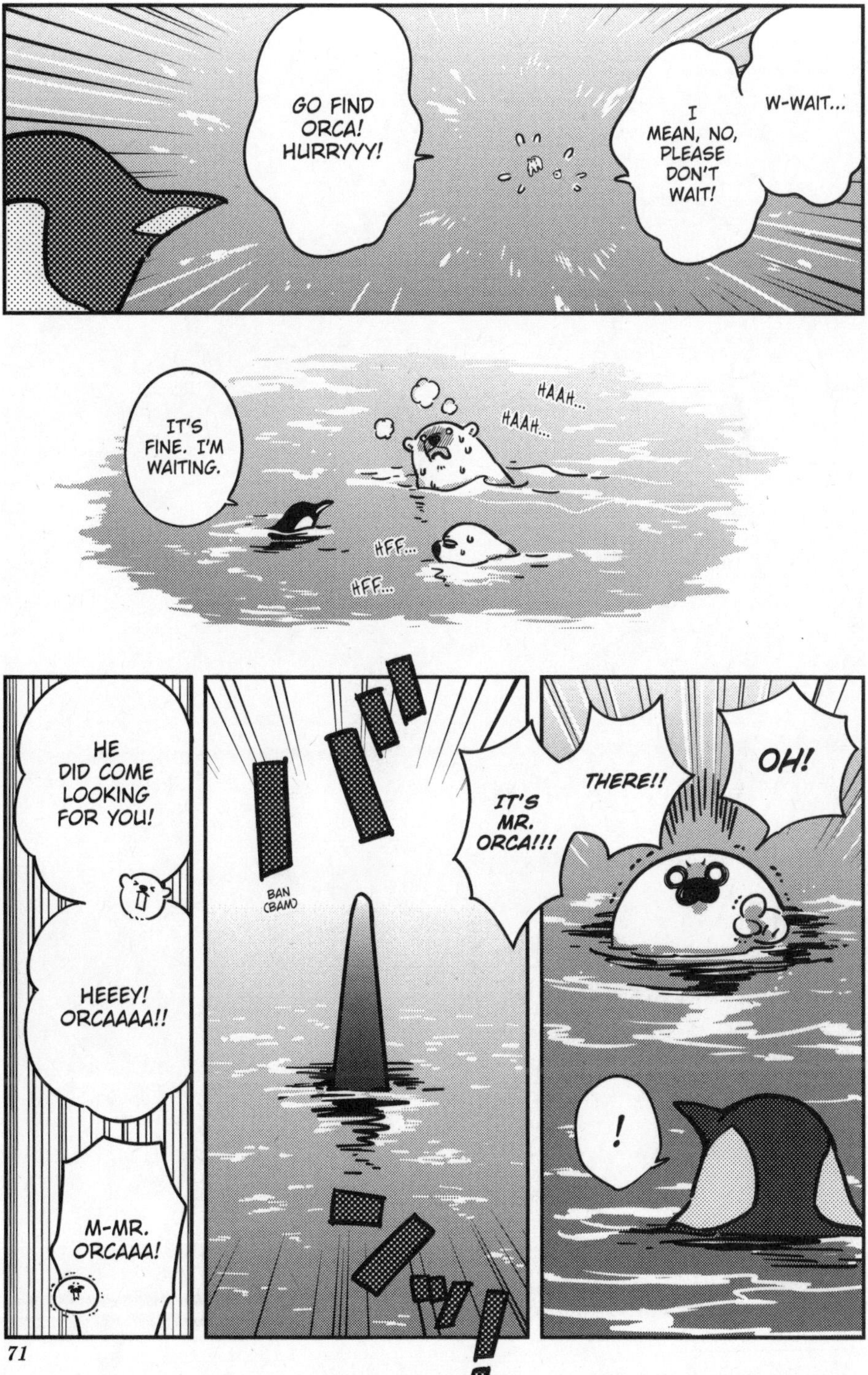
W-WAIT...
I MEAN, NO, PLEASE DON'T WAIT!
GO FIND ORCA! HURRYYY!
HAAH... HAAH...
IT'S FINE. I'M WAITING.
HFF... HFF...
OH!
THERE!!
IT'S MR. ORCA!!!
!
BAN (BAM)
HE DID COME LOOKING FOR YOU!
HEEEY! ORCAAAA!!
M-MR. ORCAAA!

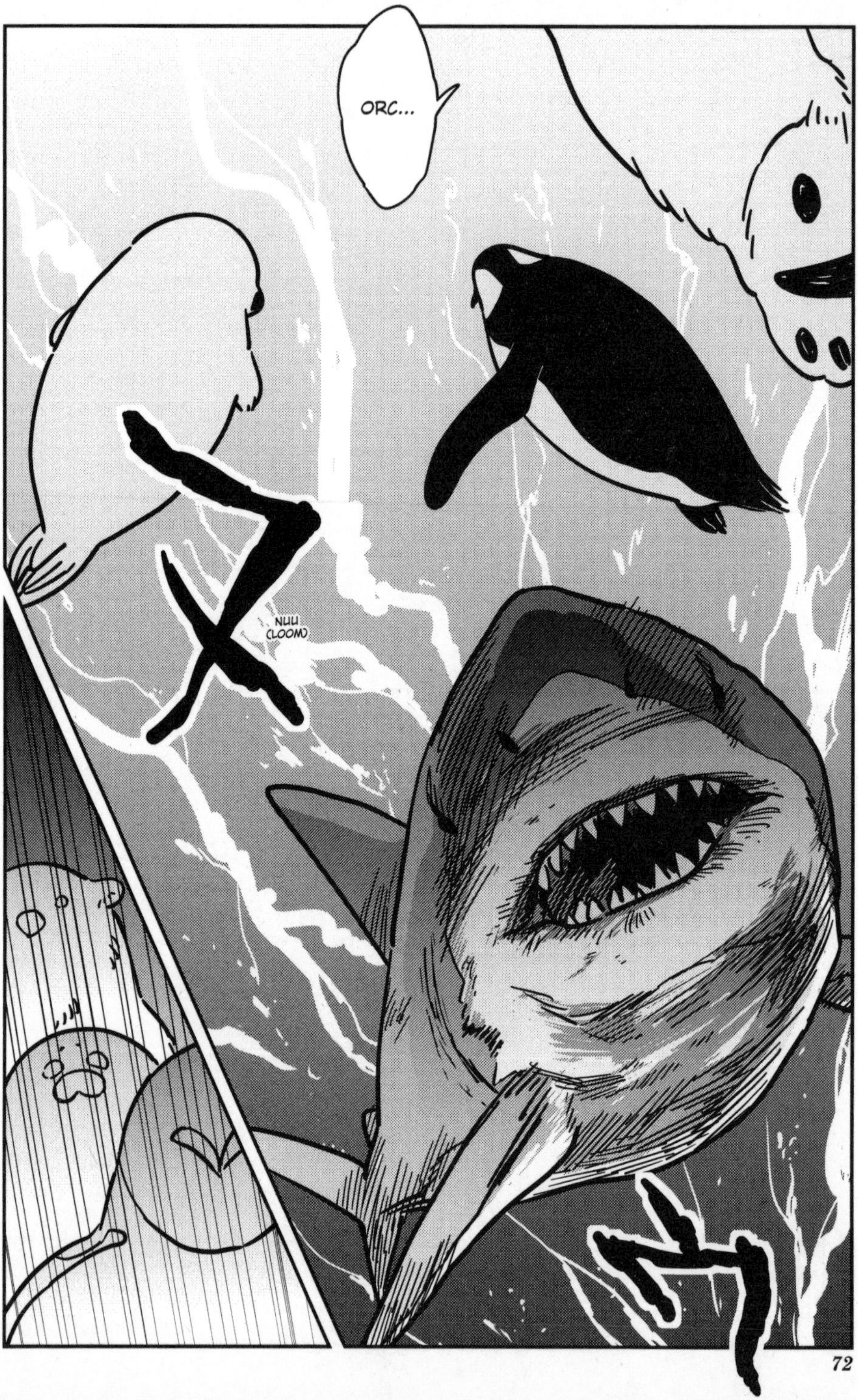
ORC...
NUU (LOOM)

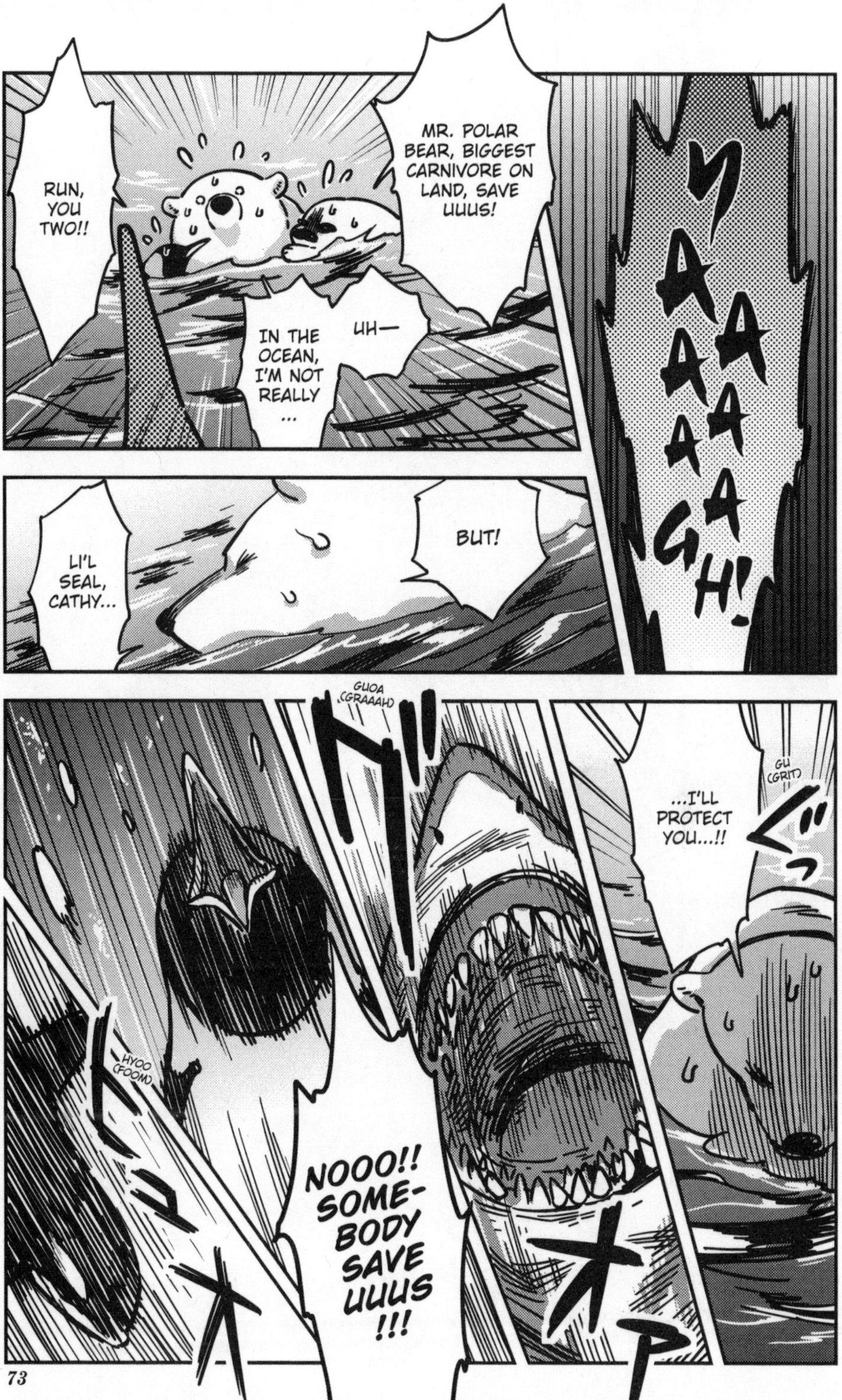
ンAAAAAAAGH!
MR. POLAR BEAR, BIGGEST CARNIVORE ON LAND, SAVE UUUS!
RUN, YOU TWO!!
UH—
IN THE OCEAN, I'M NOT REALLY ...
BUT!
LI'L SEAL, CATHY...
GU (GRIT)
...I'LL PROTECT YOU...!!
GUOA (GRAAAH)
NOOO!! SOME-BODY SAVE UUUS !!!
HYOO (FOOM)

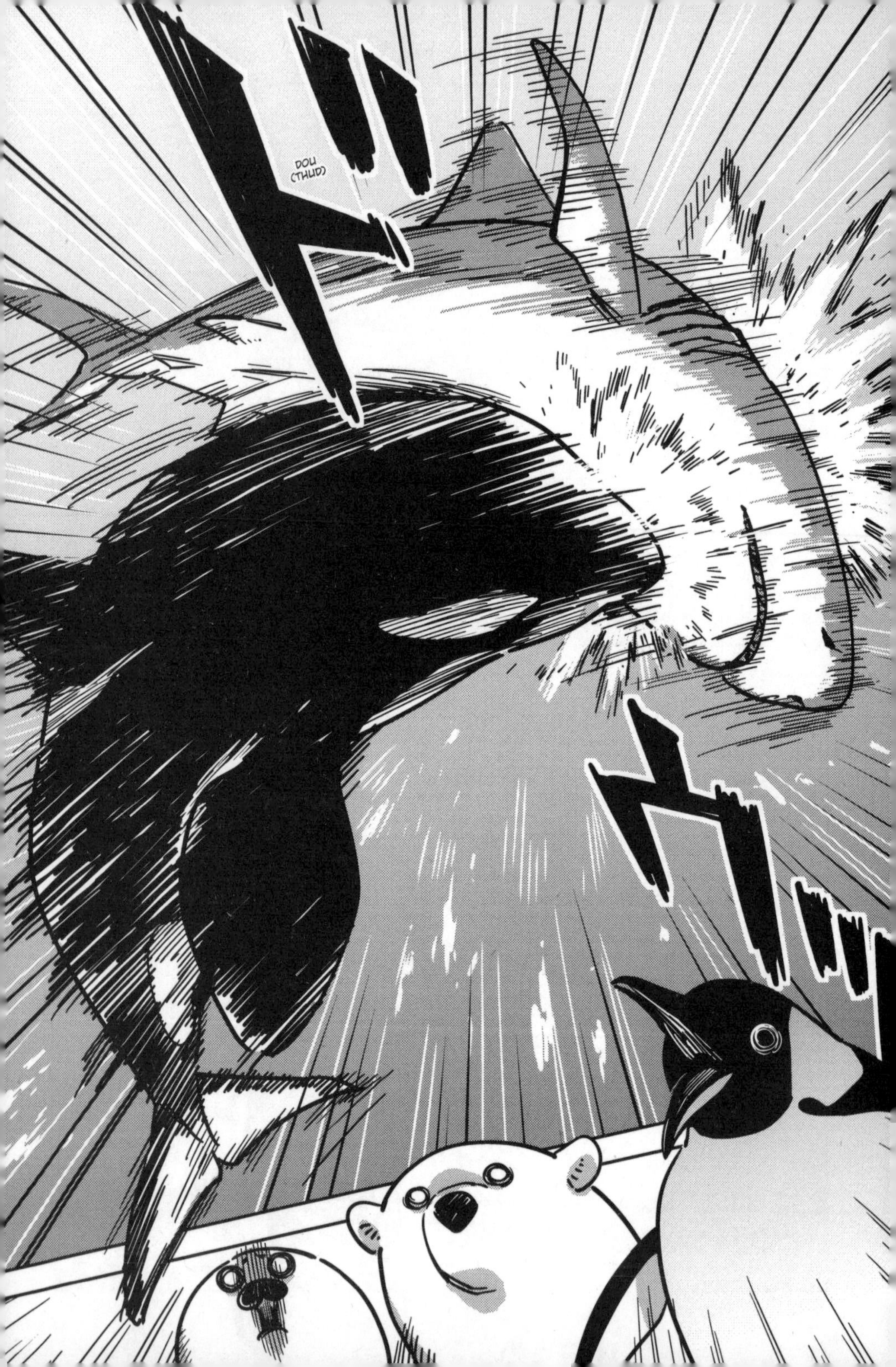
DOU
(THUD)

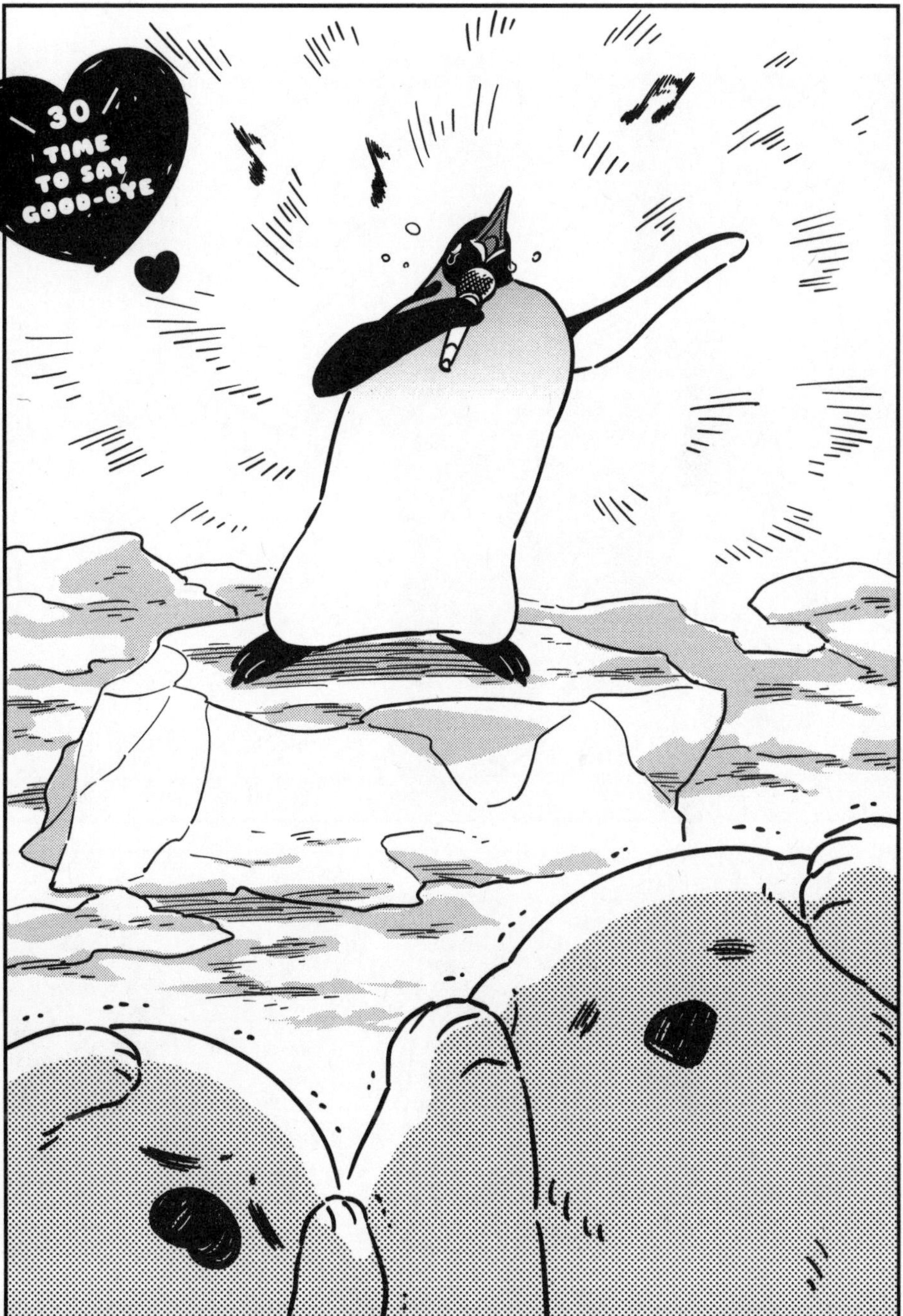
30
TIME TO SAY GOOD-BYE

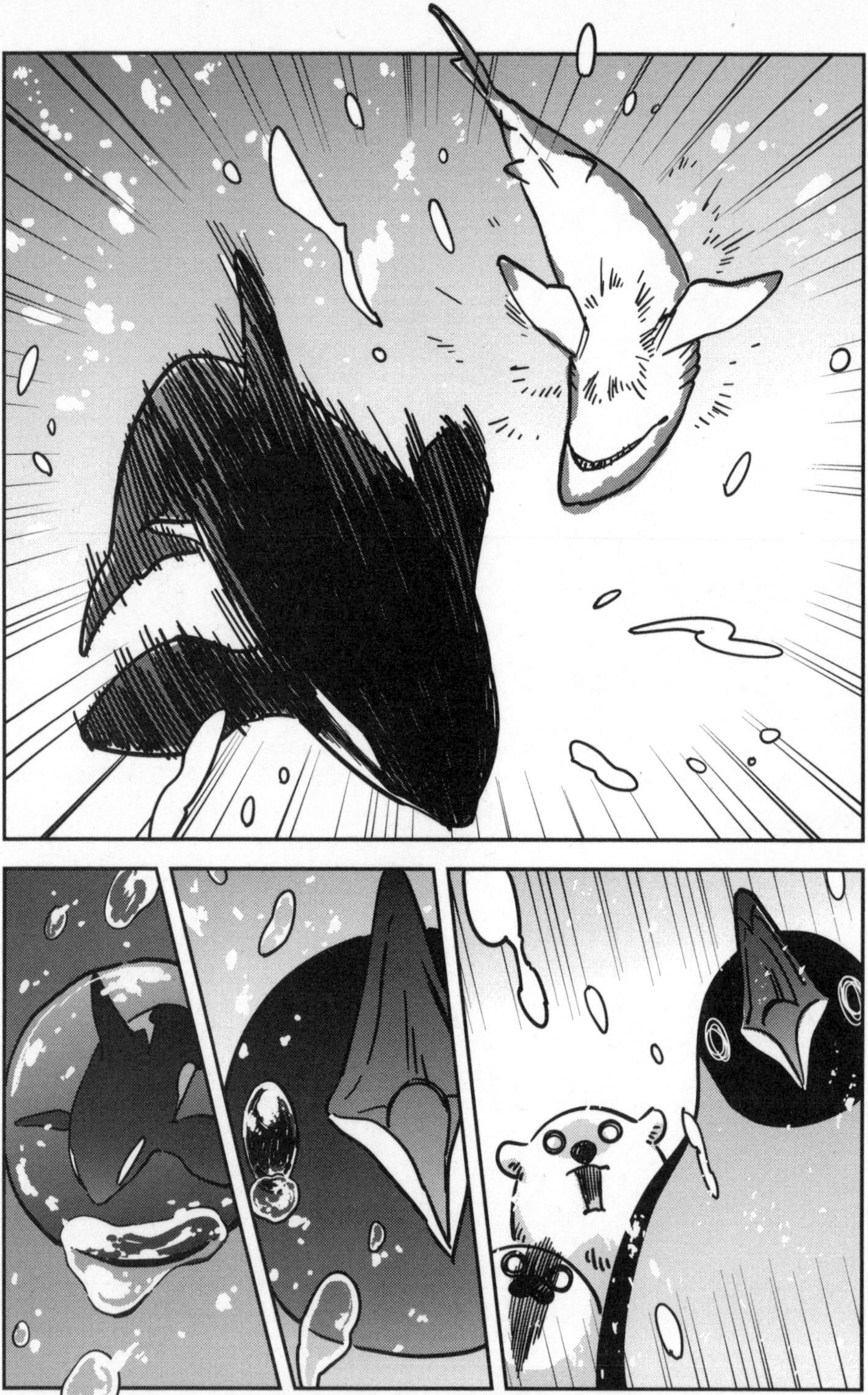

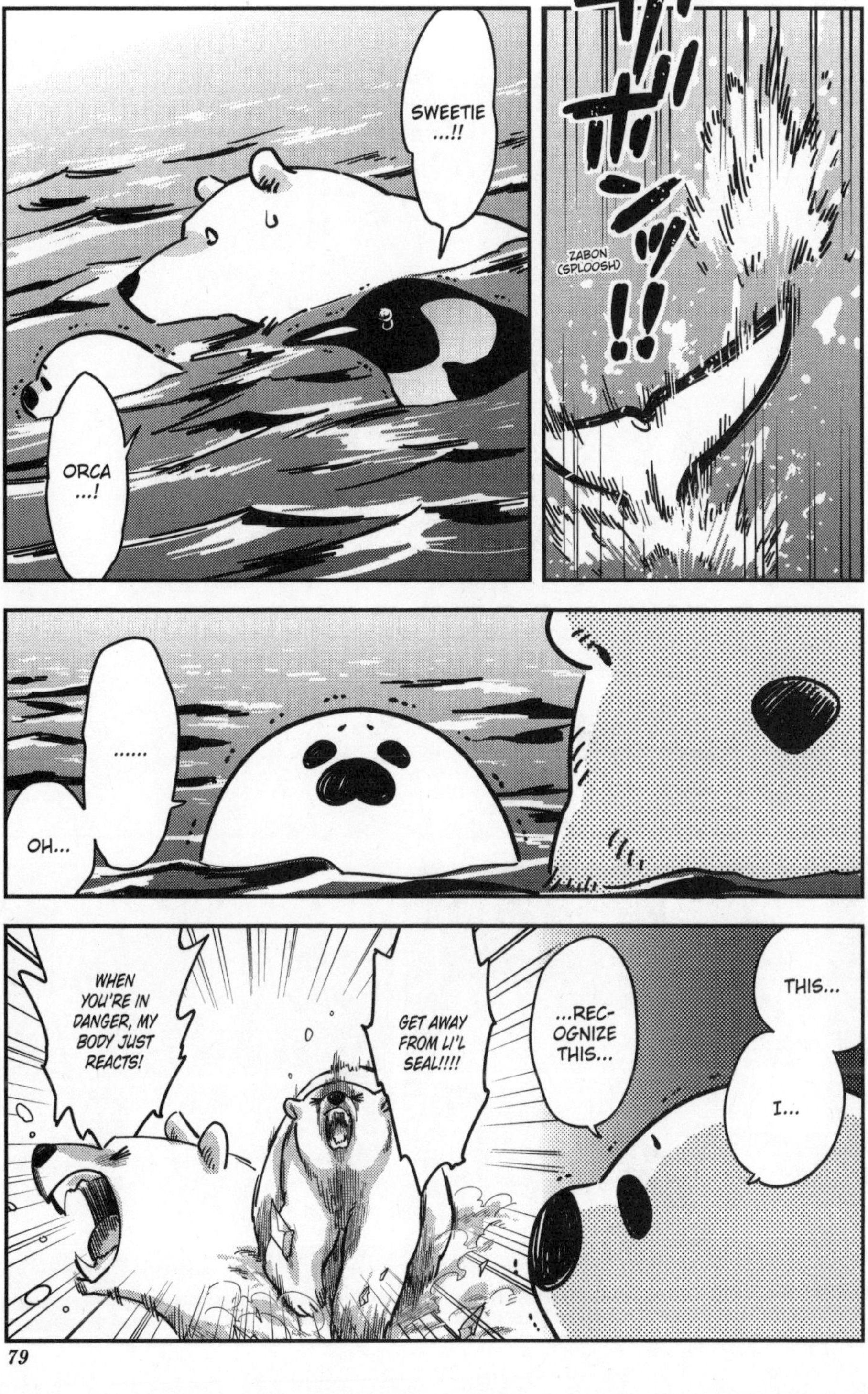
ZABON (SPLOOSH)
SWEETIE ...!!
ORCA ...!
......
OH...
THIS...
I...
...REC-OGNIZE THIS...
GET AWAY FROM LI'L SEAL!!!!
WHEN YOU'RE IN DANGER, MY BODY JUST REACTS!

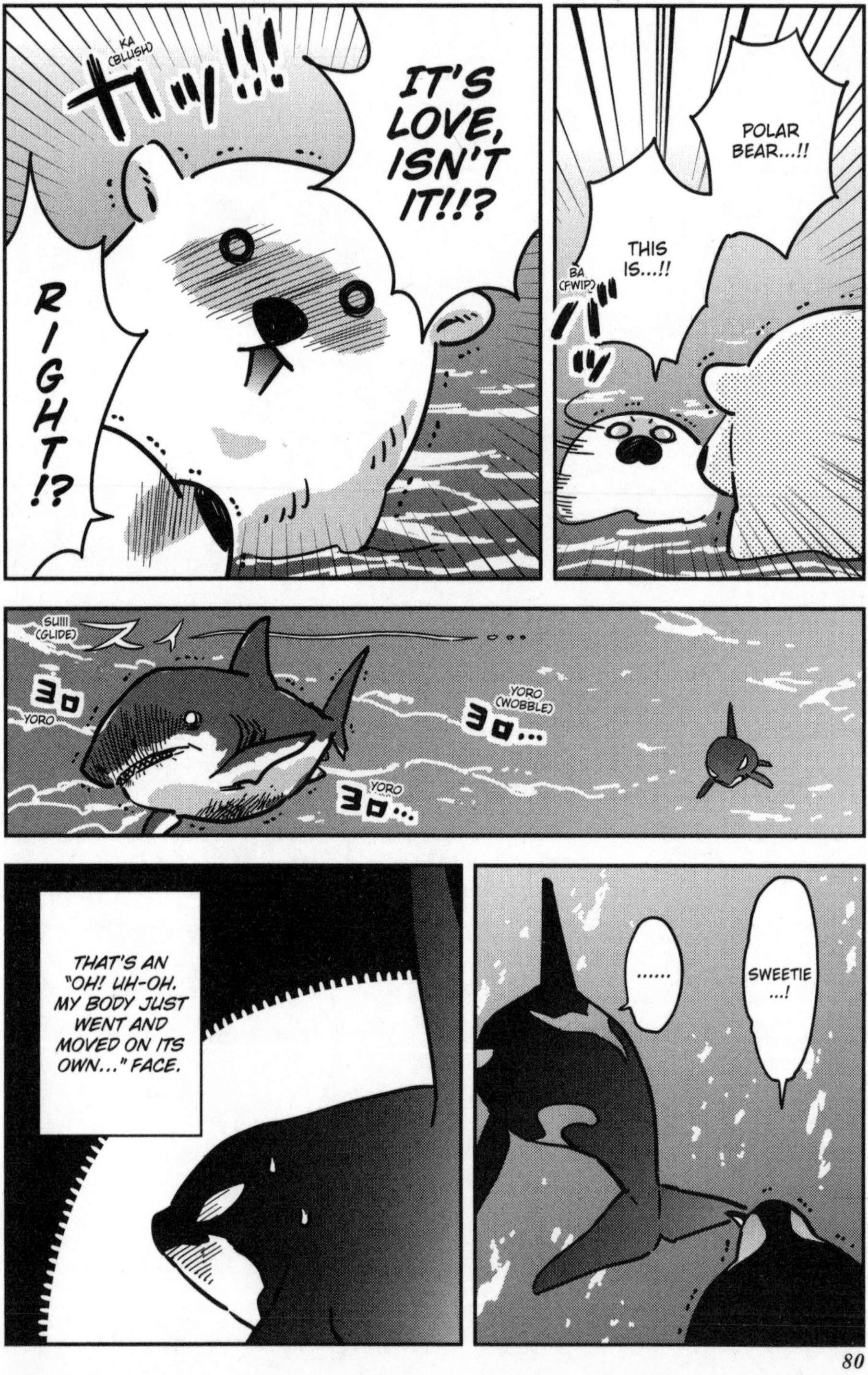
POLAR BEAR...!!
THIS IS...!!
BA (FWIP)
バッ
KA (BLUSH)
カッ!!!
IT'S LOVE, ISN'T IT!!?
RIGHT!?
SUIII (GLIDE)
スイ
ヨロ
YORO
YORO (WOBBLE)
ヨロ...
YORO
ヨロ...
SWEETIE ...!
......
THAT'S AN "OH! UH-OH. MY BODY JUST WENT AND MOVED ON ITS OWN..." FACE.

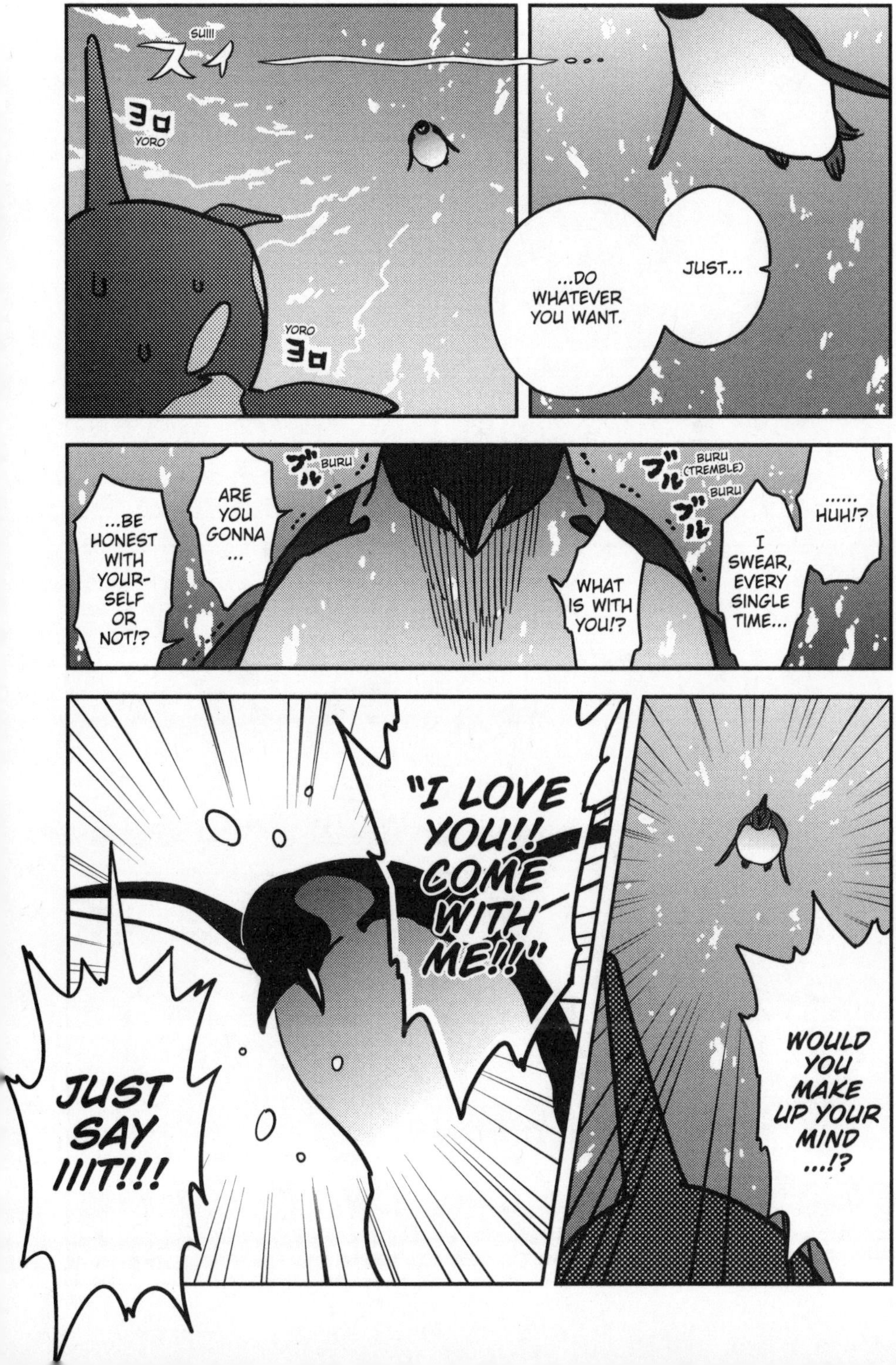
JUST...
...DO WHATEVER YOU WANT.
スイ
SUIII
...
ヨロ
YORO
YORO
ヨロ
......HUH!?
I SWEAR, EVERY SINGLE TIME...
ブル
BURU (TREMBLE)
ブル
BURU
WHAT IS WITH YOU!?
ブル
BURU
ARE YOU GONNA...
...BE HONEST WITH YOUR-SELF OR NOT!?
WOULD YOU MAKE UP YOUR MIND...!?
"I LOVE YOU!! COME WITH ME!!!"
JUST SAY IIIT!!!

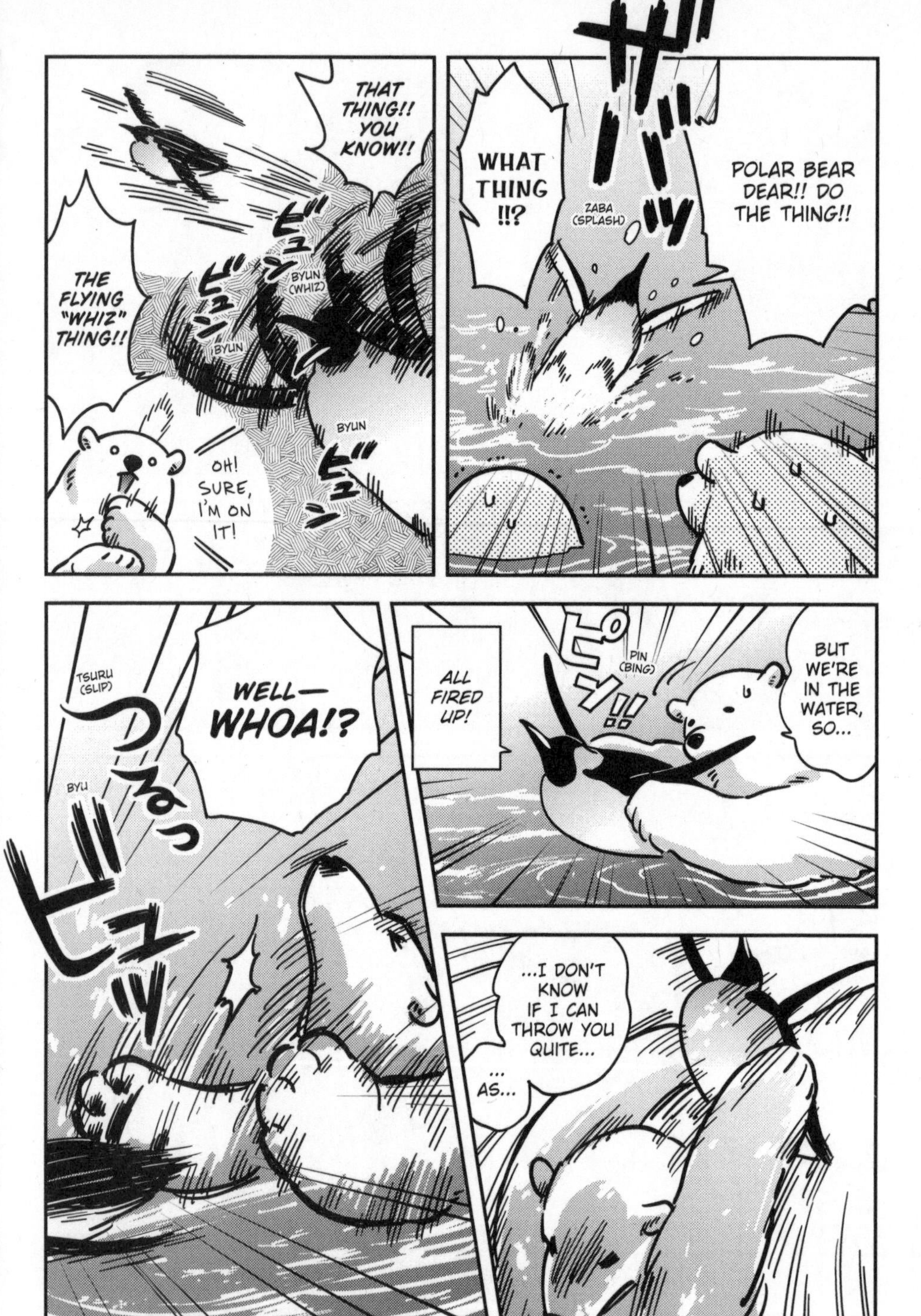
ZABA (SPLASH)
POLAR BEAR DEAR!! DO THE THING!!
WHAT THING!!?
THAT THING!! YOU KNOW!!
BYUN (WHIZ)
BYUN
THE FLYING "WHIZ" THING!!
BYUN
OH! SURE, I'M ON IT!
BUT WE'RE IN THE WATER, SO...
PIN (BING)
ALL FIRED UP!
...I DON'T KNOW IF I CAN THROW YOU QUITE...
... AS...
WELL— WHOA!?
TSURU (SLIP)
BYU

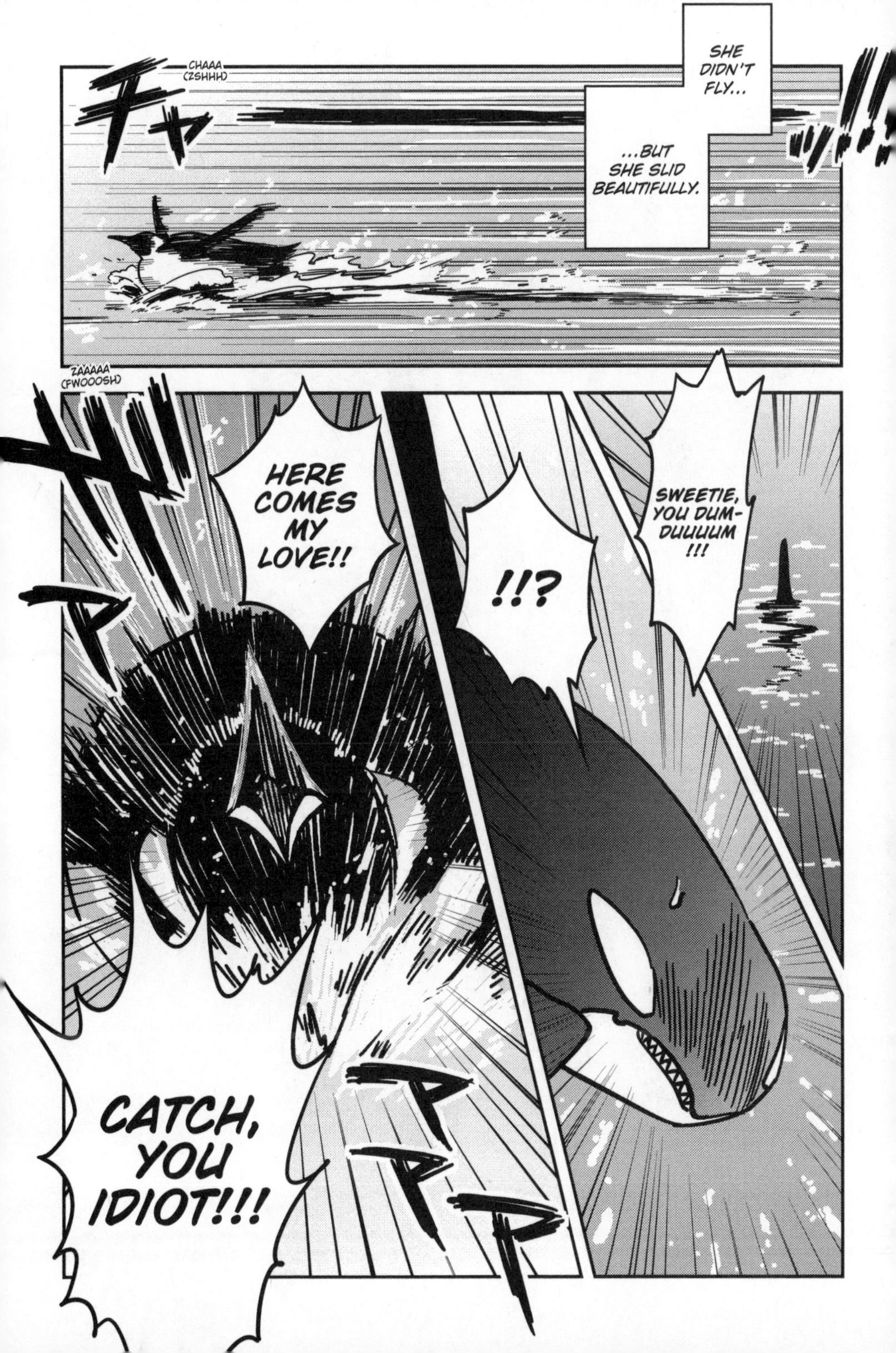
SHE DIDN'T FLY...
...BUT SHE SLID BEAUTIFULLY.
CHAAA (ZSHHH)
SWEETIE, YOU DUM-DUUUUM!!!
!!?
HERE COMES MY LOVE!!
ZAAAAA (FWOOOSH)
CATCH, YOU IDIOT!!!

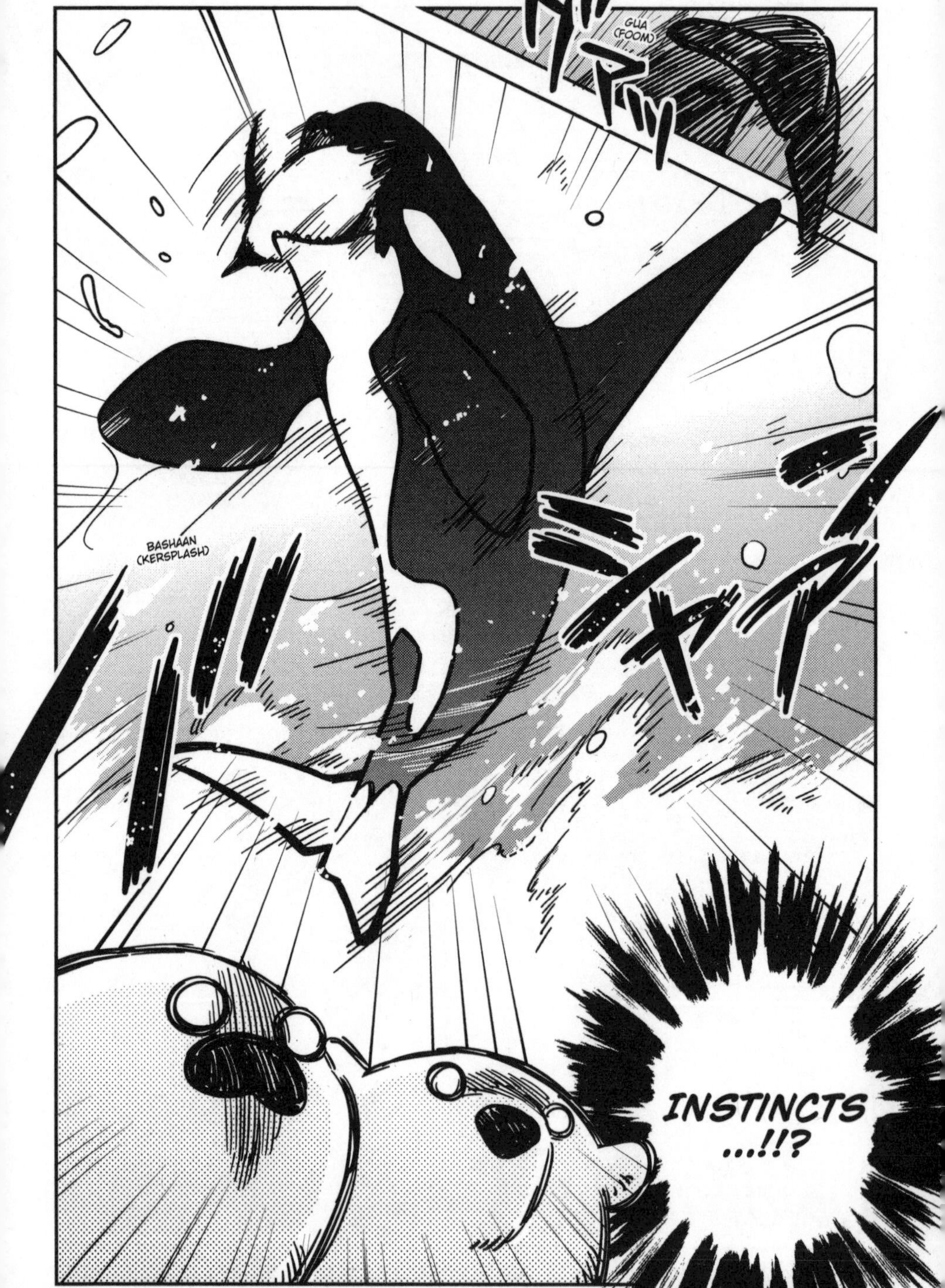
GUA (FOOM)
BASHAAN (KERSPLASH)
INSTINCTS ...!!?

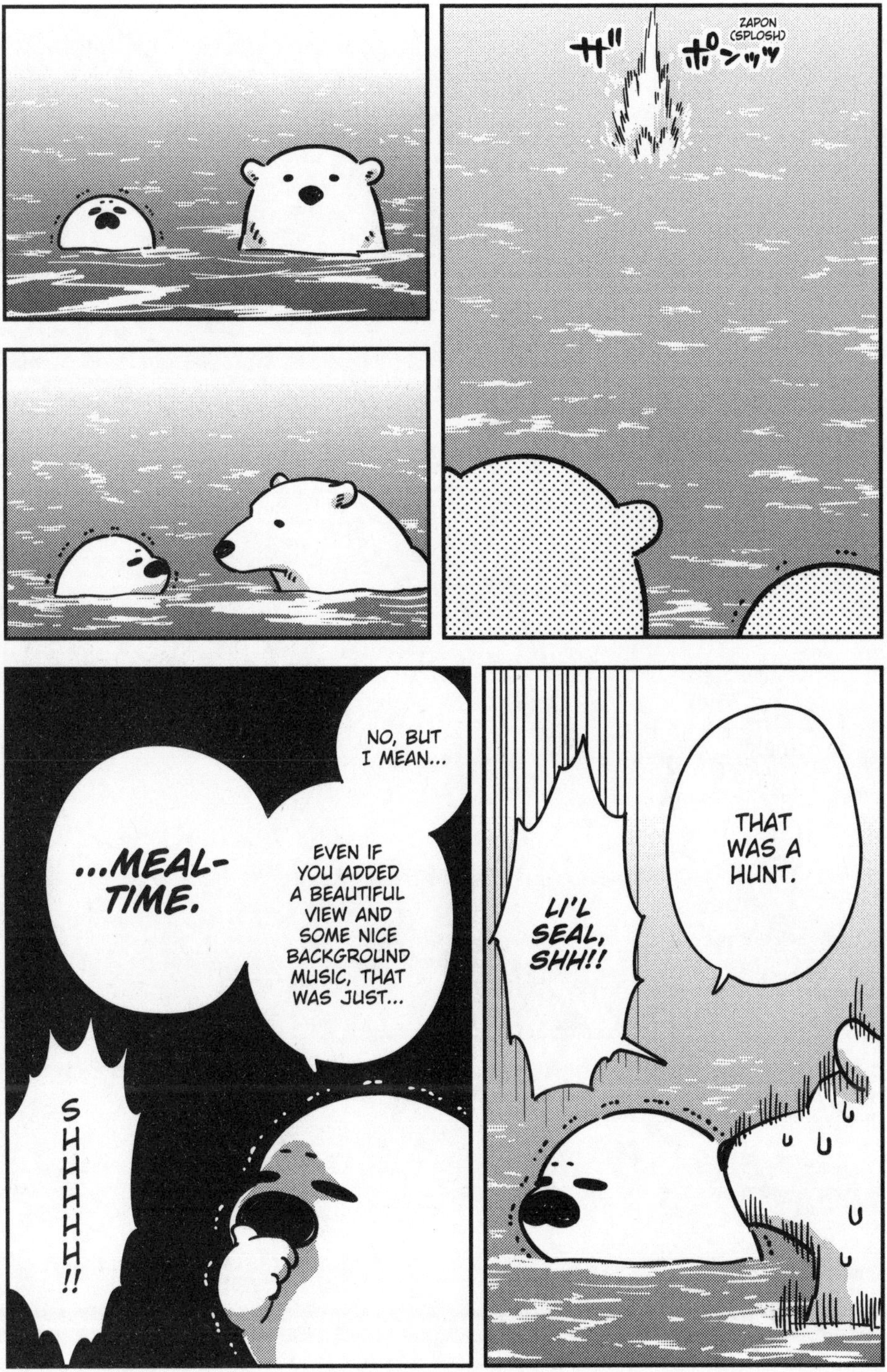
ザッポンッ
ZAPON (SPLOSH)
THAT WAS A HUNT.
LI'L SEAL, SHH!!
NO, BUT I MEAN...
EVEN IF YOU ADDED A BEAUTIFUL VIEW AND SOME NICE BACKGROUND MUSIC, THAT WAS JUST...
...MEAL-TIME.
SHHHHH!!

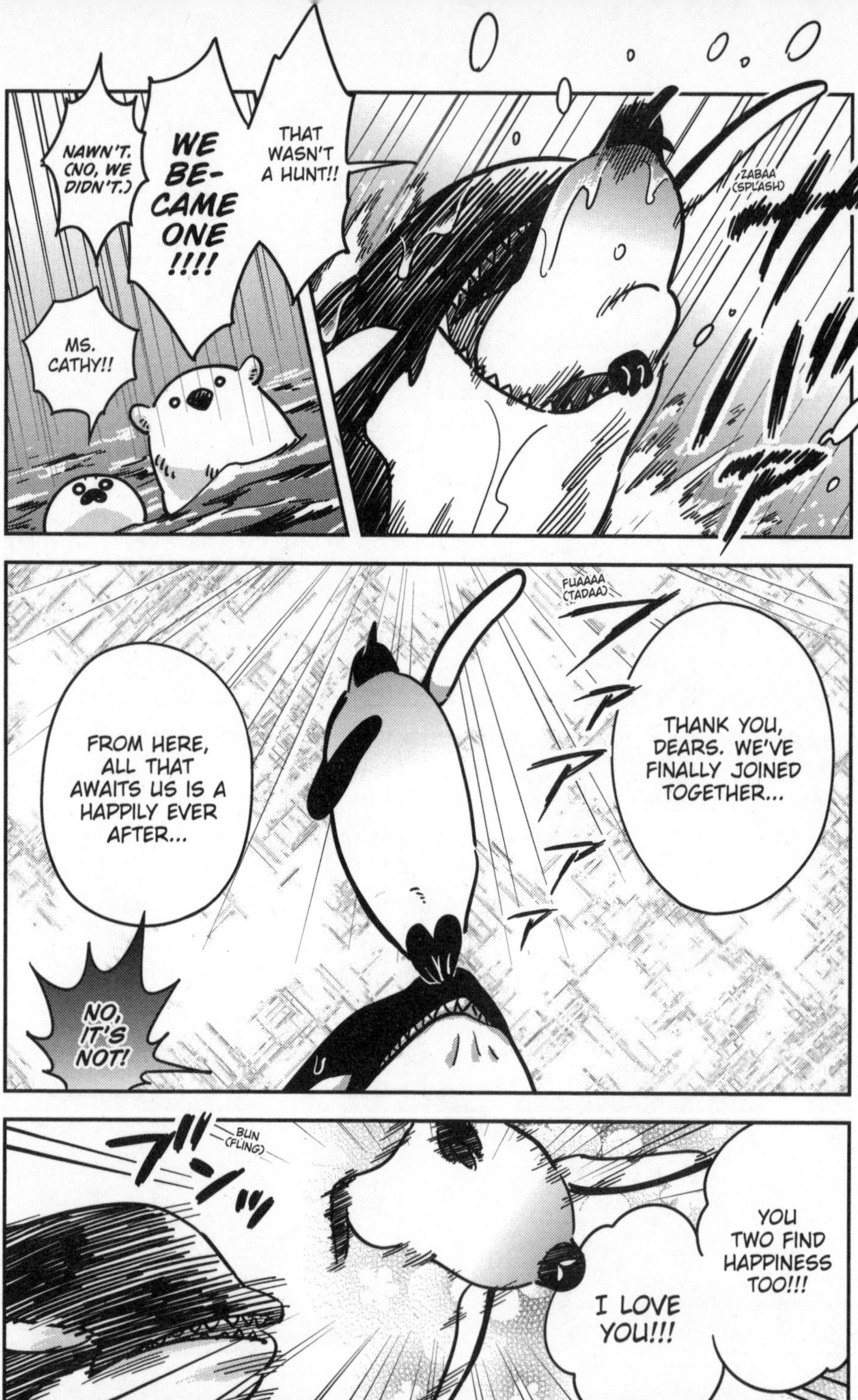
ZABAA (SPLASH)
THAT WASN'T A HUNT!!
WE BE-CAME ONE!!!!
NAWN'T. (NO, WE DIDN'T.)
MS. CATHY!!
FUAAAA (TADAA)
THANK YOU, DEARS. WE'VE FINALLY JOINED TOGETHER...
FROM HERE, ALL THAT AWAITS US IS A HAPPILY EVER AFTER...
NO, IT'S NOT!
YOU TWO FIND HAPPINESS TOO!!!
I LOVE YOU!!!
BUN (FLING)

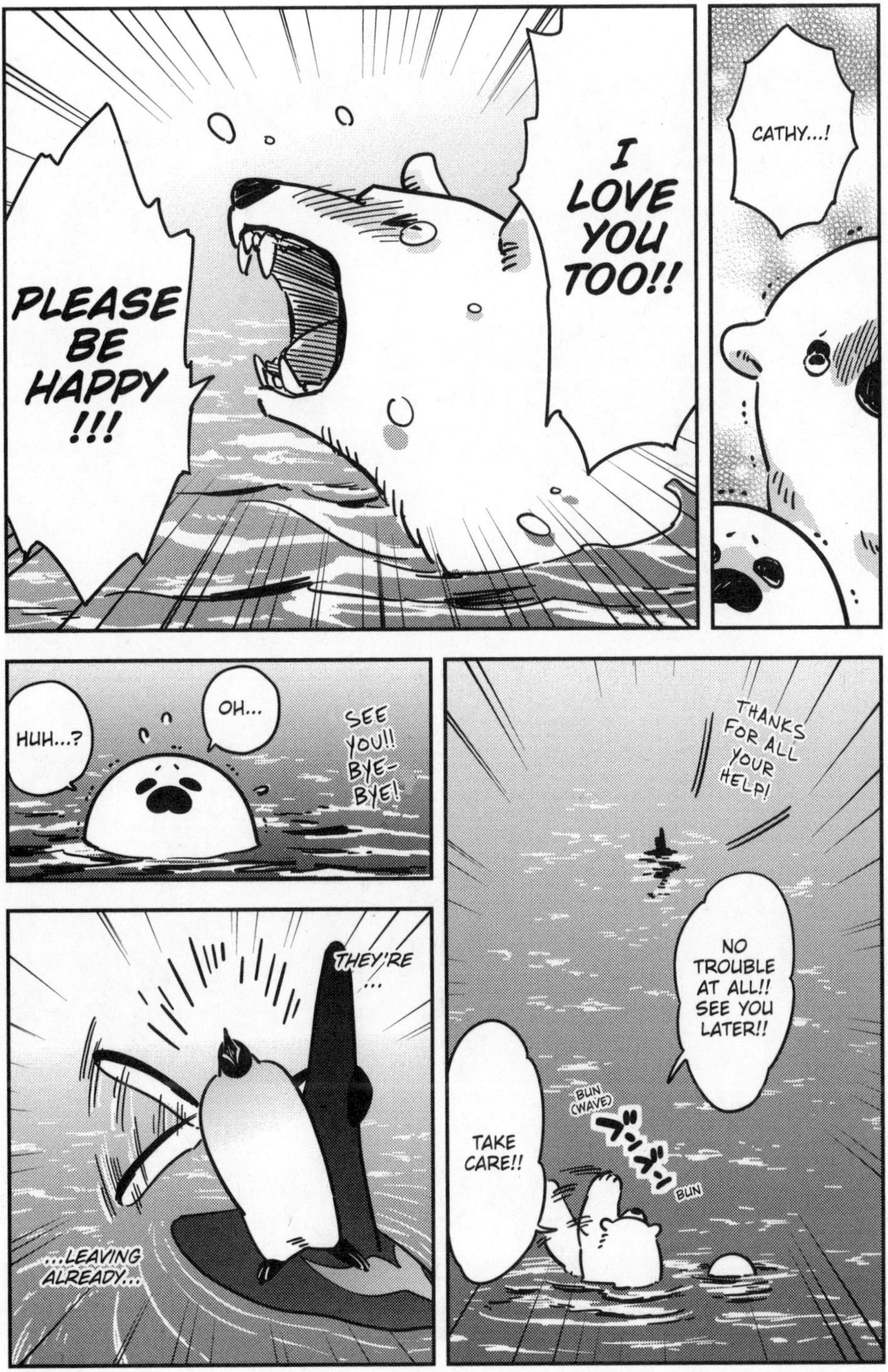
CATHY...!
I LOVE YOU TOO!!
PLEASE BE HAPPY!!!
THANKS FOR ALL YOUR HELP!
NO TROUBLE AT ALL!! SEE YOU LATER!!
BUN (WAVE)
BUN
TAKE CARE!!
SEE YOU!! BYE-BYE!
OH...
HUH...?
THEY'RE ...
...LEAVING ALREADY...

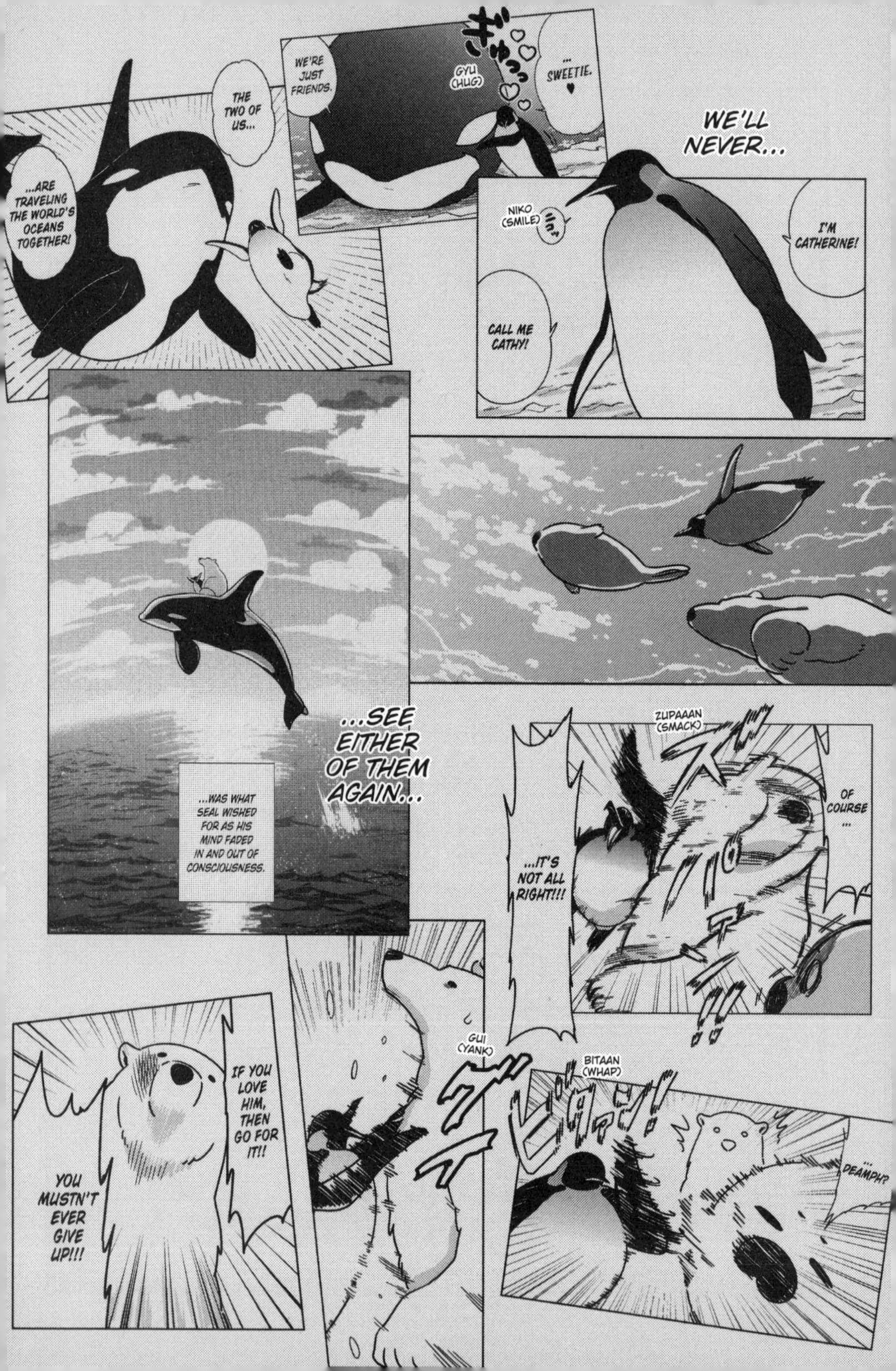
WE'LL NEVER...
I'M CATHERINE!
NIKO (SMILE)
CALL ME CATHY!
... SWEETIE.
GYU (HUG)
WE'RE JUST FRIENDS.
THE TWO OF US...
...ARE TRAVELING THE WORLD'S OCEANS TOGETHER!
...SEE EITHER OF THEM AGAIN...
...WAS WHAT SEAL WISHED FOR AS HIS MIND FADED IN AND OUT OF CONSCIOUSNESS.
ZUPAAAN (SMACK)
OF COURSE...
...IT'S NOT ALL RIGHT!!!
BITAAN (WHAP)
...DEAMPH?
GUI (YANK)
IF YOU LOVE HIM, THEN GO FOR IT!!
YOU MUSTN'T EVER GIVE UP!!!

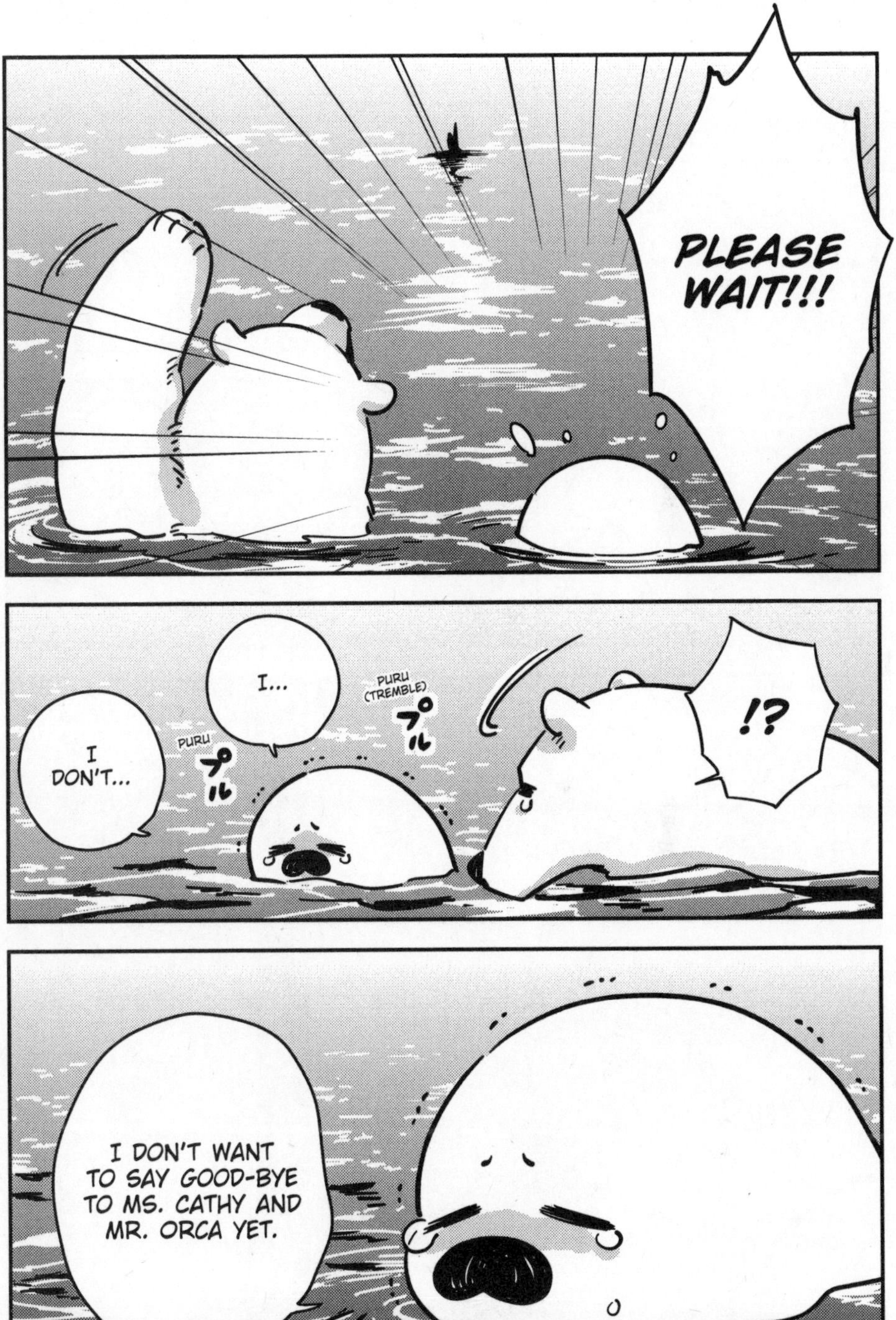
PLEASE WAIT!!!
!?
PURU (TREMBLE)
プル
I...
PURU
プル
I DON'T...
I DON'T WANT TO SAY GOOD-BYE TO MS. CATHY AND MR. ORCA YET.

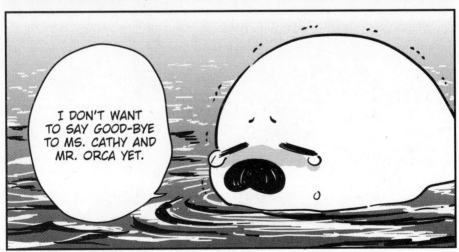

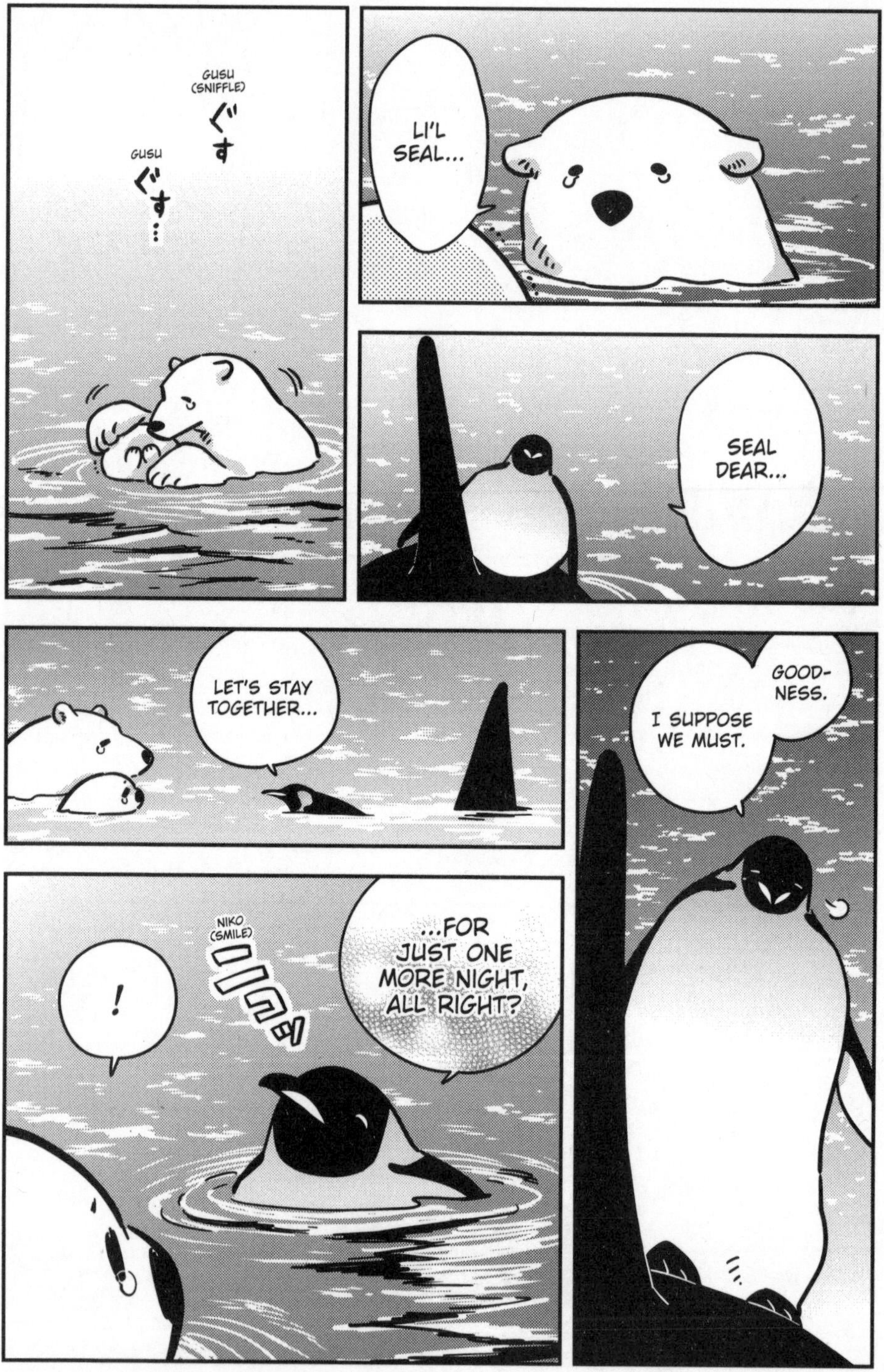
LI'L SEAL...
SEAL DEAR...
GUSU (SNIFFLE)
ぐす
GUSU
ぐす...
GOOD-NESS.
I SUPPOSE WE MUST.
LET'S STAY TOGETHER...
...FOR JUST ONE MORE NIGHT, ALL RIGHT?
NIKO (SMILE)
ニコッ
!

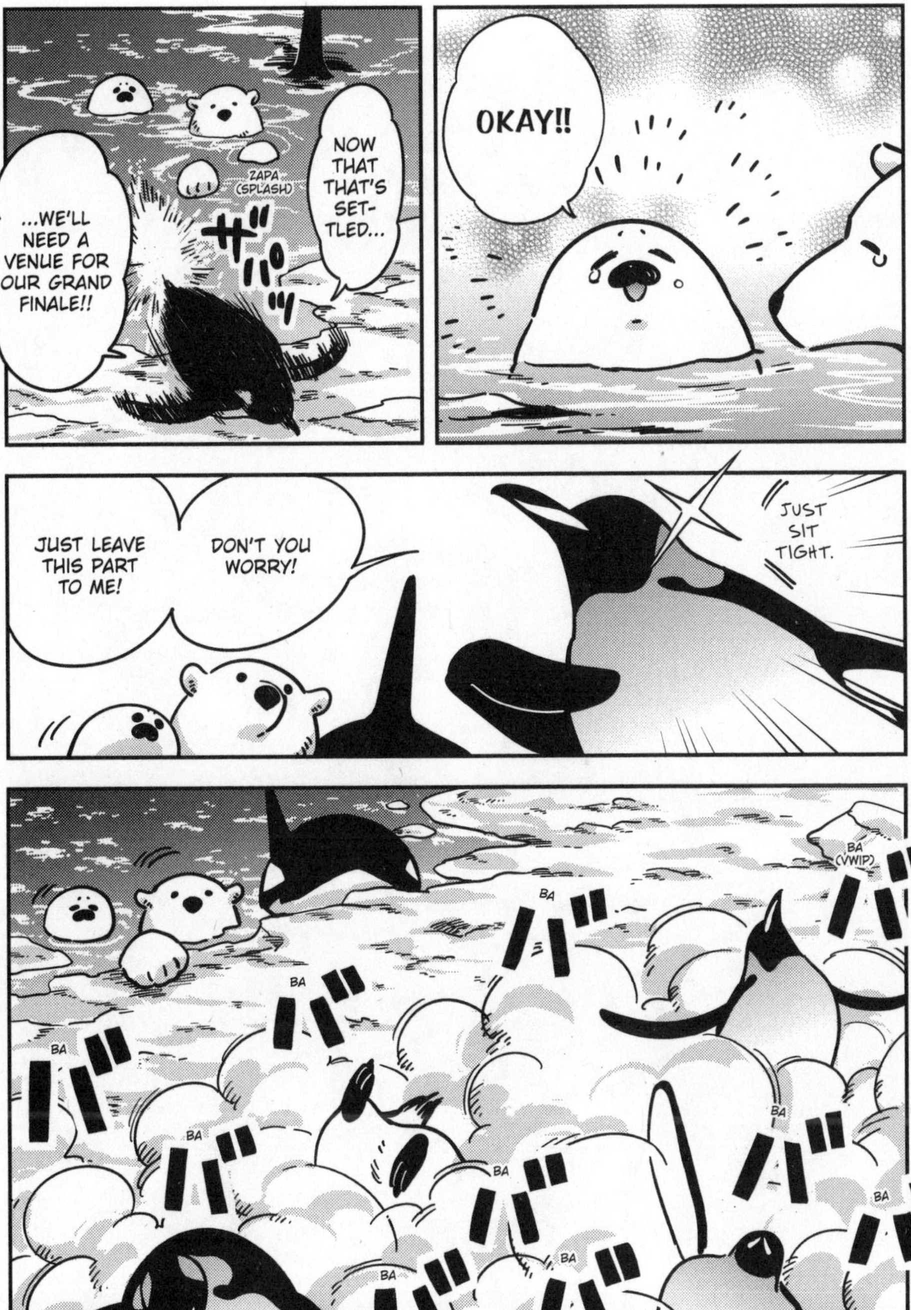
OKAY!!
NOW THAT THAT'S SET-TLED...
ZAPA (SPLASH)
...WE'LL NEED A VENUE FOR OUR GRAND FINALE!!
JUST SIT TIGHT.
DON'T YOU WORRY!
JUST LEAVE THIS PART TO ME!
BA (VWIP)
BA
BA
BA
BA
BA
BA
BA
BA
BA

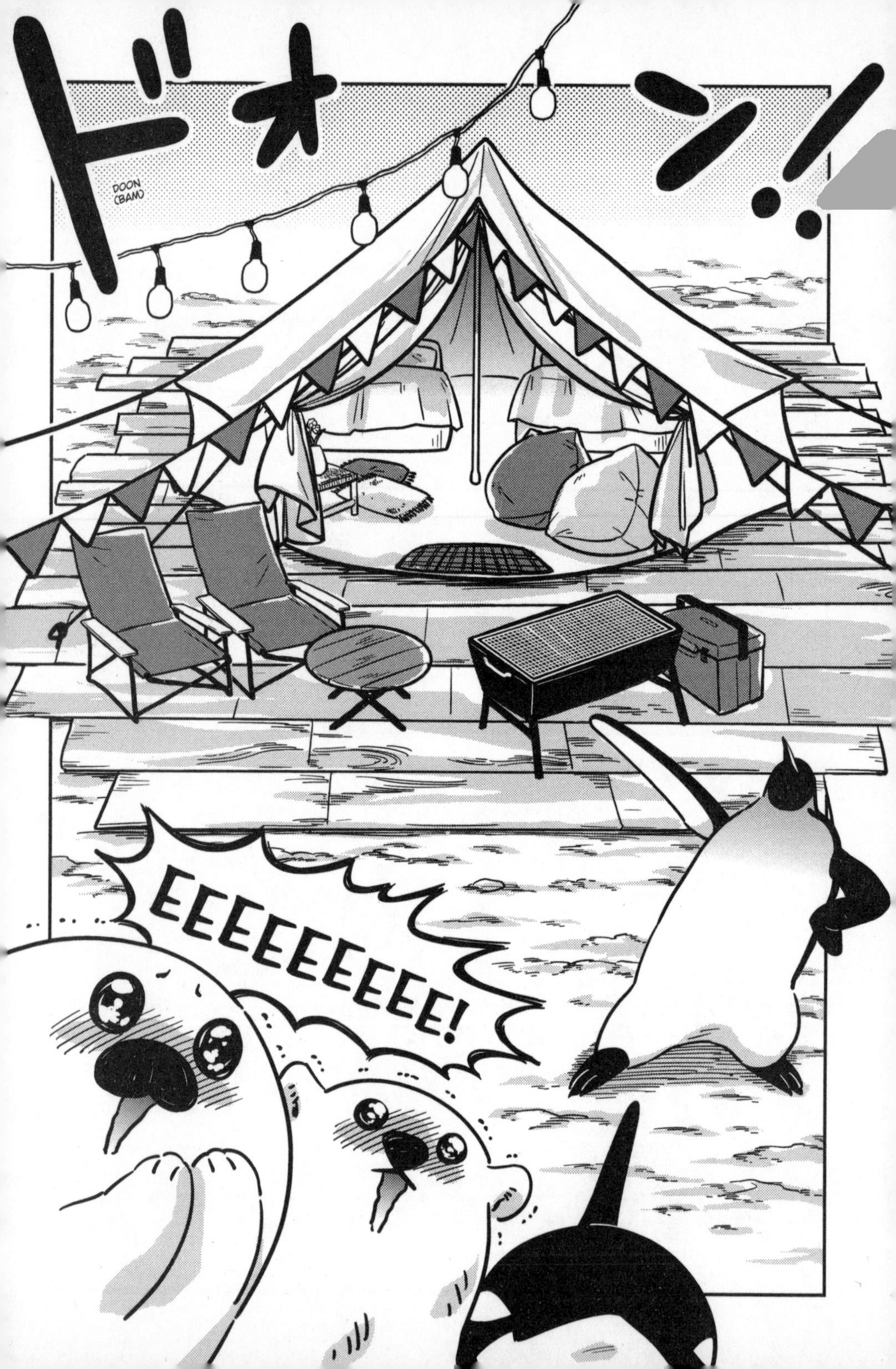
ドォン!!
DOON (BAM)
EEEEEEEEEE!

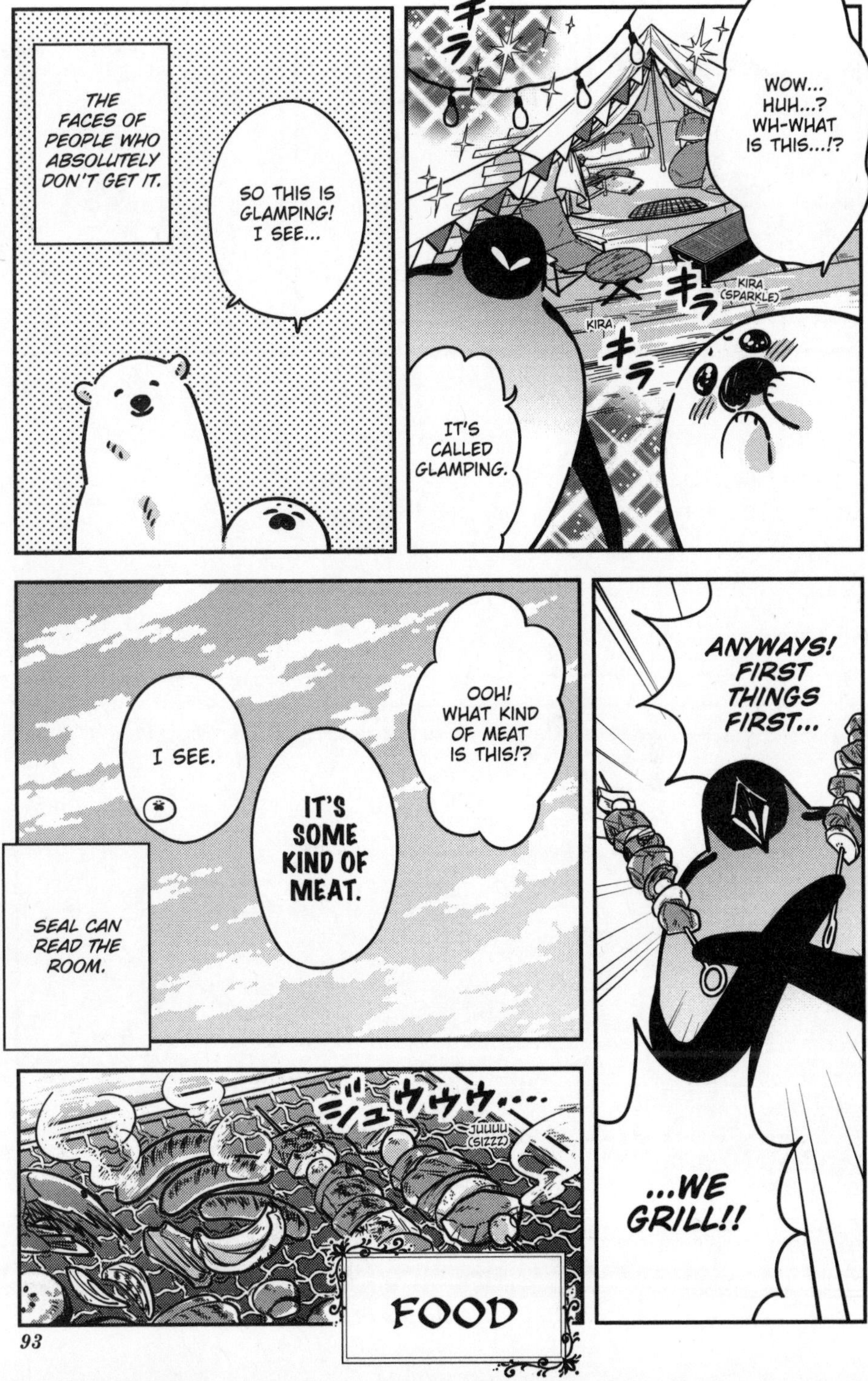
WOW... HUH...? WH-WHAT IS THIS...!?
KIRA
KIRA (SPARKLE)
KIRA
IT'S CALLED GLAMPING.
SO THIS IS GLAMPING! I SEE...
THE FACES OF PEOPLE WHO ABSOLUTELY DON'T GET IT.
ANYWAYS! FIRST THINGS FIRST...
...WE GRILL!!
OOH! WHAT KIND OF MEAT IS THIS!?
I SEE.
IT'S SOME KIND OF MEAT.
SEAL CAN READ THE ROOM.
JUUUU (SIZZZ)
FOOD

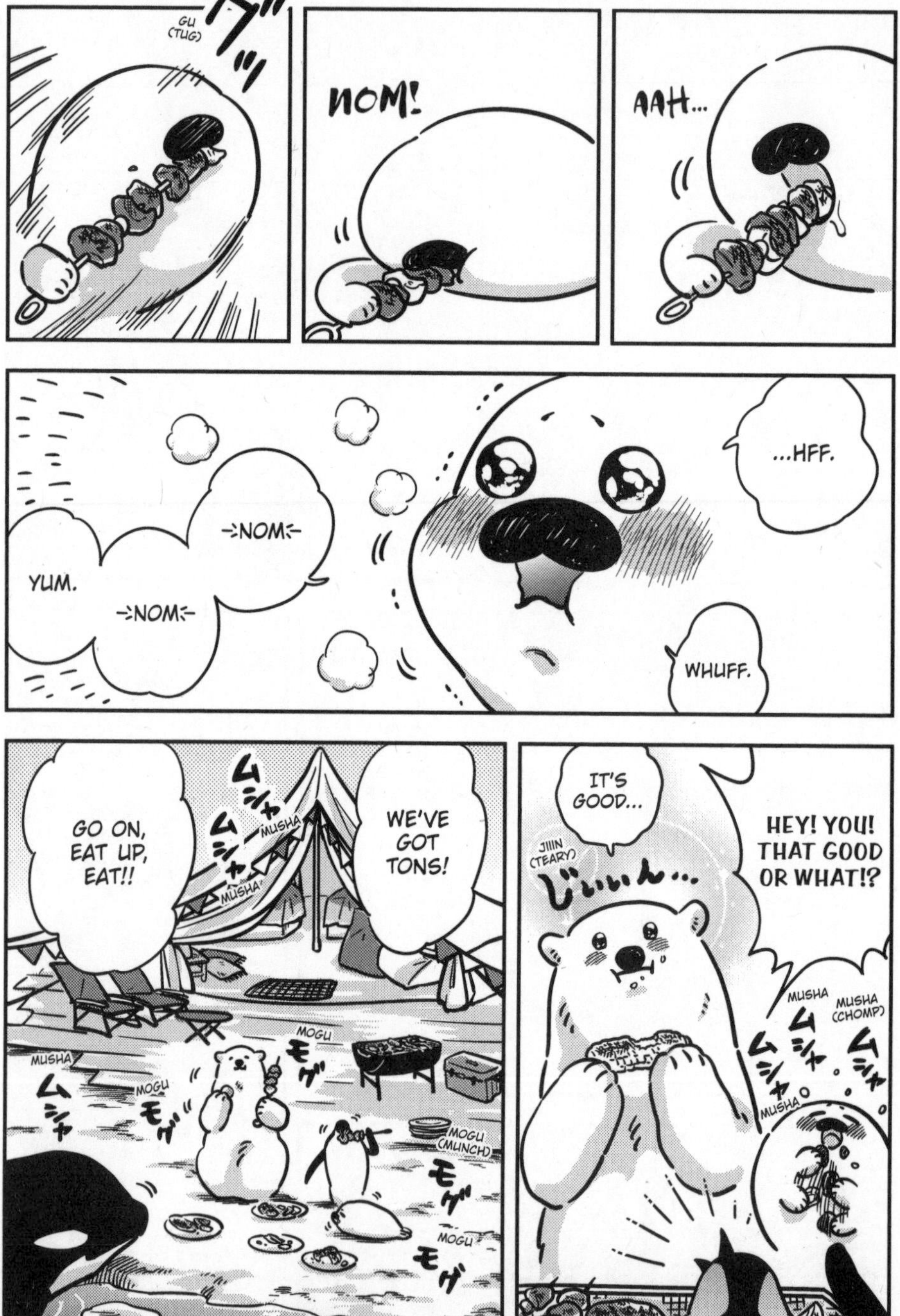
AAH...
NOM!
GU (TUG)
グッ
...HFF.
WHUFF.
YUM.
NOM
NOM
HEY! YOU! THAT GOOD OR WHAT!?
IT'S GOOD...
JIIIN (TEARY)
じいいん...
MUSHA (CHOMP)
MUSHA
MUSHA
WE'VE GOT TONS!
GO ON, EAT UP, EAT!!
MUSHA
MUSHA
MOGU
MOGU (MUNCH)
MOGU
MOGU
MUSHA

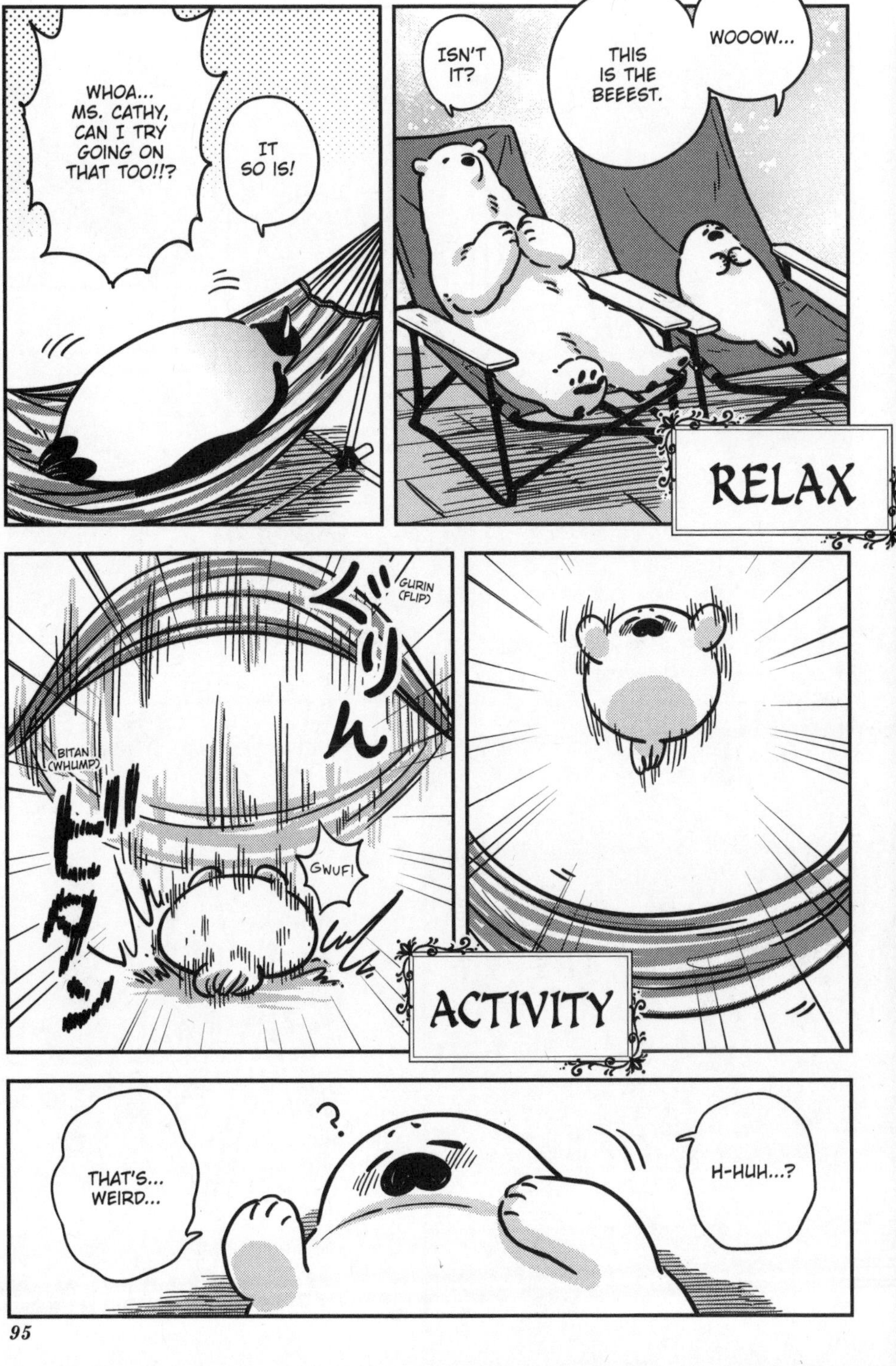
WOOOW...
THIS IS THE BEEEST.
ISN'T IT?
RELAX
IT SO IS!
WHOA... MS. CATHY, CAN I TRY GOING ON THAT TOO!!?
ACTIVITY
GURIN (FLIP)
ぐりん
BITAN (WHUMP)
ビタン
GWUF!
H-HUH...?
?
THAT'S... WEIRD...

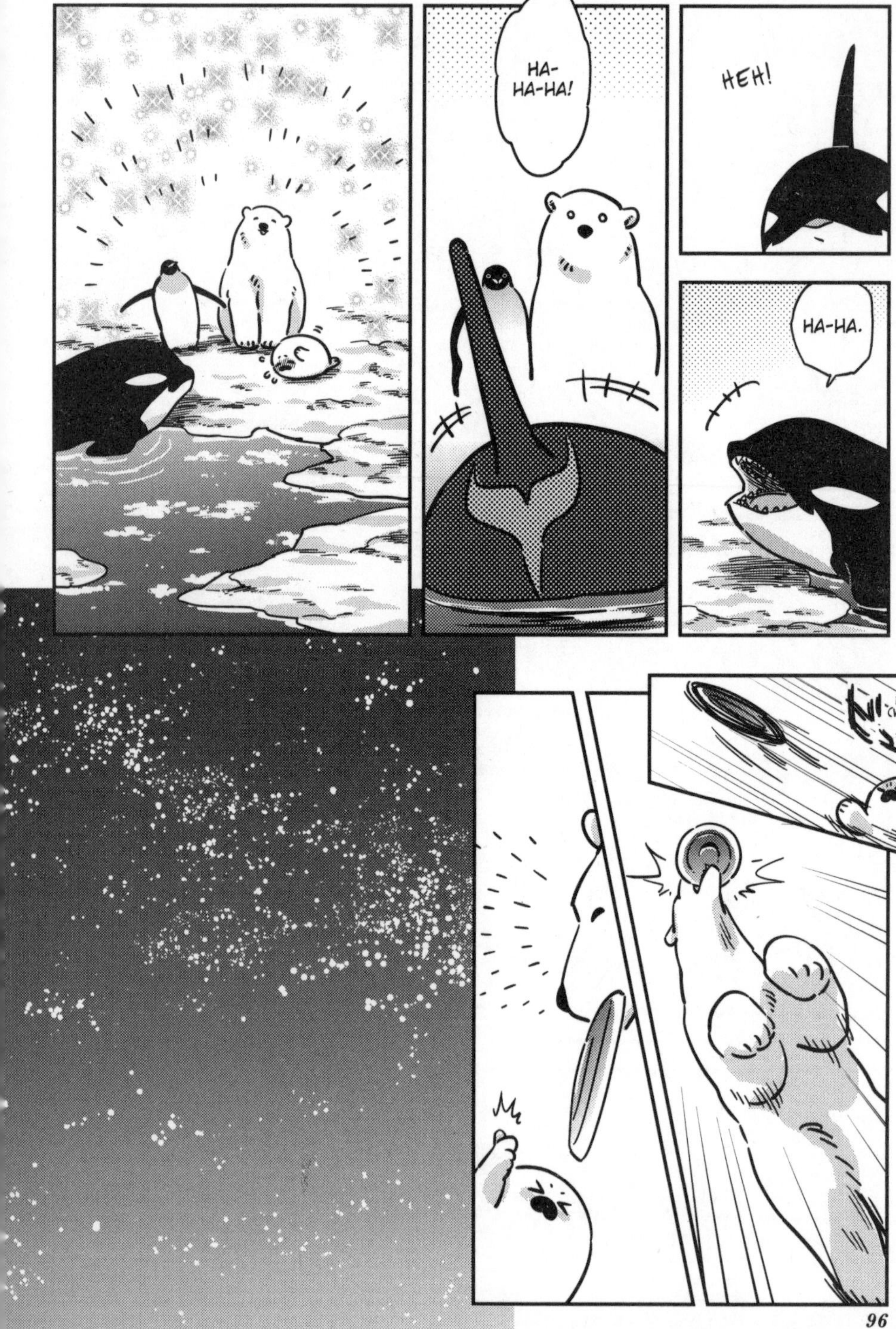
HEH!
HA-HA.
HA-HA-HA!
BYUN (WHIZZ)

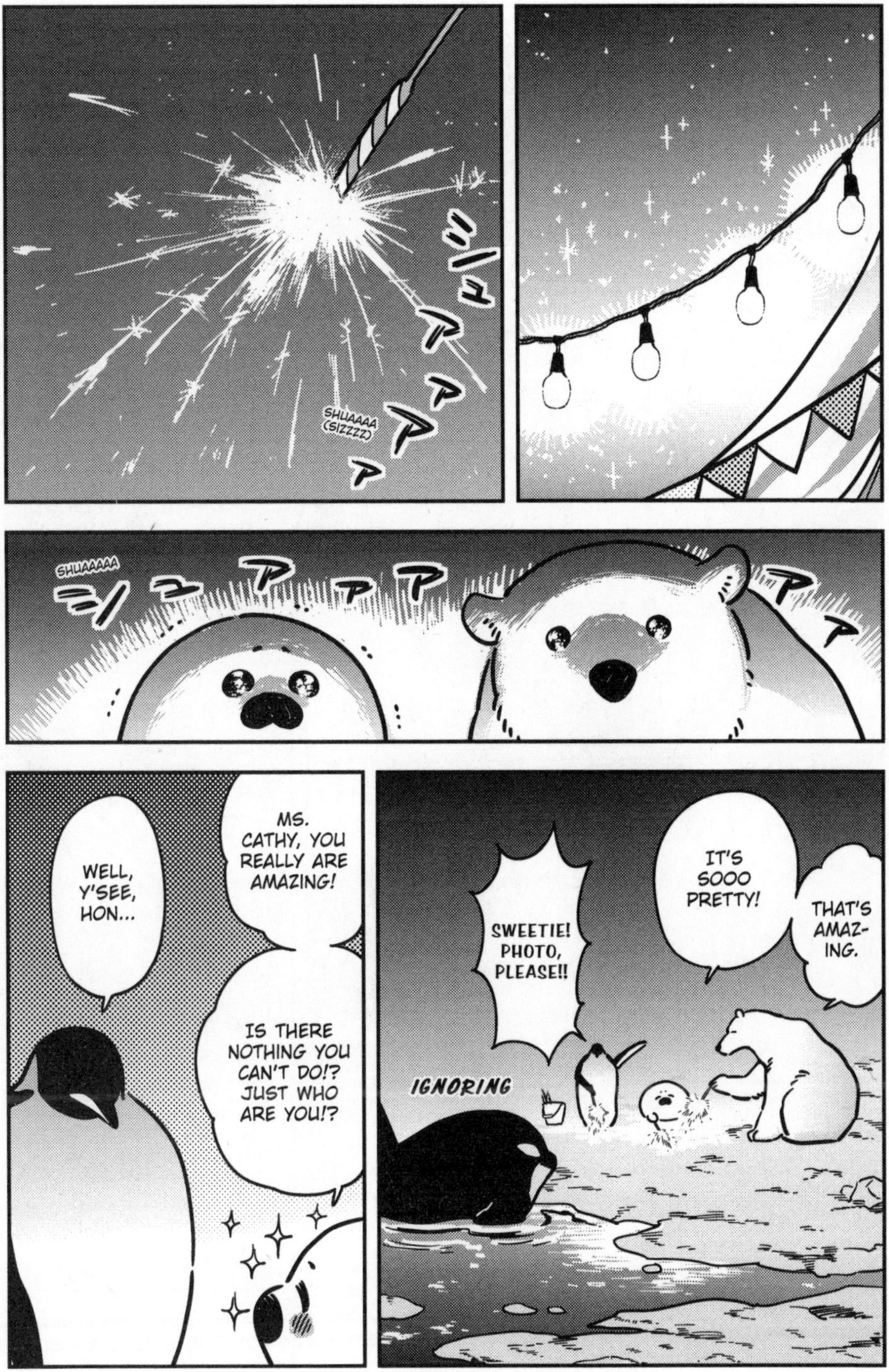
SHUAAAA (SIZZZZ)
SHUAAAAA
THAT'S AMAZ-ING.
IT'S SOOO PRETTY!
SWEETIE! PHOTO, PLEASE!!
IGNORING
MS. CATHY, YOU REALLY ARE AMAZING!
IS THERE NOTHING YOU CAN'T DO!? JUST WHO ARE YOU!?
WELL, Y'SEE, HON...

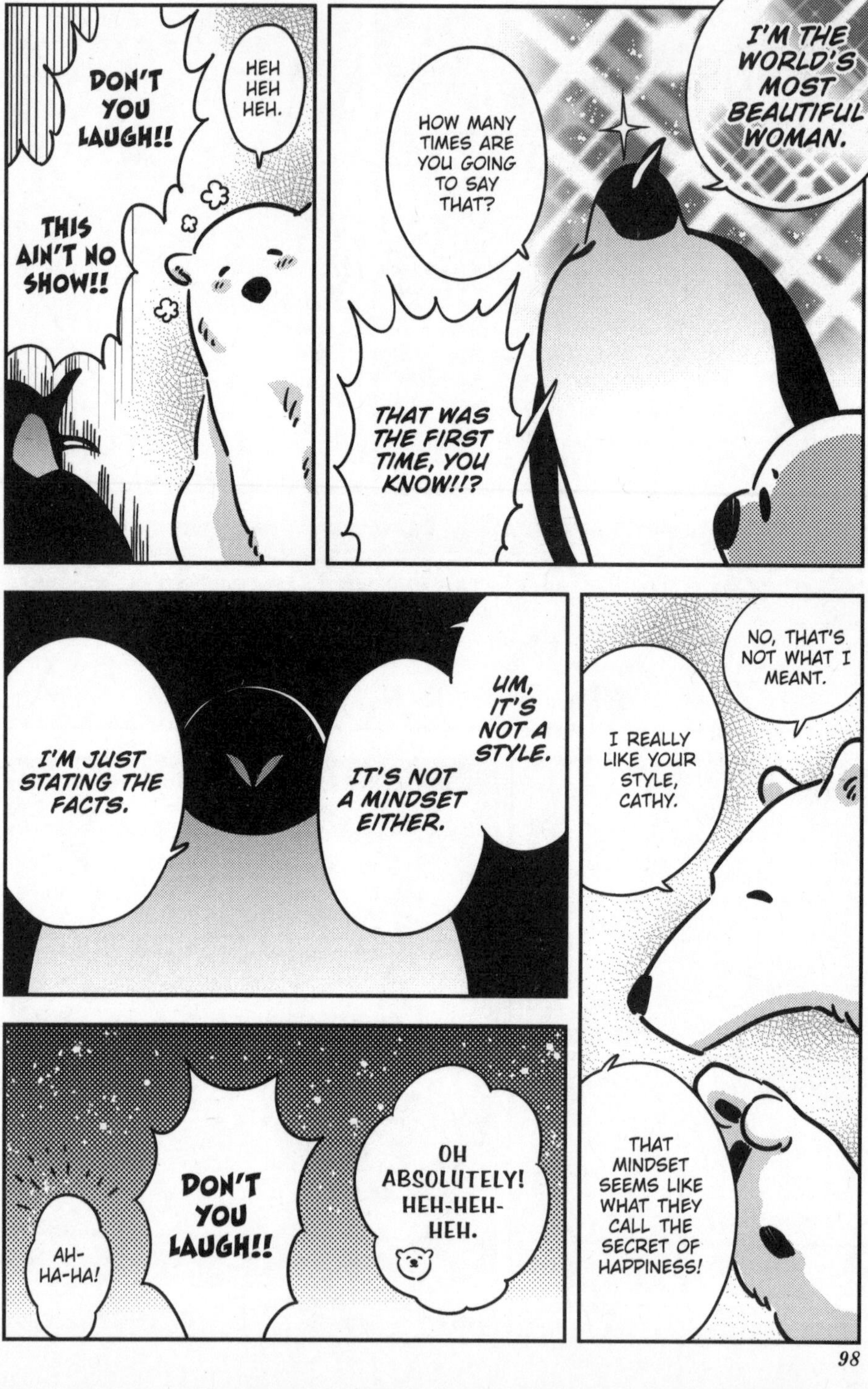
I'M THE WORLD'S MOST BEAUTIFUL WOMAN.
HOW MANY TIMES ARE YOU GOING TO SAY THAT?
THAT WAS THE FIRST TIME, YOU KNOW!!?
HEH HEH HEH.
DON'T YOU LAUGH!!
THIS AIN'T NO SHOW!!
NO, THAT'S NOT WHAT I MEANT.
I REALLY LIKE YOUR STYLE, CATHY.
THAT MINDSET SEEMS LIKE WHAT THEY CALL THE SECRET OF HAPPINESS!
UM, IT'S NOT A STYLE.
IT'S NOT A MINDSET EITHER.
I'M JUST STATING THE FACTS.
OH ABSOLUTELY! HEH-HEH-HEH.
DON'T YOU LAUGH!!
AH-HA-HA!

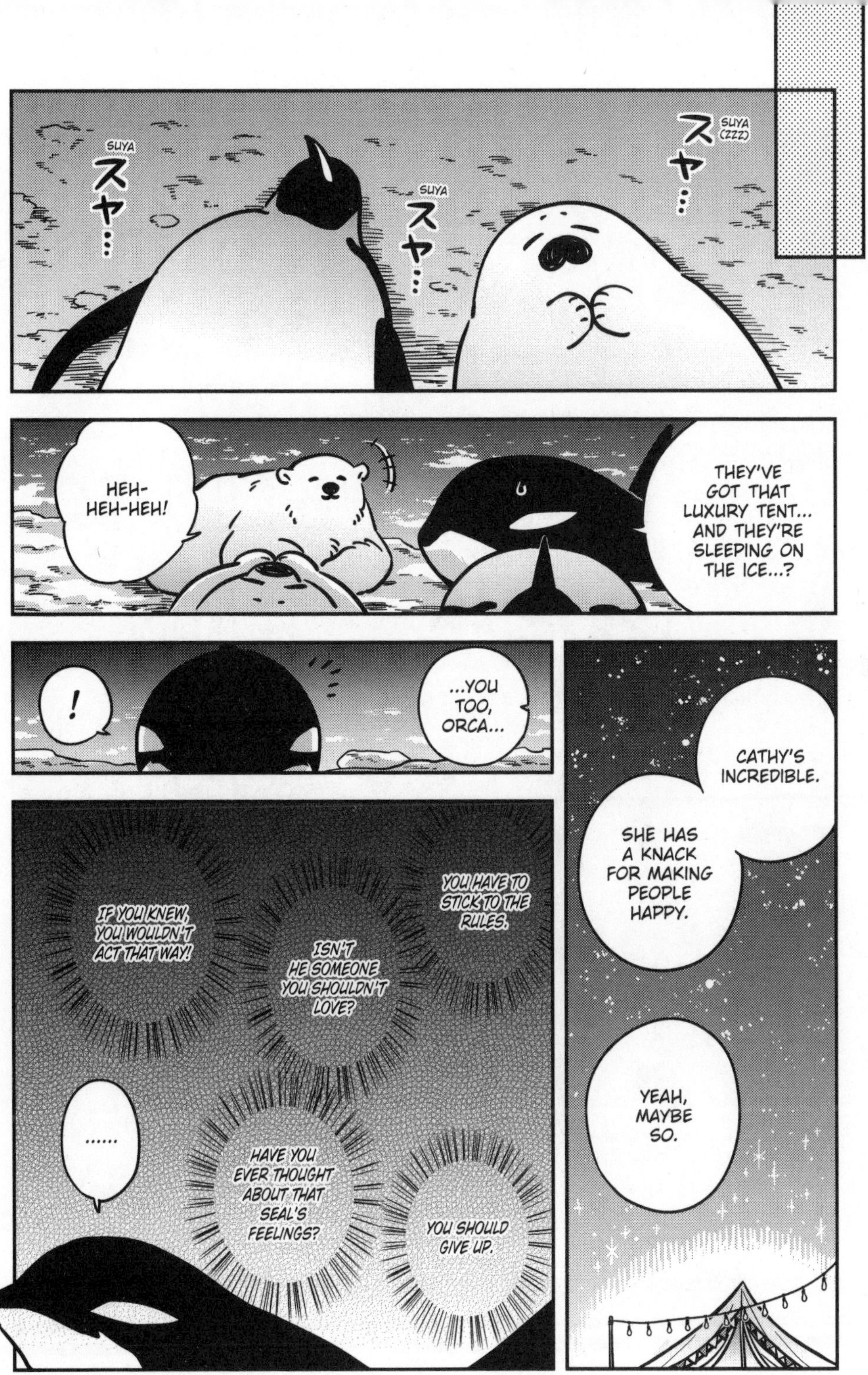
スヤ…
SUYA (ZZZ)
スヤ…
SUYA
スヤ…
SUYA
THEY'VE GOT THAT LUXURY TENT... AND THEY'RE SLEEPING ON THE ICE...?
HEH-HEH-HEH!
CATHY'S INCREDIBLE.
SHE HAS A KNACK FOR MAKING PEOPLE HAPPY.
YEAH, MAYBE SO.
...YOU TOO, ORCA...
!
YOU HAVE TO STICK TO THE RULES.
ISN'T HE SOMEONE YOU SHOULDN'T LOVE?
IF YOU KNEW, YOU WOULDN'T ACT THAT WAY!
YOU SHOULD GIVE UP.
HAVE YOU EVER THOUGHT ABOUT THAT SEAL'S FEELINGS?
......

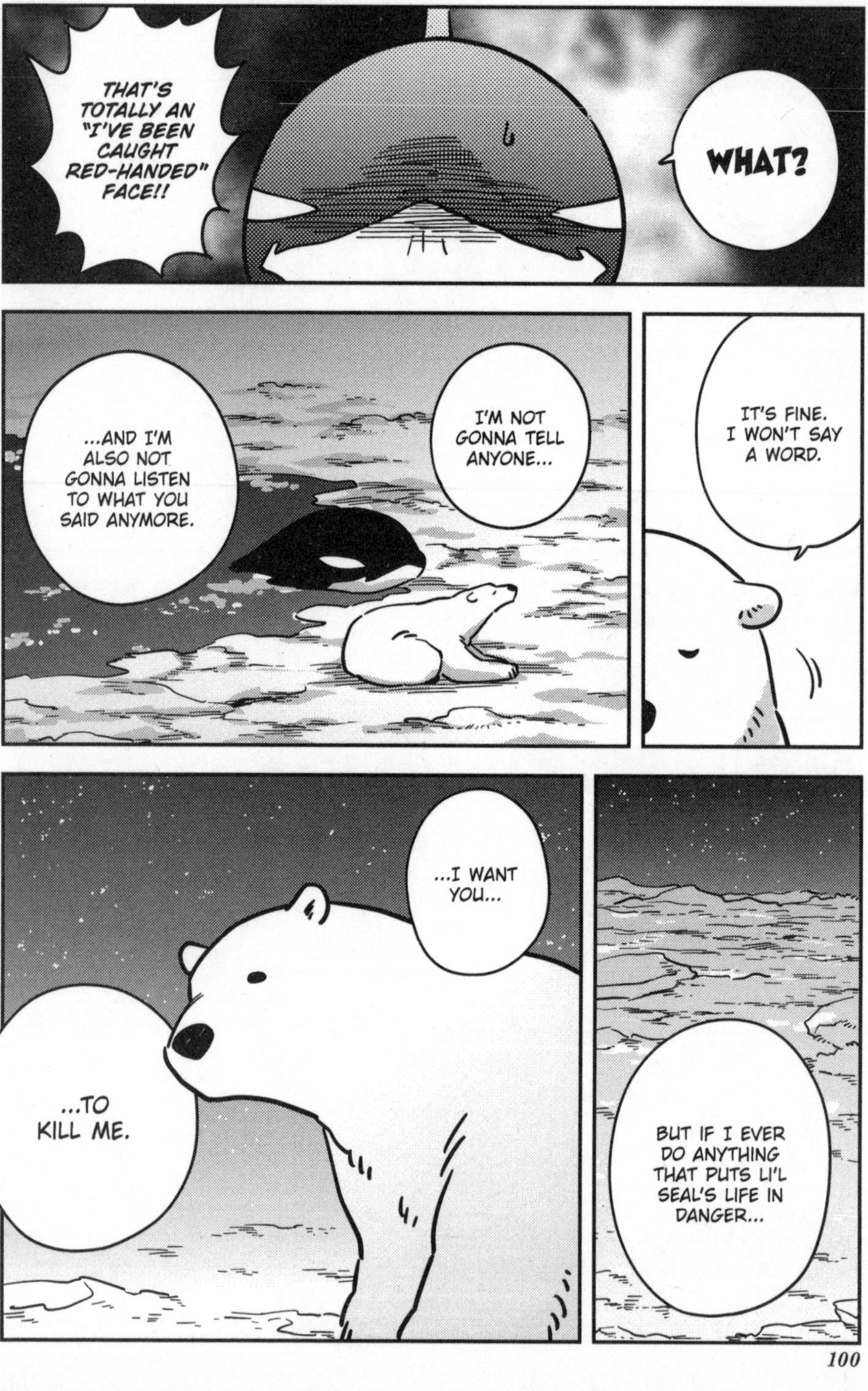
WHAT?
THAT'S TOTALLY AN "I'VE BEEN CAUGHT RED-HANDED" FACE!!
IT'S FINE. I WON'T SAY A WORD.
I'M NOT GONNA TELL ANYONE...
...AND I'M ALSO NOT GONNA LISTEN TO WHAT YOU SAID ANYMORE.
BUT IF I EVER DO ANYTHING THAT PUTS LI'L SEAL'S LIFE IN DANGER...
...I WANT YOU...
...TO KILL ME.

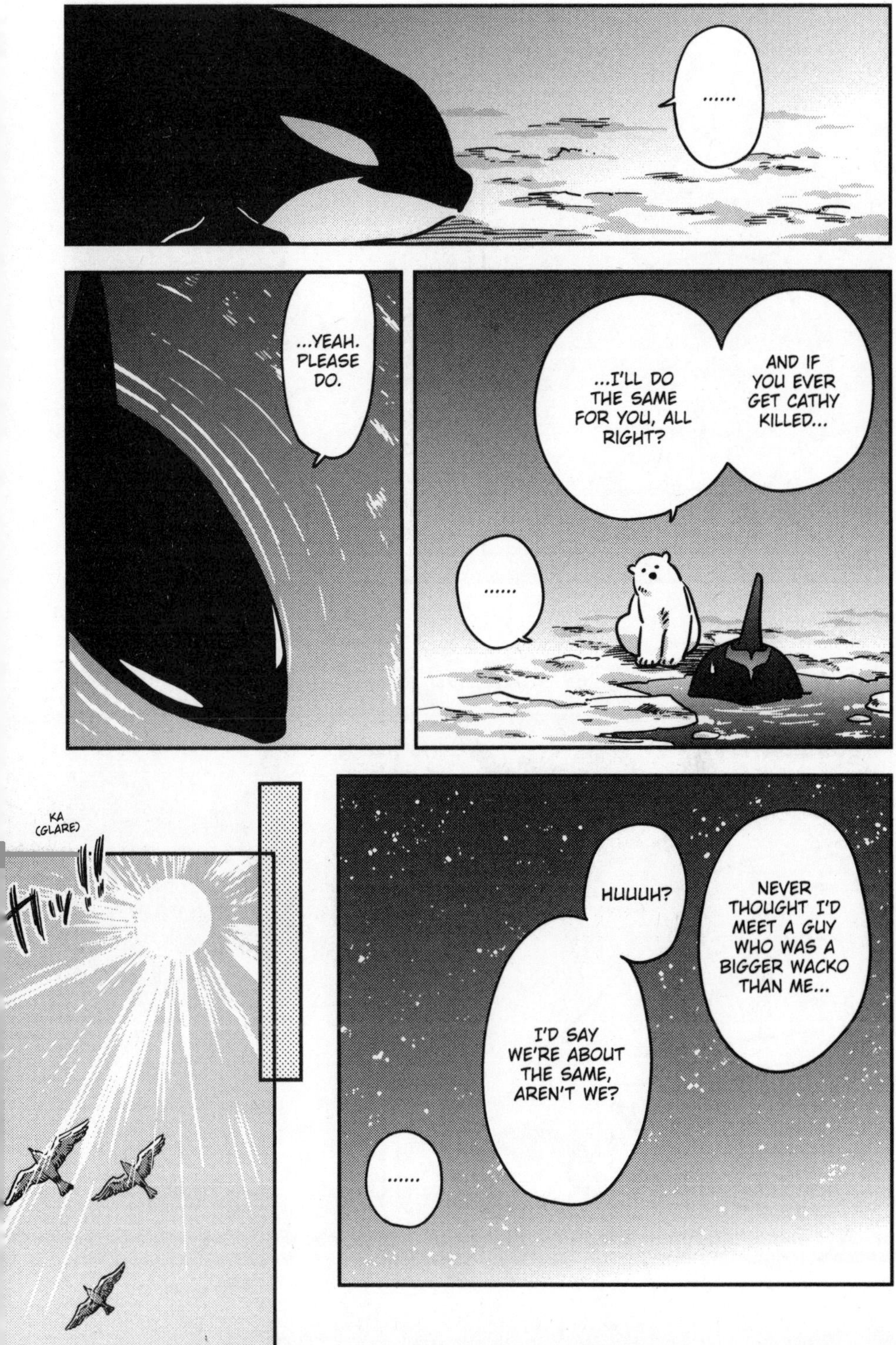
......
AND IF YOU EVER GET CATHY KILLED...
...I'LL DO THE SAME FOR YOU, ALL RIGHT?
......
...YEAH. PLEASE DO.
NEVER THOUGHT I'D MEET A GUY WHO WAS A BIGGER WACKO THAN ME...
HUUUH?
I'D SAY WE'RE ABOUT THE SAME, AREN'T WE?
......
KA (GLARE)

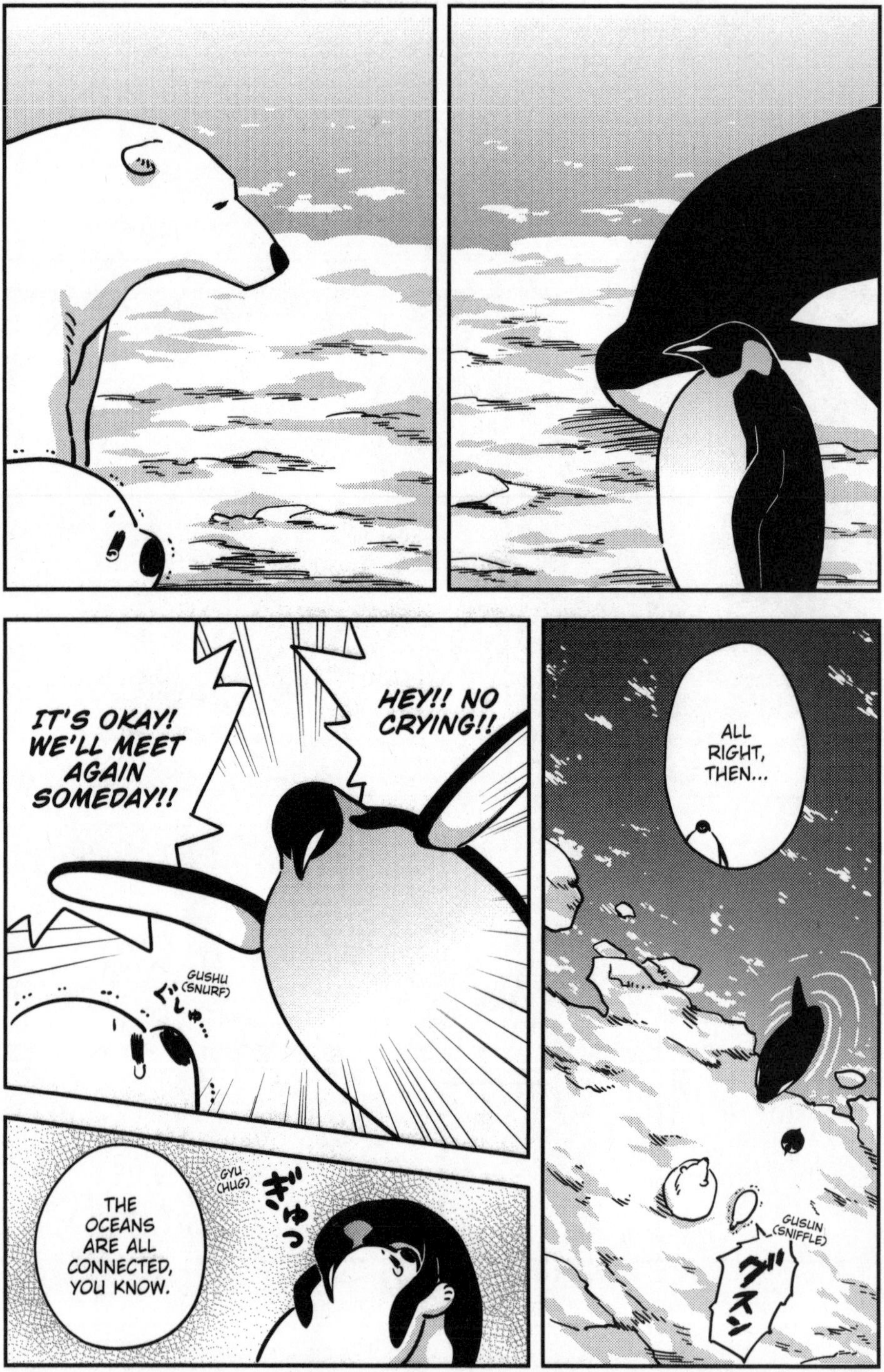
ALL RIGHT, THEN...
GUSUN (SNIFFLE)
グスン
HEY!! NO CRYING!!
IT'S OKAY! WE'LL MEET AGAIN SOMEDAY!!
GUSHU (SNURF)
ぐしゅ...
GYU (HUG)
ぎゅっ
THE OCEANS ARE ALL CONNECTED, YOU KNOW.

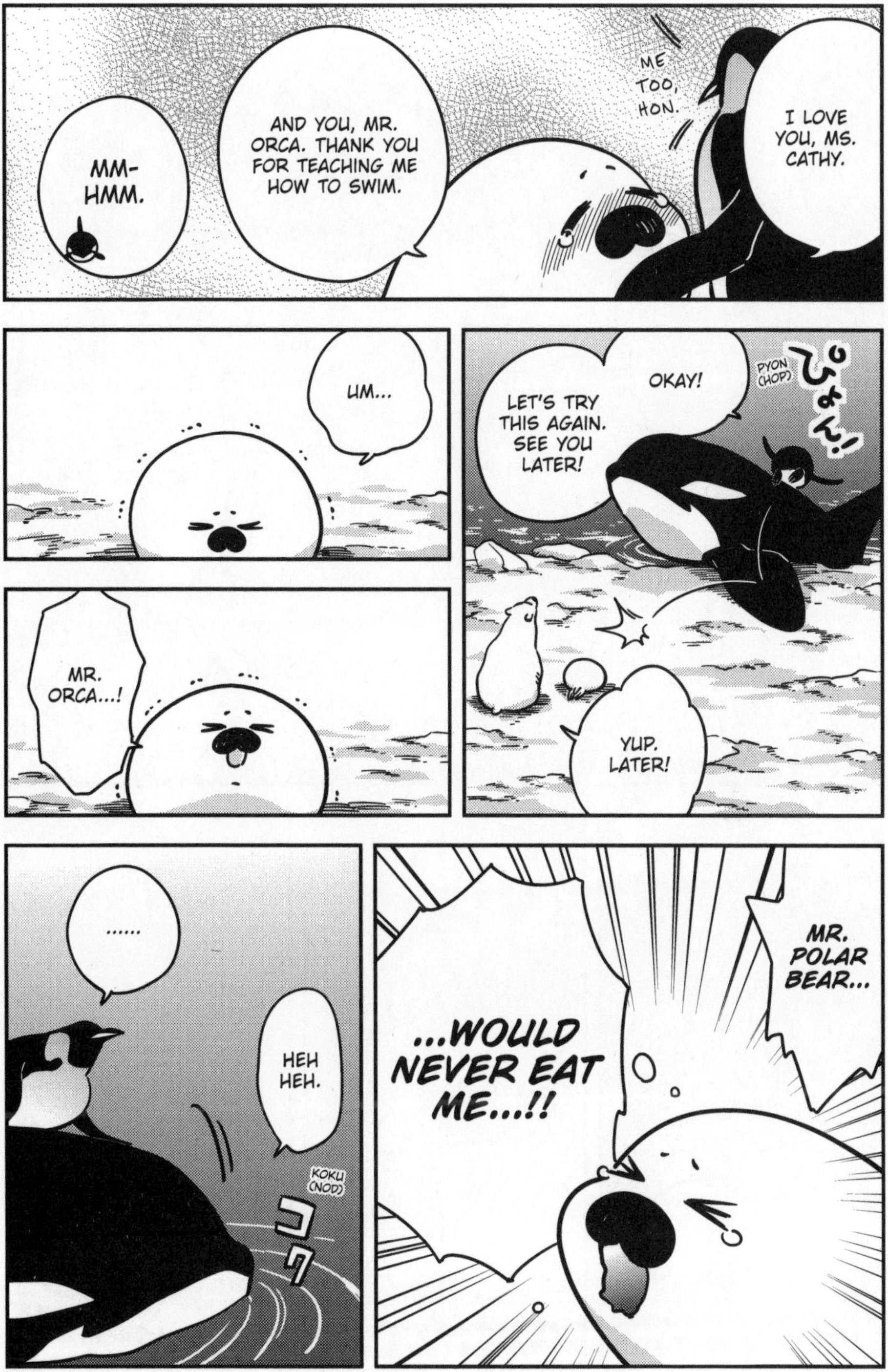
I LOVE YOU, MS. CATHY.
ME TOO, HON.
AND YOU, MR. ORCA. THANK YOU FOR TEACHING ME HOW TO SWIM.
MM-HMM.
PYON (HOP)
ぴょん!
OKAY!
LET'S TRY THIS AGAIN. SEE YOU LATER!
YUP. LATER!
UM...
MR. ORCA...!
MR. POLAR BEAR...
...WOULD NEVER EAT ME...!!
......
HEH HEH.
KOKU (NOD)
コク

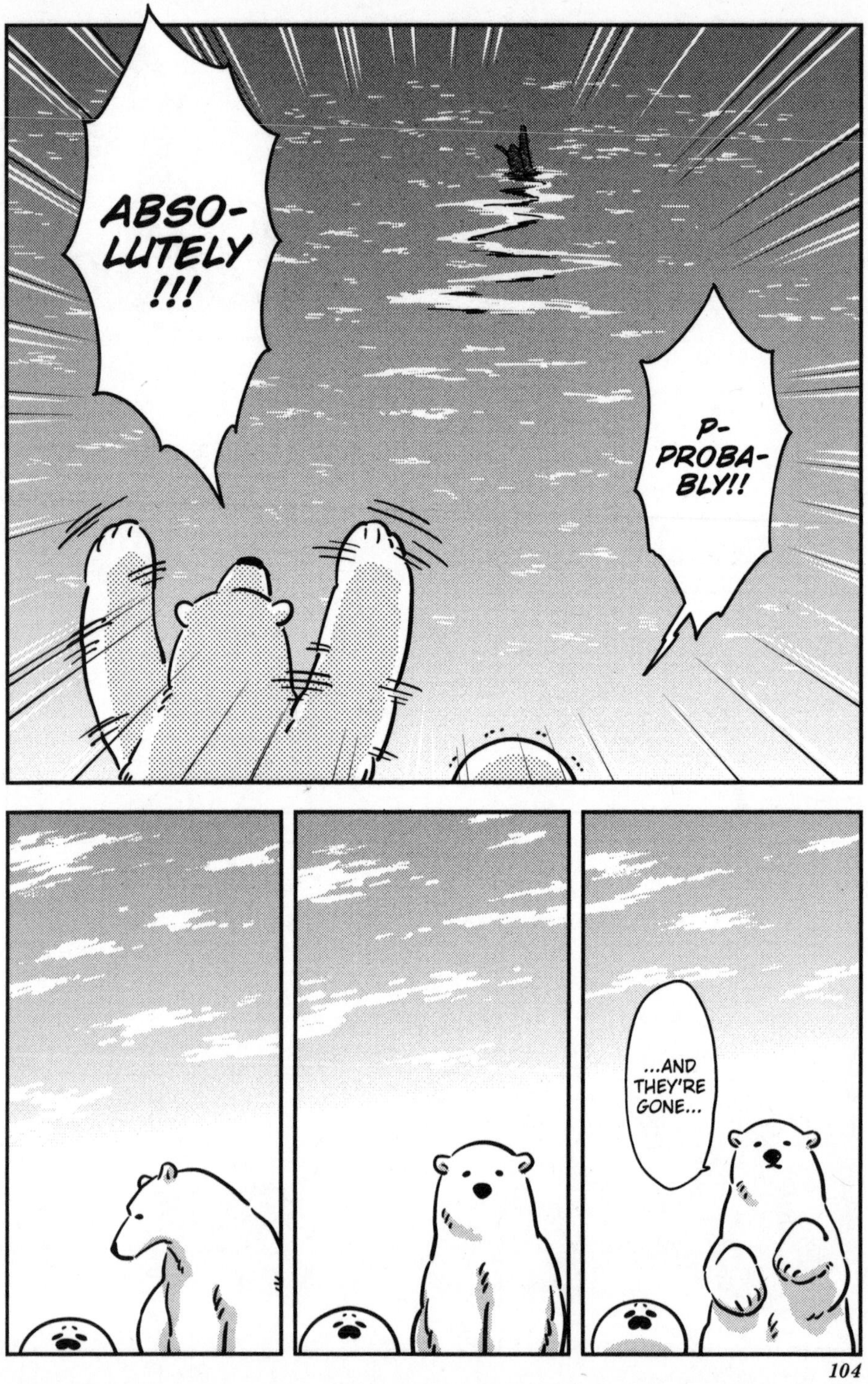
ABSO-LUTELY!!!
P-PROBA-BLY!!
...AND THEY'RE GONE...

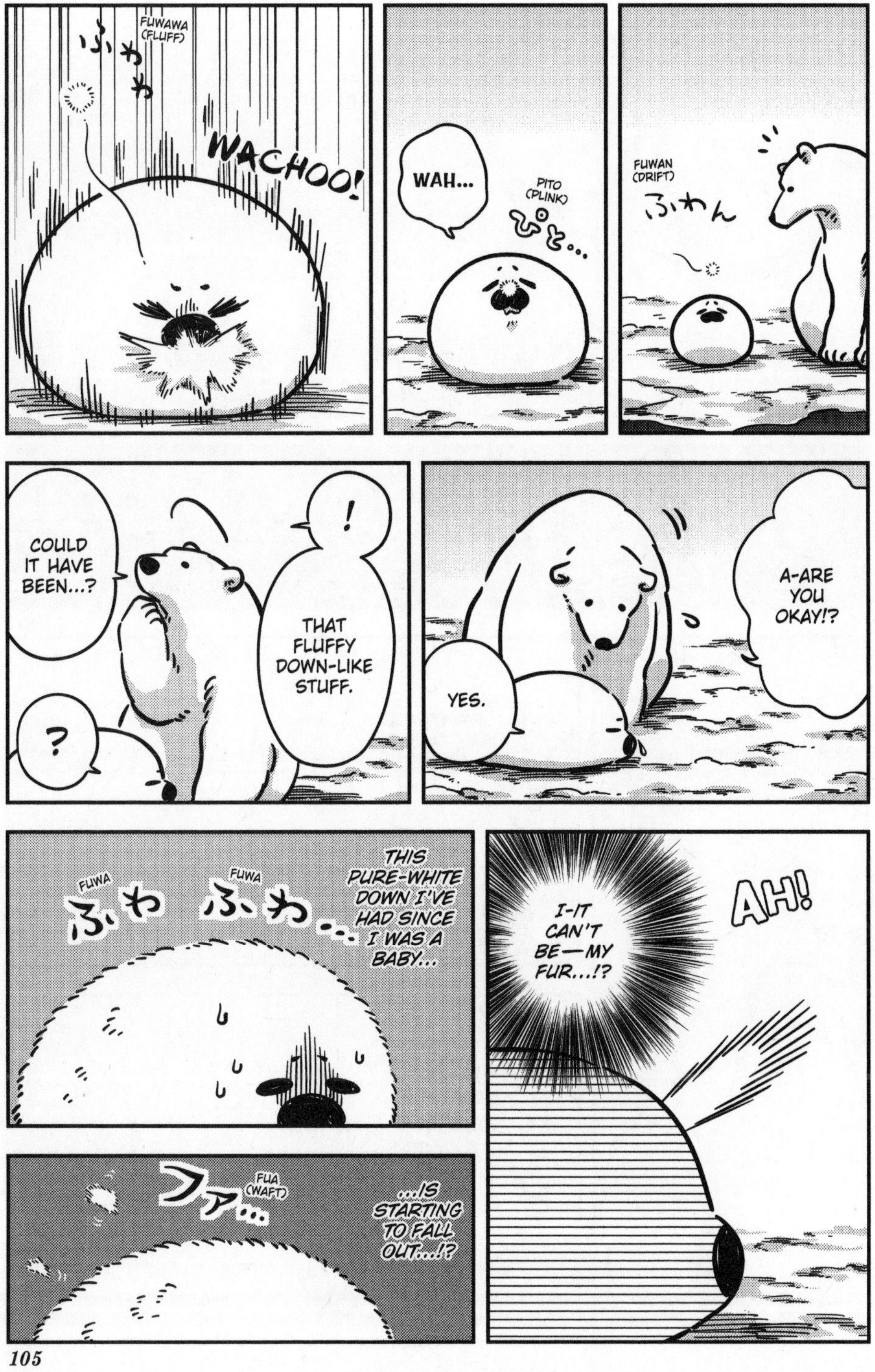
FUWAN (DRIFT)
ふわん
WAH...
PITO (PLINK)
ぴと...
FUWAWA (FLUFF)
ふわわ
WACHOO!
A-ARE YOU OKAY!?
YES.
!
COULD IT HAVE BEEN...?
THAT FLUFFY DOWN-LIKE STUFF.
?
AH!
I-IT CAN'T BE—MY FUR...!?
THIS PURE-WHITE DOWN I'VE HAD SINCE I WAS A BABY...
FUWA FUWA
ふわ ふわ...
FUA (WAFT)
ファ...
...IS STARTING TO FALL OUT...!?

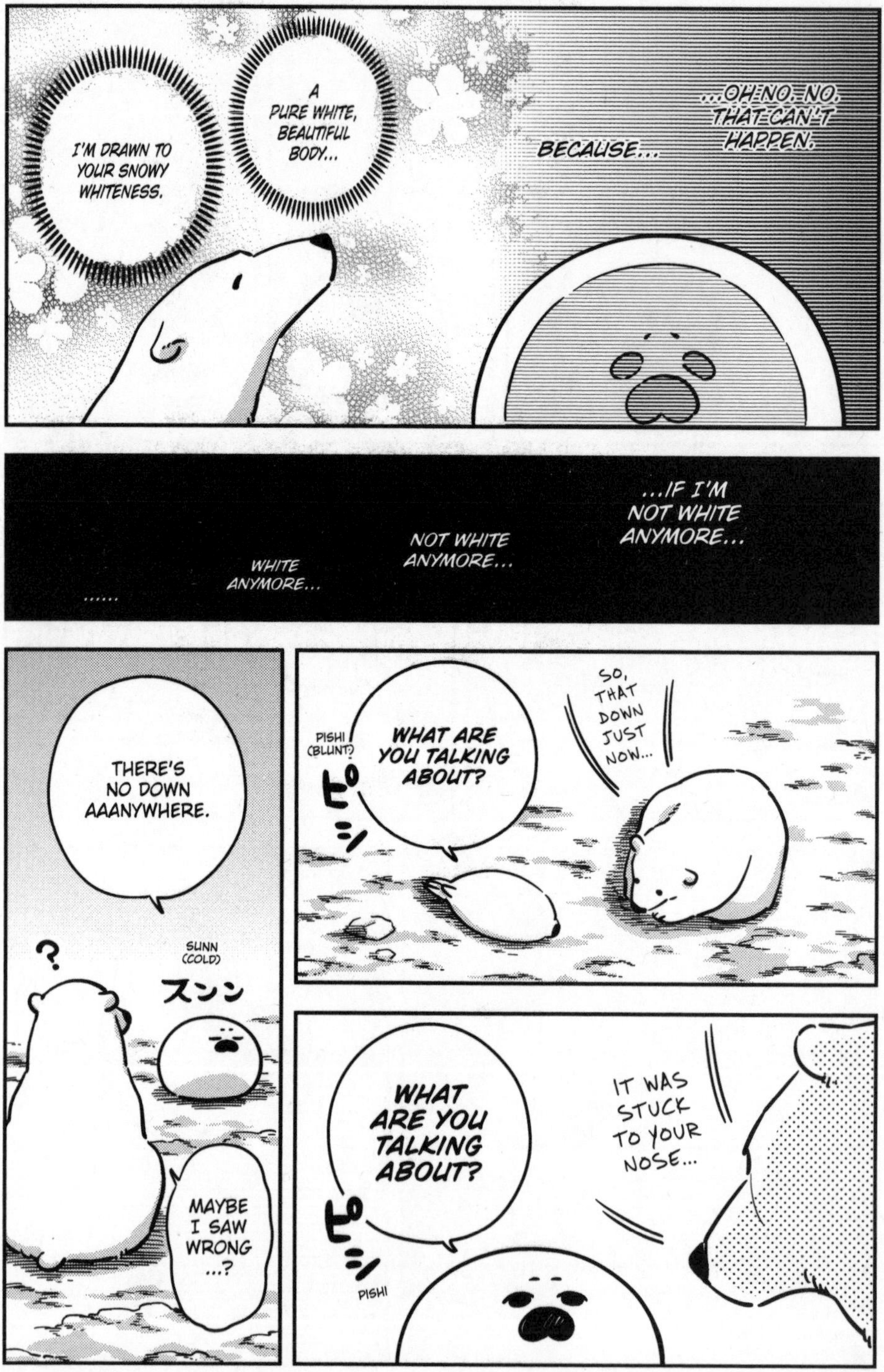
...OH NO. NO. THAT CAN'T HAPPEN.
BECAUSE...
A PURE WHITE, BEAUTIFUL BODY...
I'M DRAWN TO YOUR SNOWY WHITENESS.
...IF I'M NOT WHITE ANYMORE...
NOT WHITE ANYMORE...
WHITE ANYMORE...
......
SO, THAT DOWN JUST NOW...
WHAT ARE YOU TALKING ABOUT?
ピシ
PISHI (BLUNT?)
IT WAS STUCK TO YOUR NOSE...
WHAT ARE YOU TALKING ABOUT?
ピシ
PISHI
THERE'S NO DOWN AAANYWHERE.
スンン
SUNN (COLD)
?
MAYBE I SAW WRONG ...?

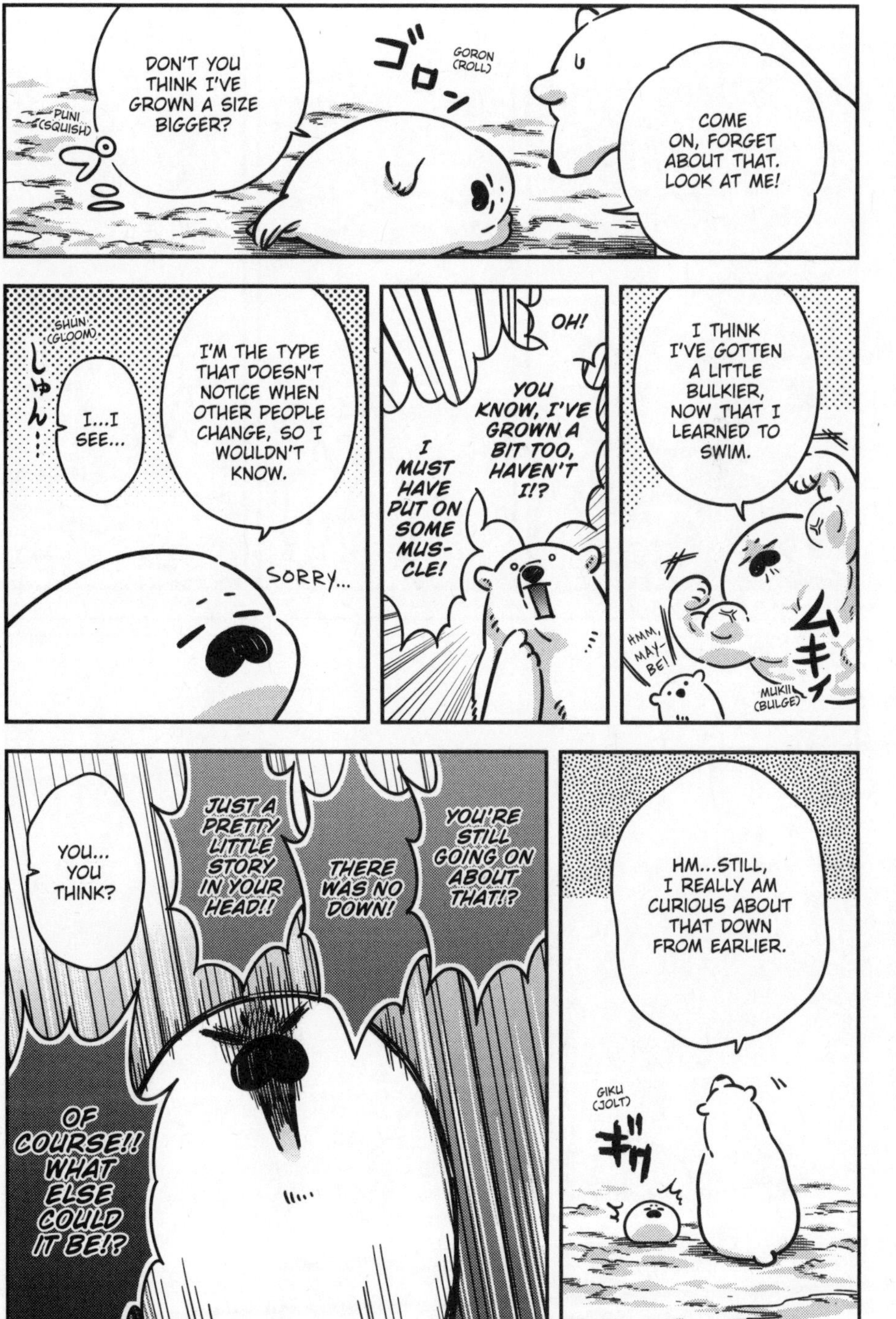
DON'T YOU THINK I'VE GROWN A SIZE BIGGER?
GORON (ROLL)
COME ON, FORGET ABOUT THAT. LOOK AT ME!
PUNI (SQUISH)
I THINK I'VE GOTTEN A LITTLE BULKIER, NOW THAT I LEARNED TO SWIM.
MUKII (BULGE)
HMM, MAY-BE!
OH!
YOU KNOW, I'VE GROWN A BIT TOO, HAVEN'T I!?
I MUST HAVE PUT ON SOME MUS-CLE!
I'M THE TYPE THAT DOESN'T NOTICE WHEN OTHER PEOPLE CHANGE, SO I WOULDN'T KNOW.
SHUN (GLOOM)
I...I SEE...
SORRY...
HM...STILL, I REALLY AM CURIOUS ABOUT THAT DOWN FROM EARLIER.
GIKU (JOLT)
YOU'RE STILL GOING ON ABOUT THAT!?
THERE WAS NO DOWN!
JUST A PRETTY LITTLE STORY IN YOUR HEAD!!
YOU... YOU THINK?
OF COURSE!! WHAT ELSE COULD IT BE!?

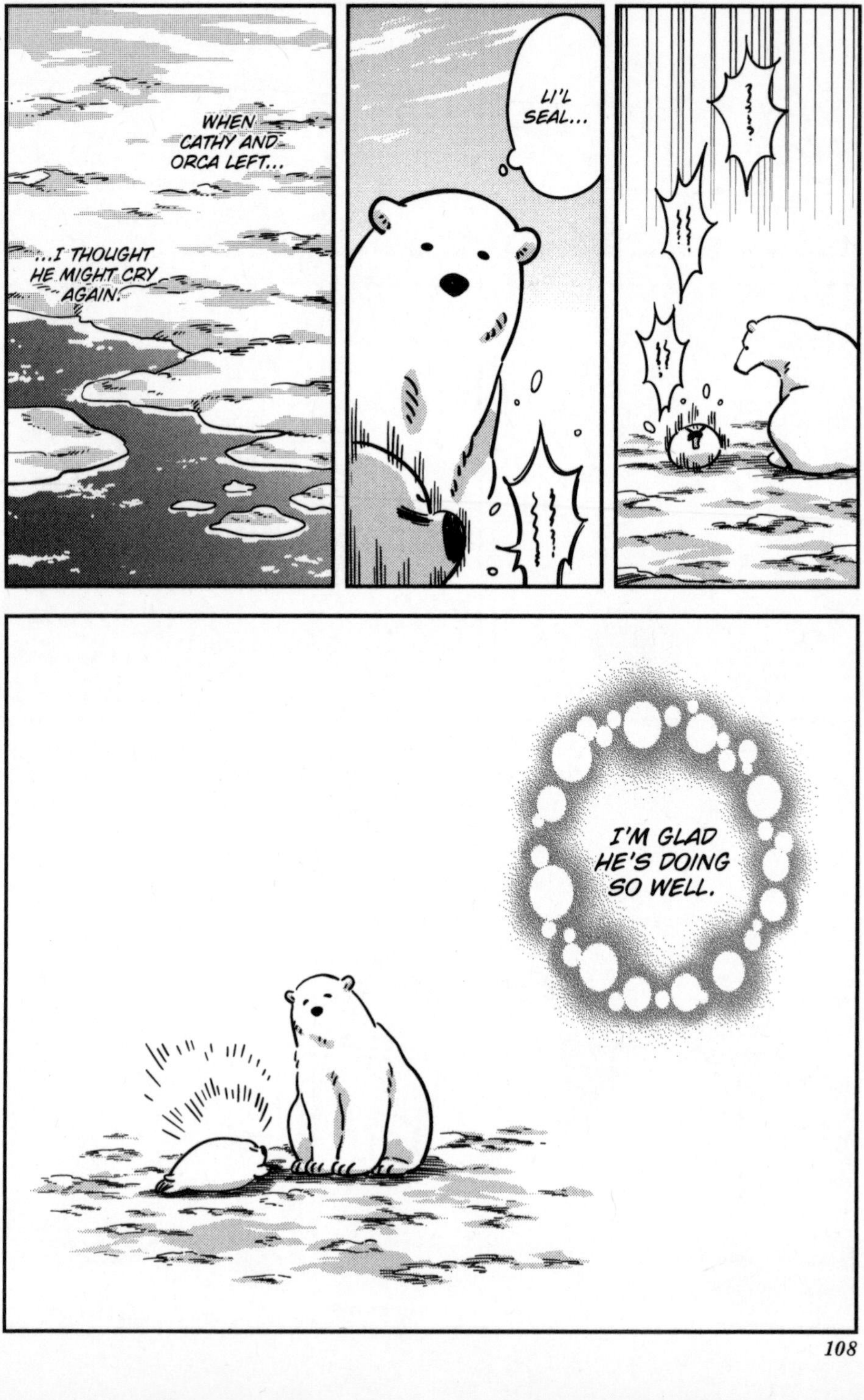
LI'L SEAL...
WHEN CATHY AND ORCA LEFT...
...I THOUGHT HE MIGHT CRY AGAIN.
I'M GLAD HE'S DOING SO WELL.

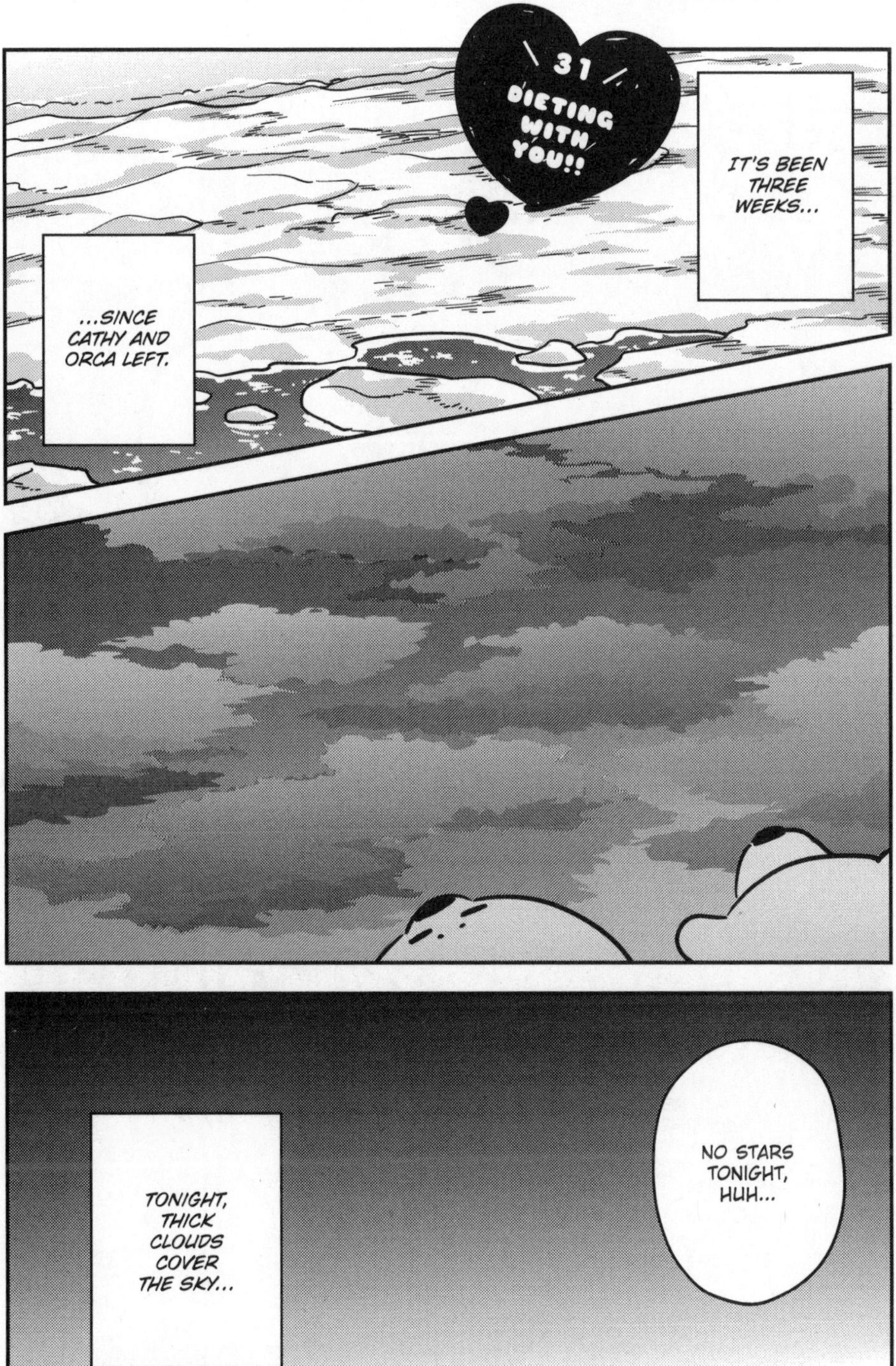
31
DIETING WITH YOU!!
IT'S BEEN THREE WEEKS...
...SINCE CATHY AND ORCA LEFT.
NO STARS TONIGHT, HUH...
TONIGHT, THICK CLOUDS COVER THE SKY...

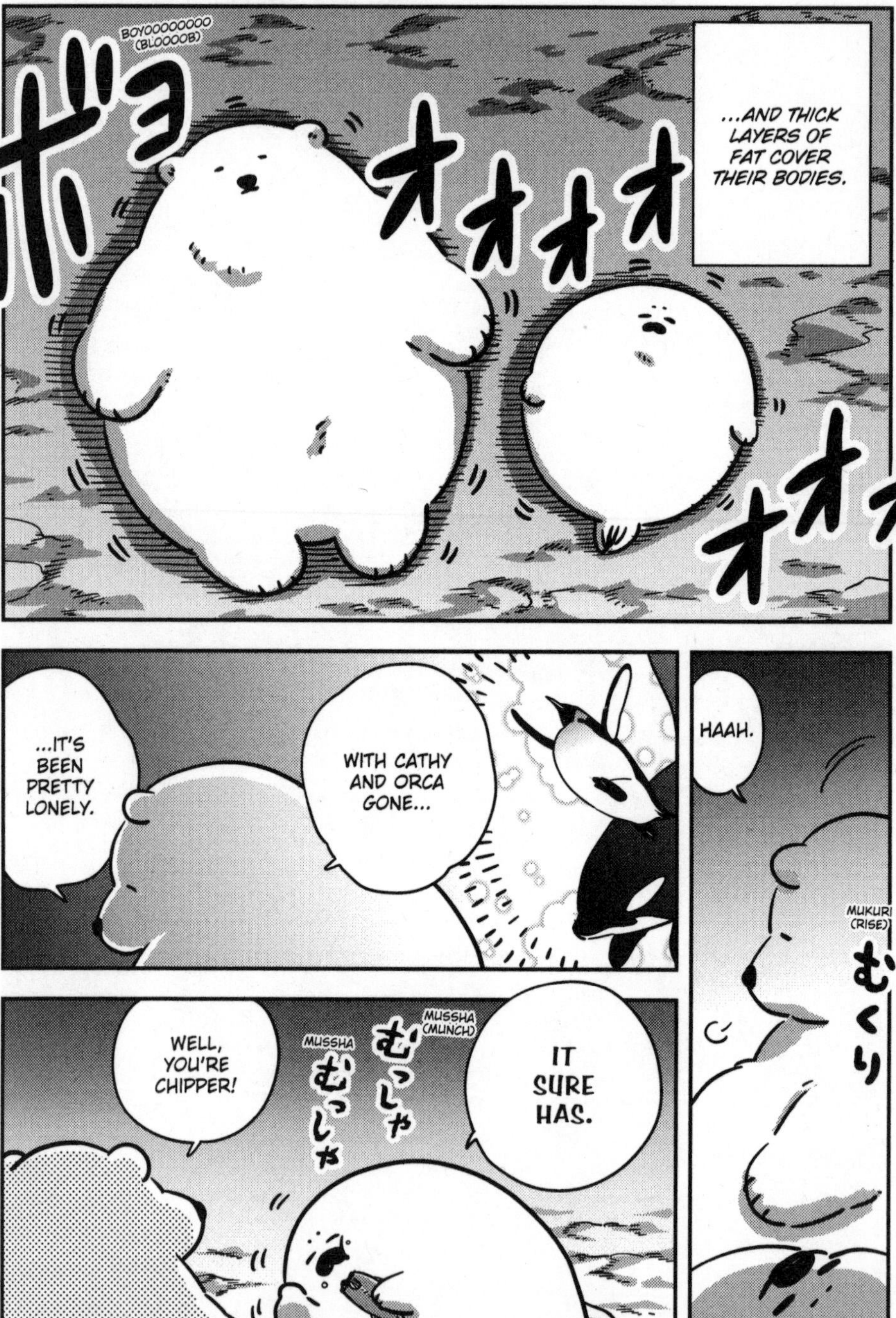
...AND THICK LAYERS OF FAT COVER THEIR BODIES.
BOYOOOOOOOO (BLOOOOB)
ボヨオオオオオオオ
HAAH.
MUKURI (RISE)
むくり
WITH CATHY AND ORCA GONE...
...IT'S BEEN PRETTY LONELY.
IT SURE HAS.
MUSSHA (MUNCH)
むっしゃ
MUSSHA
むっしゃ
WELL, YOU'RE CHIPPER!

HOW IT HAPPENED

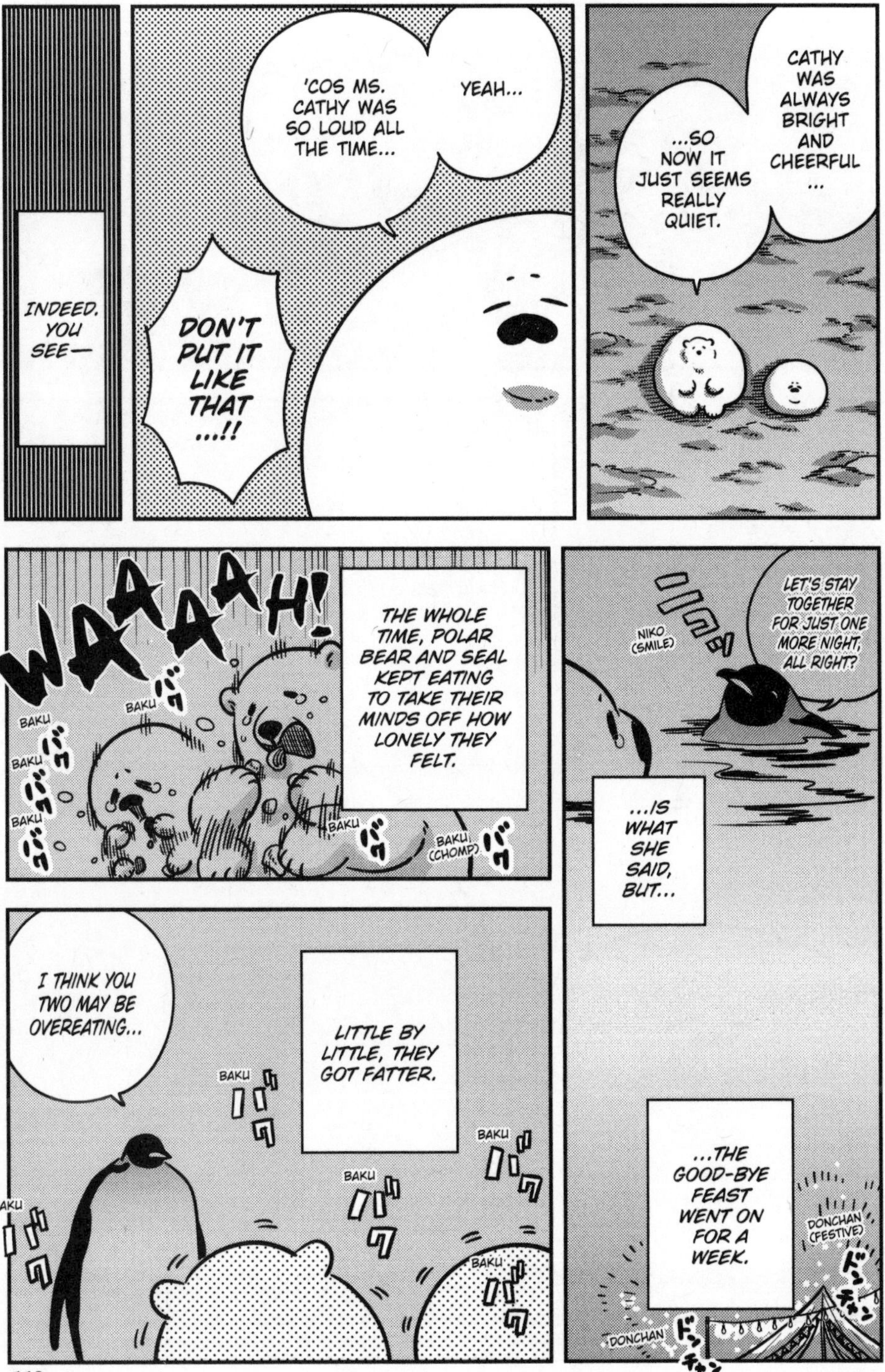
CATHY WAS ALWAYS BRIGHT AND CHEERFUL ...
...SO NOW IT JUST SEEMS REALLY QUIET.
'COS MS. CATHY WAS SO LOUD ALL THE TIME...
YEAH...
DON'T PUT IT LIKE THAT ...!!
INDEED. YOU SEE—
NIKO (SMILE)
LET'S STAY TOGETHER FOR JUST ONE MORE NIGHT, ALL RIGHT?
...IS WHAT SHE SAID, BUT...
...THE GOOD-BYE FEAST WENT ON FOR A WEEK.
DONCHAN (FESTIVE)
DONCHAN
THE WHOLE TIME, POLAR BEAR AND SEAL KEPT EATING TO TAKE THEIR MINDS OFF HOW LONELY THEY FELT.
WAAAAH!
BAKU
BAKU
BAKU
BAKU
BAKU
BAKU (CHOMP)
LITTLE BY LITTLE, THEY GOT FATTER.
I THINK YOU TWO MAY BE OVEREATING...
BAKU
BAKU
BAKU
BAKU
BAKU

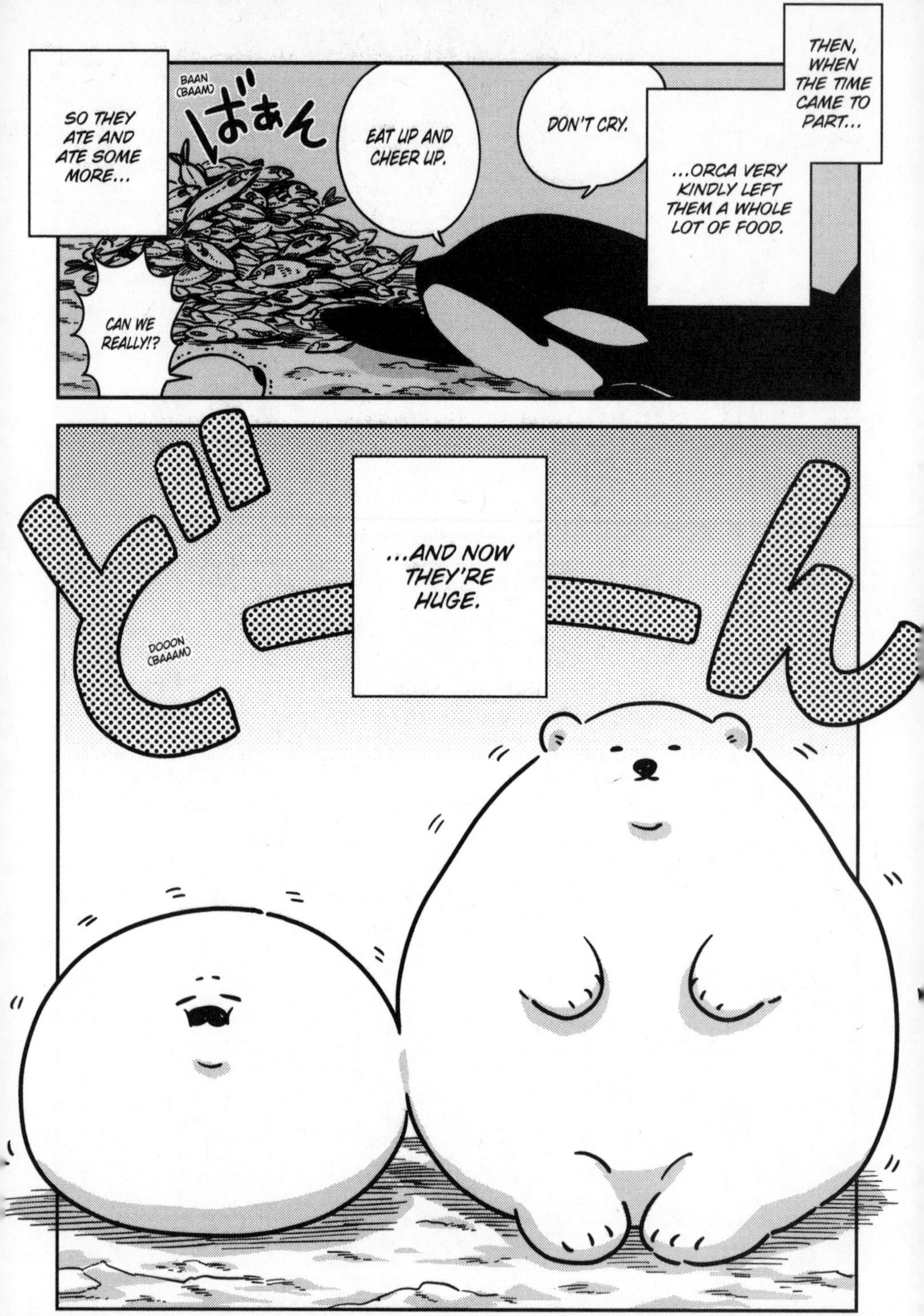
THEN, WHEN THE TIME CAME TO PART...
...ORCA VERY KINDLY LEFT THEM A WHOLE LOT OF FOOD.
DON'T CRY.
EAT UP AND CHEER UP.
BAAN (BAAM)
ばあん
SO THEY ATE AND ATE SOME MORE...
CAN WE REALLY!?
...AND NOW THEY'RE HUGE.
DOOON (BAAAM)

BURSTING AT THE SEAMS

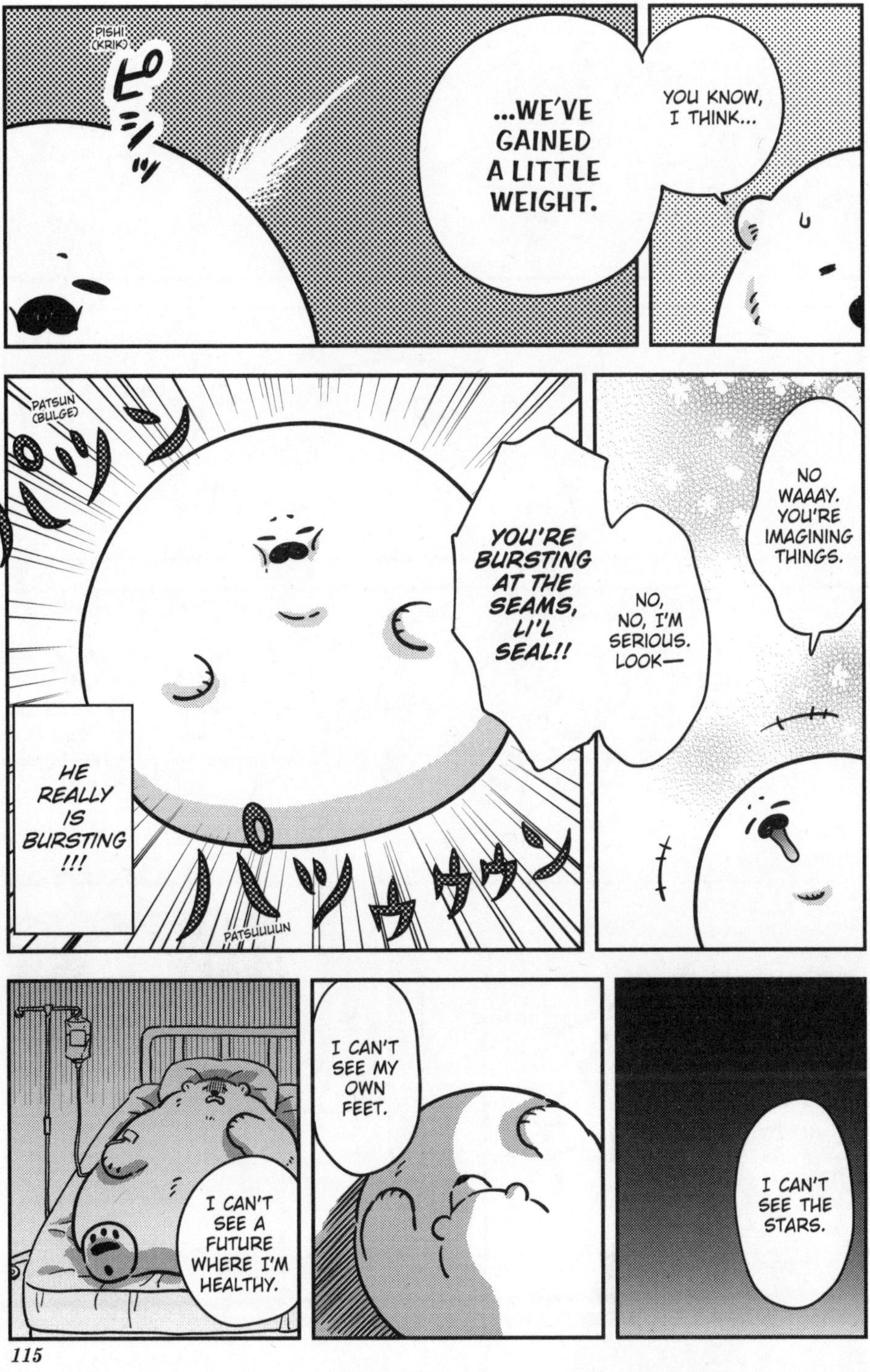

YOU KNOW, I THINK...
...WE'VE GAINED A LITTLE WEIGHT.
PISHI (KRIK)
NO WAAAY. YOU'RE IMAGINING THINGS.
NO, NO, I'M SERIOUS. LOOK—
YOU'RE BURSTING AT THE SEAMS, LI'L SEAL!!
PATSUN (BULGE)
HE REALLY IS BURSTING!!!
PATSUUUUN
I CAN'T SEE THE STARS.
I CAN'T SEE MY OWN FEET.
I CAN'T SEE A FUTURE WHERE I'M HEALTHY.

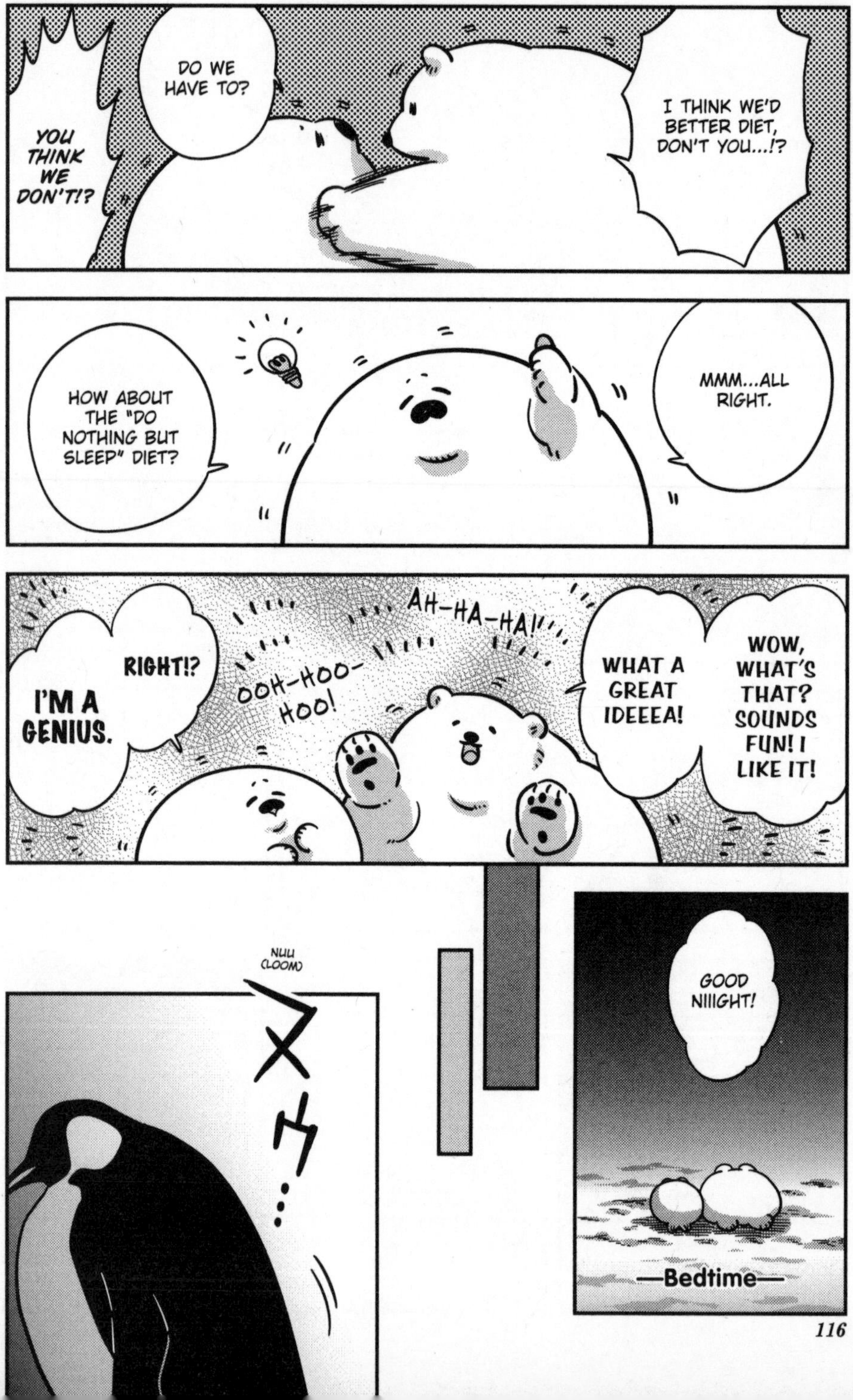
I THINK WE'D BETTER DIET, DON'T YOU...!?
DO WE HAVE TO?
YOU THINK WE DON'T!?
MMM...ALL RIGHT.
HOW ABOUT THE "DO NOTHING BUT SLEEP" DIET?
WOW, WHAT'S THAT? SOUNDS FUN! I LIKE IT!
WHAT A GREAT IDEEEA!
AH-HA-HA!
OOH-HOO-HOO!
RIGHT!?
I'M A GENIUS.
GOOD NIIIGHT!
—Bedtime—
NUU (LOOM)
ヌウ…

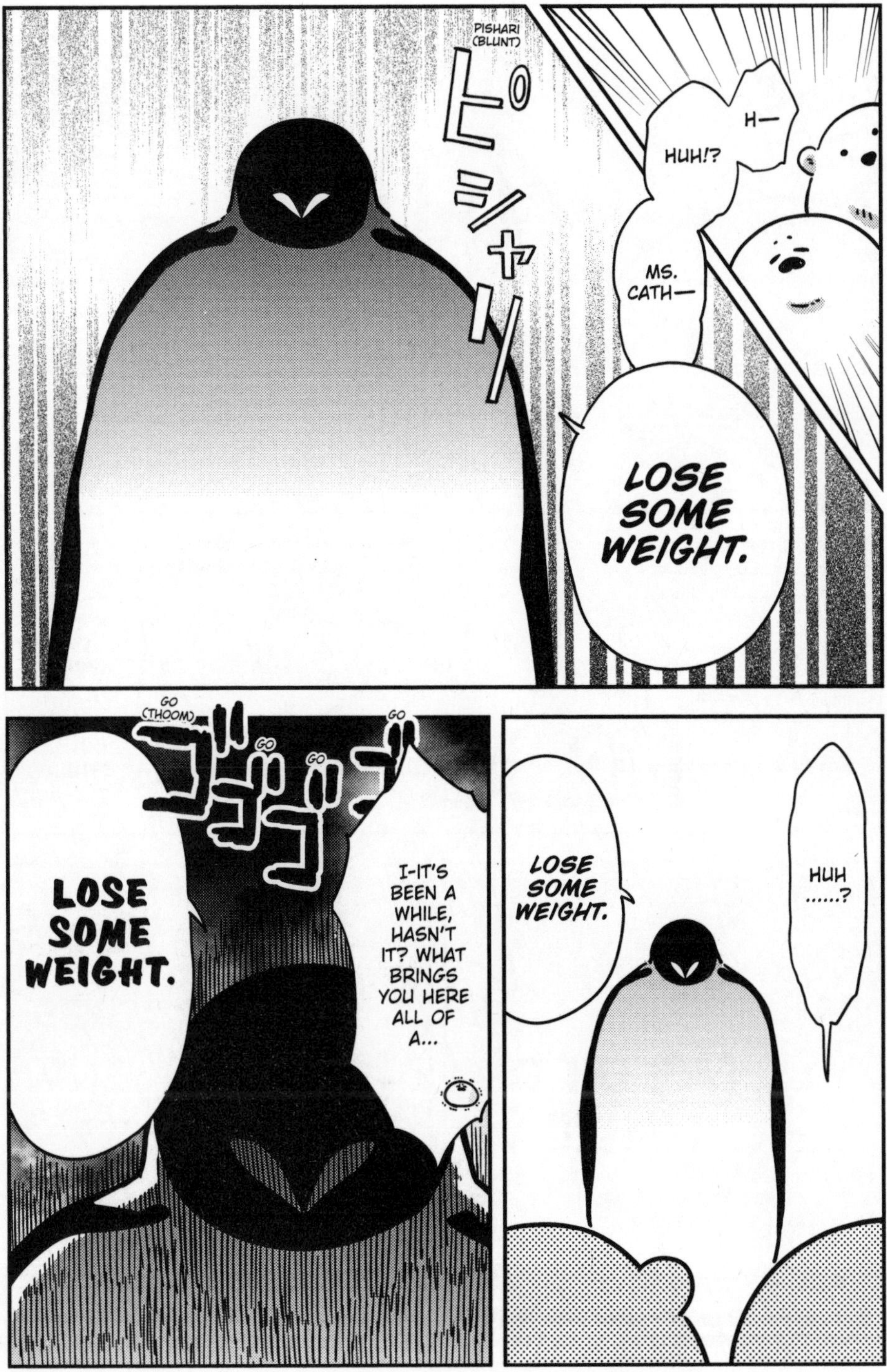
H—
HUH!?
MS. CATH—
PISHARI (BLUNT)
LOSE SOME WEIGHT.
HUH ......?
LOSE SOME WEIGHT.
GO
GO
GO
GO (THOOM)
I-IT'S BEEN A WHILE, HASN'T IT? WHAT BRINGS YOU HERE ALL OF A...
LOSE SOME WEIGHT.

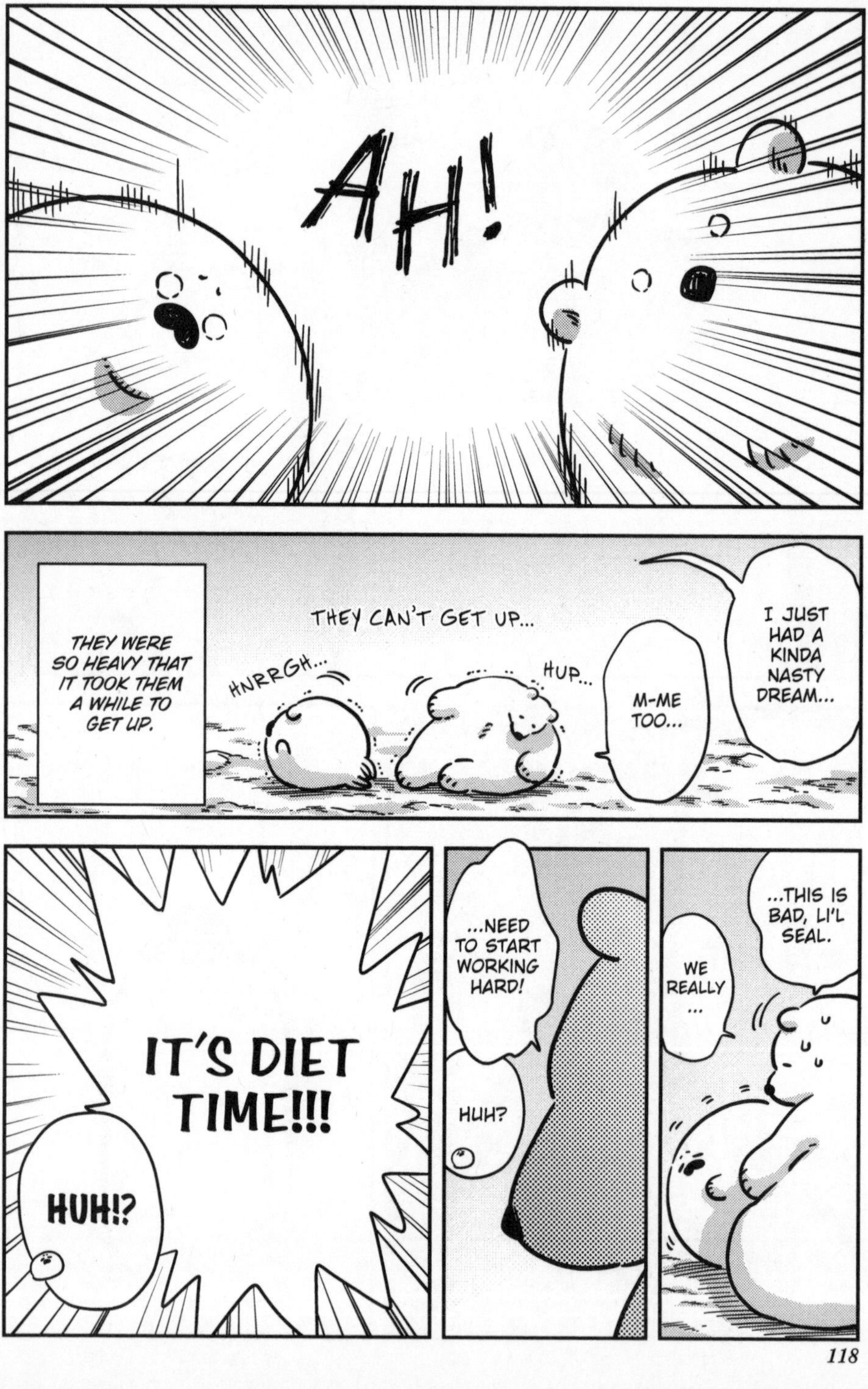
AH!
I JUST HAD A KINDA NASTY DREAM...
M-ME TOO...
HUP...
THEY CAN'T GET UP...
HNRRGH...
THEY WERE SO HEAVY THAT IT TOOK THEM A WHILE TO GET UP.
...THIS IS BAD, LI'L SEAL.
WE REALLY ...
...NEED TO START WORKING HARD!
HUH?
IT'S DIET TIME!!!
HUH!?

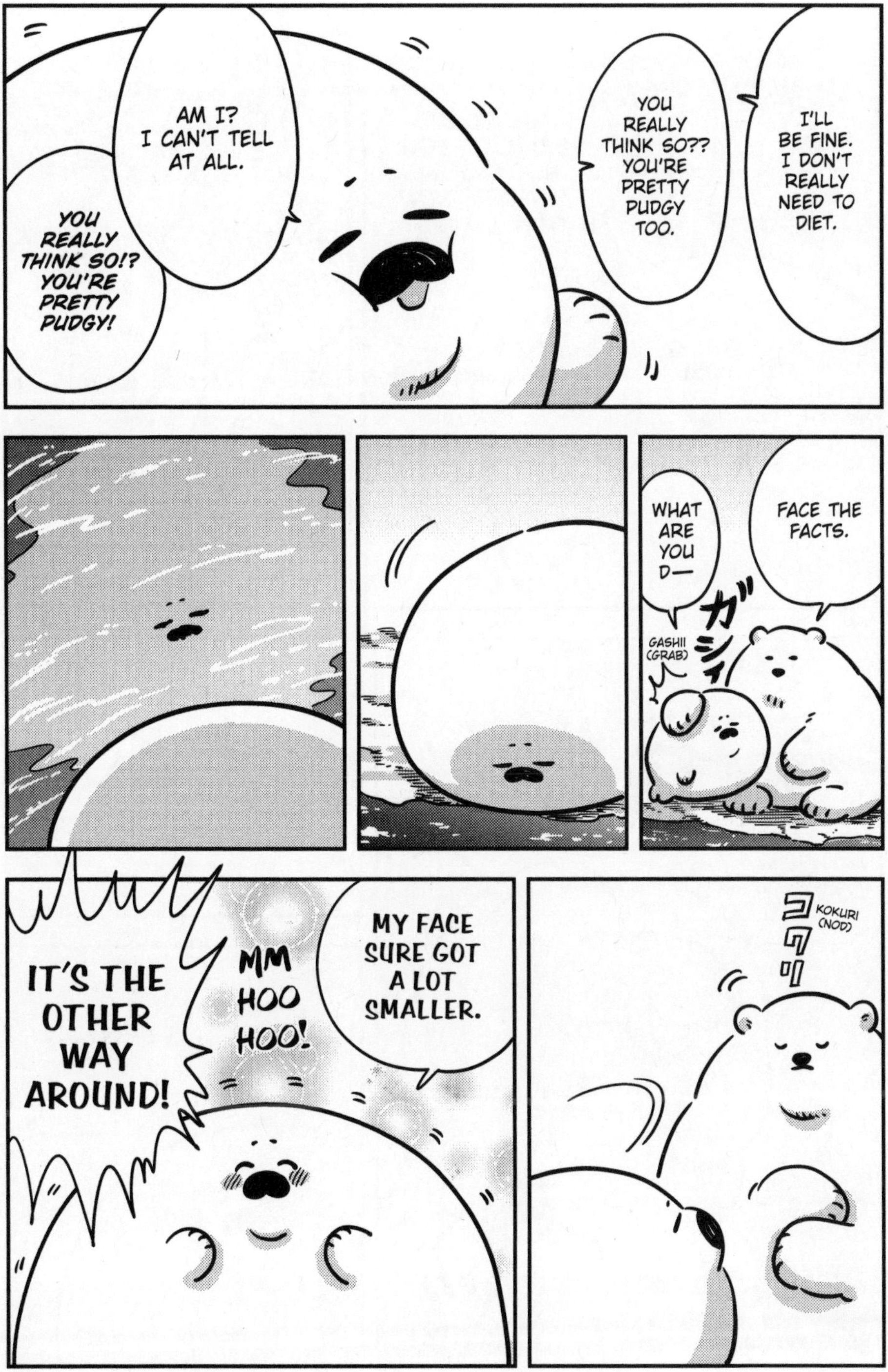
I'LL BE FINE. I DON'T REALLY NEED TO DIET.
YOU REALLY THINK SO?? YOU'RE PRETTY PUDGY TOO.
AM I? I CAN'T TELL AT ALL.
YOU REALLY THINK SO!? YOU'RE PRETTY PUDGY!
FACE THE FACTS.
WHAT ARE YOU D—
GASHII (GRAB)
KOKURI (NOD)
MY FACE SURE GOT A LOT SMALLER.
MM HOO HOO!
IT'S THE OTHER WAY AROUND!

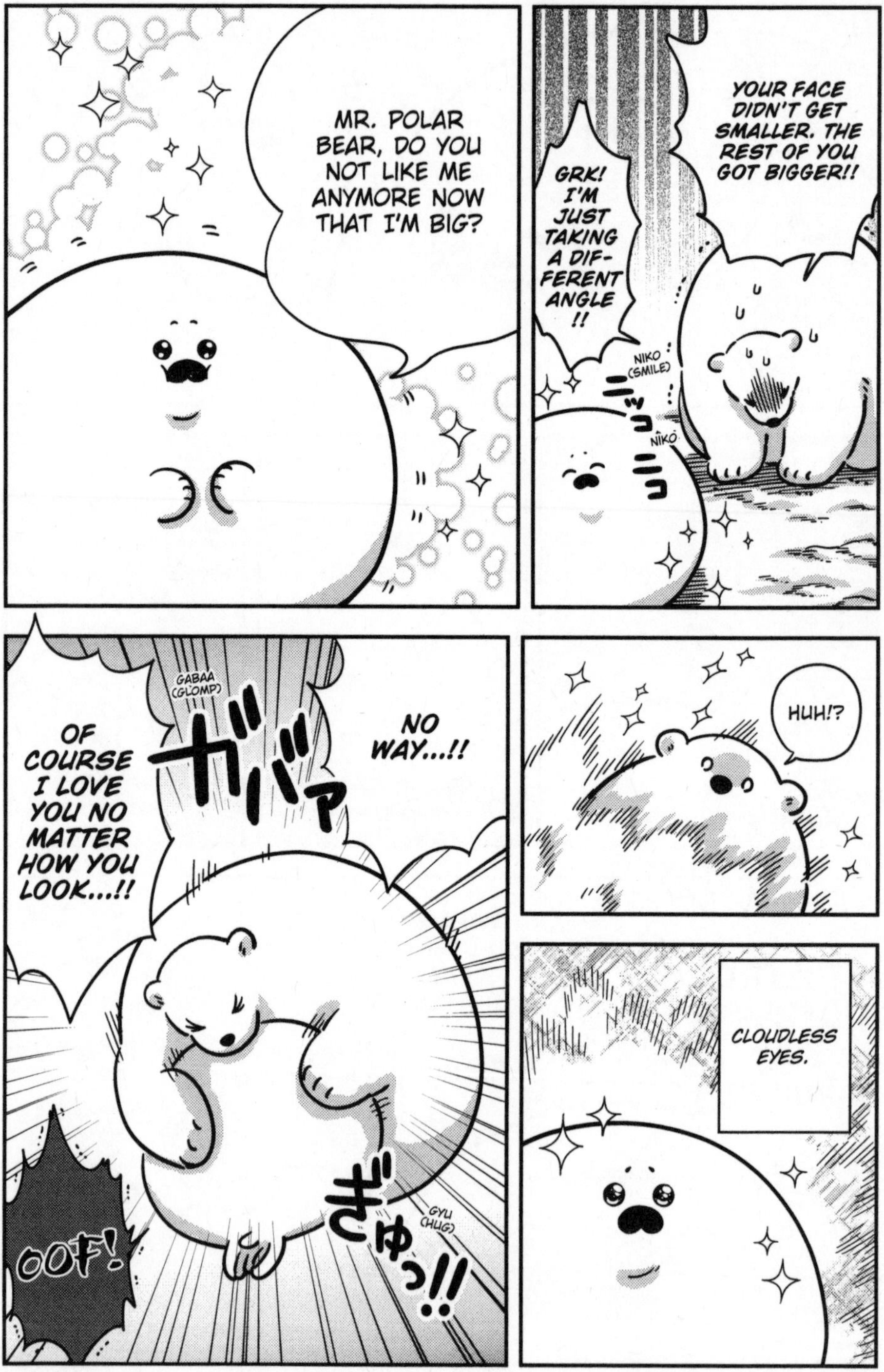
YOUR FACE DIDN'T GET SMALLER. THE REST OF YOU GOT BIGGER!!
GRK! I'M JUST TAKING A DIF-FERENT ANGLE !!
NIKO (SMILE)
ニッコ
NIKO
ニコ
MR. POLAR BEAR, DO YOU NOT LIKE ME ANYMORE NOW THAT I'M BIG?
HUH!?
CLOUDLESS EYES.
NO WAY...!!
GABAA (GLOMP)
ガバァ
OF COURSE I LOVE YOU NO MATTER HOW YOU LOOK...!!
ぎゅっ!!
GYU (HUG)
OOF!

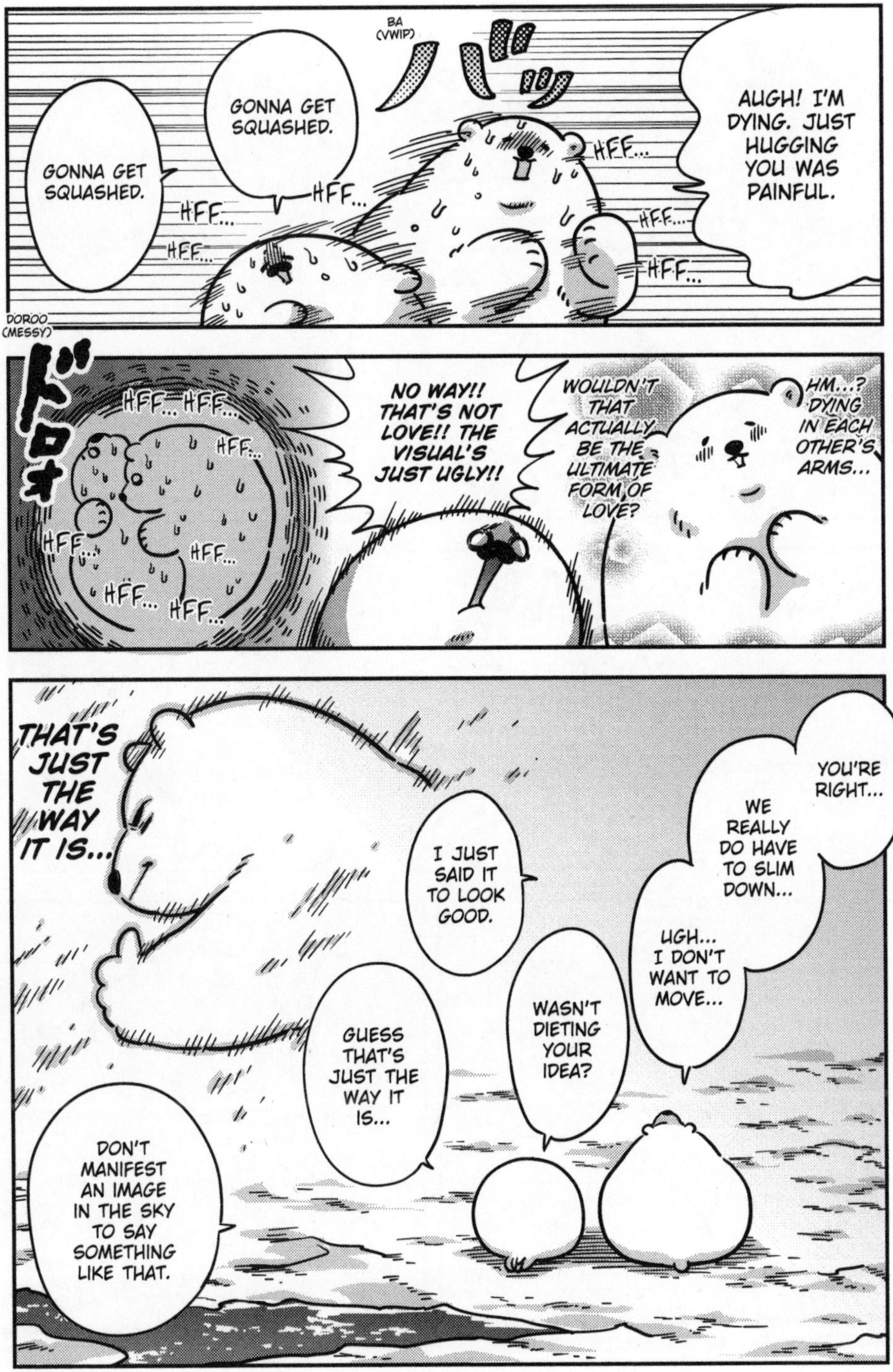
AUGH! I'M DYING. JUST HUGGING YOU WAS PAINFUL.
HFF...
HFF...
HFF...
BA (VWIP)
GONNA GET SQUASHED.
HFF...
GONNA GET SQUASHED.
HFF...
HFF...
HM...? DYING IN EACH OTHER'S ARMS...
WOULDN'T THAT ACTUALLY BE THE ULTIMATE FORM OF LOVE?
NO WAY!! THAT'S NOT LOVE!! THE VISUAL'S JUST UGLY!!
DOROO (MESSY)
HFF... HFF... HFF... HFF... HFF... HFF... HFF...
YOU'RE RIGHT...
WE REALLY DO HAVE TO SLIM DOWN...
UGH... I DON'T WANT TO MOVE...
I JUST SAID IT TO LOOK GOOD.
WASN'T DIETING YOUR IDEA?
GUESS THAT'S JUST THE WAY IT IS...
THAT'S JUST THE WAY IT IS...
DON'T MANIFEST AN IMAGE IN THE SKY TO SAY SOMETHING LIKE THAT.

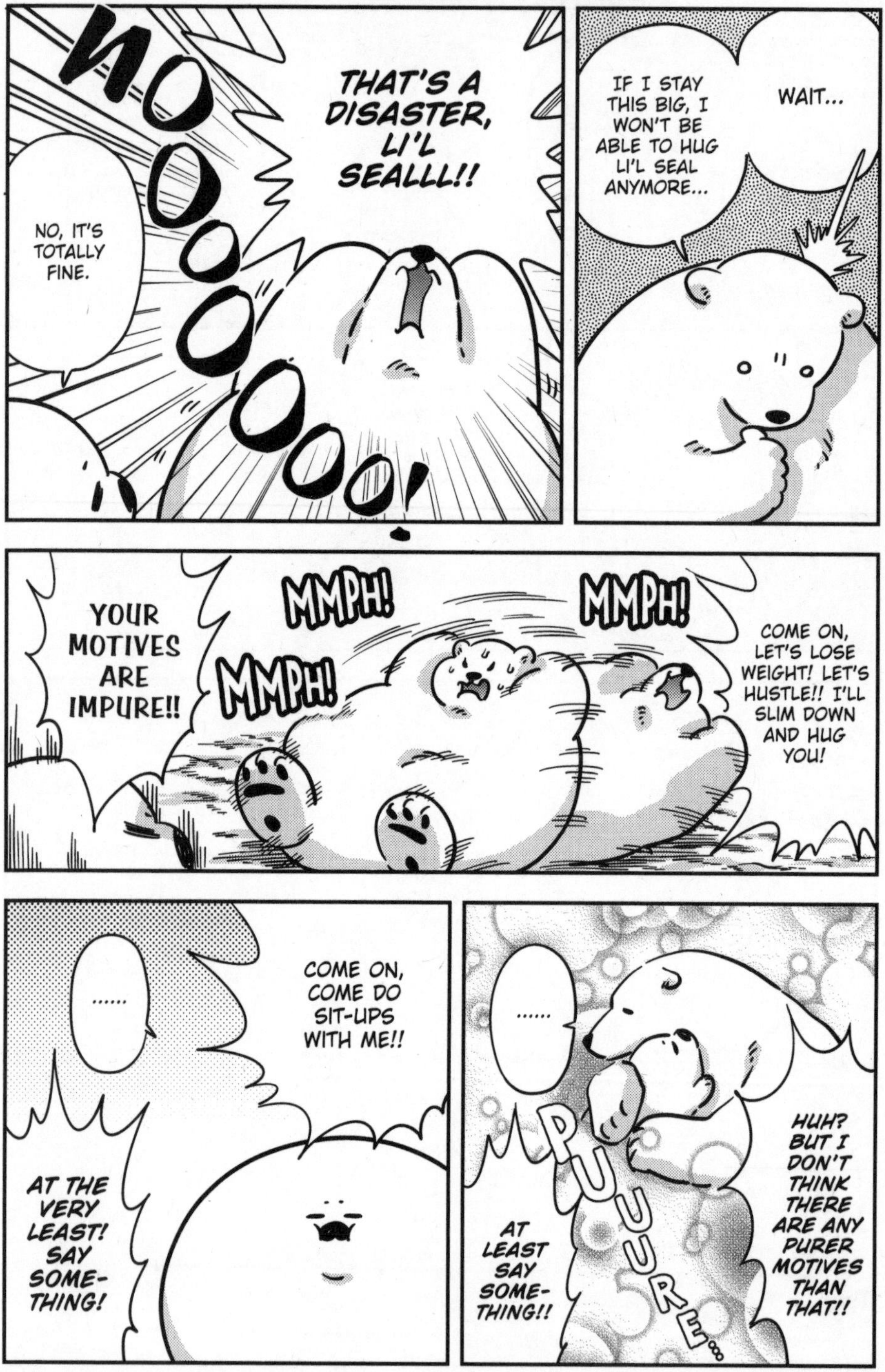
WAIT...
IF I STAY THIS BIG, I WON'T BE ABLE TO HUG LI'L SEAL ANYMORE...
THAT'S A DISASTER, LI'L SEALLL!!
NOOOOOOOOOO!
NO, IT'S TOTALLY FINE.
COME ON, LET'S LOSE WEIGHT! LET'S HUSTLE!! I'LL SLIM DOWN AND HUG YOU!
MMPH!
MMPH!
MMPH!
YOUR MOTIVES ARE IMPURE!!
HUH? BUT I DON'T THINK THERE ARE ANY PURER MOTIVES THAN THAT!!
......
PUUURE...
AT LEAST SAY SOME-THING!!
COME ON, COME DO SIT-UPS WITH ME!!
......
AT THE VERY LEAST! SAY SOME-THING!

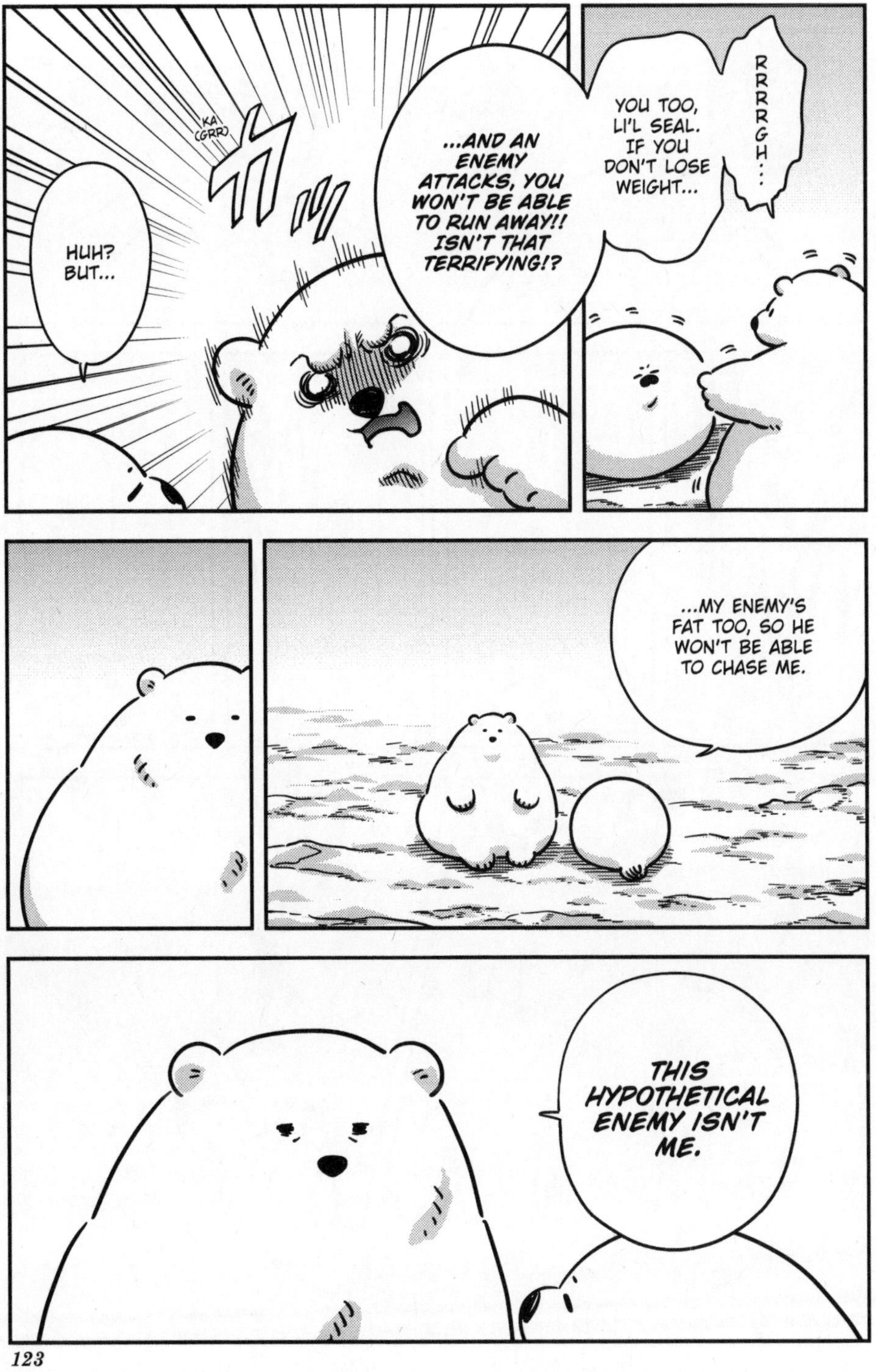
RRRRGH...
YOU TOO, LI'L SEAL. IF YOU DON'T LOSE WEIGHT...
...AND AN ENEMY ATTACKS, YOU WON'T BE ABLE TO RUN AWAY!! ISN'T THAT TERRIFYING!?
KA (GRR)
HUH? BUT...
...MY ENEMY'S FAT TOO, SO HE WON'T BE ABLE TO CHASE ME.
THIS HYPOTHETICAL ENEMY ISN'T ME.

IT'S ALL RIGHT

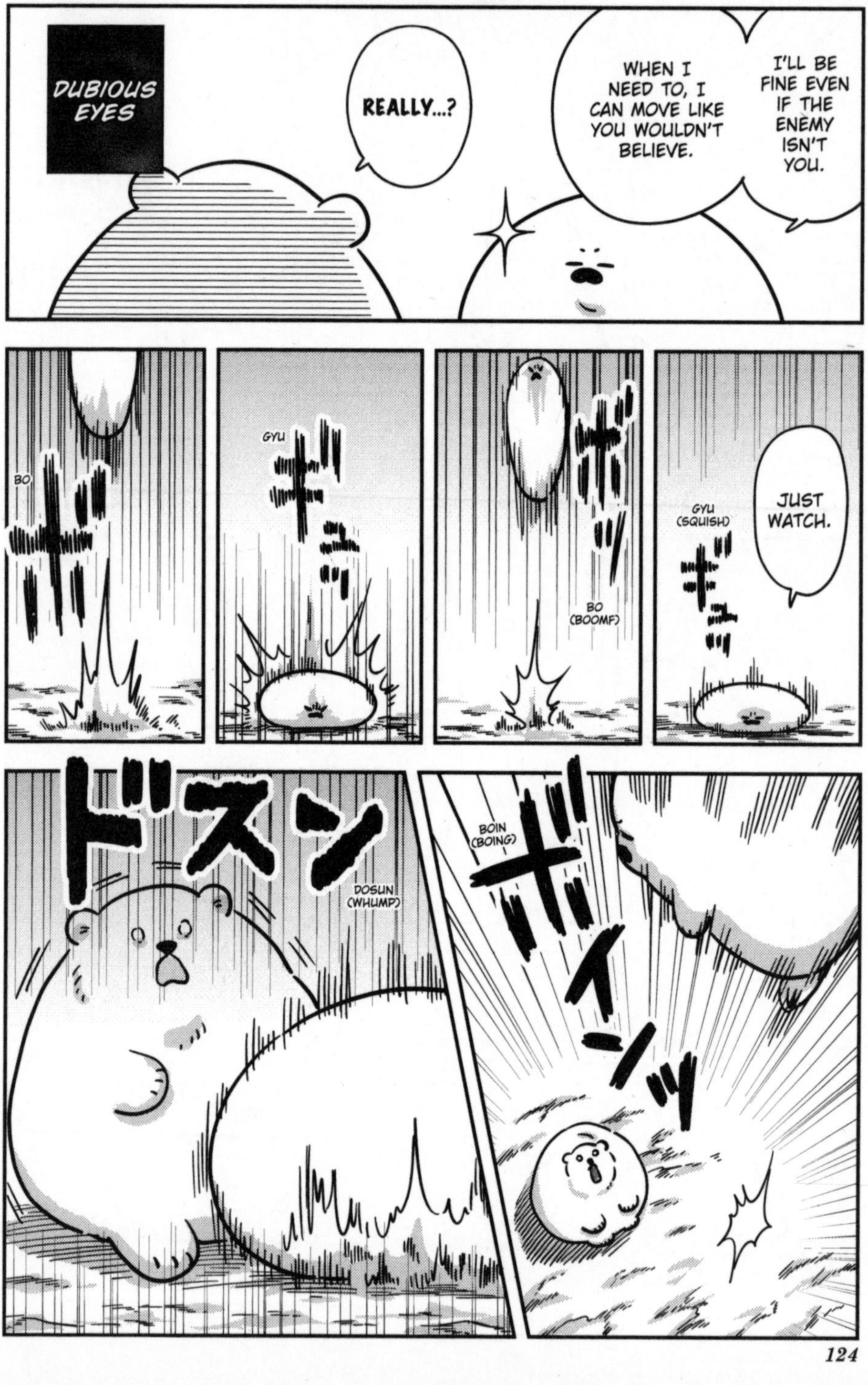
I'LL BE FINE EVEN IF THE ENEMY ISN'T YOU.
WHEN I NEED TO, I CAN MOVE LIKE YOU WOULDN'T BELIEVE.
REALLY...?
DUBIOUS EYES
JUST WATCH.
GYU (SQUISH)
BO (BOOMF)
GYU
BO
ボイーンッ
BOIN (BOING)
ドスン
DOSUN (WHUMP)

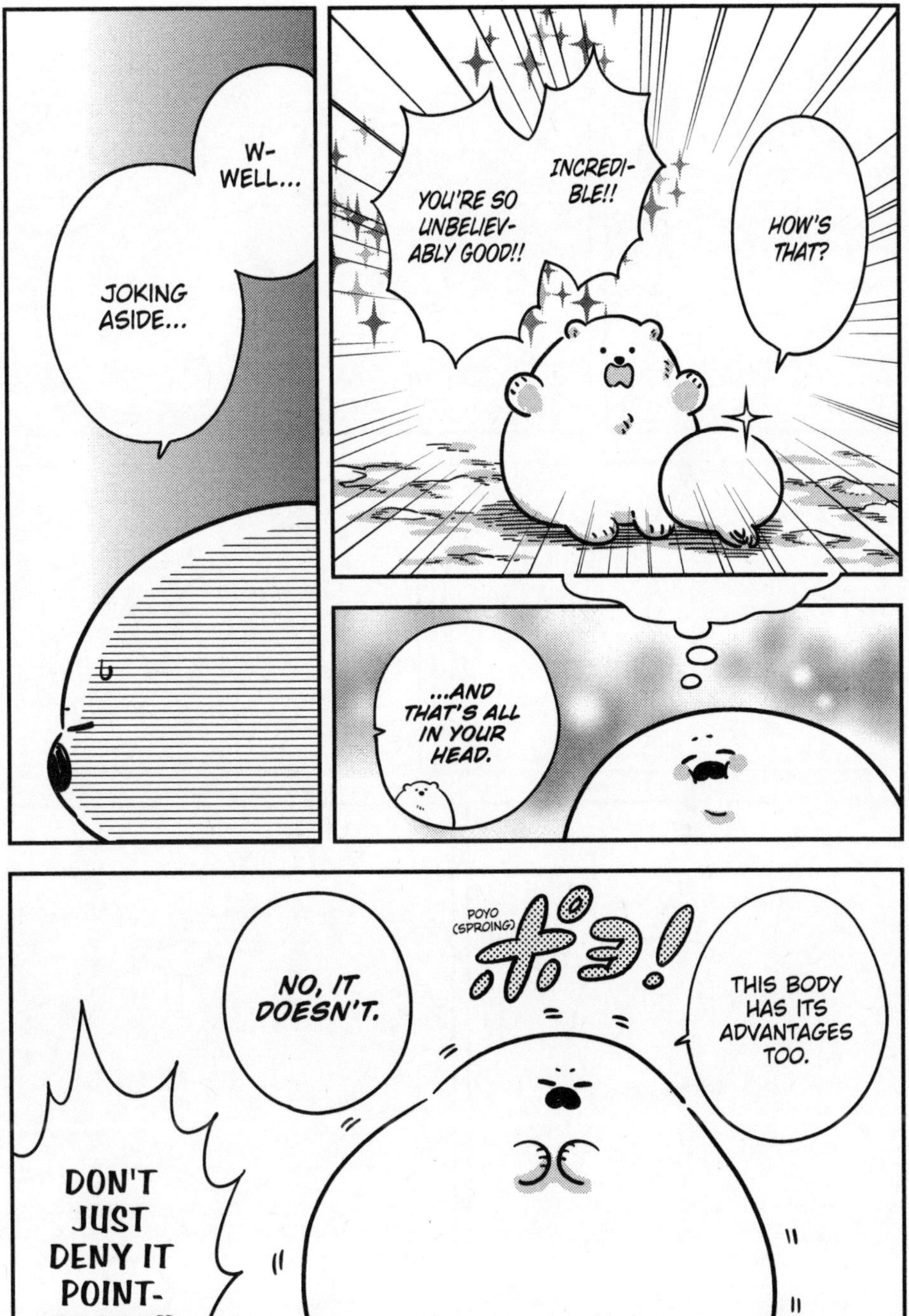
HOW'S THAT?
INCREDI-BLE!!
YOU'RE SO UNBELIEV-ABLY GOOD!!
...AND THAT'S ALL IN YOUR HEAD.
W-WELL...
JOKING ASIDE...
THIS BODY HAS ITS ADVANTAGES TOO.
POYO (SPROING)
NO, IT DOESN'T.
DON'T JUST DENY IT POINT-BLANK!!

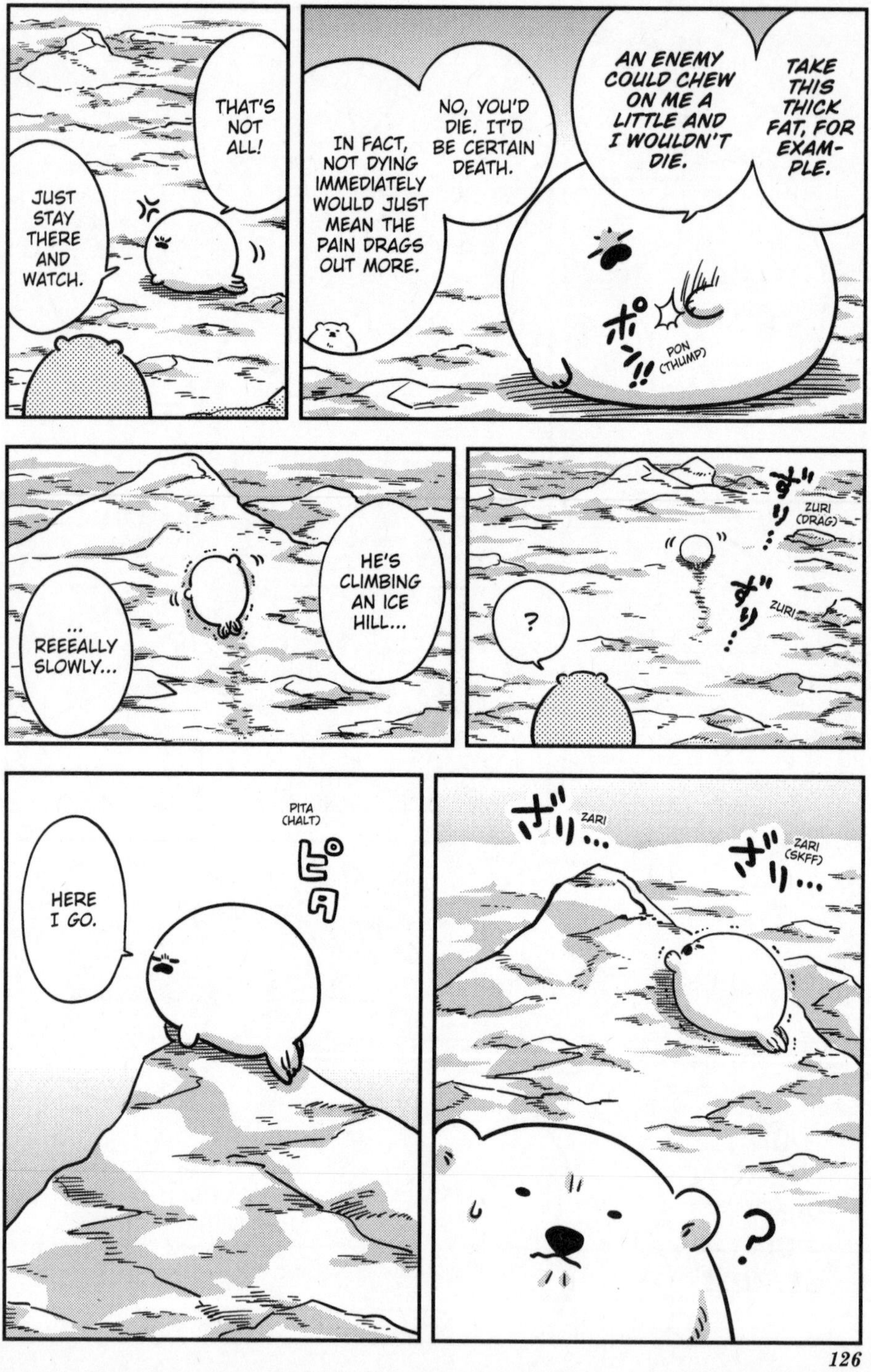
TAKE THIS THICK FAT, FOR EXAMPLE.
AN ENEMY COULD CHEW ON ME A LITTLE AND I WOULDN'T DIE.
PON (THUMP)
NO, YOU'D DIE. IT'D BE CERTAIN DEATH.
IN FACT, NOT DYING IMMEDIATELY WOULD JUST MEAN THE PAIN DRAGS OUT MORE.
THAT'S NOT ALL!
JUST STAY THERE AND WATCH.
ZURI (DRAG)
ZURI
?
HE'S CLIMBING AN ICE HILL...
... REEEALLY SLOWLY...
ZARI (SKFF)
ZARI
?
PITA (HALT)
HERE I GO.

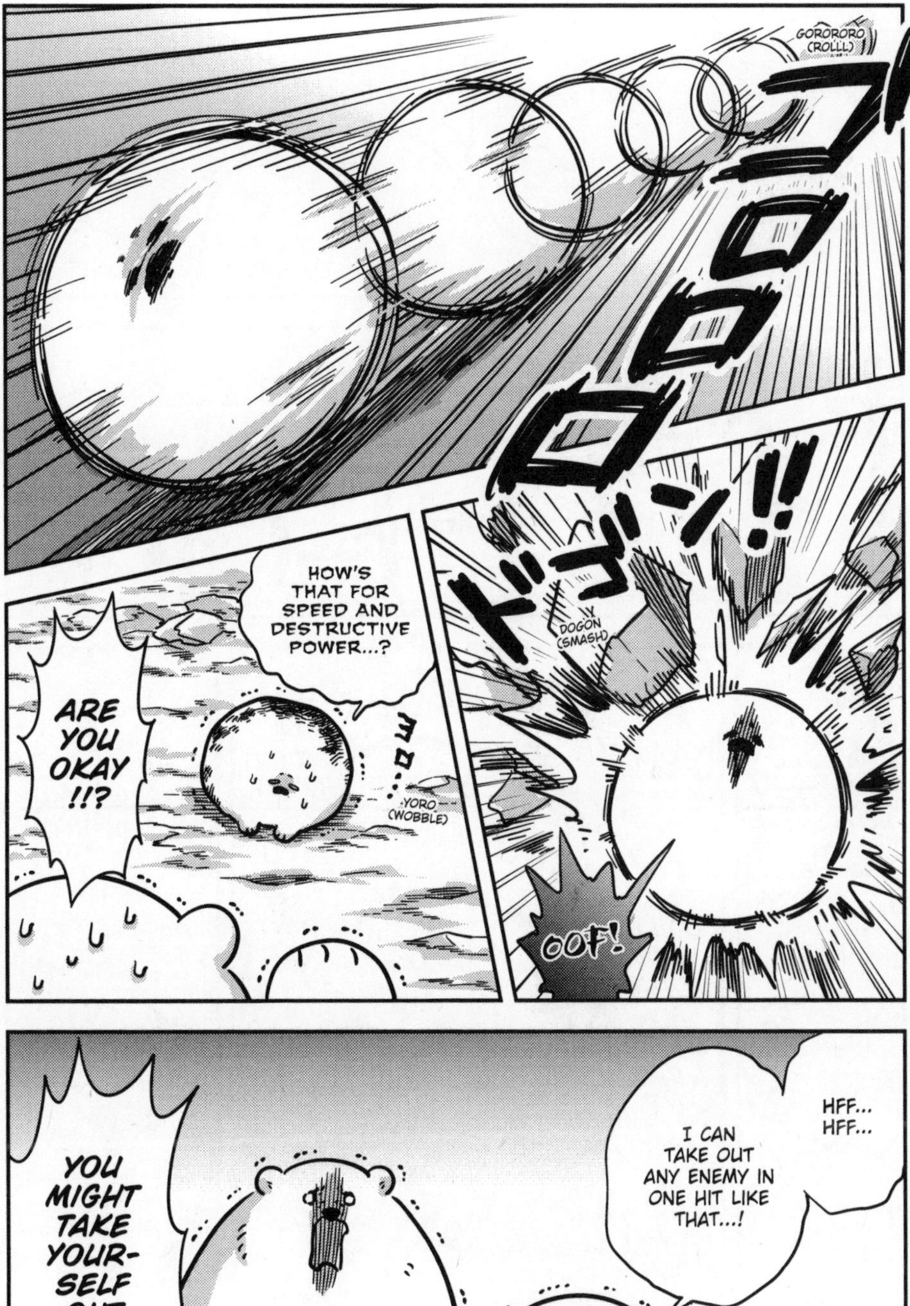

GOROROROR (ROLLL)
ゴロロロ
ドゴン!!
DOGON (SMASH)
OOF!
HOW'S THAT FOR SPEED AND DESTRUCTIVE POWER...?
ヨロ...
YORO (WOBBLE)
ARE YOU OKAY!!?
HFF... HFF...
I CAN TAKE OUT ANY ENEMY IN ONE HIT LIKE THAT...!
YOU MIGHT TAKE YOURSELF OUT TOO!!

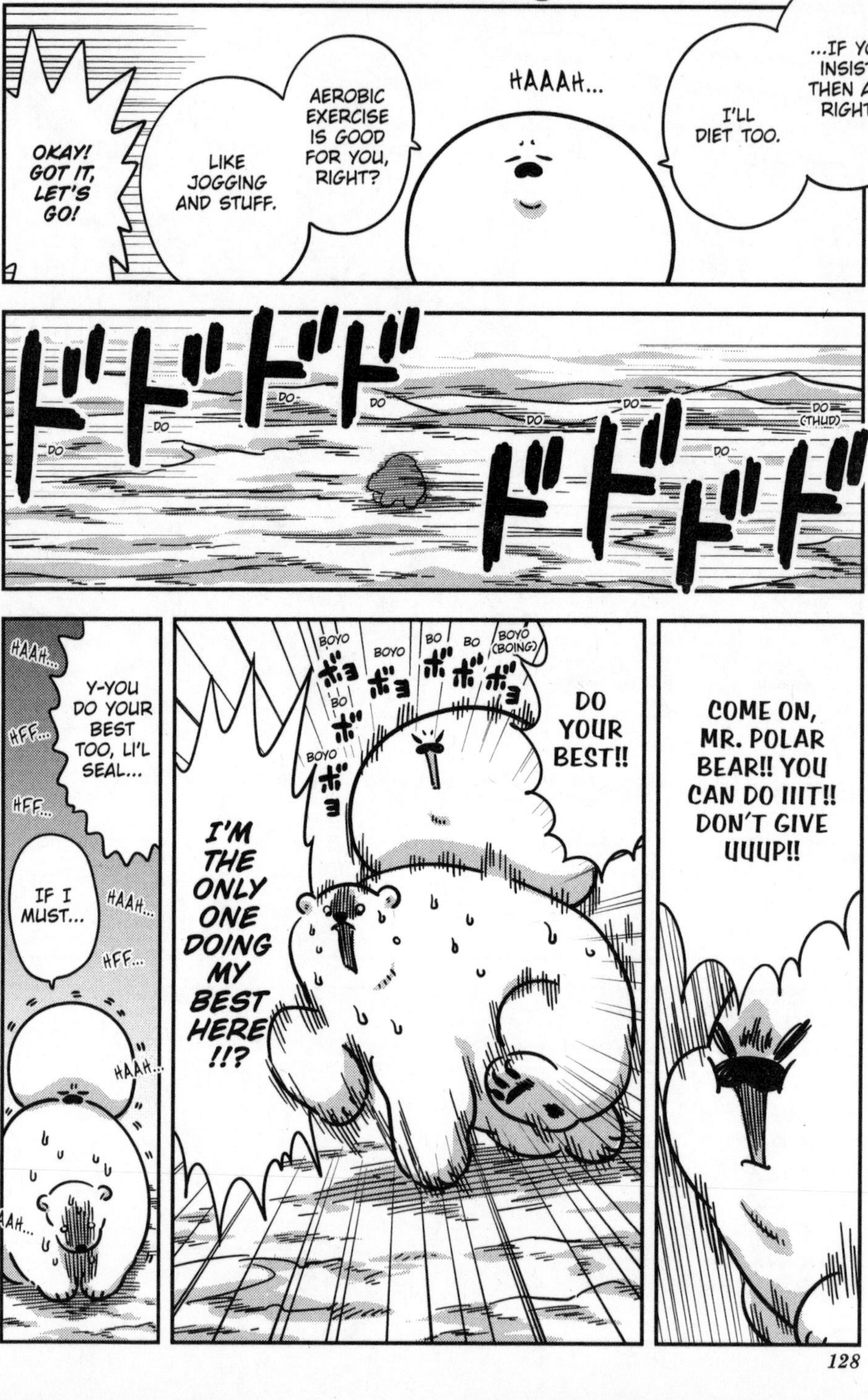
...IF YOU INSIST, THEN ALL RIGHT.
I'LL DIET TOO.
HAAAH...
AEROBIC EXERCISE IS GOOD FOR YOU, RIGHT?
LIKE JOGGING AND STUFF.
OKAY! GOT IT, LET'S GO!
ドドドドド
ドドドドド
DO DO DO DO DO DO DO DO DO (THUD)
COME ON, MR. POLAR BEAR!! YOU CAN DO IIIT!! DON'T GIVE UUUP!!
ボヨ ボヨ ボボボヨ ボ ボヨ
BOYO BOYO BO BO BOYO (BOING) BO BOYO
DO YOUR BEST!!
I'M THE ONLY ONE DOING MY BEST HERE!!?
HAAAH...
Y-YOU DO YOUR BEST TOO, LI'L SEAL...
HFF...
HFF...
IF I MUST...
HAAH...
HFF...
HAAH...
HAAH...

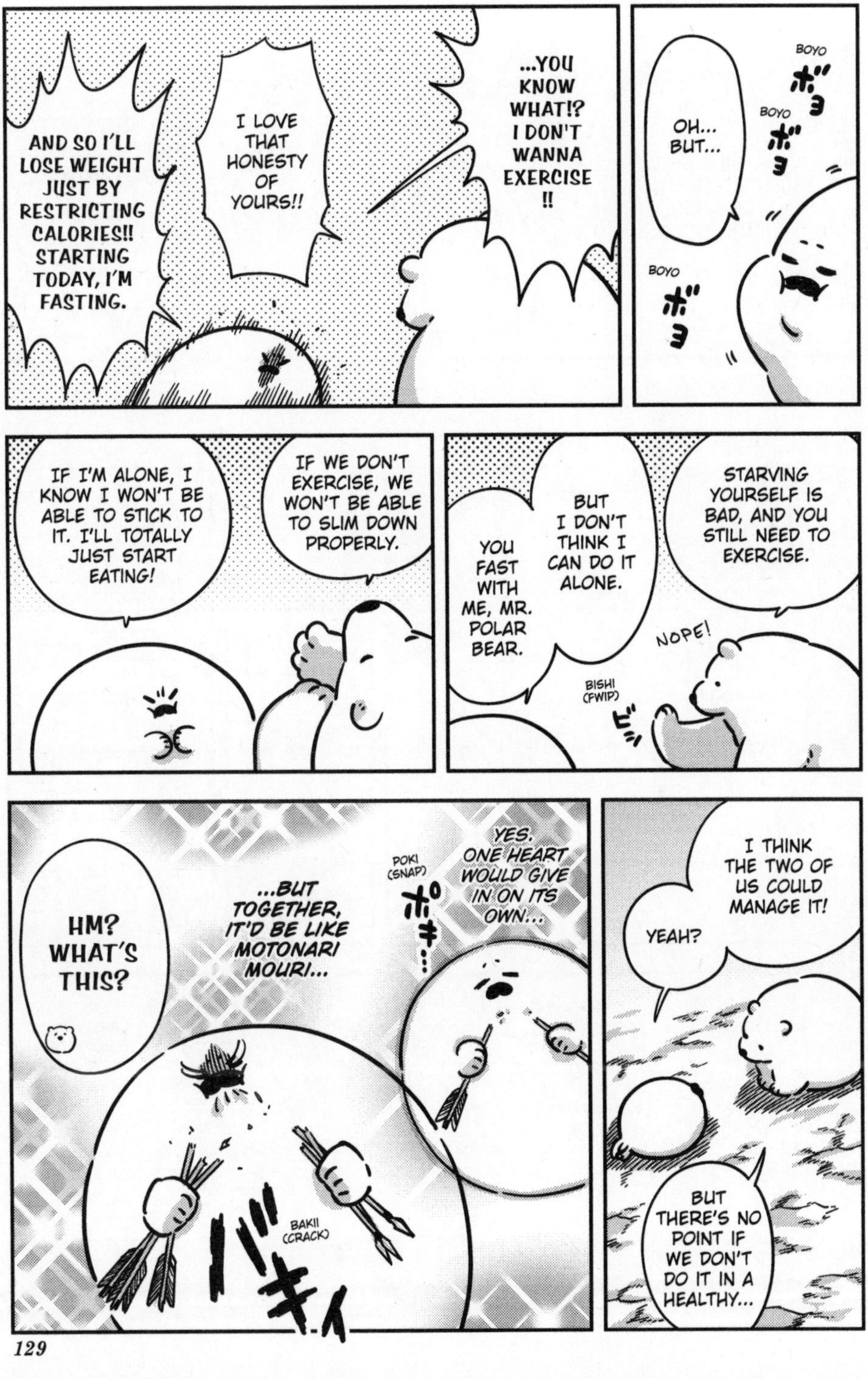
OH... BUT...
BOYO
ボヨ
BOYO
ボヨ
BOYO
ボヨ
...YOU KNOW WHAT!? I DON'T WANNA EXERCISE!!
I LOVE THAT HONESTY OF YOURS!!
AND SO I'LL LOSE WEIGHT JUST BY RESTRICTING CALORIES!! STARTING TODAY, I'M FASTING.
STARVING YOURSELF IS BAD, AND YOU STILL NEED TO EXERCISE.
NOPE!
BUT I DON'T THINK I CAN DO IT ALONE.
YOU FAST WITH ME, MR. POLAR BEAR.
BISHI (FWIP)
ビシ
IF WE DON'T EXERCISE, WE WON'T BE ABLE TO SLIM DOWN PROPERLY.
IF I'M ALONE, I KNOW I WON'T BE ABLE TO STICK TO IT. I'LL TOTALLY JUST START EATING!
I THINK THE TWO OF US COULD MANAGE IT!
YEAH?
BUT THERE'S NO POINT IF WE DON'T DO IT IN A HEALTHY...
YES. ONE HEART WOULD GIVE IN ON ITS OWN...
POKI (SNAP)
ポキ...
...BUT TOGETHER, IT'D BE LIKE MOTONARI MOURI...
HM? WHAT'S THIS?
BAKII (CRACK)
バキイ

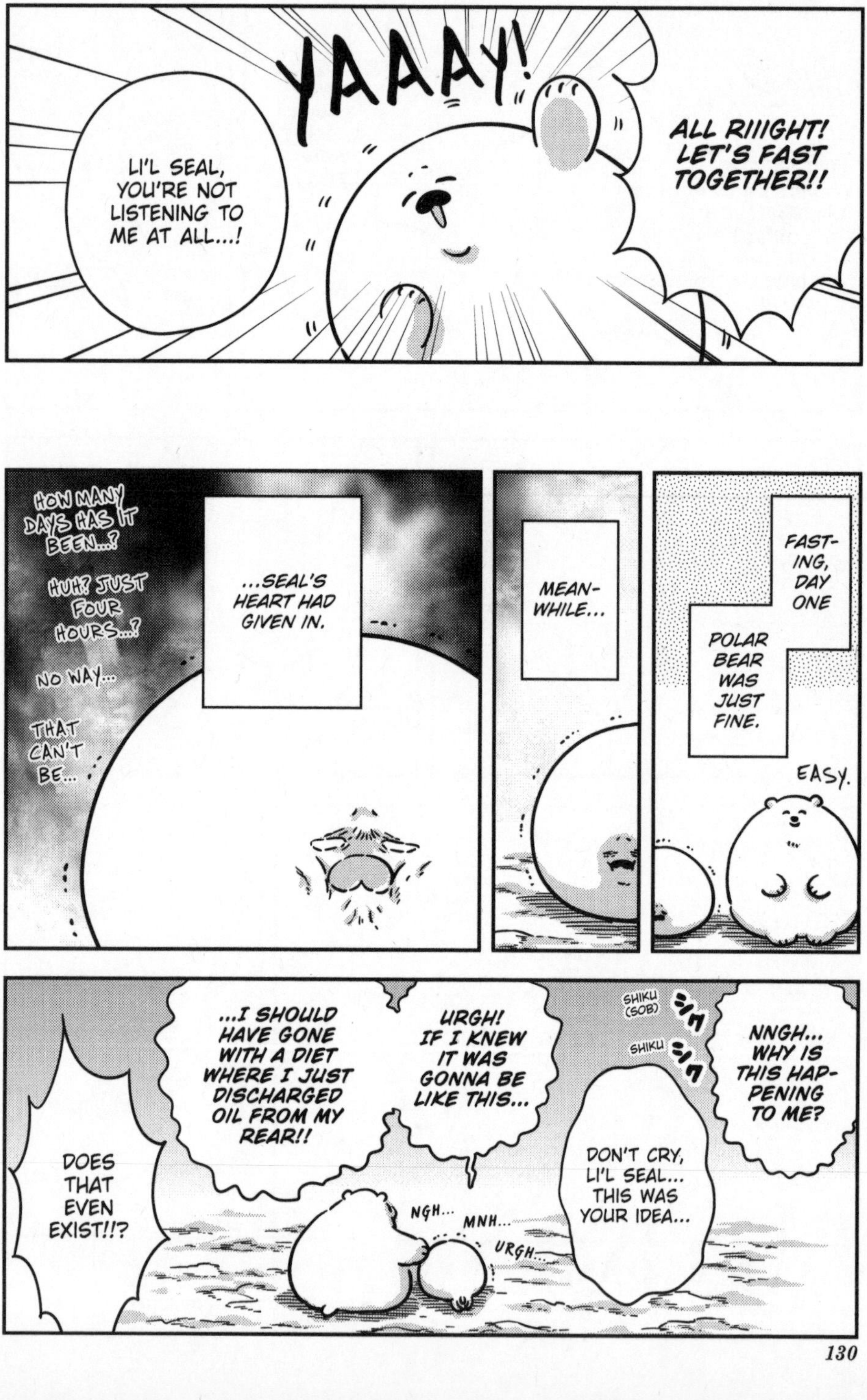
YAAAY!
ALL RIIIGHT! LET'S FAST TOGETHER!!
LI'L SEAL, YOU'RE NOT LISTENING TO ME AT ALL...!
FASTING, DAY ONE
POLAR BEAR WAS JUST FINE.
EASY.
MEANWHILE...
...SEAL'S HEART HAD GIVEN IN.
HOW MANY DAYS HAS IT BEEN...?
HUH? JUST FOUR HOURS...?
NO WAY...
THAT CAN'T BE...
NNGH... WHY IS THIS HAPPENING TO ME?
SHIKU (SOB)
SHIKU
URGH! IF I KNEW IT WAS GONNA BE LIKE THIS...
...I SHOULD HAVE GONE WITH A DIET WHERE I JUST DISCHARGED OIL FROM MY REAR!!
DON'T CRY, LI'L SEAL... THIS WAS YOUR IDEA...
NGH...
MNH...
URGH...
DOES THAT EVEN EXIST!!?

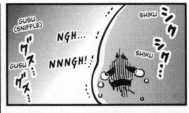

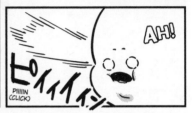

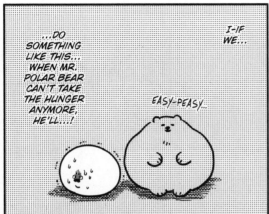

SHIKU
シク シク…
SHIKU
NGH…
NNNGH!
GUSU (SNIFFLE)
グス…
GUSU
グス…
AH!
ピィィィィン
PIIIIIN (CLICK)
I-IF WE…
…DO SOMETHING LIKE THIS… WHEN MR. POLAR BEAR CAN'T TAKE THE HUNGER ANYMORE, HE'LL…!
EASY-PEASY…
WH-WHAT HAVE I DONE…
…BY SUG-GESTING THIS …!!?
MR. POLAR BEAR, LET'S…STOP FASTING.
HM? OKAY, BUT WHY THE SUDDEN CHANGE OF HEART?
THE SEALS WILL GO EXTINCT.
HUH? WHAT?

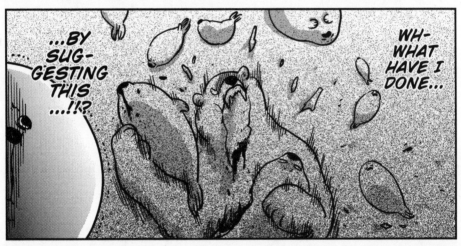

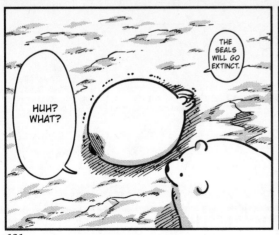

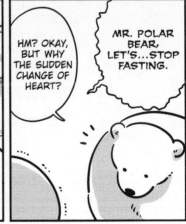

ALLURING VR

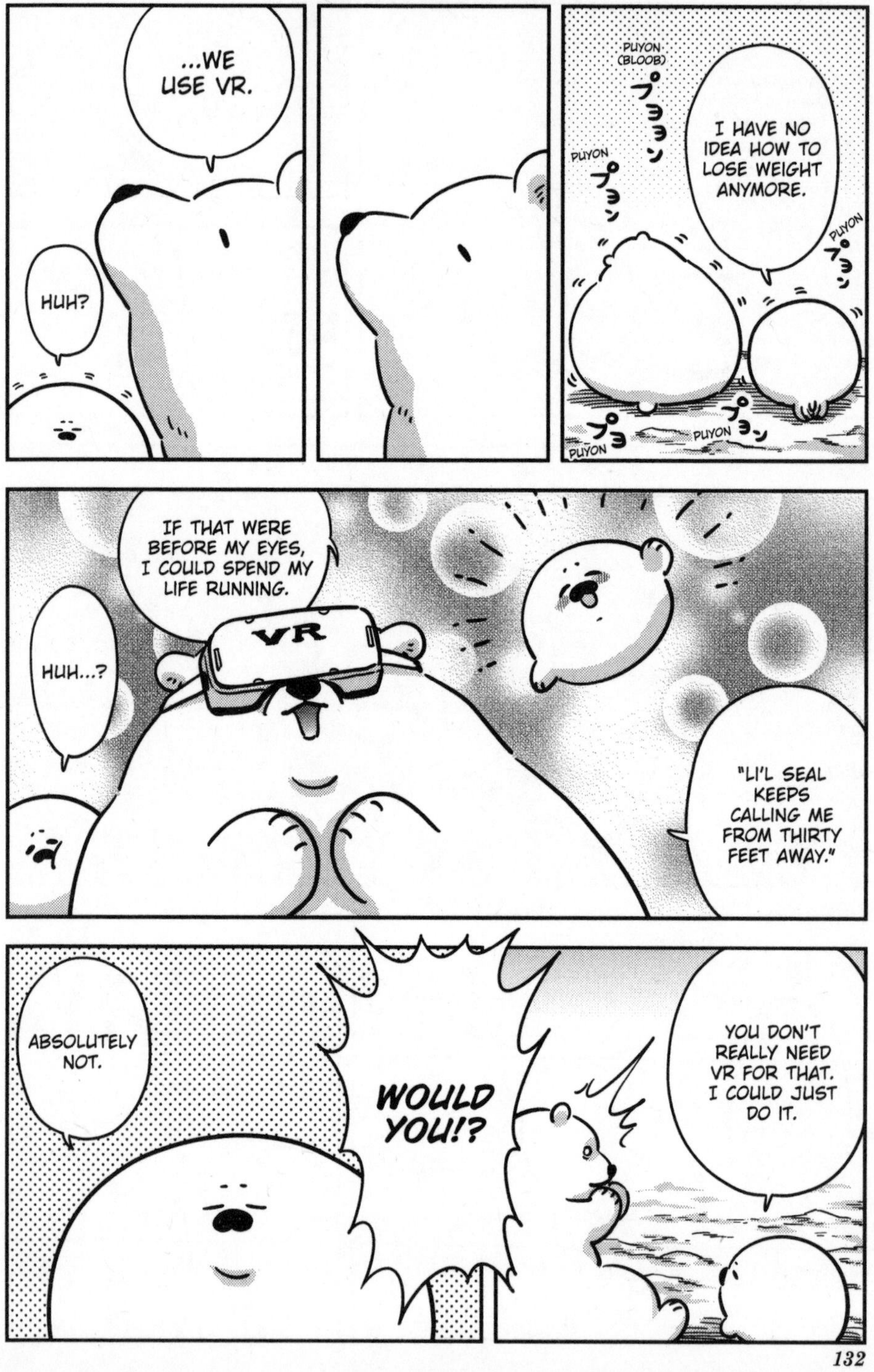

PUYON プヨン
I HAVE NO IDEA HOW TO LOSE WEIGHT ANYMORE.
PUYON (BLOOB) プヨン
PUYON プヨン
PUYON プヨン
PUYON プヨ
...WE USE VR.
HUH?
"LI'L SEAL KEEPS CALLING ME FROM THIRTY FEET AWAY."
IF THAT WERE BEFORE MY EYES, I COULD SPEND MY LIFE RUNNING.
VR
HUH...?
YOU DON'T REALLY NEED VR FOR THAT. I COULD JUST DO IT.
WOULD YOU!?
ABSOLUTELY NOT.

THE ANNOYING ONE

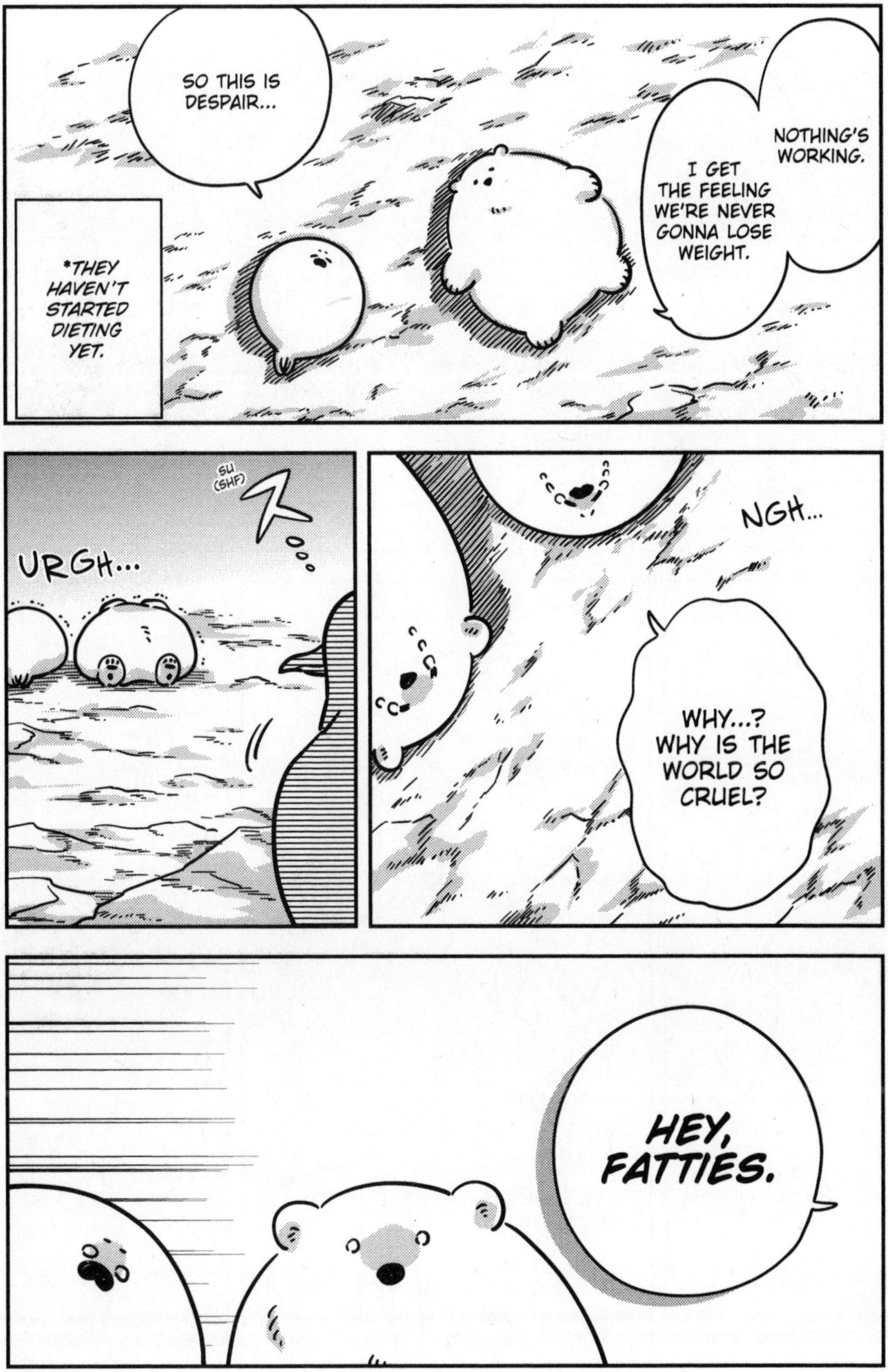

NOTHING'S WORKING.
I GET THE FEELING WE'RE NEVER GONNA LOSE WEIGHT.
SO THIS IS DESPAIR...
*THEY HAVEN'T STARTED DIETING YET.
NGH...
WHY...? WHY IS THE WORLD SO CRUEL?
SU (SHF)
URGH...
HEY, FATTIES.

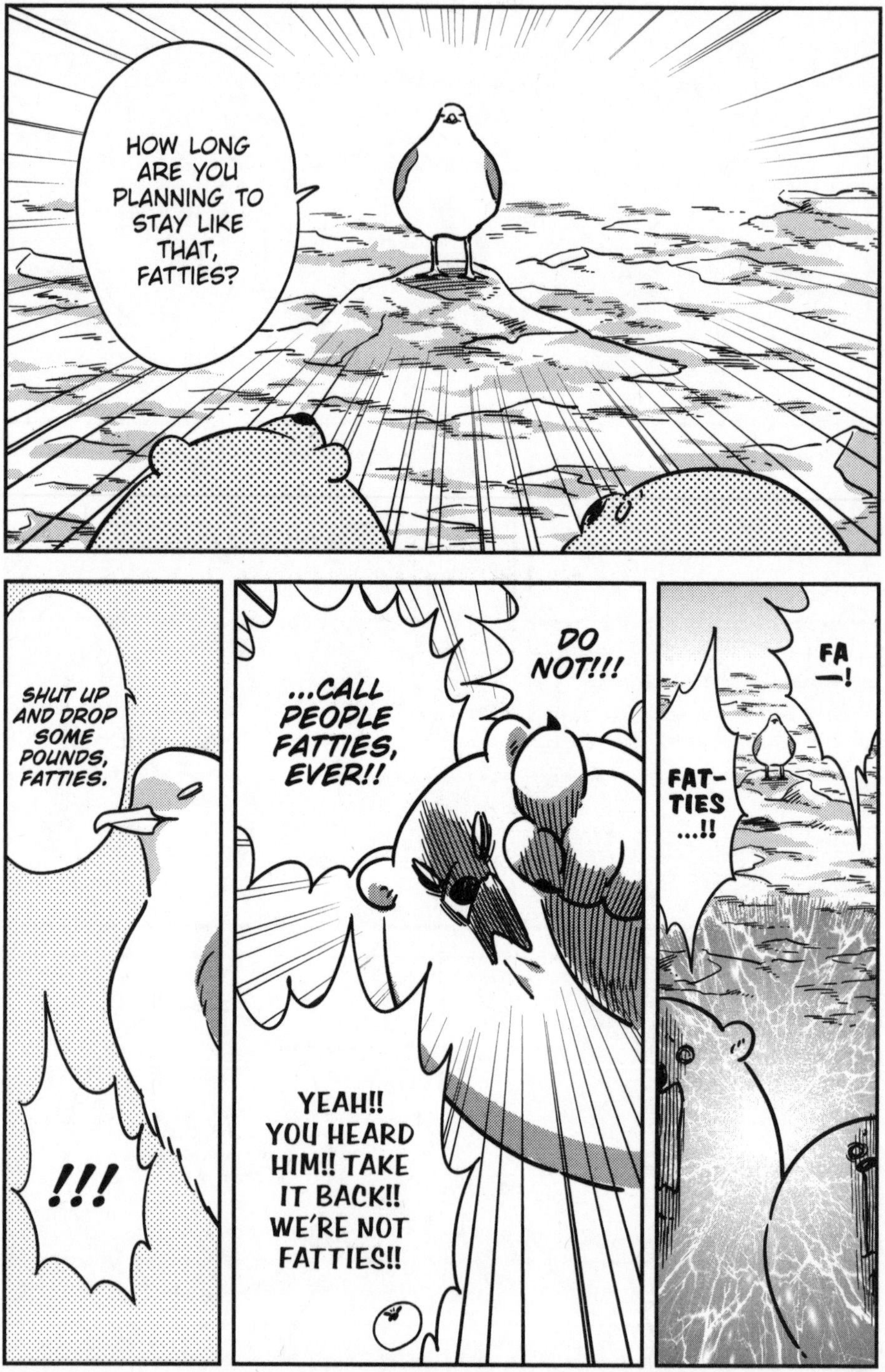
HOW LONG ARE YOU PLANNING TO STAY LIKE THAT, FATTIES?
FA—!
FAT-TIES...!!
DO NOT!!!
...CALL PEOPLE FATTIES, EVER!!
YEAH!! YOU HEARD HIM!! TAKE IT BACK!! WE'RE NOT FATTIES!!
SHUT UP AND DROP SOME POUNDS, FATTIES.
!!!

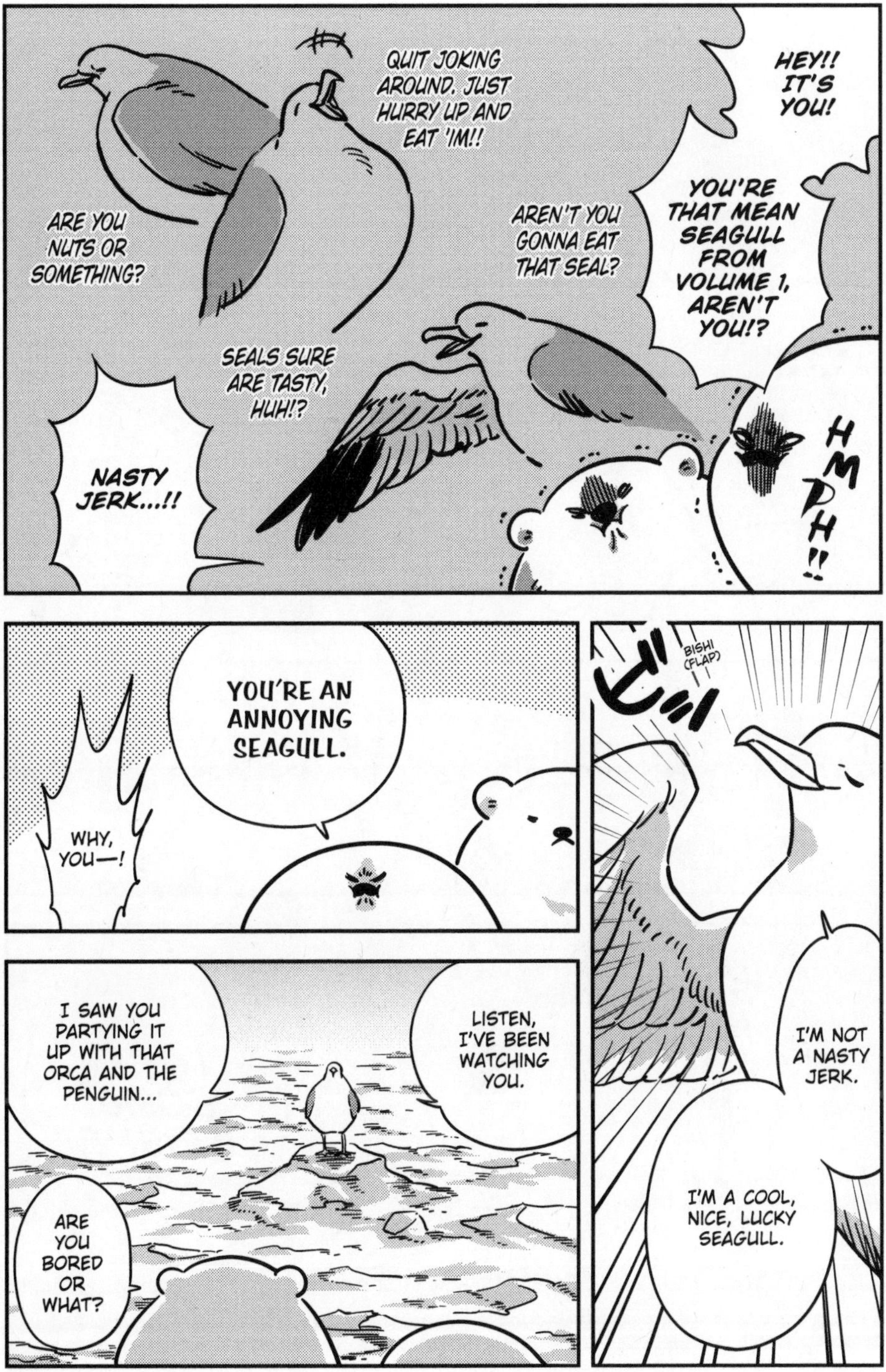
HEY!! IT'S YOU!
YOU'RE THAT MEAN SEAGULL FROM VOLUME 1, AREN'T YOU!?
HMPH!!
QUIT JOKING AROUND. JUST HURRY UP AND EAT 'IM!!
AREN'T YOU GONNA EAT THAT SEAL?
ARE YOU NUTS OR SOMETHING?
SEALS SURE ARE TASTY, HUH!?
NASTY JERK...!!
BISHI (FLAP)
I'M NOT A NASTY JERK.
I'M A COOL, NICE, LUCKY SEAGULL.
YOU'RE AN ANNOYING SEAGULL.
WHY, YOU—!
LISTEN, I'VE BEEN WATCHING YOU.
I SAW YOU PARTYING IT UP WITH THAT ORCA AND THE PENGUIN...
ARE YOU BORED OR WHAT?

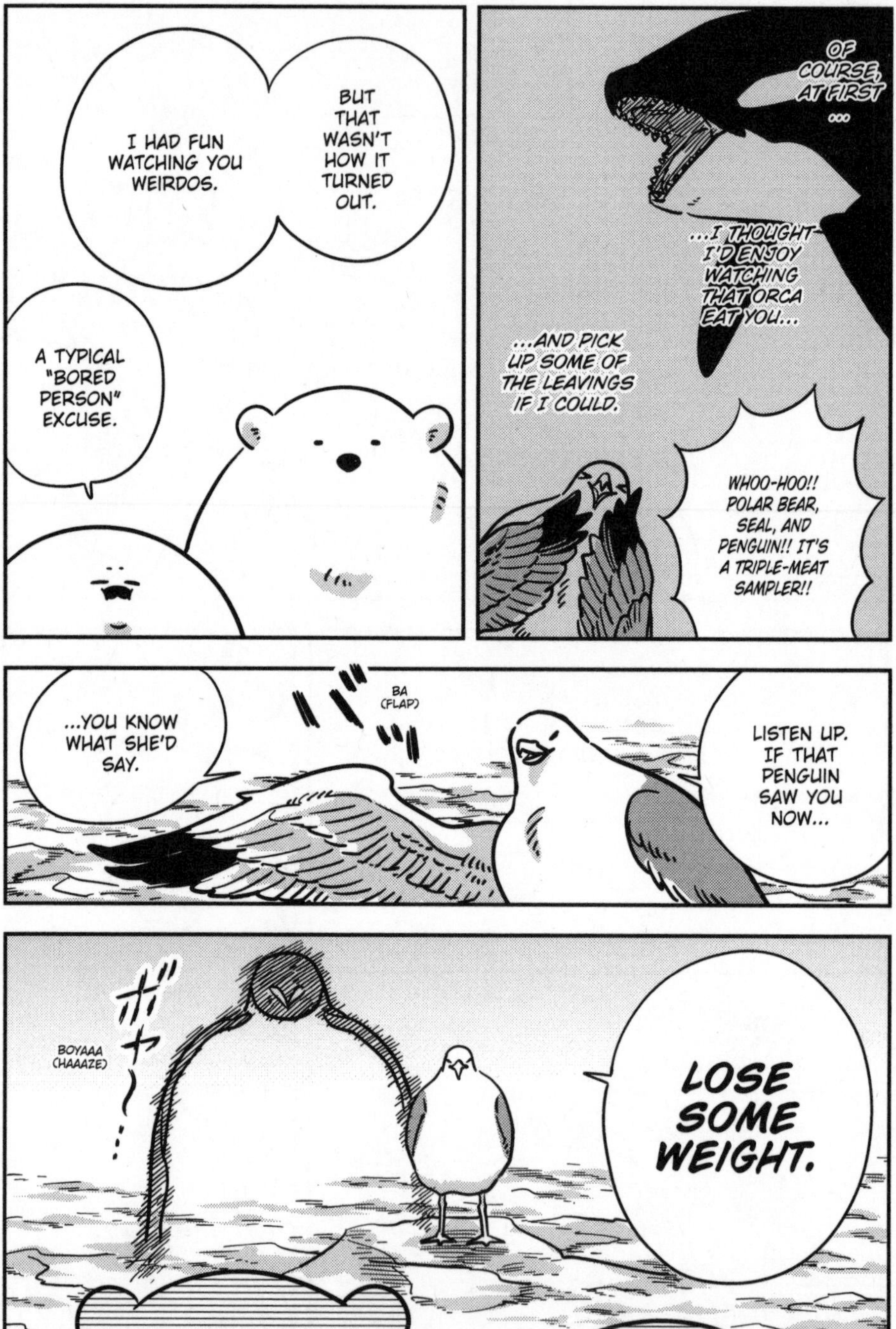
OF COURSE, AT FIRST ...
...I THOUGHT I'D ENJOY WATCHING THAT ORCA EAT YOU...
...AND PICK UP SOME OF THE LEAVINGS IF I COULD.
WHOO-HOO!! POLAR BEAR, SEAL, AND PENGUIN!! IT'S A TRIPLE-MEAT SAMPLER!!
BUT THAT WASN'T HOW IT TURNED OUT.
I HAD FUN WATCHING YOU WEIRDOS.
A TYPICAL "BORED PERSON" EXCUSE.
LISTEN UP. IF THAT PENGUIN SAW YOU NOW...
BA (FLAP)
...YOU KNOW WHAT SHE'D SAY.
LOSE SOME WEIGHT.
ボヤ～…
BOYAAA (HAAAZE)

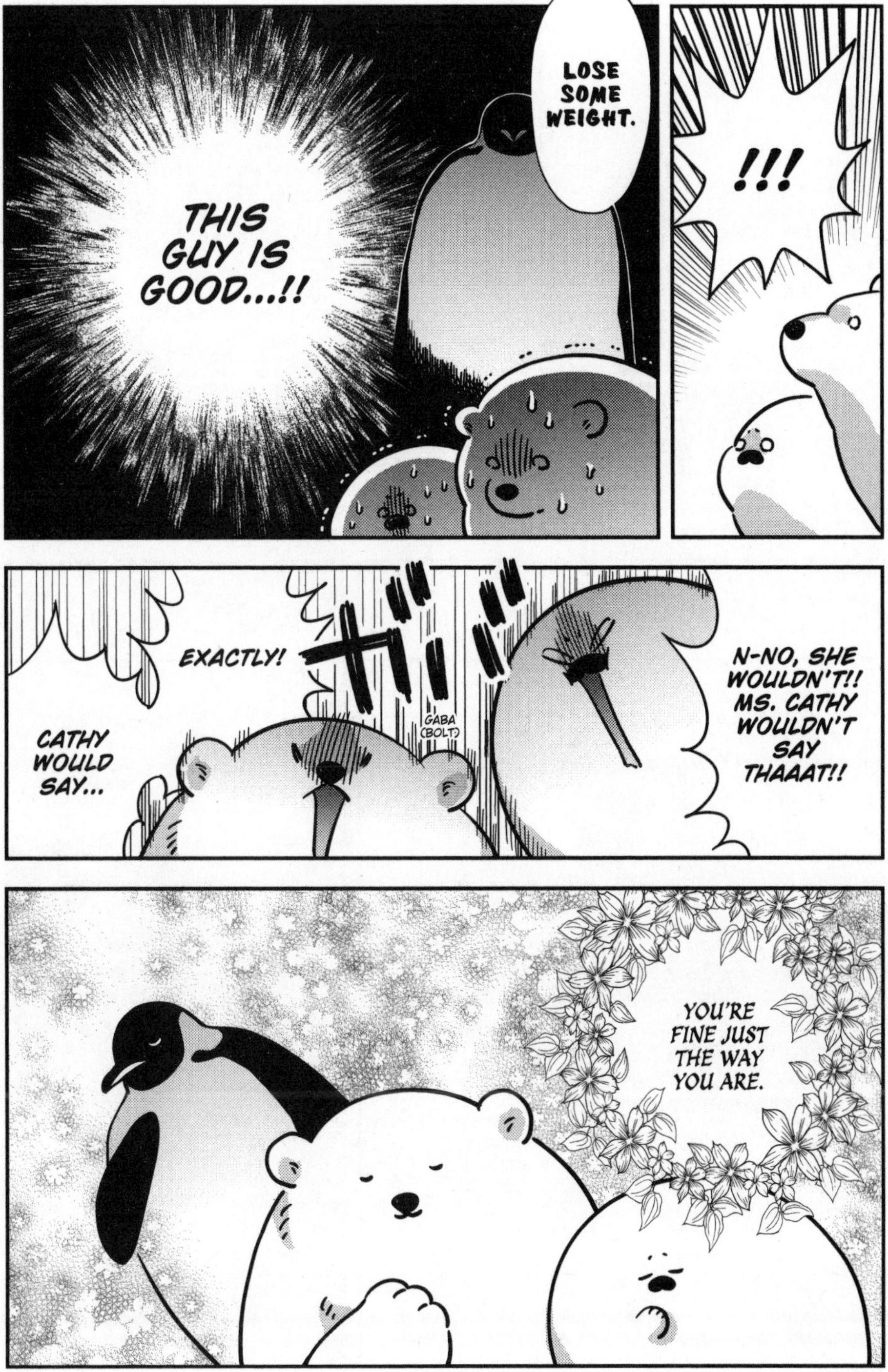
!!!
LOSE SOME WEIGHT.
THIS GUY IS GOOD...!!
N-NO, SHE WOULDN'T!! MS. CATHY WOULDN'T SAY THAAAT!!
ガバ
GABA (BOLT)
EXACTLY!
CATHY WOULD SAY...
YOU'RE FINE JUST THE WAY YOU ARE.

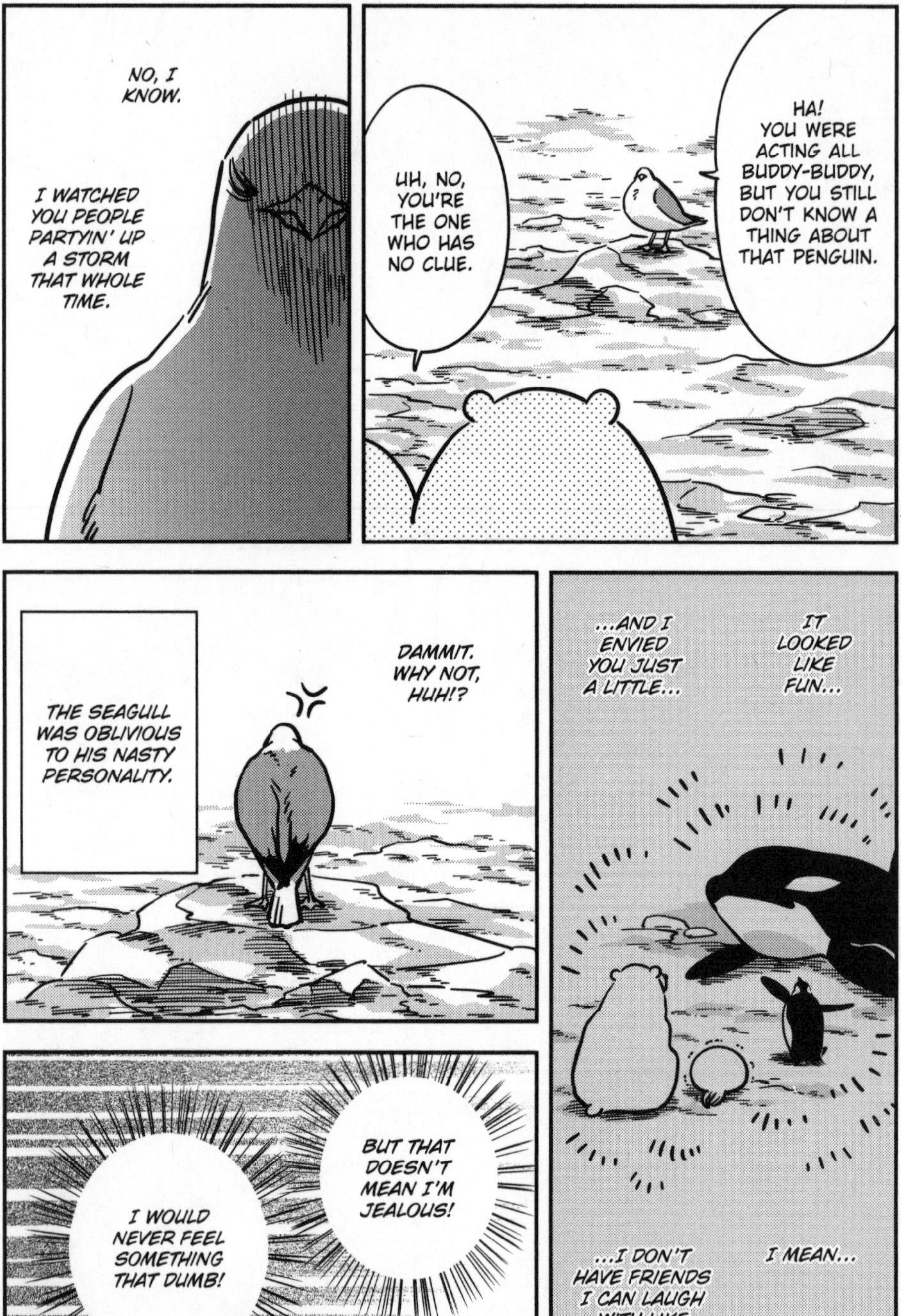
HA! YOU WERE ACTING ALL BUDDY-BUDDY, BUT YOU STILL DON'T KNOW A THING ABOUT THAT PENGUIN.
UH, NO, YOU'RE THE ONE WHO HAS NO CLUE.
NO, I KNOW.
I WATCHED YOU PEOPLE PARTYIN' UP A STORM THAT WHOLE TIME.
IT LOOKED LIKE FUN...
...AND I ENVIED YOU JUST A LITTLE...
I MEAN...
...I DON'T HAVE FRIENDS I CAN LAUGH WITH LIKE THAT.
DAMMIT. WHY NOT, HUH!?
THE SEAGULL WAS OBLIVIOUS TO HIS NASTY PERSONALITY.
BUT THAT DOESN'T MEAN I'M JEALOUS!
I WOULD NEVER FEEL SOMETHING THAT DUMB!

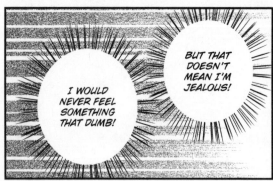

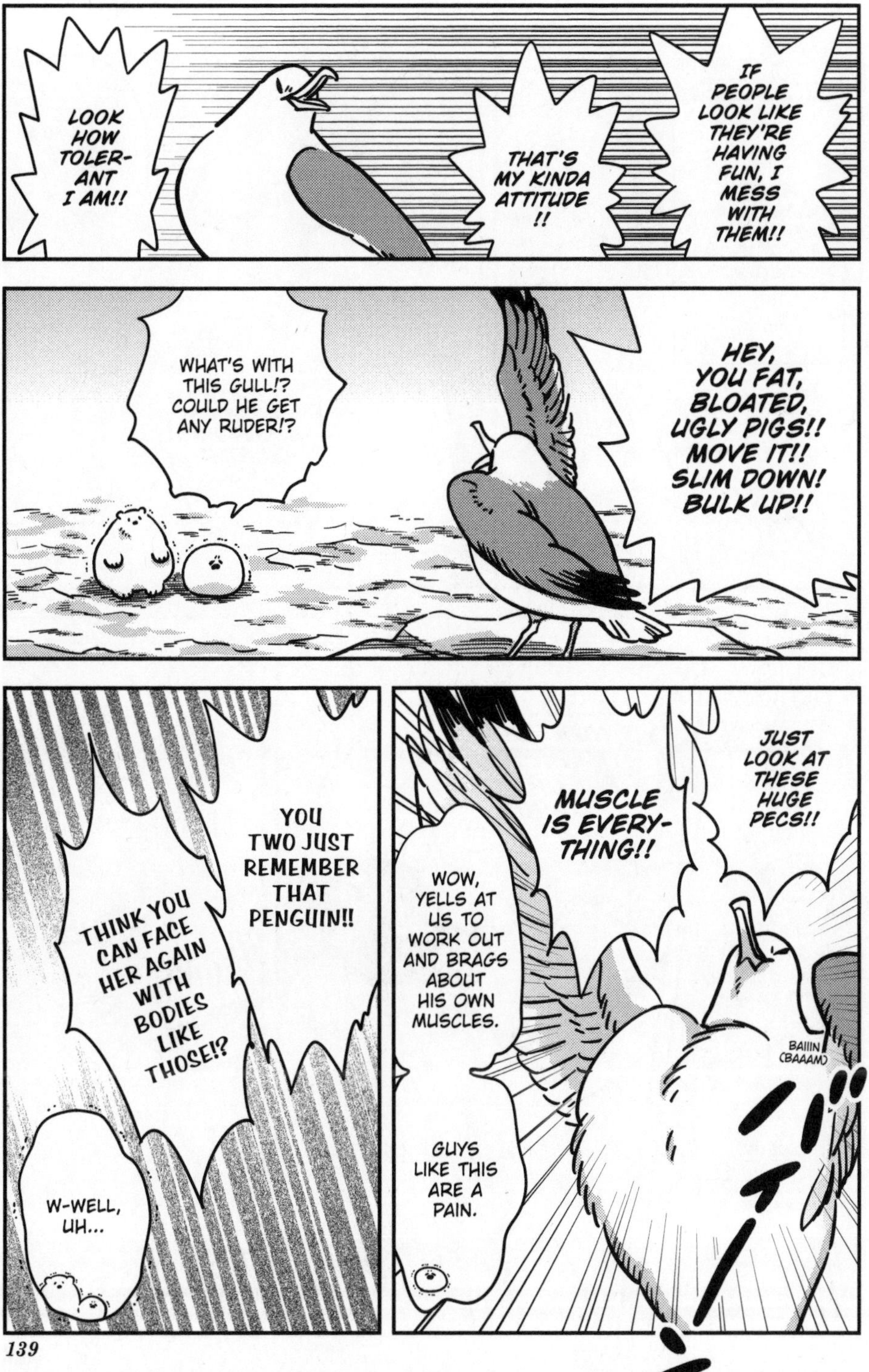

IF PEOPLE LOOK LIKE THEY'RE HAVING FUN, I MESS WITH THEM!!
THAT'S MY KINDA ATTITUDE!!
LOOK HOW TOLER-ANT I AM!!
HEY, YOU FAT, BLOATED, UGLY PIGS!! MOVE IT!! SLIM DOWN! BULK UP!!
WHAT'S WITH THIS GULL!? COULD HE GET ANY RUDER!?
JUST LOOK AT THESE HUGE PECS!!
MUSCLE IS EVERY-THING!!
WOW, YELLS AT US TO WORK OUT AND BRAGS ABOUT HIS OWN MUSCLES.
BAIIIN (BAAAM)
GUYS LIKE THIS ARE A PAIN.
YOU TWO JUST REMEMBER THAT PENGUIN!!
THINK YOU CAN FACE HER AGAIN WITH BODIES LIKE THOSE!?
W-WELL, UH...

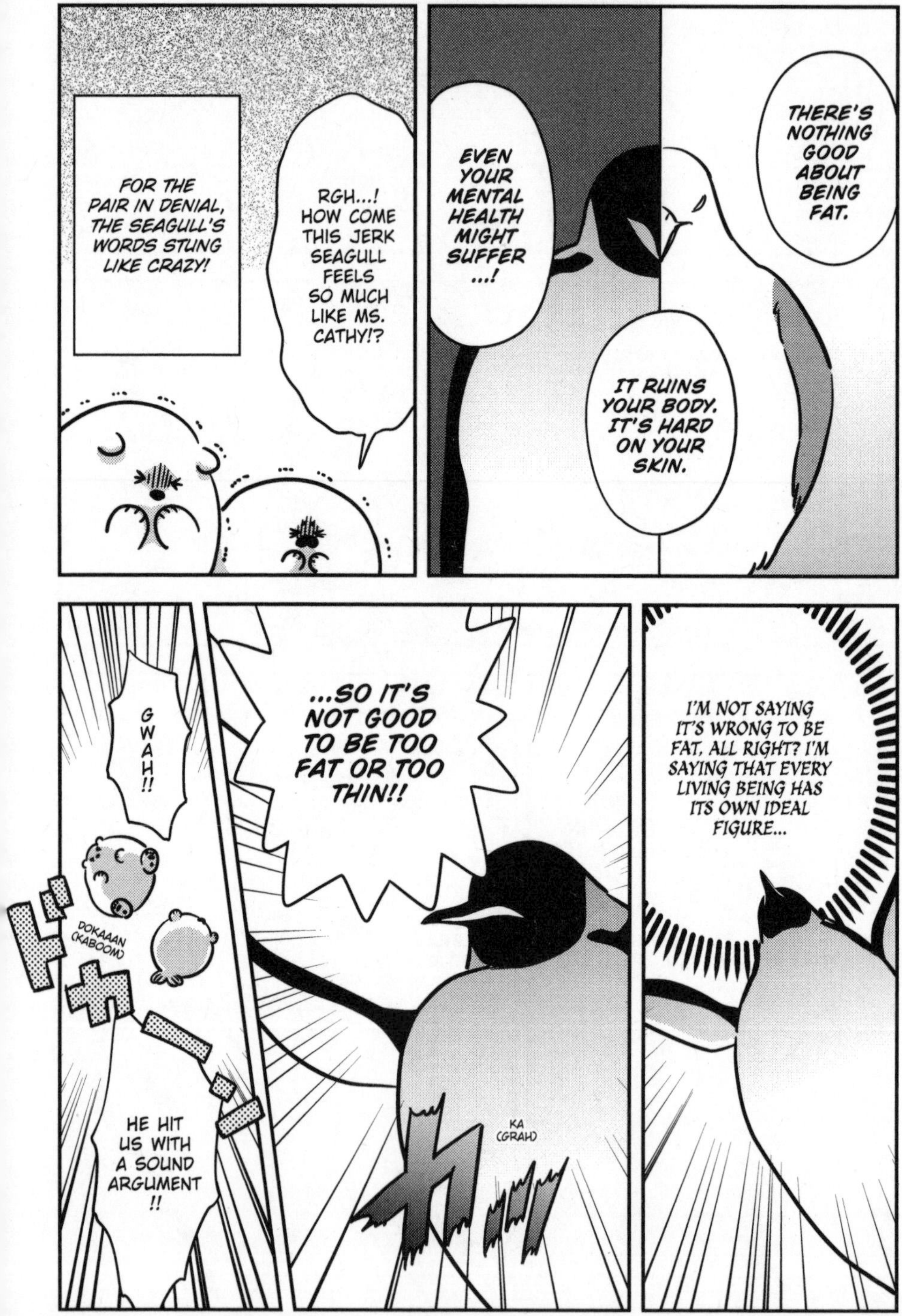
THERE'S NOTHING GOOD ABOUT BEING FAT.
IT RUINS YOUR BODY. IT'S HARD ON YOUR SKIN.
EVEN YOUR MENTAL HEALTH MIGHT SUFFER ...!
RGH...! HOW COME THIS JERK SEAGULL FEELS SO MUCH LIKE MS. CATHY!?
FOR THE PAIR IN DENIAL, THE SEAGULL'S WORDS STUNG LIKE CRAZY!
I'M NOT SAYING IT'S WRONG TO BE FAT, ALL RIGHT? I'M SAYING THAT EVERY LIVING BEING HAS ITS OWN IDEAL FIGURE...
...SO IT'S NOT GOOD TO BE TOO FAT OR TOO THIN!!
KA (GRAH)
GWAH!!
DOKAAAN (KABOOM)
HE HIT US WITH A SOUND ARGUMENT !!

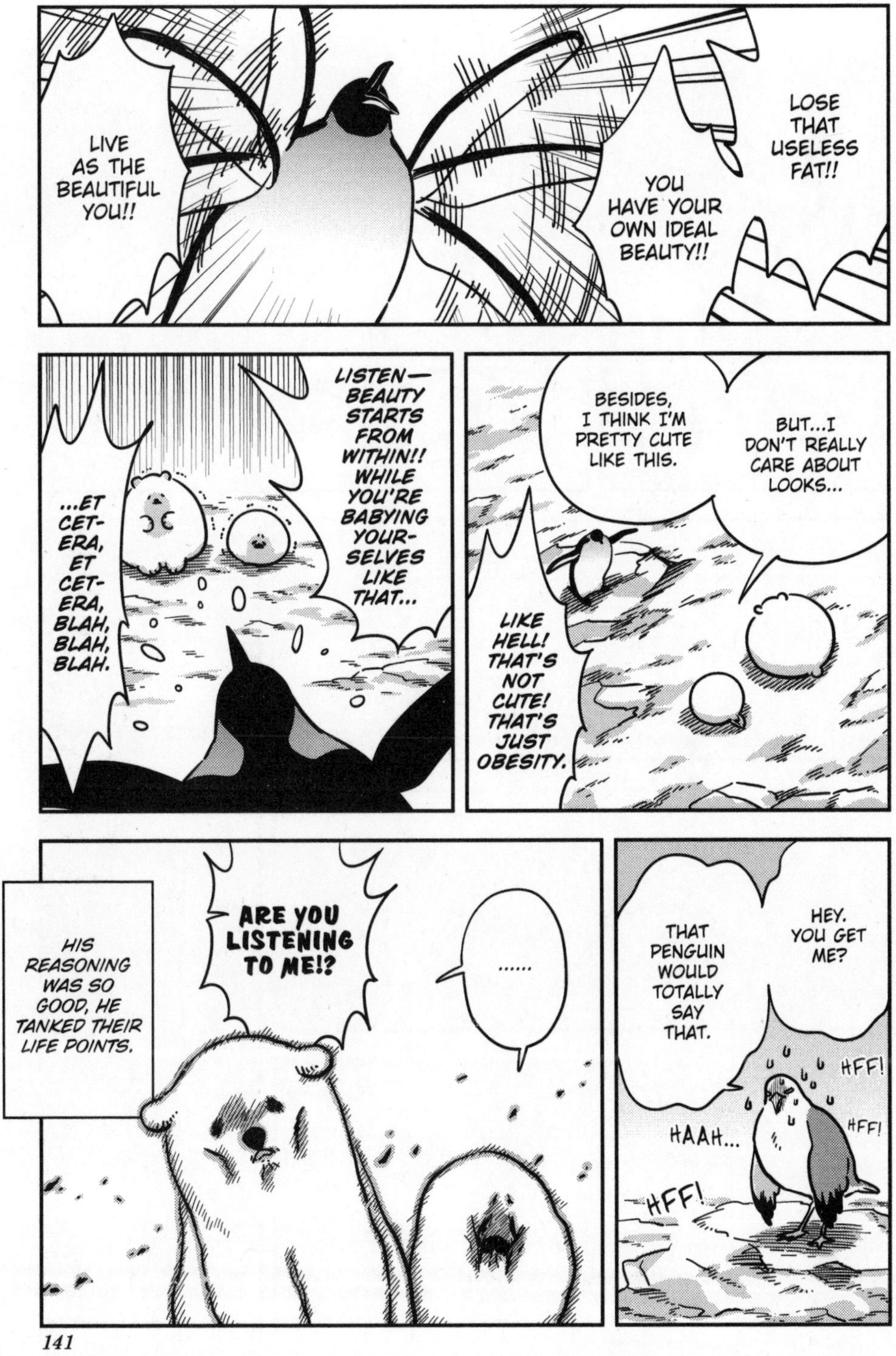
LOSE THAT USELESS FAT!!
YOU HAVE YOUR OWN IDEAL BEAUTY!!
LIVE AS THE BEAUTIFUL YOU!!
BUT...I DON'T REALLY CARE ABOUT LOOKS...
BESIDES, I THINK I'M PRETTY CUTE LIKE THIS.
LIKE HELL! THAT'S NOT CUTE! THAT'S JUST OBESITY.
LISTEN—BEAUTY STARTS FROM WITHIN!! WHILE YOU'RE BABYING YOURSELVES LIKE THAT...
...ET CETERA, ET CETERA, BLAH, BLAH, BLAH.
HEY. YOU GET ME?
THAT PENGUIN WOULD TOTALLY SAY THAT.
HFF!
HFF!
HAAH...
HFF!
......
ARE YOU LISTENING TO ME!?
HIS REASONING WAS SO GOOD, HE TANKED THEIR LIFE POINTS.

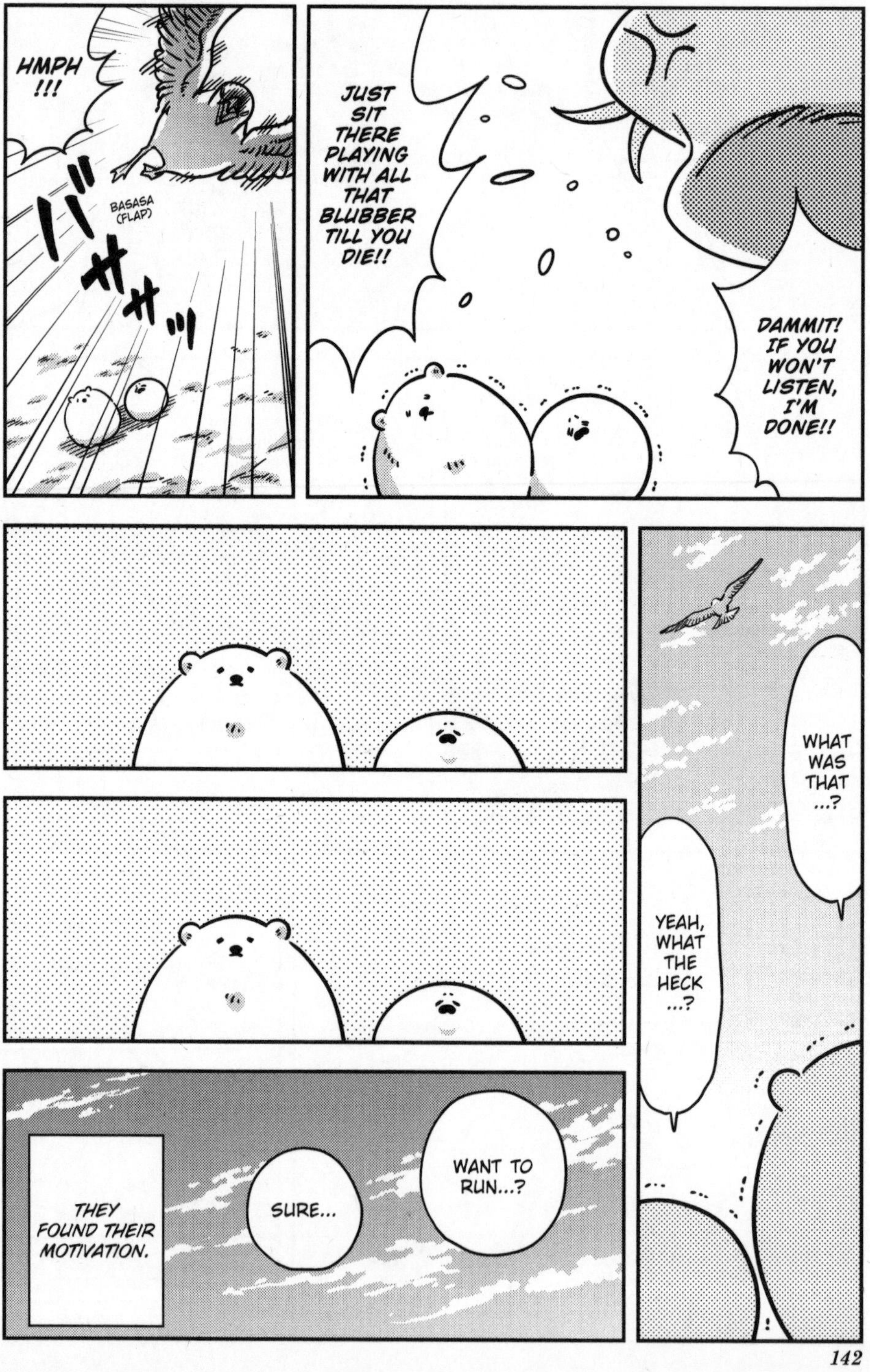
DAMMIT! IF YOU WON'T LISTEN, I'M DONE!!
JUST SIT THERE PLAYING WITH ALL THAT BLUBBER TILL YOU DIE!!
HMPH !!!
BASASA (FLAP)
バササッ
WHAT WAS THAT ...?
YEAH, WHAT THE HECK ...?
WANT TO RUN...?
SURE...
THEY FOUND THEIR MOTIVATION.

CHALLENGE ②

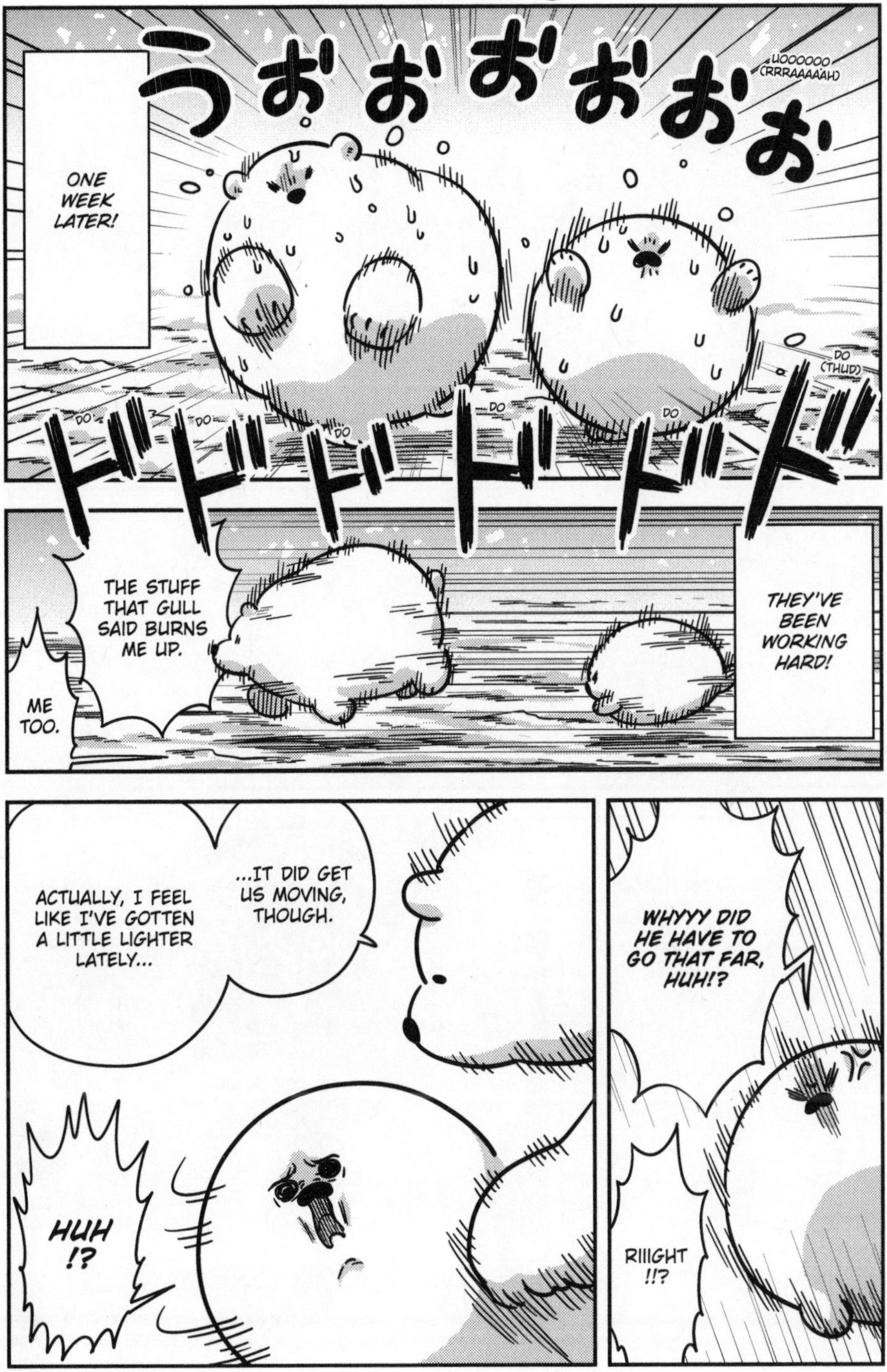
UOOOOOO (RRRAAAAAH)
ONE WEEK LATER!
DO (THUD)
DO DO DO DO DO
THEY'VE BEEN WORKING HARD!
THE STUFF THAT GULL SAID BURNS ME UP.
ME TOO.
WHYYY DID HE HAVE TO GO THAT FAR, HUH!?
RIIIGHT !!?
...IT DID GET US MOVING, THOUGH.
ACTUALLY, I FEEL LIKE I'VE GOTTEN A LITTLE LIGHTER LATELY...
HUH !?

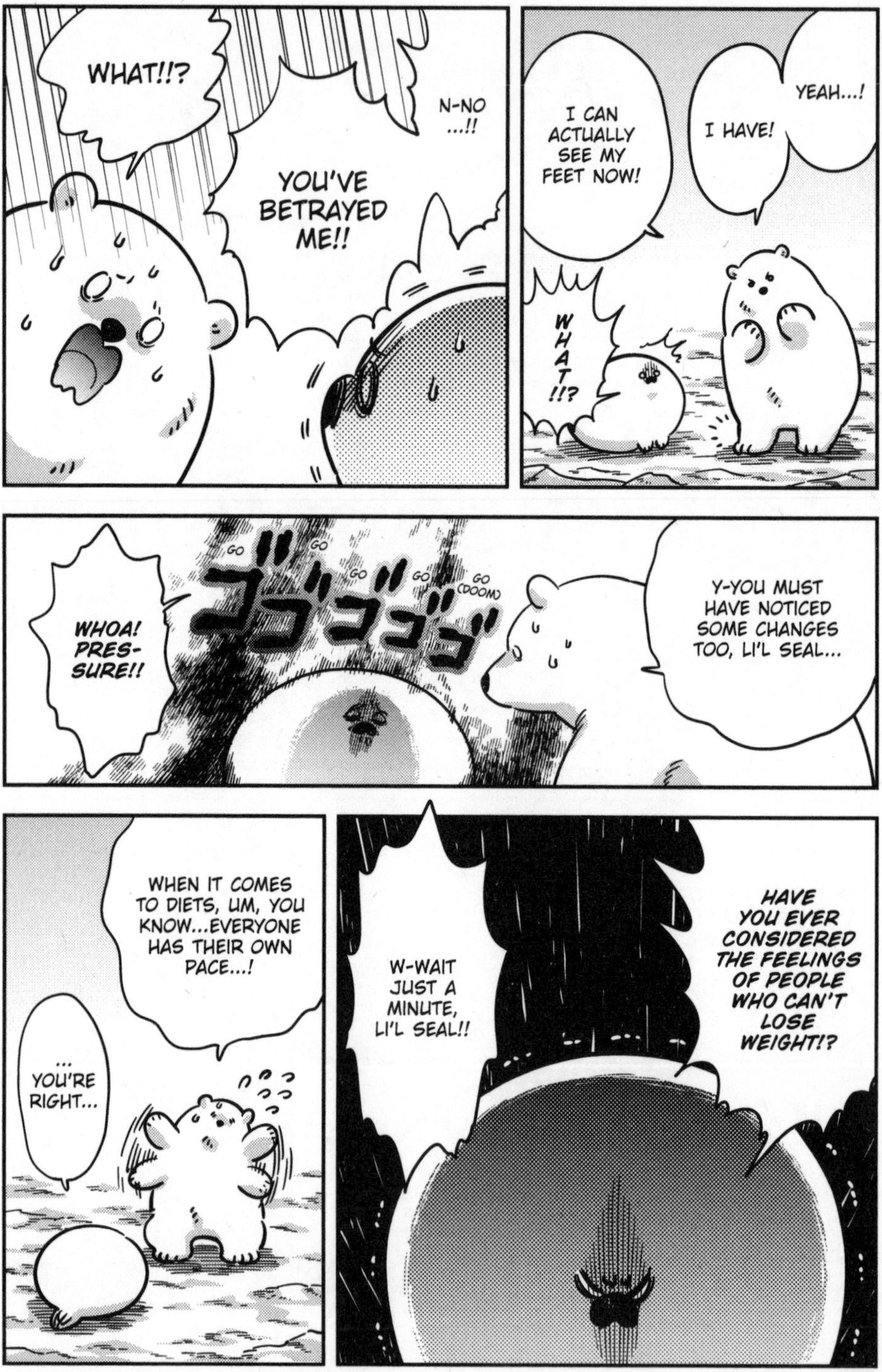
YEAH...!
I HAVE!
I CAN ACTUALLY SEE MY FEET NOW!
WHAT!!?
N-NO ...!!
YOU'VE BETRAYED ME!!
WHAT!!?
Y-YOU MUST HAVE NOTICED SOME CHANGES TOO, LI'L SEAL...
GO GO GO GO GO (DOOM)
WHOA! PRES-SURE!!
HAVE YOU EVER CONSIDERED THE FEELINGS OF PEOPLE WHO CAN'T LOSE WEIGHT!?
W-WAIT JUST A MINUTE, LI'L SEAL!!
WHEN IT COMES TO DIETS, UM, YOU KNOW...EVERYONE HAS THEIR OWN PACE...!
... YOU'RE RIGHT...

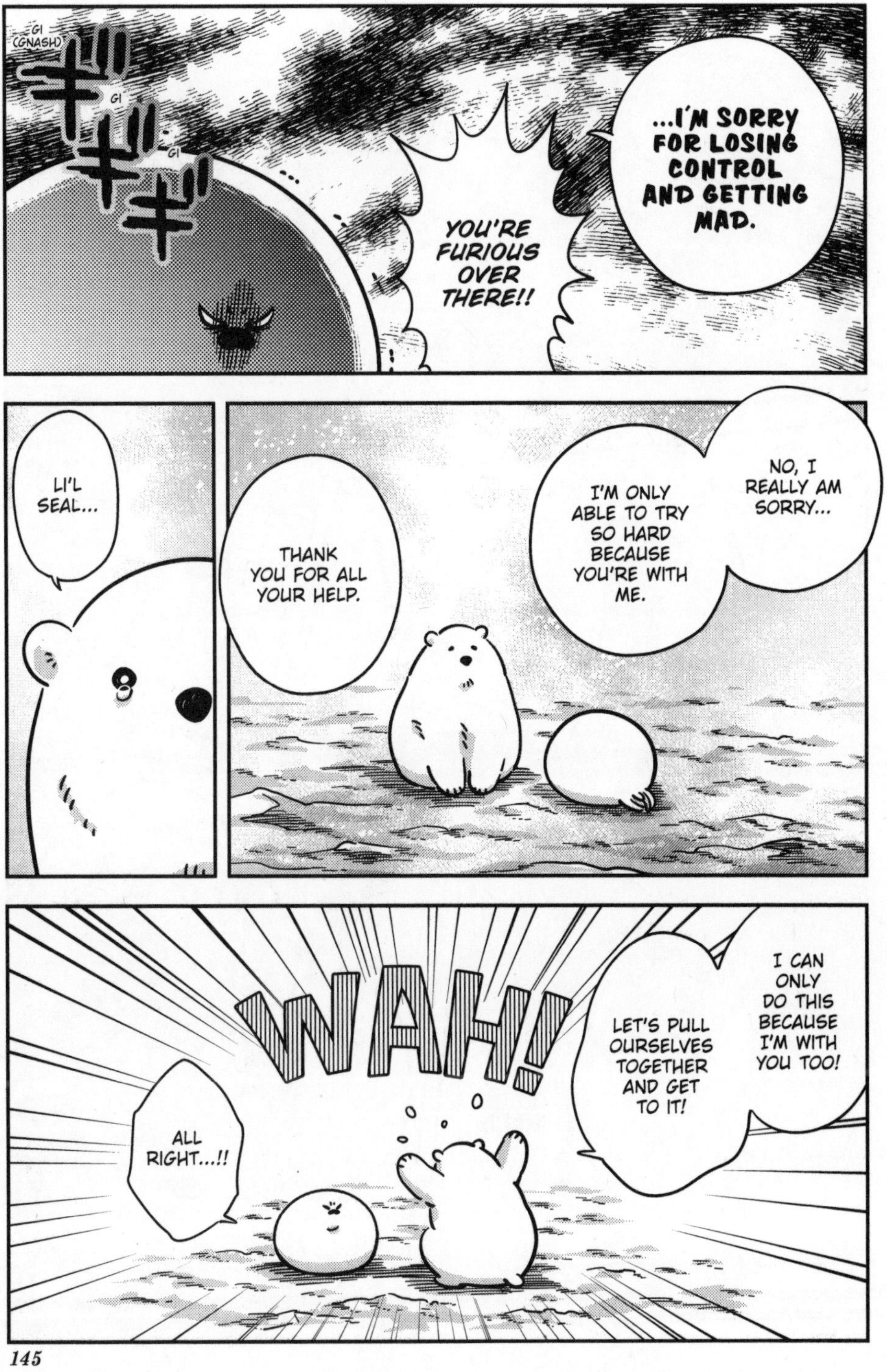
...I'M SORRY FOR LOSING CONTROL AND GETTING MAD.
YOU'RE FURIOUS OVER THERE!!
GI (GNASH)
GI
GI
NO, I REALLY AM SORRY...
I'M ONLY ABLE TO TRY SO HARD BECAUSE YOU'RE WITH ME.
THANK YOU FOR ALL YOUR HELP.
LI'L SEAL...
I CAN ONLY DO THIS BECAUSE I'M WITH YOU TOO!
LET'S PULL OURSELVES TOGETHER AND GET TO IT!
WAH!
ALL RIGHT...!!

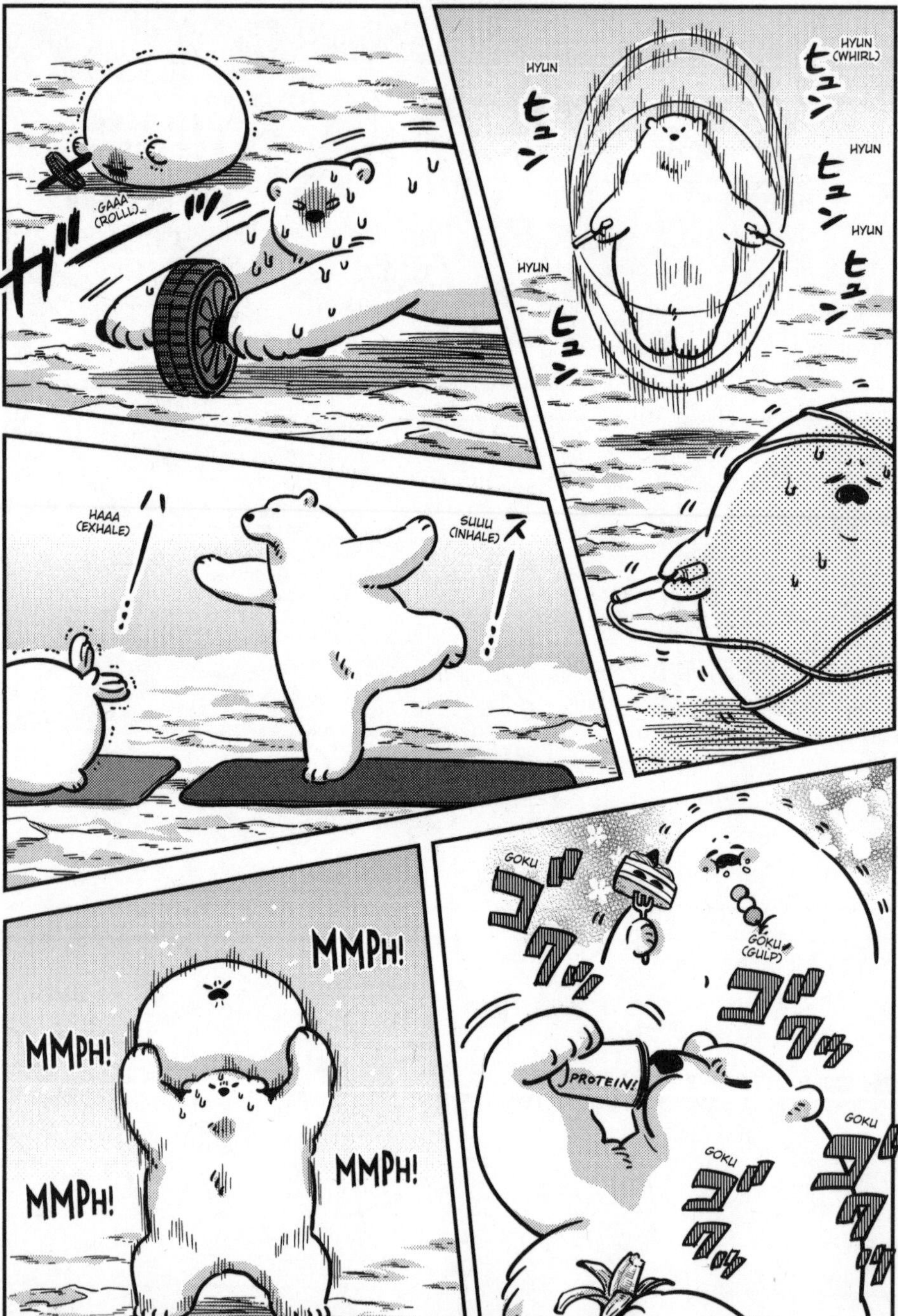
ヒュン
HYUN (WHIRL)
ヒュン
HYUN
ヒュン
HYUN
ヒュン
HYUN
ヒュン
HYUN
ガー
GAAA (ROLLL)
ス
SUUU (INHALE)
ハ
HAAA (EXHALE)
ゴクッ
GOKU
ゴクッ
GOKU (GULP)
PROTEIN!
ゴクッ
GOKU
ゴクッ
GOKU
MMPH!
MMPH!
MMPH!
MMPH!

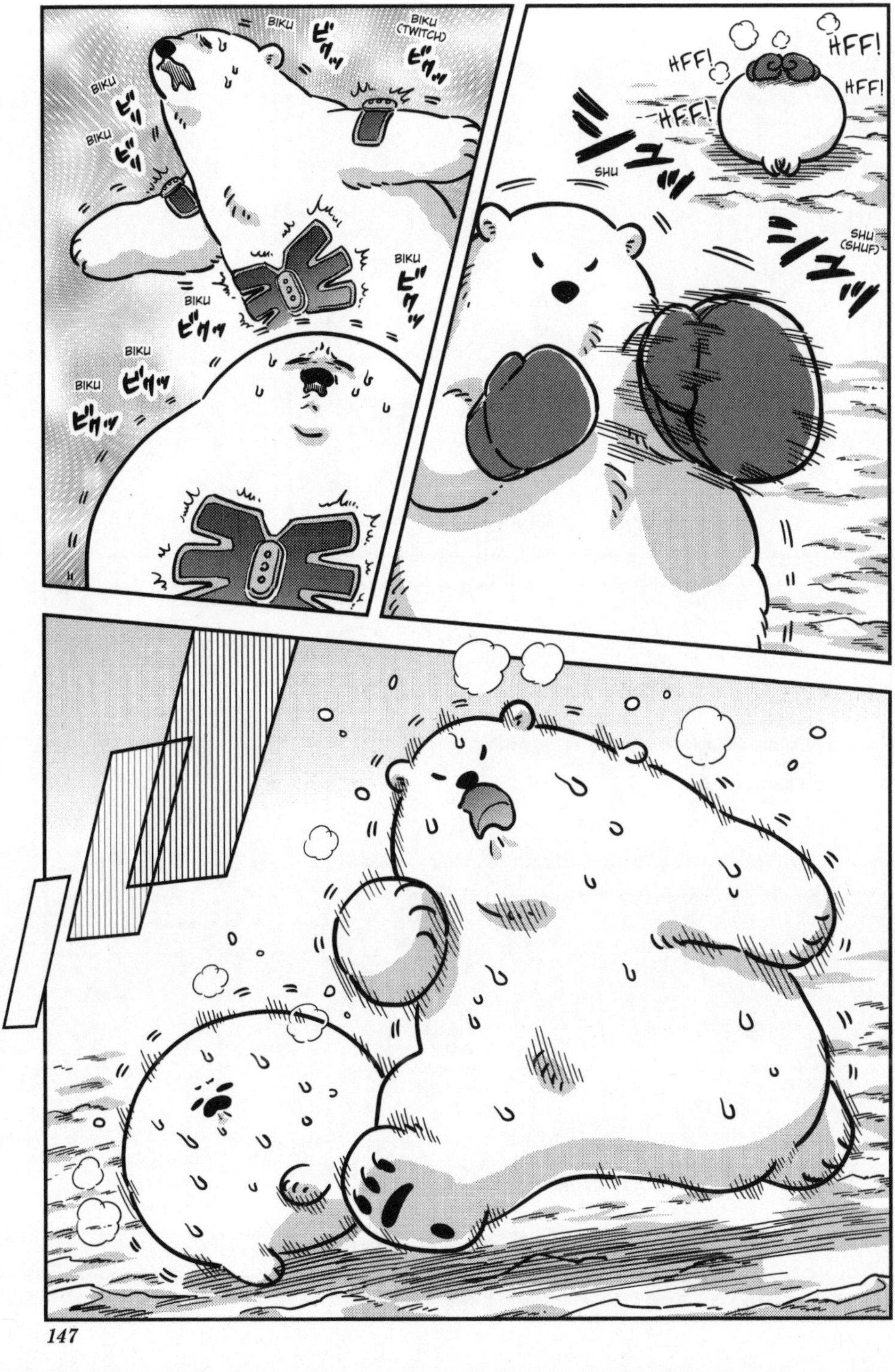
HFF!
HFF!
HFF!
HFF!
SHU
シュッ
SHU (SHUF)
シュッ
BIKU (TWITCH)
ビクッ
BIKU
ビクッ
BIKU
ビッ
BIKU
ビッ
BIKU
ビクッ
BIKU
ビクッ
BIKU
ビクッ
BIKU
ビクッ

NICE BULK!

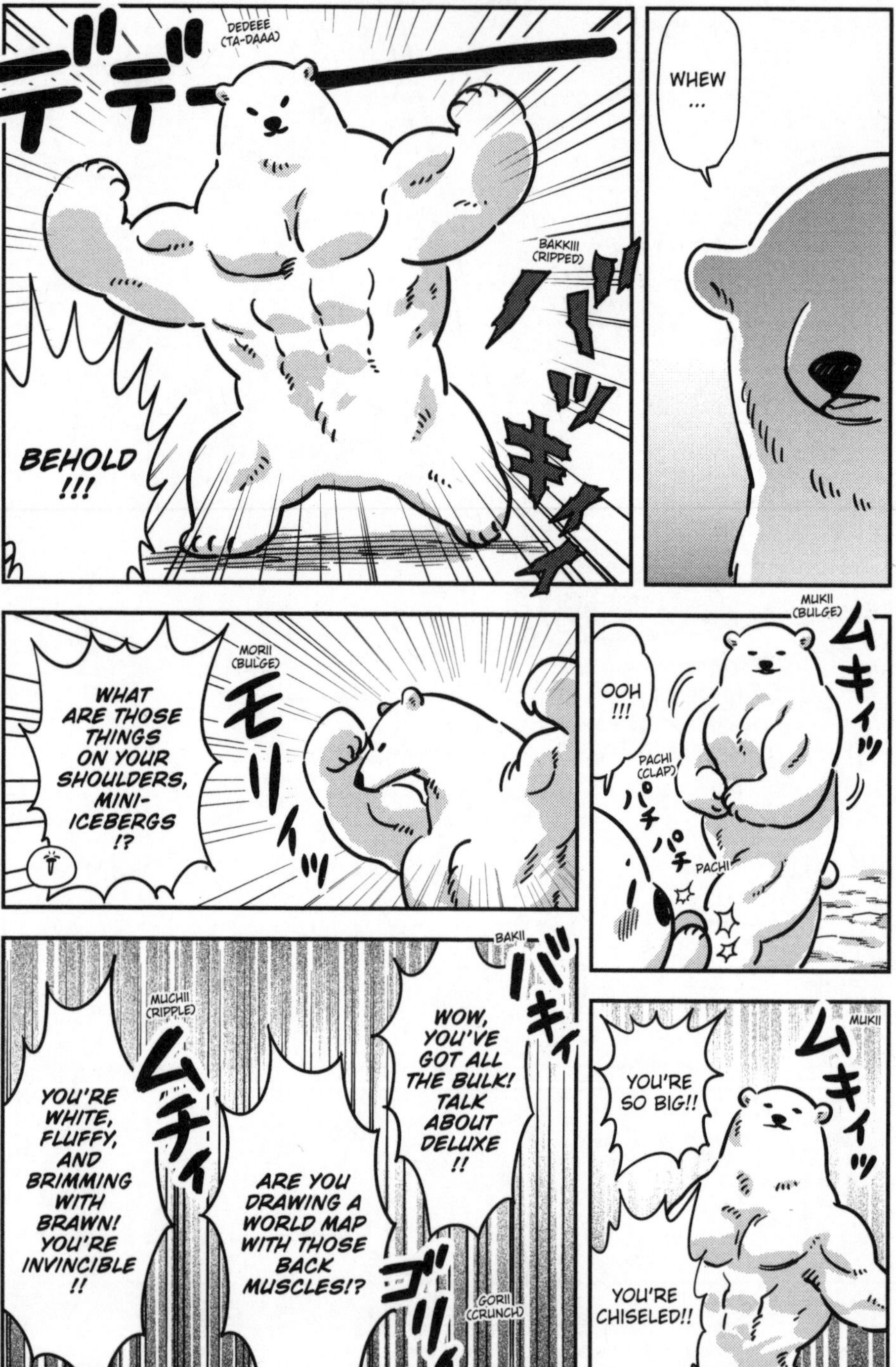
WHEW ...
DEDEEE (TA-DAAA)
BAKKIII (RIPPED)
BEHOLD !!!
MUKII (BULGE)
OOH !!!
PACHI (CLAP)
PACHI
MORII (BULGE)
WHAT ARE THOSE THINGS ON YOUR SHOULDERS, MINI-ICEBERGS !?
MUKII
YOU'RE SO BIG!!
YOU'RE CHISELED!!
BAKII
WOW, YOU'VE GOT ALL THE BULK! TALK ABOUT DELUXE !!
ARE YOU DRAWING A WORLD MAP WITH THOSE BACK MUSCLES!?
GORII (CRUNCH)
MUCHII (RIPPLE)
YOU'RE WHITE, FLUFFY, AND BRIMMING WITH BRAWN! YOU'RE INVINCIBLE !!

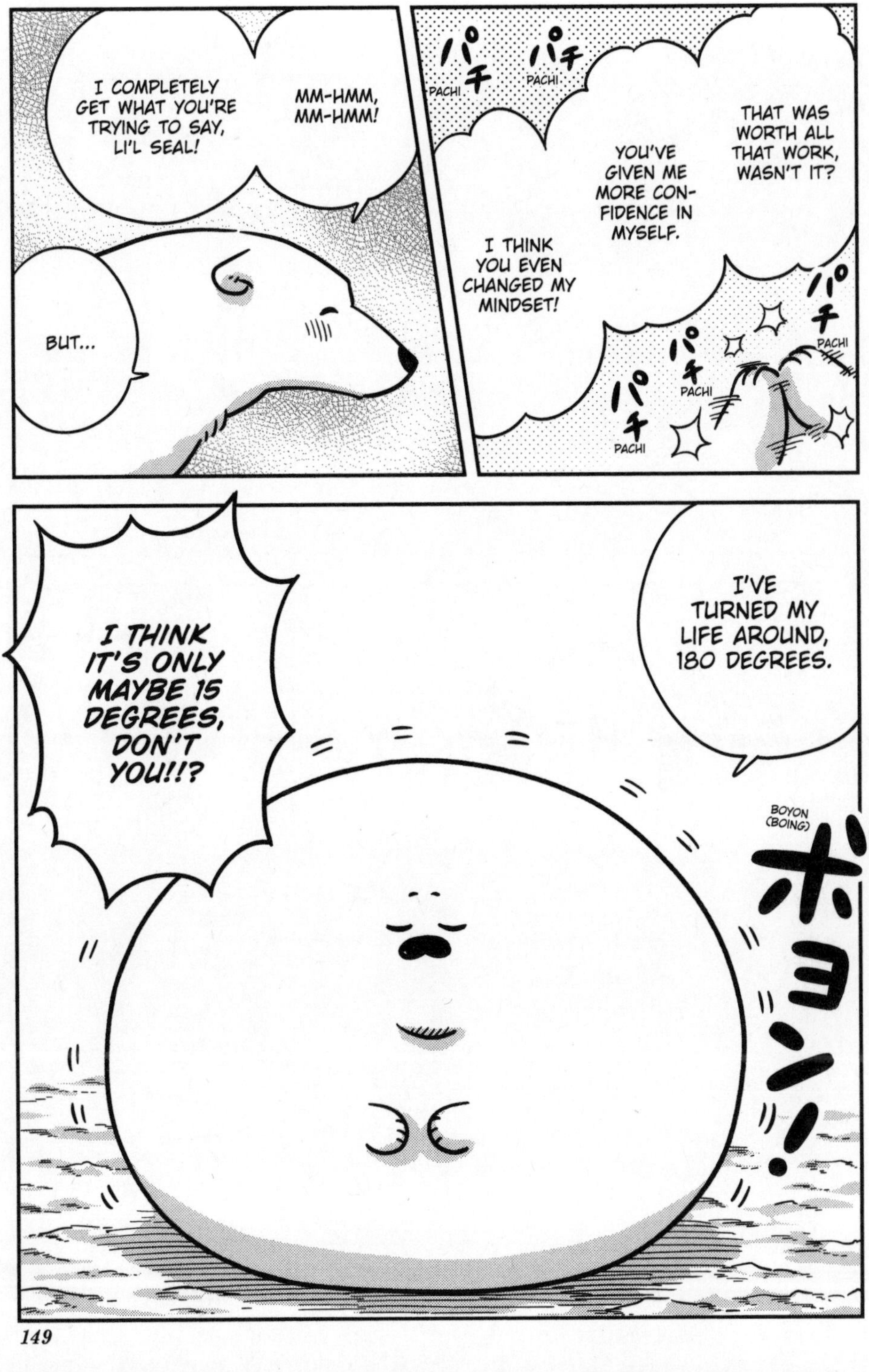
パチ PACHI
パチ PACHI
THAT WAS WORTH ALL THAT WORK, WASN'T IT?
YOU'VE GIVEN ME MORE CON-FIDENCE IN MYSELF.
I THINK YOU EVEN CHANGED MY MINDSET!
パチ PACHI
パチ PACHI
パチ PACHI
MM-HMM, MM-HMM!
I COMPLETELY GET WHAT YOU'RE TRYING TO SAY, LI'L SEAL!
BUT...
I'VE TURNED MY LIFE AROUND, 180 DEGREES.
ボヨン!! BOYON (BOING)
I THINK IT'S ONLY MAYBE 15 DEGREES, DON'T YOU!!?

TO BE CONTINUED IN VOLUME 6 ♥

[BONUS MANGA] A SPECIAL ANNIVERSARY ♥

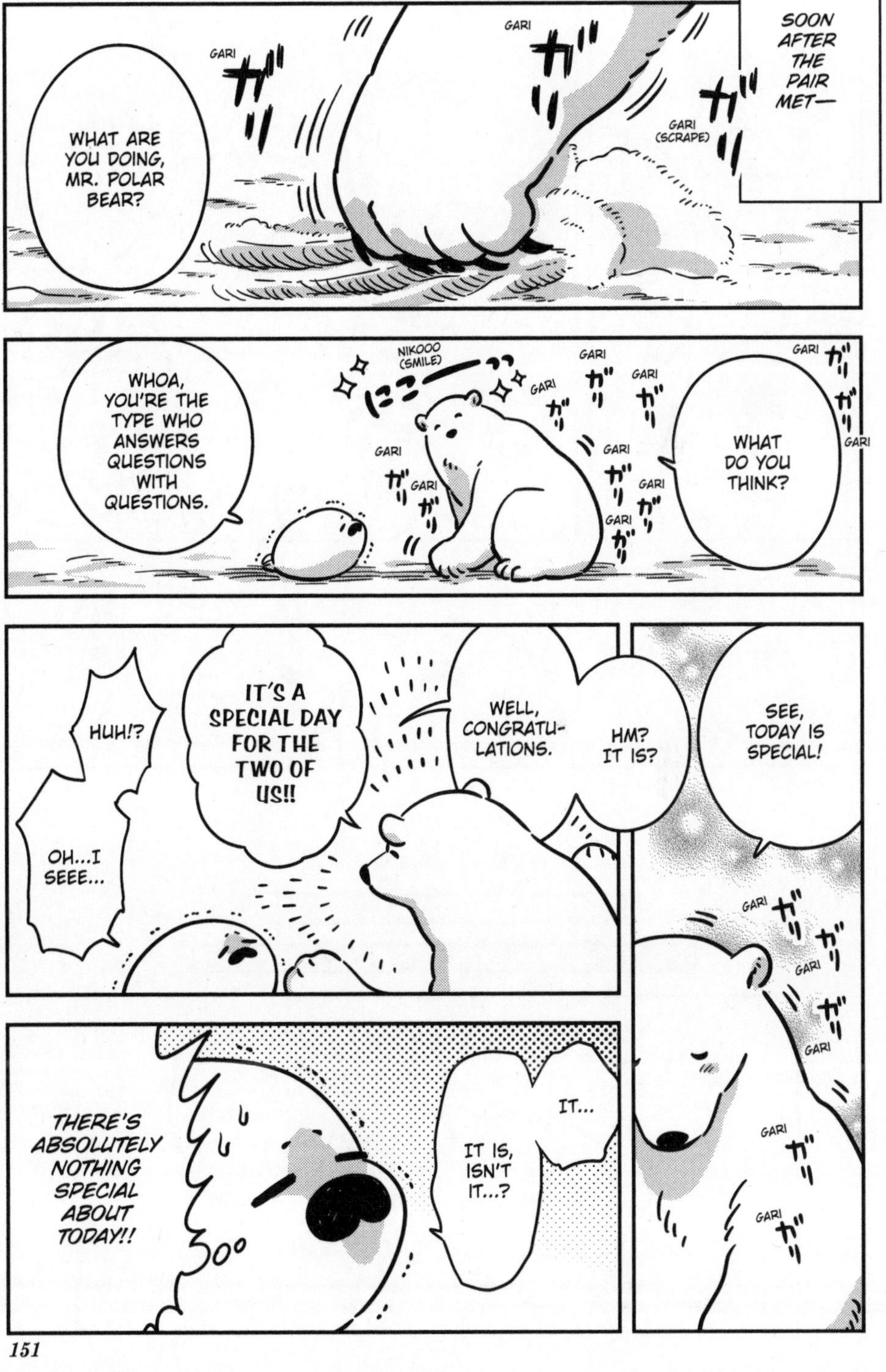
SOON AFTER THE PAIR MET—
GARI (SCRAPE)
GARI
GARI
WHAT ARE YOU DOING, MR. POLAR BEAR?
WHAT DO YOU THINK?
GARI
GARI
NIKOOO (SMILE)
GARI
GARI
WHOA, YOU'RE THE TYPE WHO ANSWERS QUESTIONS WITH QUESTIONS.
SEE, TODAY IS SPECIAL!
GARI
GARI
GARI
GARI
GARI
HM? IT IS?
WELL, CONGRATULATIONS.
IT'S A SPECIAL DAY FOR THE TWO OF US!!
HUH!?
OH...I SEEE...
IT...
IT IS, ISN'T IT...?
THERE'S ABSOLUTELY NOTHING SPECIAL ABOUT TODAY!!

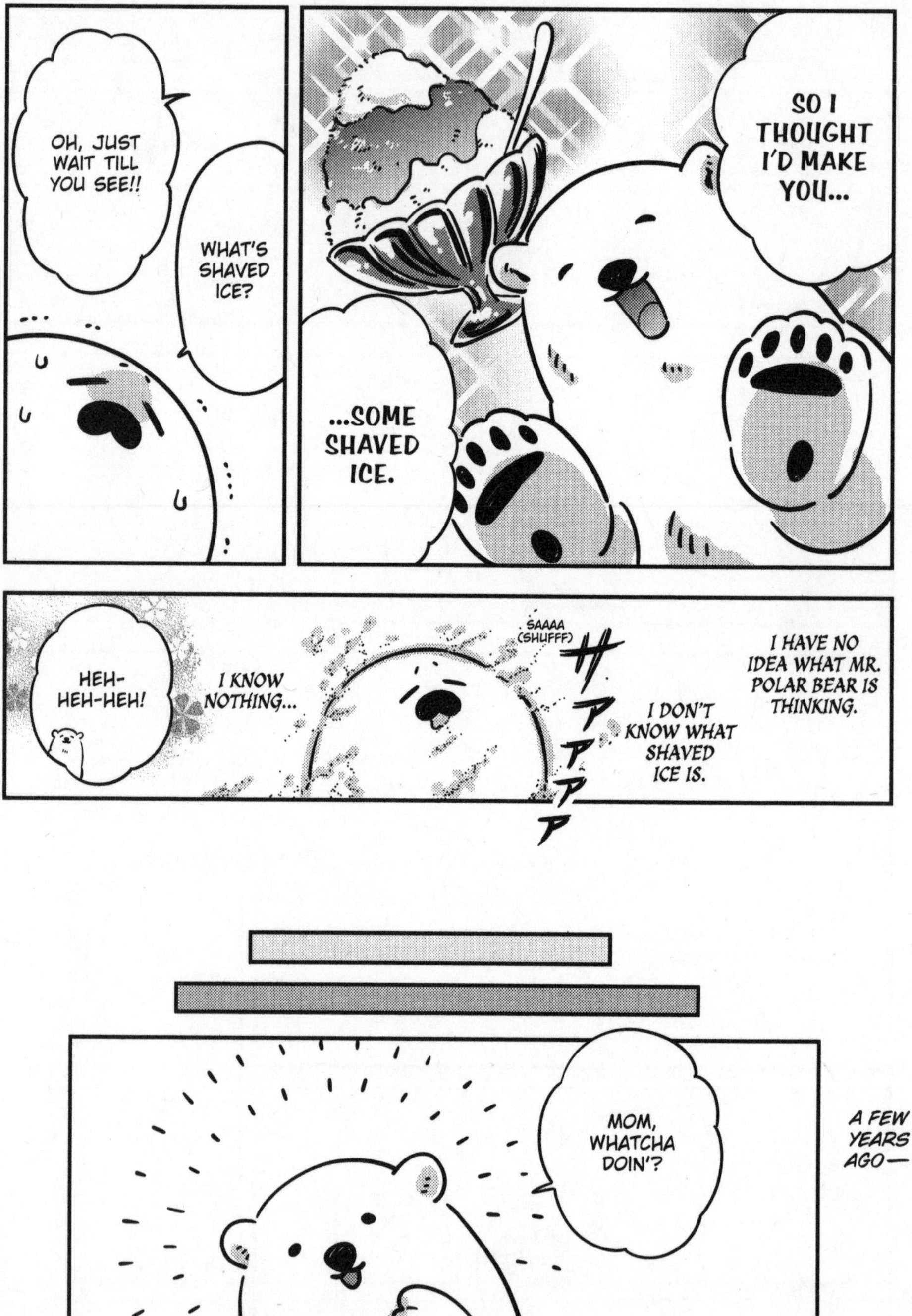
SO I THOUGHT I'D MAKE YOU...
...SOME SHAVED ICE.
WHAT'S SHAVED ICE?
OH, JUST WAIT TILL YOU SEE!!
I HAVE NO IDEA WHAT MR. POLAR BEAR IS THINKING.
I DON'T KNOW WHAT SHAVED ICE IS.
SAAAA (SHUFFF)
I KNOW NOTHING...
HEH-HEH-HEH!
A FEW YEARS AGO—
MOM, WHATCHA DOIN'?

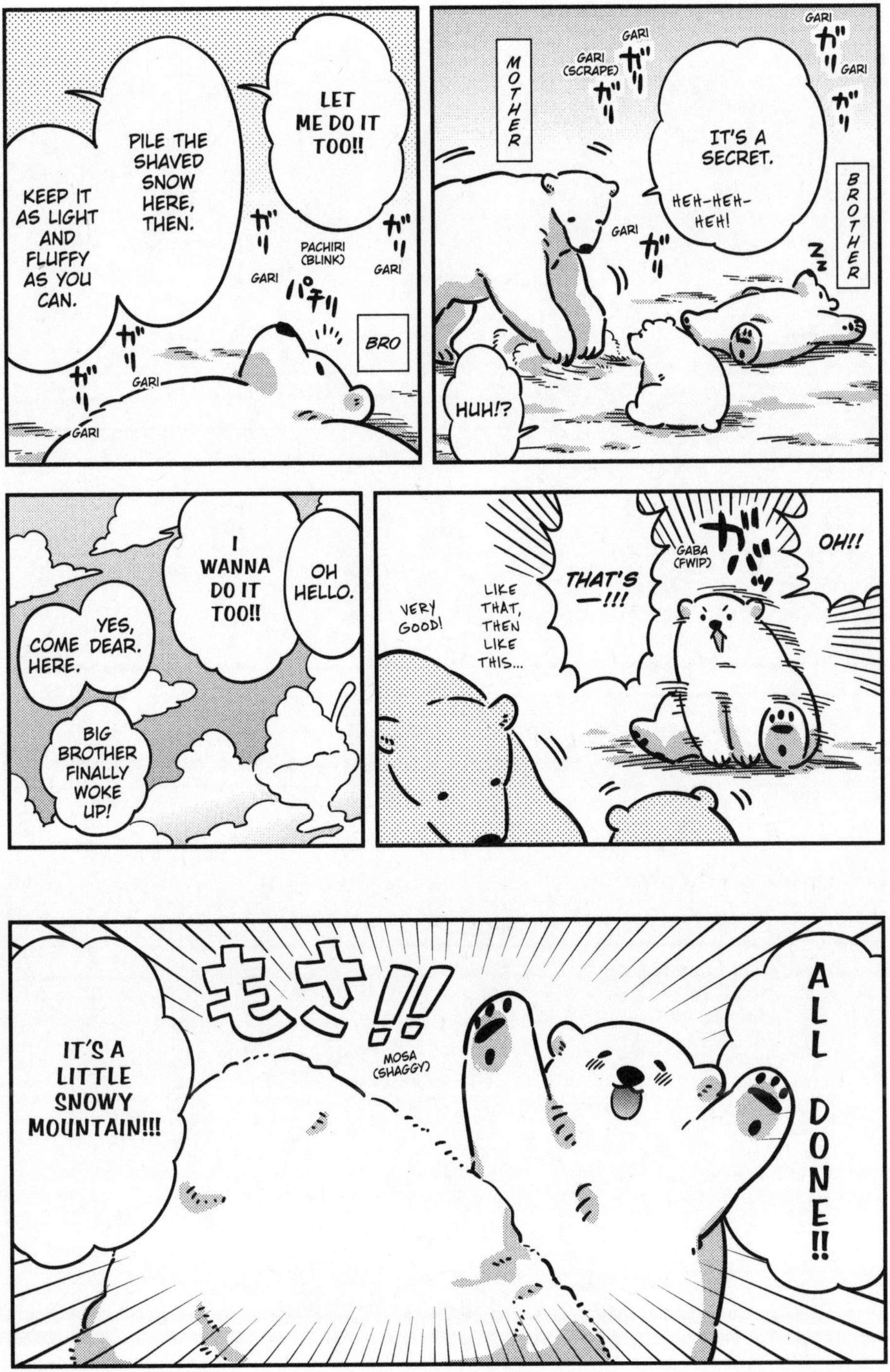
GARI ガリ GARI ガリ
IT'S A SECRET.
BROTHER
HEH-HEH-HEH!
MOTHER
GARI ガリ
GARI (SCRAPE) ガリ
GARI ガリ
HUH!?
LET ME DO IT TOO!!
PILE THE SHAVED SNOW HERE, THEN.
KEEP IT AS LIGHT AND FLUFFY AS YOU CAN.
GARI ガリ
PACHIRI (BLINK) パチリ
GARI ガリ
BRO
GARI ガリ
GARI ガリ
OH!!
GABA (FWIP) ガバッ
THAT'S—!!!
LIKE THAT, THEN LIKE THIS...
VERY GOOD!
OH HELLO.
I WANNA DO IT TOO!!
YES, DEAR. COME HERE.
BIG BROTHER FINALLY WOKE UP!
ALL DONE!!
もさ!!
MOSA (SHAGGY)
IT'S A LITTLE SNOWY MOUNTAIN!!!

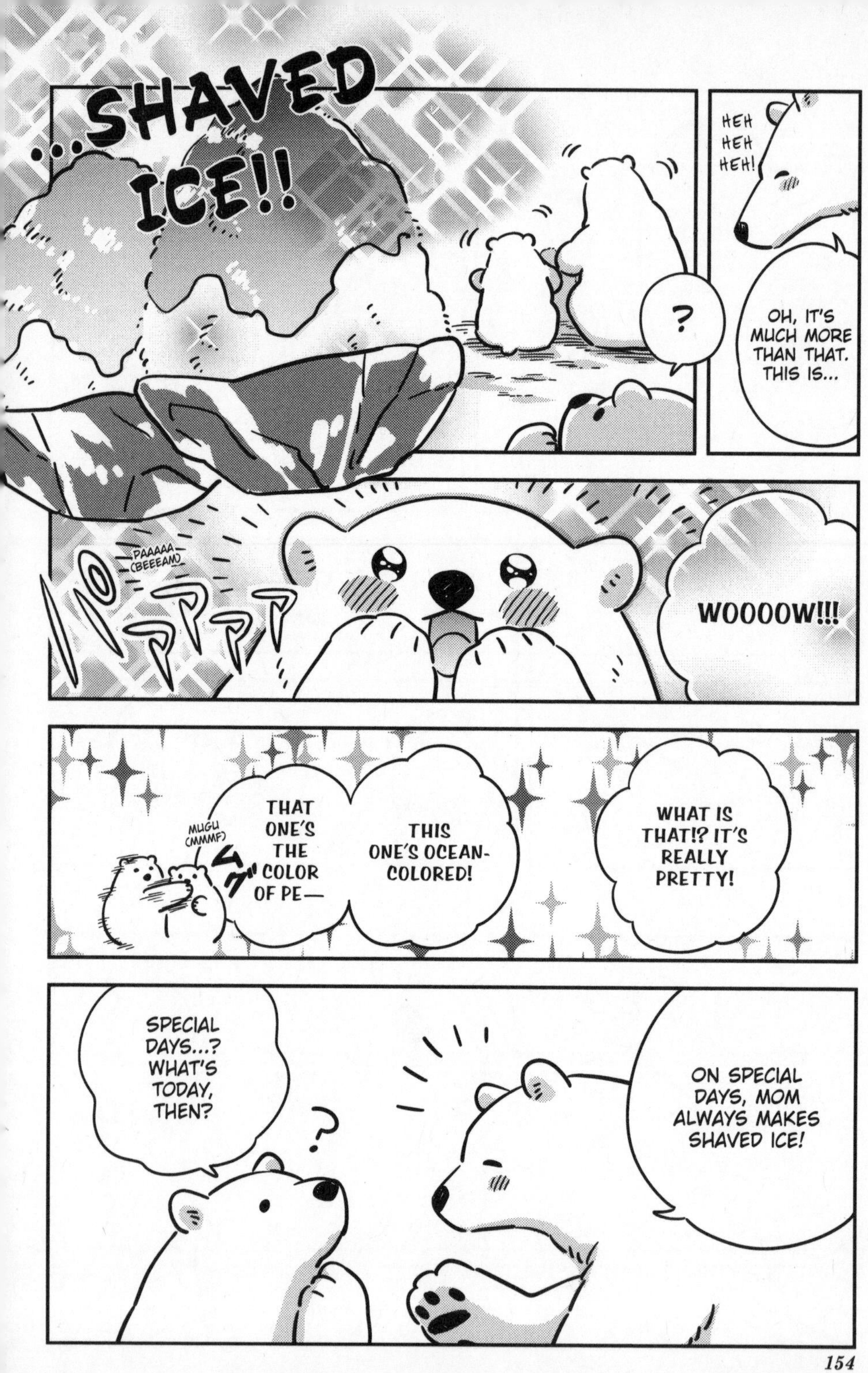
HEH HEH HEH!
OH, IT'S MUCH MORE THAN THAT. THIS IS...
...SHAVED ICE!!
?
WOOOOW!!!
PAAAAA (BEEEAM)
WHAT IS THAT!? IT'S REALLY PRETTY!
THIS ONE'S OCEAN-COLORED!
THAT ONE'S THE COLOR OF PE—
MUGU (MMMF)
ON SPECIAL DAYS, MOM ALWAYS MAKES SHAVED ICE!
SPECIAL DAYS...? WHAT'S TODAY, THEN?
?

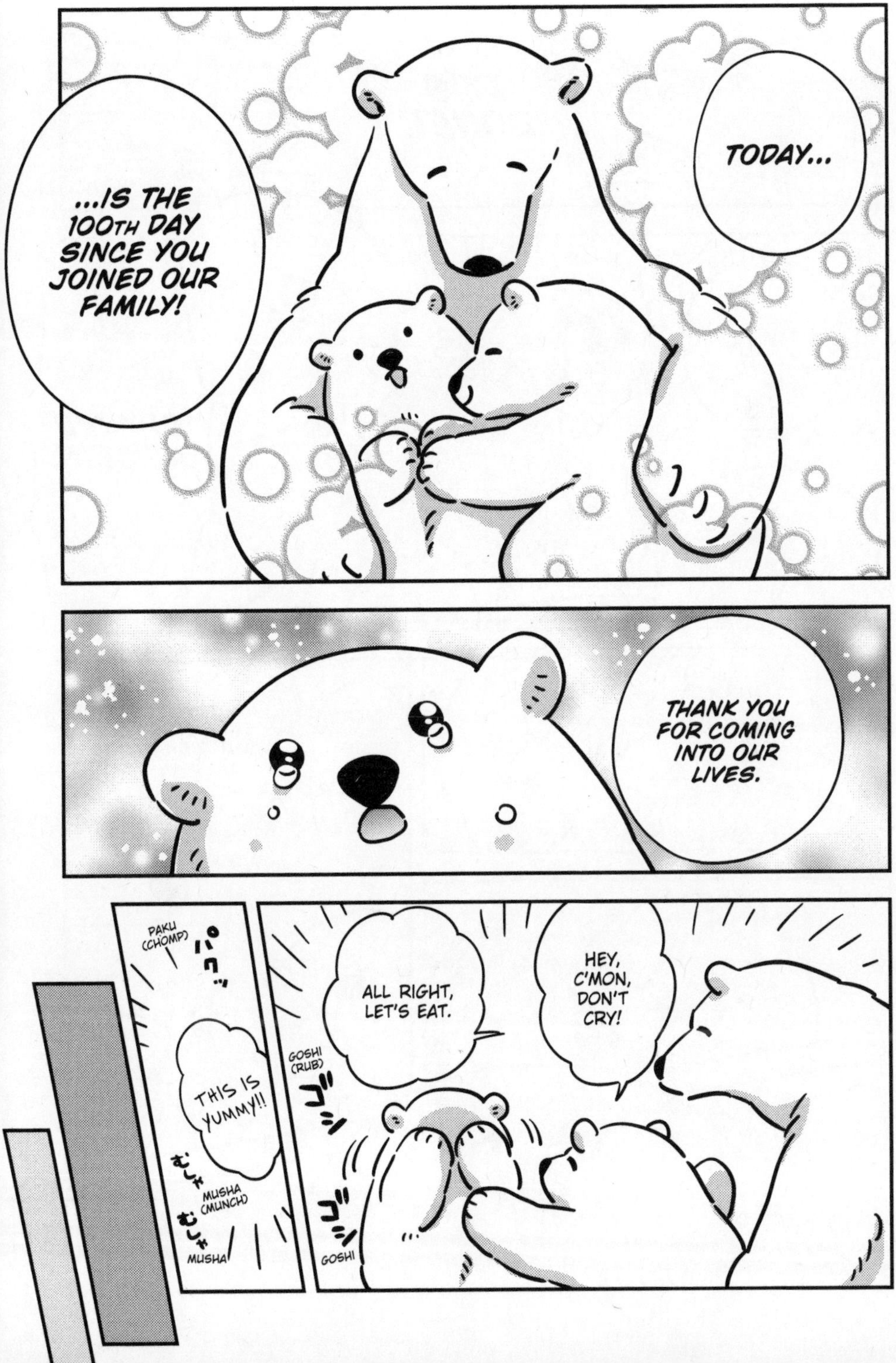
TODAY...
...IS THE 100TH DAY SINCE YOU JOINED OUR FAMILY!
THANK YOU FOR COMING INTO OUR LIVES.
HEY, C'MON, DON'T CRY!
ALL RIGHT, LET'S EAT.
GOSHI (RUB)
ゴシッ
ゴシッ
GOSHI
PAKU (CHOMP)
パクッ
THIS IS YUMMY!!
むしゃ
MUSHA (MUNCH)
むしゃ
MUSHA

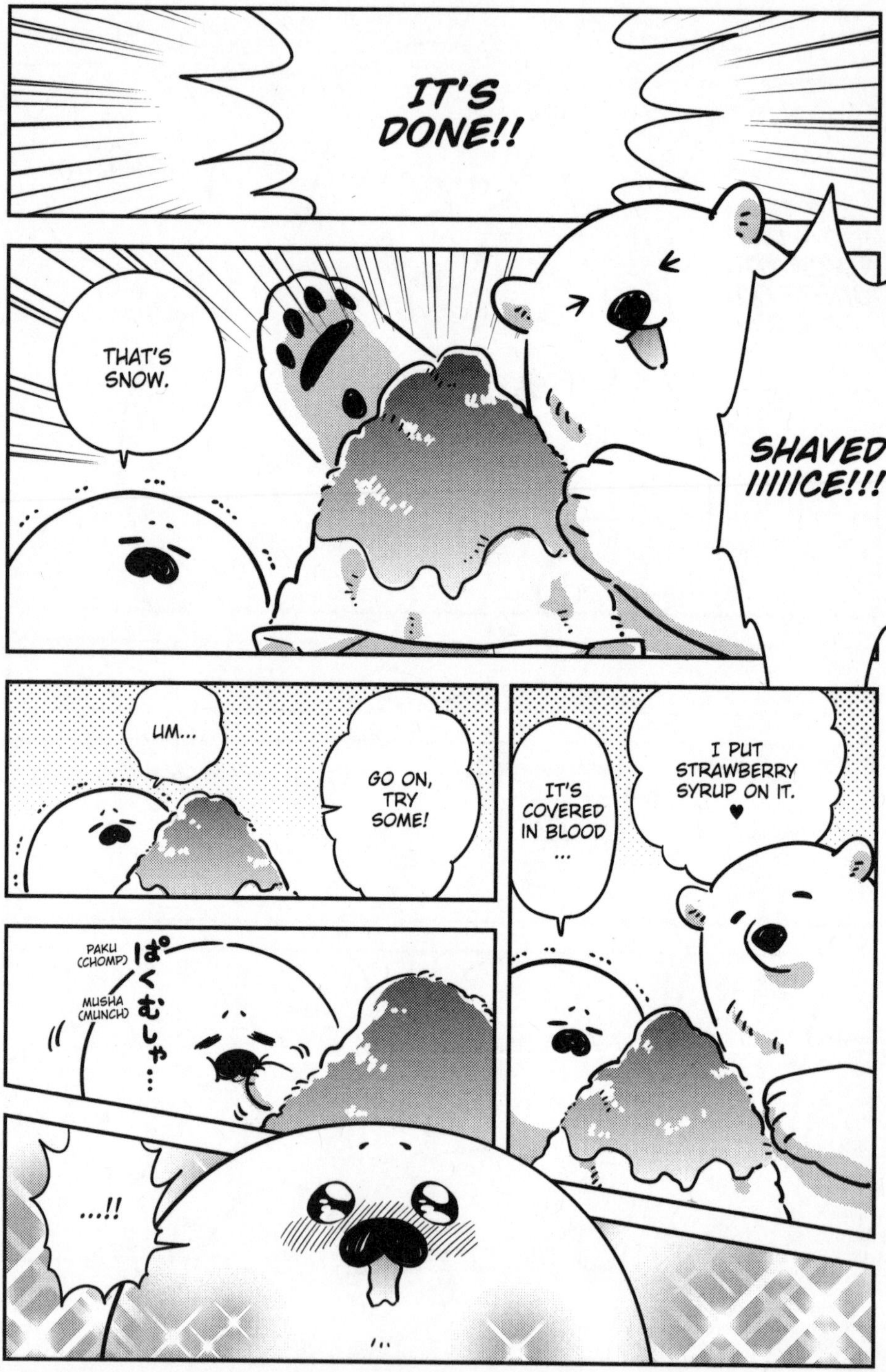
IT'S DONE!!
SHAVED IIIIICE!!!
THAT'S SNOW.
I PUT STRAWBERRY SYRUP ON IT. ♥
IT'S COVERED IN BLOOD ...
GO ON, TRY SOME!
UM...
PAKU (CHOMP)
MUSHA (MUNCH)
ぱくむしゃ…
...!!

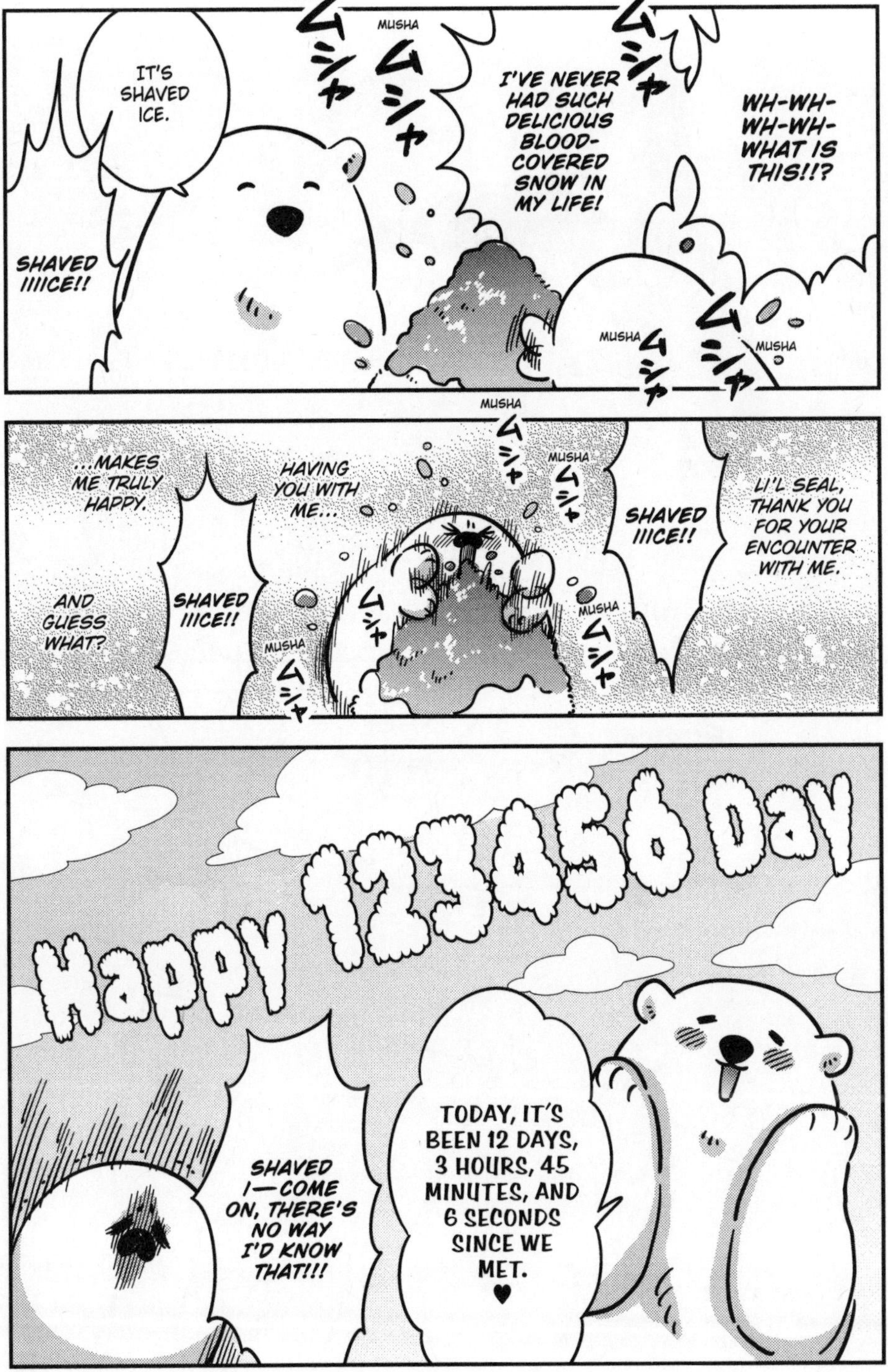

MUSHA ムシャ
WH-WH-WH-WH-WHAT IS THIS!!?
MUSHA ムシャ
I'VE NEVER HAD SUCH DELICIOUS BLOOD-COVERED SNOW IN MY LIFE!
MUSHA ムシャ
MUSHA ムシャ
MUSHA ムシャ
IT'S SHAVED ICE.
SHAVED IIIICE!!
LI'L SEAL, THANK YOU FOR YOUR ENCOUNTER WITH ME.
SHAVED IIICE!!
MUSHA ムシャ
MUSHA ムシャ
MUSHA ムシャ
HAVING YOU WITH ME...
...MAKES ME TRULY HAPPY.
SHAVED IIICE!!
AND GUESS WHAT?
MUSHA ムシャ
Happy 123456 Day
TODAY, IT'S BEEN 12 DAYS, 3 HOURS, 45 MINUTES, AND 6 SECONDS SINCE WE MET. ♥
SHAVED I—COME ON, THERE'S NO WAY I'D KNOW THAT!!!

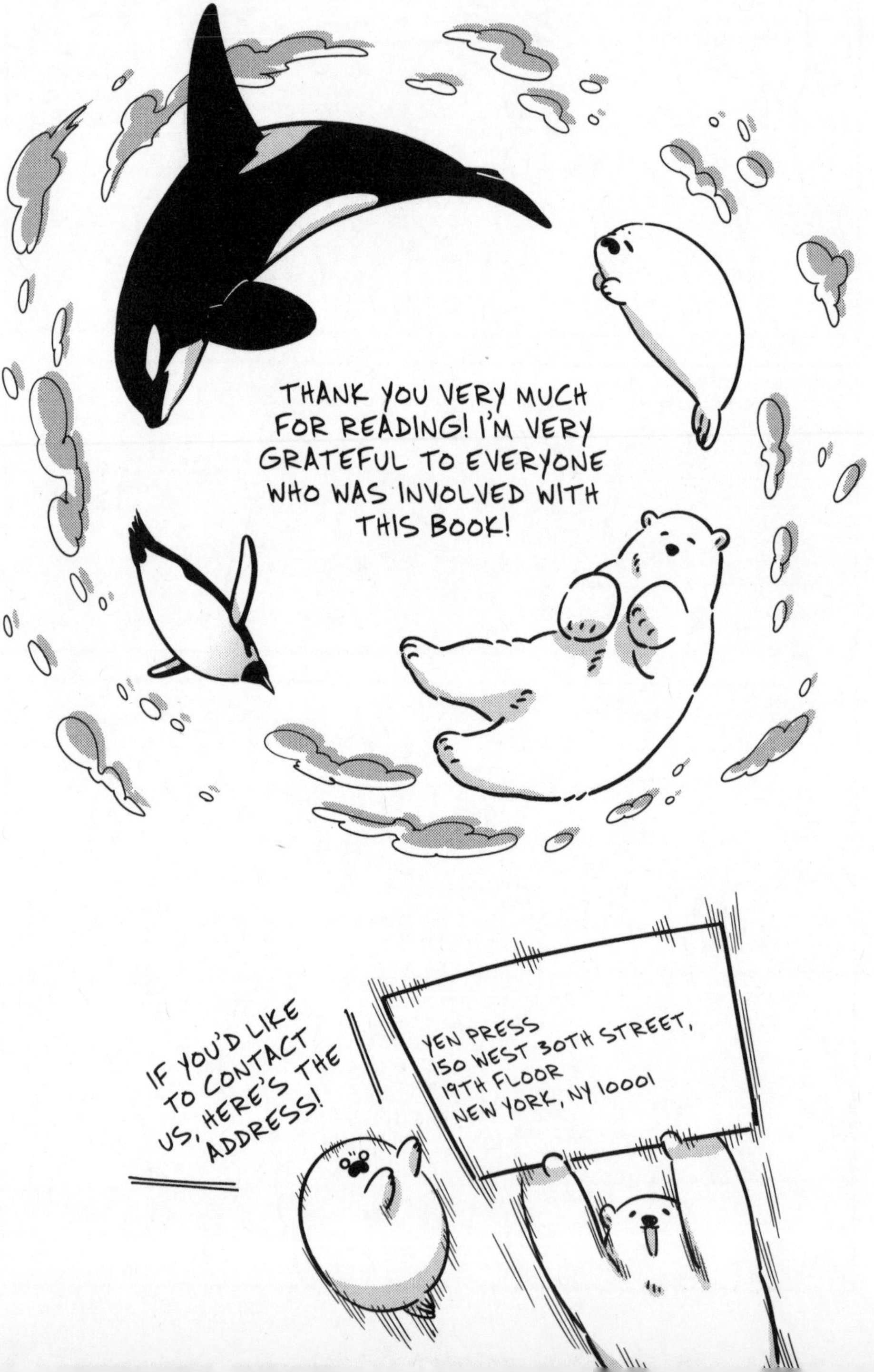
THANK YOU VERY MUCH FOR READING! I'M VERY GRATEFUL TO EVERYONE WHO WAS INVOLVED WITH THIS BOOK!
YEN PRESS
150 WEST 30TH STREET,
19TH FLOOR
NEW YORK, NY 10001
IF YOU'D LIKE TO CONTACT US, HERE'S THE ADDRESS!

AUTHOR'S NOTE

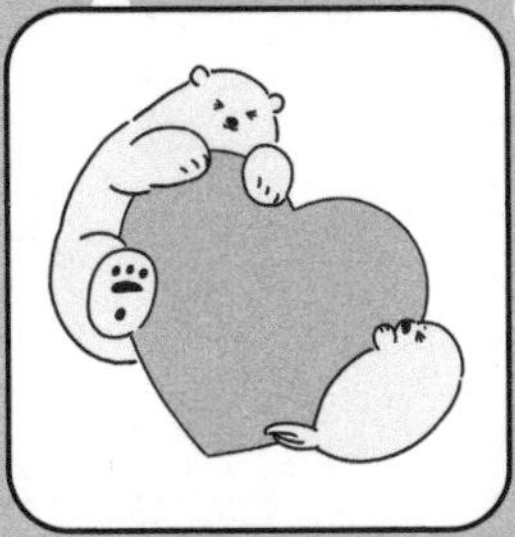

Koromo

VOLUME 5 IS OUT!
I DIDN'T THINK IT WAS GOING
TO HAPPEN EITHER...
IT'S BEEN, WHAT, THREE OR
FOUR YEARS...?
IF ANYONE'S READING THIS NOW,
IT'S A MIRACLE, AND I THANK YOU
FROM THE BOTTOM OF MY HEART.
SERIOUSLY, THANK YOU SO, SO MUCH...
I HOPE YOU ENJOY VOLUME 5.
...HAAAH, THAT WAS SCARY.

SWEETIE'S...

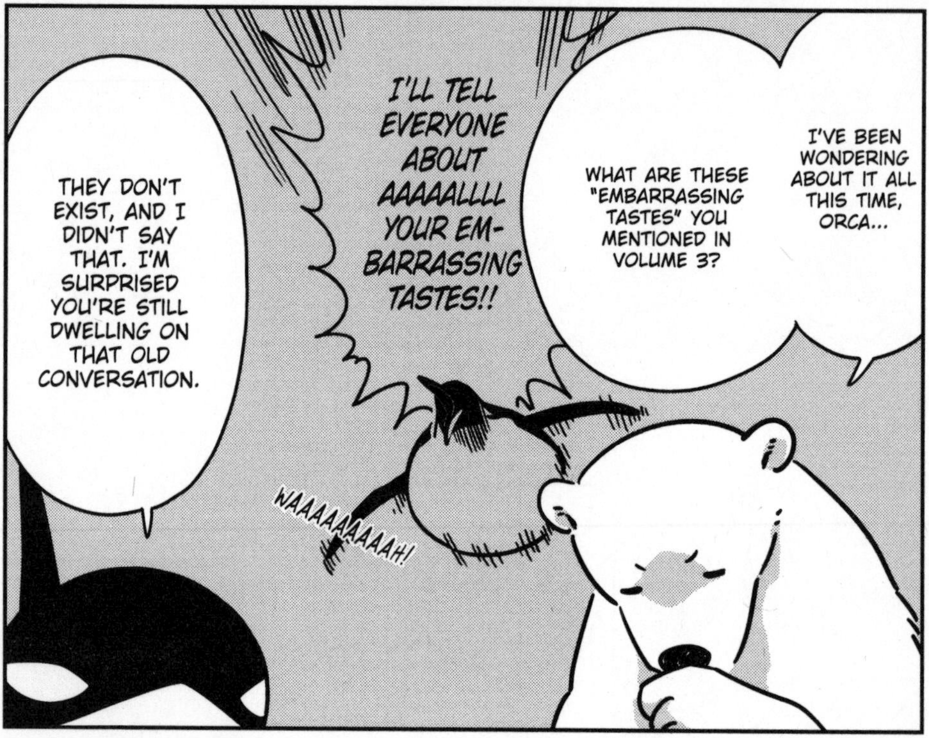

I'VE BEEN WONDERING ABOUT IT ALL THIS TIME, ORCA...
WHAT ARE THESE "EMBARRASSING TASTES" YOU MENTIONED IN VOLUME 3?
I'LL TELL EVERYONE ABOUT AAAAALLLL YOUR EM-BARRASSING TASTES!!
WAAAAAAAAAAH!
THEY DON'T EXIST, AND I DIDN'T SAY THAT. I'M SURPRISED YOU'RE STILL DWELLING ON THAT OLD CONVERSATION.

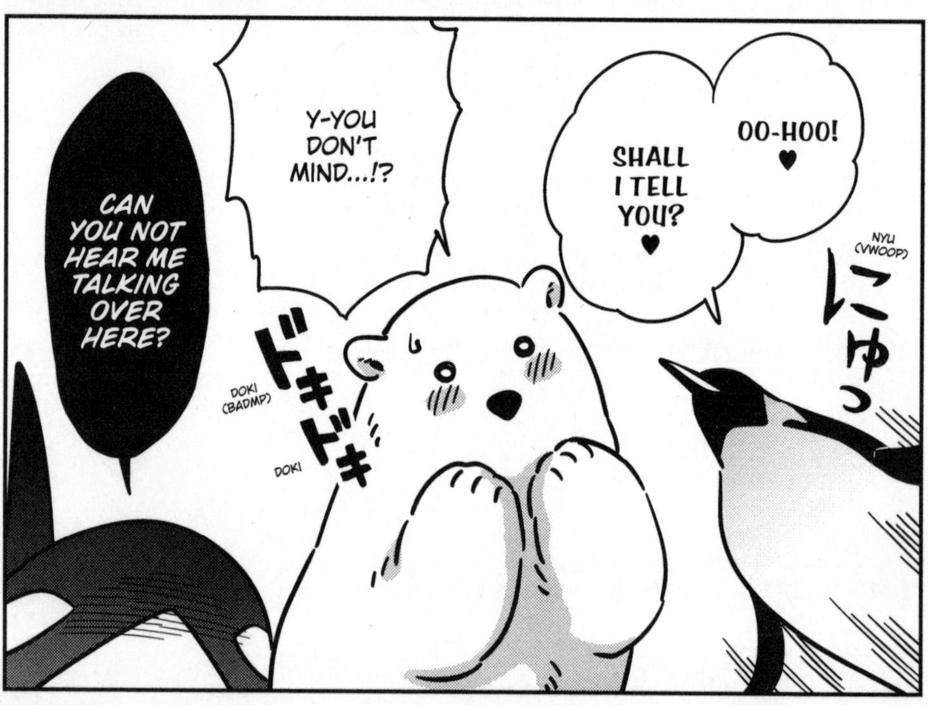

OO-HOO! ♥
SHALL I TELL YOU? ♥
NYU (VWOOP)
にゅっ
Y-YOU DON'T MIND...!?
DOKI (BADMP)
ドキドキ
DOKI
CAN YOU NOT HEAR ME TALKING OVER HERE?

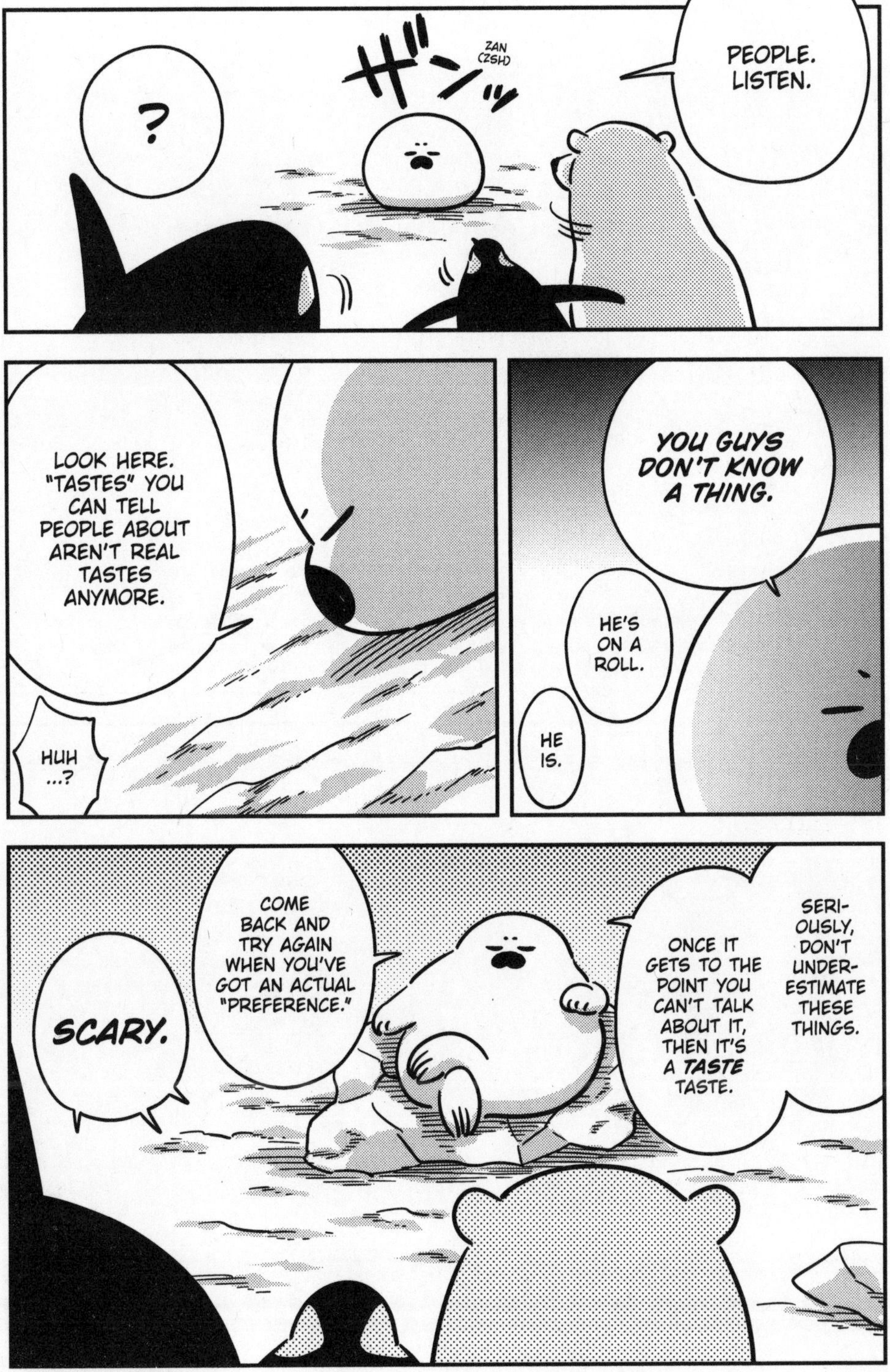
PEOPLE. LISTEN.
ザンッ
ZAN (ZSH)
?
YOU GUYS DON'T KNOW A THING.
HE'S ON A ROLL.
HE IS.
LOOK HERE. "TASTES" YOU CAN TELL PEOPLE ABOUT AREN'T REAL TASTES ANYMORE.
HUH ...?
SERI-OUSLY, DON'T UNDER-ESTIMATE THESE THINGS.
ONCE IT GETS TO THE POINT YOU CAN'T TALK ABOUT IT, THEN IT'S A TASTE TASTE.
COME BACK AND TRY AGAIN WHEN YOU'VE GOT AN ACTUAL "PREFERENCE."
SCARY.

THE END

TRANSLATION NOTES

PAGE 67
Power harassment is a type of workplace bullying in which those with power, such as managers or senior employees, treat those in a lower position unjustly. It's been recognized as a particularly serious issue in Japan, and legislation has been passed in an attempt to address it.

PAGE 129
Motonari Mouri is known for, among other things, demonstrating to three of his sons that they would be stronger together than apart. He did this by giving them each an arrow, which they broke easily, and then giving them three arrows bundled together, which they were unable to break. While this event may or may not have actually happened, the lesson it contains is still taught to Japanese schoolkids.

So I'm a Spider, So What?

I'M GONNA SURVIVE—JUST WATCH ME!

I was your average, everyday high school girl, but now I've been reborn in a magical world...as a spider?! How am I supposed to survive in this big, scary dungeon as one of the weakest monsters? I gotta figure out the rules to this QUICK, or I'll be kissing my short second life good-bye...

MANGA VOL. 1-11

LIGHT NOVEL VOL. 1-15

AVAILABLE NOW!

YOU CAN ALSO KEEP UP WITH THE MANGA SIMUL-PUB EVERY MONTH ONLINE!

YenPress.com

TRANSLATION: Sarah Neufeld ❤ LETTERING: Viet Vu

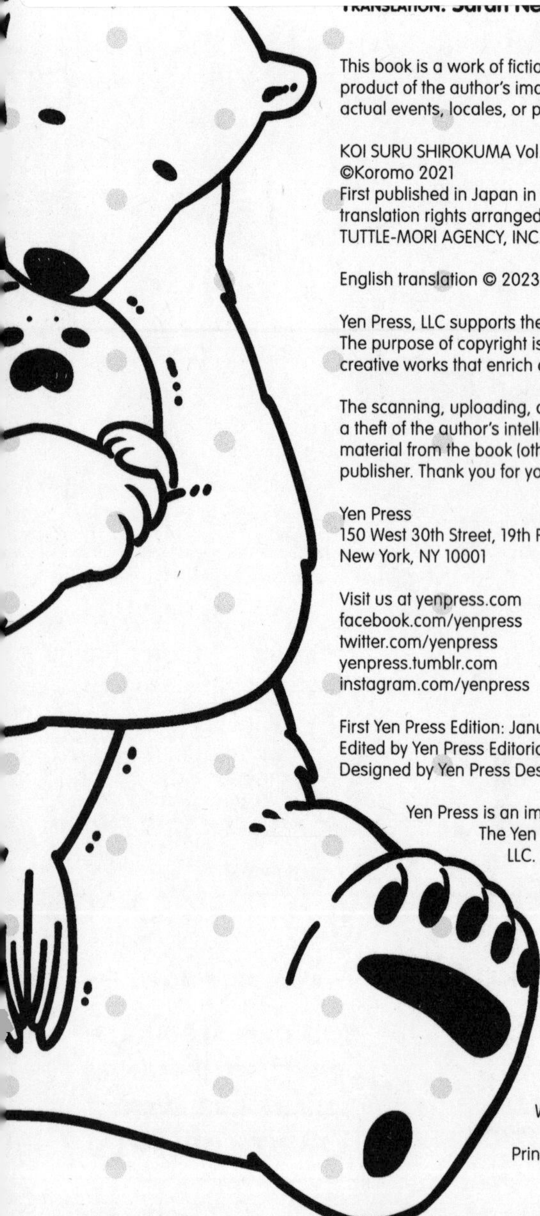

This book is a work of fiction. Names, characters, places, and incidents are the product of the author's imagination or are used fictitiously. Any resemblance to actual events, locales, or persons, living or dead, is coincidental.

KOI SURU SHIROKUMA Vol.5
©Koromo 2021
First published in Japan in 2021 by KADOKAWA CORPORATION, Tokyo. English translation rights arranged with KADOKAWA CORPORATION, Tokyo through TUTTLE-MORI AGENCY, INC., Tokyo.

English translation © 2023 by Yen Press, LLC

Yen Press
150 West 30th Street, 19th Floor
New York, NY 10001

Visit us at yenpress.com
facebook.com/yenpress
twitter.com/yenpress
yenpress.tumblr.com
instagram.com/yenpress

First Yen Press Edition: January 2023
Edited by Yen Press Editorial: Jacquelyn Li, Carl Li
Designed by Yen Press Design: Lilliana Checo, Wendy Chan

Yen Press is an imprint of Yen Press, LLC.
The Yen Press name and logo are trademarks of Yen Press, LLC.

The publisher is not responsible for websites (or their content) that are not owned by the publisher.

Library of Congress Control Number: 2017949438

ISBNs: 978-1-9753-6115-0 (paperback)
       978-1-9753-6116-7 (ebook)

10 9 8 7 6 5 4 3 2 1

WOR

Printed in the United States of America